Resonance

Dora M Raymaker

AUTON OMOUS PRESS

Weird Books for Weird People

2022

INTRO

"The lungs of the sky made whistles of the wheat."

"What?"

"You asked me to do an intro for the archive, a beginning. That's the beginning: the lungs of the sky made whistles of the wheat. On Agrippa, in the Iae-Kuat star system. Agrippa's classified Colonial, and it's a shit-hole ass-pit-back-water crap-stop—except for the sounds. The sounds are great! The sounds started everything. I made up a little song about them, as the intro." Caran Watts slouches on the couch with his bare feet on the table between us, like he's fourteen not forty.

He does not realize he's misinterpreted my request to "do an intro for the archive." *Note to self: have research assistant pull info re. Operator language impairments.*

He leans his head to the side and blinks his beautiful black eyes.

At me.

The curve of his mouth shifts between warmth and pain, like clouds in a brisk wind, as he pokes tangled black hair from his face.

His movements fascinate me; if they were more awkward, they might disturb me. Instead, the awkwardness reads as grace. Of course, I'm not the first fascinated by every flutter-of-an-eyelash over those disarming eyes and golden skin.

He's an indeterminate ancestral mix, like most people, and half-bare in a sleeveless, shapeless, cream-colored dress and nothing else. The light in my office hits his forehead at just the right angle reveal the iridescent pale blue sheen of taboo technology beneath the surface of his skin. Describing him in my notes feels silly. How could anyone not know what he looks like? But then, most people don't observe him alone and barefoot in their office.

I've conducted qualitative interviews for over two decades, with subjects ranging from the isolationist monks of Mau to the ten most popular corporate CEOs. But I've never interviewed an Operator before—or "nauta," as they prefer. Sure, I've collaborated with plenty of nauta. All Worlds Scientific is one of the few places where those genetically able to use quantum brain computers are treated like human beings and not machines. But working with someone and interviewing them for a research study are very different activities. How little we "normals" understand the nauta, despite their omnipresence. Despite the fact that without their abilities to manipulate quantum code, all life originating on Earth would likely be extinct.

"Okay," I say. I can obtain a formal, written introduction for the archive later. "Tell me more about that. About the wind in the wheat."

He closes his eyes and whistles atonally, fingers tapping pat-pat on his breastbone. "On Agrippa, near harvest, the wheat grows into reeds. When the wind blows, it whistles. I'd talk to it. Add the bass-beat of my heart, hum in my throat, birds in the sky, tuning to that place where sound becomes music. Have to avoid hitting the same notes as the wind, though, that shit makes your teeth vibrate." He grins, showing me his teeth.

Music leaks between his words, in the cadence of his speech, in the colors of his once-in-a-century voice. The hairs on my arms stand on end as the invisible alien creature in the room raises a faint static field, choosing this moment to make its presence felt.

Caran sways on-beat as he speaks. "The wind in the wheat, the wind in my hair, dirty, tangled, I was a mess back then but who cares, no one, I didn't care, what matters is I could sing. I could sing with the wheat. The wheat sang back."

The alien creature, the élan vital, the first meta-intelligent life like us we've found, begins to enter my head. It's making a link between me and my research participant, manipulating the slow end of the electromagnetic spectrum to create a conduit between us. I've practiced this, but I'm not used to it. I'm not supposed to fight it; I'm supposed to let it match my frequencies, my bio-feedbacks, for it to adjust itself to align to me, and me to it, and us to Caran until all three of us resonate together—

"I am not alone!" Caran shouts.

<!*joylovesong*!>

From what context did that shout, and the emphatic echo from the alien, originate? Did it come from their memories, out in the fields of Agrippa? Or from here, now, in my office at All Worlds Scientific on Mars?

Or, perhaps, an overlapping of both times and places?

It's hard to sort through the hair-tickling static field the creature has raised. I take a deep breath and try to surrender. That's what Cami kept saying during training. *Surrender. A resonant link created by an élan vital is disorienting, even for people who have practiced it.* I've only had Cami's hasty lessons.

"Did you tell anyone on Agrippa about the alien, about Muse?" I probe for more detail. Or, at least I think I do. In the buzzing and the overlapping I can't tell where my body begins or ends.

"Even if I could talk, even if I'd had the words—which you know fuck-all-well I didn't—what would've been the point in telling?

Another black eye? Another turned back? Another couldn't-do-anything-right?"

Disorientation fades as the telempathic link with the alien stabilizes. Caran's pressed back in the sofa, legs curled to his chest, black eyes glinting angry in the light. I have to remember who I'm talking to. I've been assured the emotional minefield of his psyche is, these days, under control, but that was from people unfamiliar with qualitative research methods. I will need to push his buttons to get the rich data I want, while also respecting his experiences. It's a line that ordinarily I'm comfortable navigating, but this is not an ordinary set of interviews, and Caran Watts is not an ordinary man. And, ordinarily, I am not in psychic resonance with my research participants, able to feel what they feel, and, perhaps, project some of my own feelings back—all of which I'm told I'll have limited control over.

"I'm sorry." I reestablish my manners, remember my responsibilities as a scientist. "I want to remind you that you don't have to answer any questions you don't feel comfortable with. Any time you need a break, you just tell me."

His shiny black eyes narrow to cruel lines, but through the link with the alien he calls Muse I know that glare protects a complicated dance of art and wounds.

"It's okay." He relaxes, knees coming down and feet going back onto the top of the coffee table. He waves away the tension with a hand, like his overreaction was no big deal. "I want the story out. It's time it comes out."

I take a deep breath and nod. "So, then, the wind in the wheat. Your intro. You said you made a song. Sorry I interrupted, go on."

He closes his eyes and picks the atonal whistle back up. The room warms as the alien creature emits an infrared glow of <*pleasure*>.

He stands, slapping rhythm with his hands and feet. Slap-pound-pat.

The whistle turns tonal, melodic, with the om-thrill-wheet of the birdsong in the rush, the swish-click-hiss of static-electric underbrush—

(I telempathically live the memories of a ten-year-old boy beside an alien entity, dancing under setting twin stars, shedding a world too loud, too hard, too bright, like wheat in the thresher, wordless and laughing—)

I emerge from the memory and he goes silent. The light dims in Muse's sudden shadows.

He snarls. "I didn't let go. Not that day. Not ever. That meal bar was mine."

I feel the meal bar curled in my fist. "You got it from Mx. Chandiramani?" The name comes to me, a memory not my own, stirred up through the link. With it, a tsunami of emotion leaves me coughing, shaking, sweating, missing anything he might be saying in love/fear/loneliness/fight-or-flight/hope—The emotions pass into a bitter-sweet ache, and I've a face full of tears for feelings not my own.

Caran does not seem to notice. Or, if he does, he does not seem to care. He must be used to living with these feelings.

His eyes look into memories. "I would've starved to death without Mx. Chandiramani. I didn't know shit back then, but I knew that. Plus, he loved music like I did."

"But Agrippa is a Federal Banking World, it has subsistence, no one starves—" I start.

He scoffs. "You starve if you're a kid who can't form logical sequences and no one bothers to feed you. You think my sod of a mother hated me any less than the rest of them on that rock? I made her skin crawl just as much. All of them. Everyone on Agrippa. They sensed what I was even if they couldn't finger it."

"How'd that even happen in the first place?"

"That no one knew I was nauta?"

"Yes. You got the full genetic battery at birth, like everyone. The markers for K-syndrome are hardly subtle."

"One-in-ten-thousand chance of a false negative. I won the lotto, yeah? Just a statistical winner all round, me." He shrugs.

"Wow. Just think if you'd been sent to a Nursery and put into a sponsored programming job." I choke on the improbability of it all. I can't imagine a world without his music—or without his role in the Great Changes. "So, Mx. Chandiramani, tell me more about him."

Caran stands, and puts on a grand voice and bows, gesturing large to present me with an invisible item. "Behold! The Flute!" He sits, and in a normal voice continues. "He was one of the original settlers on Agrippa, taught music, maths, and mechanics at that shit-pit six-room schoolhouse. Must've been over a hundred by the time I met him. Had this wall of drawers full of instruments. Didn't let him get near me at first because no one had much touched me unless it was a smack. But he was patient, taught me that it was possible for someone to be decent to me. He'd ask my permission to mold my fingers around the reeds, or brass, or sticks, trying to teach me how to play something, anything. I'd lean in, make it last, closest thing I ever got to a parent's touch. We worked through every drawer and still I never learned shit. But he fed me. Cared for me. Gave me those meal bars. He was the only person on that assrock who didn't tell me I was a useless fuck-up every day."

Tears roll down his face, but he holds his voice steady. I sense a devastating will holding back his feelings so he can function. "Guess he knew what it was like to be unpopular considering what he taught. Couldn't wrap at the time how an advanced spacefaring civilization could hate maths and mechs so much and still be advanced and spacefaring. I knew it had to do with the woman they kept locked up in the old granary on Blavatsky Street, the one they called 'feeble.' She was, of course, the nauta in command of Agrippa's computer systems, but I didn't know it then, just knew she was the only person on the planet they hated more than me. Kept her in chains, like a beast, like five hundred years of institutionalized oppression wouldn't keep her in line just fine."

"No one drew the connection between you two? That you had the same symptoms she did?"

"They might've." Caran shrugs and I feel his impatience groaning through the telempathic link. "But it would've inconvenienced them to admit it. They'd have to contact Fed Med, arrange a re-test, who knows what else, and that's a lot of quality pub time to give up. Plus, Agrippa's second generation agro-Colonial. Only a hundred thousand on the whole rock, and most of them immigrated because they hate tech extra-much, beyond the normal hate. They saw nauta as unhousebroken animals with the power to obliterate humanity, held in check only by our tendency to spend our free time drooling on ourselves. Not like anyone saw much of our assigned Operator, so no one got the reality check that we're, you know, people."

"You've been asked about that a lot, haven't you, about why no one realized what you were?"

He scoffs, and even that brief annoyed sound is musical. "Just a bit, yeah. Plus the endless speculation for years while I was at 100 Worlds Music. But Mx. Chandiramani,"—his face breaks into a huge grin—"I think he stole those meal bars!"

He darkens again, closes his eyes, closes his fist white-knuckled around his memories, his voice a whisper. "He'd put the bar in my hand and close my fingers around it just like this, and he'd say, 'Don't let anyone take it from you.'"

He pauses, shivering, though the environmentals in the room would have adapted a comfortable microclimate around him to suit his biofeedbacks. "And they would, they would try to take it from me, the bullies in the schoolyard. Smack-crack of Riley's fist on my face and they'd get me on the ground, kick my ribs, dig my tendons, try to get my hand open. I'm small and clumsy, but I'm tough, always been tough. I don't feel most pain, hyposensitive to it, and I had Muse too. Muse would radiate infrared heat, they'd get uneasy, back off. We had no idea what we could do back then; Muse was as young and stupid as I was.

"We'd run away, into the wheat, unwrap the bar. Sweet and salt, heart-beat, up-tempo, all those sugars and proteins hitting my bloodstream ooh-eee!" He belts a note so high I can't believe he can make it happen in full voice with no warm-up.

The note ends in the whistle-rush-hush (of the wind), his hands slapping in a swish-pat (of the wheat), a birdsong (from the thrush calling high above).

The telempathic resonance of the alien Muse sends me these images from Caran's memories, though I might have imagined something like them anyway. His specialty is painting landscapes with sound.

"Muse would manifest full-visible then," he keeps up the slap-pat, swish-hush with his hands and feet, voice in a spoken-word poem, "a point of light unfolding, static charge a-sparking, and then the field—ZAM!—is full of prisms!"

A long, lovely, longing hum.

"This is the intro. The start. When I was ten years old, the start, the beginning, the wish. The intro you asked for."

He's a hundred thousand light years away, pulling me deeper into story, deeper into nightmare, sound, and beauty. I cannot stop the vector, even if I wanted to. I fall fully inside his memory.

◊

*<*JOY!*> Muse emotes.*
The first star winks on in the heavens.
<should we wish on it?> I think/feel to Muse.
<!!!!!!!!*>*
<i wish my voice to be good for something, for kindness and freedom, to make people happy. i wish to be a star!>

Electricity arcs through the wheat, setting the tips of the grasses smoking. Muse picks up the wish and thrusts it into space on alien breath, broadcasting the future far and loud.

◊

Greetings.

You have accessed All Worlds Anthropological Archive number 24190-A, entitled "Narrative Voices in a Phenomenological Study of the Great Changes of the Early 26th Century: Part One, 'Resonance.'" This is an archive of interviews conducted by Principal Investigator Dr. Steven Kwon, PhD during his data collection for a large analysis of events entitled "The Great Changes." The interviews occurred in Dr. Kwon's office at All Worlds Scientific on Mars and describe events on Jupiter's moons of Europa, Io, Ganymede, and Callisto.

Dr. Kwon uses an inductive approach at both semantic and latent levels, seeking to understand first-person experiences both by allowing themes to emerge organically from the speaker's own words, and by interpreting stories within broader social contexts. To access Dr. Kwon's scientific research, please exit this Popular Media area and re-enter through the Scientific Gateway.

This Popular Media Archive contains the first-person experiences of the key instigators of the Great Changes—Caran Watts, Jordis Ansari, Noa Oki, and Camilla Morgan—along with questions, observations, and reflexive journaling by Dr. Kwon. It remains our most-accessed popular science archive.

This archive is available in a variety of formats.

1. 2V audio only

2. 3V holographic playback

3. 4V interactive mode

4. 5V+ adaptive-enhanced mode with optional telempathic resonators for unique first-person immersive perspectives. Note: If you wish the 5V+ experience, please swipe your thumb to indicate you understand human-élan hybrid technology is in its early stages and may have as-yet unknown side-effects.

Please make your selection now.

Thank you.

5V+ adaptive-enhanced experience: START.

PART 1:

SOL SYSTEM,
JUPITER ORBIT: EUROPA

"Let's start with your arrival on Europa for the *Two Shades of Blue* tour."

Caran sings to me.

◊

"Dancing in ether
dancing in sleep
dancing in memories
of my days in the deep
I called your name
but nobody came
guess that's ok
I never needed to be real..."

◊

The song is eerie and hearing it so close and live and acapella sets me shivering, like a lover touching that place on my neck.

"That's from 'Dancing in Deep' off my *Two Shades of Blue* set release," Caran says, upbeat, with a satisfied smile. "Produced and distributed by 100 Worlds Music Corporation on Cassiopeia Prime, thirty years after we wished in the wheat." He sits across from me, bare feet up and black eyes catching light I didn't even know was in the room.

"Yes, I have listened to a few of your set releases." I take the edge off my shivers with a dry tone and a smile. Who hasn't listened to them all? He's a seven-time Galaxy Award winner.

He laughs. He's lighthearted this morning, free with his smiles as he apologized for being late and, with uncharacteristic shyness, asked for a glass of water.

"So what happened on your arrival at Europa?" I ask again.

He cocks his head and squints at me. "How close to arrival? Like an hour before? When *Sonica's* realspace engines cut in the Europa City docking bay? 'Cause we were in orbit around Callisto, more than a million kilometers from Europa, for hours because of that fucking bomb, almost missed my events. Might've been better if I had missed my events, but I made my events, and anyway that's when I started composing Callisto's song because we were orbiting for hours and there she was through the window, the hard, round moon Callisto, most beautiful, all dark, no lights, no colony then"—he hums a few bars of the Callisto movement of the Jovian Symphony.

"The two biggest things to understand about nauta and language," my research assistant said, *"is one, that they don't think in any language we—or even each other—understand. And two, their visual-associative intelligence is at least a standard deviation better than ours— more than just one for Caran. The programming in their navi translates between their own language and ours, but it doesn't always get it right. You're going to get a lot of weird associative rambling but be patient; it'll make sense. Get used to clarifying a lot of misunderstandings."* But I don't want to clarify; I don't want to give him *my* idea about where to start *his* story. As an anthropologist I facilitate, I don't lead, so I formulate a probe based on his "weird rambling" instead. I ask,

"The explosion that kept you from docking in Europa City, was that the explosion in Hangar 19? The one they blamed on the Genetic Liberation Front?"

"Yeah. Though I'd no clue at the time. No clue how important it was either, besides getting between me and the wet bar in my hotel room. No one told me anything. I wouldn't have cared anyway." Urgency pulses through the telempathic link <*hunger pressure nEEEEEEd*>—he tamps it down.

I swallow. "So you were orbiting Callisto, waiting for clearance to approach Europa."

"Yeah. Europa City. The Dreaming City. You been there? Europa's all liquid water beneath her ice crust. City's the shape of a torus, like a big donut, and it floats around her hard core. Entry's impressive—sparkling swoop through a huge ice tunnel and then smack! Into the water where you follow strings of lights to the floating city. It's neat. I wasn't watching. I didn't care." <*pressure-Need—TAMP*>

"No? Where were you?"

"In my cabin on Sonica." <*pr—TAMP*>

"What were you doing?"

I clutch my chest like I'm having a heart attack. <*NEEED pleasure pressure resentment relief*>

"Eight drops," Caran says. "Eight drops of dark blue lies."

(I am he, we, the élan pulls me into his memories.)

◊

(We are on Sonica, waiting for clearance to land.)
A-one and a-two and a-three and a-four;
Five, six, seven, eight!

Eight drops of nyquolium quadrolate!

Suck it up onto the crystal dropper, suck it up, chin up, be a good trooper, make the music, make the money, make them all believe the lies—

Dose it.

Dose it now.

Yow.

Wow.

YOW!

My tongue burns as the liquid spreads and the rush starts and wow-fucking-shit I can move and speak and come up with words that aren't songs, and the world coming through the senses makes sense. This is what it's like for normals, except for the associative connections, pre-verbal intuitive soundscapes, shouting songs, a million things that normals just can't do.

"But artists can; artists can do anything!" I laugh at my reflection, ugly, sneering, jutting my hip out to mimic my manager Jonathan LaRoque. I see every gilded curve and baroque detail of the mirror-frame, who the fuck picked this thing out for me anyway?

Manager LaRoque and Security Head Mindy Ming had another one of their "conversations" about me in the common area right before I escaped to my room to dose, like I wasn't standing right the fuck there.

I shift my weight to center, pretending to be Mindy, matching her over-burdened tone. "Gods, LaRoque, he's a space-wreck."

Shift back to LaRoque. " Deal with it, Min. Artists are like that." Aping their voices is easy, perfect pitch and all—but the hip jut, the rat-looking face of LaRoque, that's harder to get right.

I can't go on. I'm giggling. My bones are singing. My song is rushing. I'm fucking giggling. I snap my head back and forth, the spikes of dark purple hair making whips on my shoulder blades.

I'm not wearing any clothes.

I was supposed to put on clothes.

That's how I managed to get back to my room alone so I could dose; that's why I'm here.

For clothes, for clothes! Pants, pants is a funny word, patter-patter pants, pants-less-ness!

My giggling echoes off the walls and floor and hard surfaces of the cabin.

Walking out to media naked is just the sort of thing I'd do too. "My fans want me to be fucked-up." I mimic myself now instead of LaRoque, pacing short, sharp strides. "And you know what's perfect? I am!" Media's replayed the clip of me saying that five years running. Never gets old.

Clothes. Where are the clothes? Figure / ground resolves itself as the drug takes hold.

Across the bed there's a long, form-fitting, sharp-cut jacket. Its surface crawls like mercury. Pants glitter like ice at the bottom of a tumbler of vodka. A black shirt tight enough to suggest physique but loose enough to hide the bones that I can never cover, doesn't matter how much food I eat or how many weights I lift. Ankle-height shiny black boots to match my eyes, with eight-centimeter heels like someone thought that would compensate for my runtiness.

I can't stop giggling. I have to dress. I have to stop giggling. This is so much fun. We are all such beautiful people.

All the beautiful people are back in the common area, rushing me like iron to a magnet, fussing over hair, face, fold of cuff.

"Guess I got dressed!" I'm still giggling.

Muse shows up, drinking the emotional high and feeding it back, increasing the glow, the flow, the rush. The joy. We're all giggling. Everyone's giggling.

◊

"Wait, your handlers, did they know the élan was there? In feedback with their feelings?" Sweat stings my right eye. The surface of my skin buzzes, riding the edge between pleasurable and unbearable. I can't sit still. I'm not sure if I have to pee. That's not me; it's him, his feelings. The sensations fade, the resonance between the three of us weakening as I reassert my individuality.

"Course they didn't know." Caran is no longer on the couch. He's standing; I think he might have been pacing. He's stopped by the chair beside the sofa, slender frame held in a taut, dancer-like posture, like he's paused mid-ballet move. He cocks his head toward me with a snappy glare of his eyes, "If they'd known Muse was there, the Great Changes wouldn't have been nearly so great now, would they?"

"But it felt so obvious." There's a defensiveness to my reaction that leaves me wincing. Whatever would I have to feel defensive about? This isn't my story. I am just an instrument of the research. Or is Caran feeling defensive, and I'm feeling his feelings through Muse? That kind of feedback loop—that alignment and amplification of thoughts and feelings between human and alien—is exactly what happened with the handlers.

"It was obvious they adored working for me—before the show at any rate. After the show," he laugh-sneers, "was a different matter because Muse was gone. It liked to go play with the fans. Then the crew would make their malice known. Whisper down low where no normal could hear, but I wasn't no normal now was I. I heard everything. I saw the sullen glares. Fickle fuckers." Anger roils across his eyes and clears, almost in synch with the sun and clouds flickering on fast wind through the window behind him. "The telempathic feedbacks of the élans are usually subtle. For most of them, they're too alien, finding resonance with us only an accident. They hook in, we align, make the link—then poof! slip away as the frequency shifts a few nano-Hertz. In Muse's case though, it's just a subtle creature. When it wants to be."

I feel the alien now, a flash of heat on my face that dries my sweat instantly.

<i'm an obvious creature when i want to be, too>

I gasp. It's like a thought of my own from outside myself—and cocky.

Caran comes un-stuck in his posture. He shakes out his hands and laughs at me, though this time there's no accompanying emotion through the link so I'm uncertain as to why. "Muse likes you. It doesn't share its thoughts directly with just anyone."

I swallow. "So the handlers and Muse. The amplification of thoughts and emotions through alignment and resonant feedback. You'd just been cleared for landing on Europa."

◊

"Caran!" Mindy Ming, security-head-cum-tour-mom, olive cheeks, red flush. She's twice everyone's bulk and legal for retractable liteguns implanted where her ulnae used to be. She's taken a bullet for me, more than once. That doesn't make us friends. She's corporate through-and-through. "We're landed in ten."

"Yeah. Hey thanks Min, thanks for canceling the opening night party thing."

"LaRoque isn't happy about it."

Jonathan LaRoque is half everyone's bulk and shaped like the rat he is, but it's not like I've any say in managers.

"LaRoque can bite me." I've no say in schedule either, so what all's left except expressing my feelings to the fullest extent possible. Sure, I've got my own corporate identity under the swirly "CW" sigil clipped to the webbing of my right thumb, but that's still a sub-charter of 100 Worlds Music. Don't forget, don't ever forget, it's the price to keep the music. They own me, but I own my songs. No one owns my songs. Like music could ever belong to anyone at all. It's like owning atmosphere.

Mindy squeezes my shoulder though not hard enough for me to feel it with my hyposensitive sense of touch. "And now we're landed in nine."

Got to take a few deep breaths. Got to get ready for show time in seven. Six. Five. Four. Three. Two—

I step onto the landing platform whistling, handlers surging from all sides; security, local and mine, pushing back media to make a path to the secure sonic VIP tube.

"Welcome to—"

"You got a—"

"Is the kinetikosonus really—"

"Are the rumors—"

"Can I have your—"

Wave big, smile bigger, don't show, don't blow. "Coming to the gig tonight sweetie? Kiss kiss!" Inane whatevers. Never answer a question directly, redirectly. "Love the shirt! Did you buy the 2V of my set?" Wink-wink, flirt-flirt.

Next: Whisking down a blur of passageways on a private sonic tube, surrounded by—what are all these people for again?

For shoving food at me, water, prep for sound check, makeup in five, press your corpin to this form, you-need-to-see-this-media!, food, more food, vitamin water juice prep time, don't forget your stretches, here's a new shirt you like it huh?, put this on, sound-check, check-check, kinetikosonus has a hitch here can you tell the tech guys to, check check check—

Thirty minutes later: Mainfeed all the way, and Bobbie from the Europan Monitor stands on the gold-sparkle Studio Six set. The beads of goldstuff on tracks running up and down the walls should have kicked me into sensory overload, except the drug puts that sharp edge of dull over everything making it clear what's going on. I can see each tiny bead, and at the same time really see it without losing my shit into screaming, biting, fight-or-flight. Might be frying my nerves on the down-spin but the up-spin sure does sing! Sparkle for the holocams pointed at the chairs, stage over to the right.

"Mx. Watts! May I call you Caran?" Bobbie looks female, sounds male.

"Yeah, sure." I lean forward so Bobbie can catch my cheek. "You can call me anything as long as you give me kisses." The cameras roll, seeking a candid of something hypeable. I shoot them a crooked smile to show I'm onto the game. Doesn't matter what I say or do, media will spin it however it hooks the most consumers.

Bobbie flutters impotently near my cheek and retreats. Bobbie's braver than most since the time I told everyone I couldn't handle yellow and then my six-o-clock from Red City Reporter had worn yellow, the worst kind of yellow, all sharp and off-key screaming in my eyes, just one thing too much. Bit that reporter's ear right the fuck off. Now fans scream and clap every time reporters cover their ears. They say lightning never strikes the same place twice, and neither does Caran Watts in meltdown mode; Bobbie you're safe. "Don't I get a wetter kiss. I won't bite. Not you, anyway." Oh yeah, they'll buzz over that when they run the backstage holo later.

"Very funny," Bobbie says but doesn't come closer. Instead they gesture to the clear easy-chair-shaped thing with pink and green glowstripes around the arms and edges. I'd been right to wear the shifting metallic jacket, swirling colors in the glowstripes. Wrong to sit in the chair, cold and hard as a block of iron. Impossible not to fidget.

"Three... two... one..." studio staff counts and we're live.

Bobbie to the camera: "I'm here at the Europan Monitor's Studio Six Entertainment Stage with the famous—or should I say infamous—Caran Watts, who is starting a week of sold-out performances here at Europa's Mnemosyne Theatre. Hope you're one of the lucky few with a ticket!"

Bobbie to me: "So, I was at your *Two Shades of Blue* preview in Red City last week, very impressive."

"Yeah, what'd you expect?" Flash, flash, the rakish grin.

Bobbie laughs, then gets Serious Reporter Face, brows in and down, eyes bright, mouth a fake-concerned line that says: I'm going to invade your privacy now; it'll be fun. "The song about the boy who jacked in—'Blood Deeps'—that's a reference to 20th century notions of brain computers?"

"Could be. Could be a reference to sex too." I wink. Try to get comfortable in the chair. Back in the 20th century the scandal would have been the sex, not the tech. Fuck this chair itches.

"You know here on Europa there have been some recent, and very serious, terror threats by the Genetic Liberation Front, so there's a lot of concern about anything that promotes mental control of computers. In fact, there was a bomb scare linked to the GLF just this afternoon, I think it delayed your landing? How would you respond to the Parent Monitor Association Corporation's recommendation to tag the new track for age major-only?"

"More power to 'em! It'll only make the sales jack!"

More Bobbie laughter. Reporter laughter. They all have the same laugh. Fuck, this is boring. "Great laugh Bobbie, you got a great laugh."

"Seriously though, here are some of the lyrics," Bobbie recites with no sense of rhythm, "'Burning up for jacking in / See the sea and live again / Down in dirt I bite my tongue / Jack the sea and live again.' You're aware that some Operators refer to the information-space of the Mem as 'sea' and the real world as 'land?' Still say the song's about sex?"

I smirk at them. "Yeah. Sex is wet. Like the sea. Like the kisses you didn't give me."

"There are some people who say the kinetikosonus is either smoke and mirrors or uses some very questionable technology. How would you say your unique instrument operates?"

"Magic!" I shake my hands in the air, poof! *No, Bobbie, no, the instrument actually runs on quantum code. I program it myself. That's what's really on the dataslip around my neck, not your stupid-fucking-normal 21st century silicon-chip code like you've been told every single fucking day, for the past ten years, when you and your ilk have asked that same, dumb fucking question. Oops, Bobbie, big oops; I'm everything you fear and hate! Take that, Bobbie! Take that, world! Take that, truth!*

Bobbie opens their mouth, but I'm done with Bobbie, so I gesture at the stage which is entirely taken up and then some by the kinetikosonus, all taboo naked circuit boards and valves and shimmering brass and glass and wire. "We gonna sing here today?"

Bobbie gives a hopeful nod, but I can see from their twitching right eye they're pissed as shit there wouldn't be more interview. Doesn't matter what you want Bobbie! You've come at me too hard too fast with the dangerous questions; you know better. Three questions about the tech is all you get! My PR guy insists! Plus you're damn boring for an entertainment reporter.

I finger the warm, heavy surfaces of the platinum-coated dataslip around my neck. The fast-talk and the walk-walk and the sparkle-tolerance are dark blue lies. But not the music. The music always tells the truth.

I stand and step onto the stage—OUT OF THAT FUCKING CHAIR, THANKS—by way of an impossibly small corridor between the eight meters of 4V projection plates upstage and the banks of electronics and acoustics downstage. The kinetikosonus is getting too big; time to strip away some of the sections. Maybe I can do with less brass. I don't use the tuba-thing much because of the electronic effect that makes the bass-chest rumble.

All right.

All right.

Let's do this thing.

The dataslip slots into the reader and the interactive 4V display turns on over the holoplates.

Awash in color.

Step within, moving my hands through sienna swirls to initiate a back-drone and all the tension goes.

Lashes wet on cheeks in sonic relief.

My skin shivers with the static tingle of Muse manifesting invisibly around, within.

<hhhhhiiiiiii soon sound satisfaction> it whispers to me, sharing the sensation of curling its consciousness into the amplifiers. <*warm eager* music good we agree?>

<yes, on music we agree> Fucking thing sure didn't agree with

me when I tried to down the whole vial of dark blue lies earlier. Zap-snapped my hand with so many amps I almost dropped it. Fucking thing won't even let me die.

<not while we've music>

"Seeing as you liked my sex song so much, here it is, 'Blood Deeps.'" No solutions, just a thousand shimmering paths to denial. Cover it all over in sound.

I blink the resonators on; my voice reacts with the drones, non-linear sine-wave feedbacks. "Hear that, kids, turn on your main-feed recorders, catch the tune before they ban it!" I sweep on the visualizers for the gestural controls. "Never let 'em take your sweet freedom!" Colors spray and the drones change pitch. I blow a not-wet kiss to the cameras, to the invisible crowds gathered at the local mainfeed terminals through the Europa torus and Ganymede too, standing in information hotspots, staring up at media projected onto the ceilings of tube stations and public ways. Everything bad washes away in sound. Whatever else happens, the music is mine. No, not mine. Ours, yours, hope, my gift to the world.

<*love*> echoes Muse.

"Blood Deeps." The instrument picks up my voice and carries it with layers of whisper-tones, eerie ambience as I move and sway and the electronics rise, and I twirl on the woodwinds and air rushes through the reeds.

Smash into the dance.

A wall of sound blasting from a tiny stage

splashing from living light

sharing symphonies inside my head

clear

brutal

torched with power.

◇

"Okay, back up a moment, say more about the dataslip. It becomes very important later, so I want to make sure I understand it correctly."

"You can't possibly be serious." He responds to my question, flipping his head back, rolling his eyes. "Are you even getting my thoughts?"

"Oh, I'm getting them all right, and I don't need to be in your head to know how often the media pressed you about the contents of your dataslip, or how the kinetikosonus works. But sometimes new details or insights come out through the format of an interview. It helps frame your stories and helps ensure I understand your experience."

"Okay," he says at the start of a long-suffering exhale that goes on forever because he's got enormous lungs. He tilts his attention toward the table between us, activating its 3V projection plate with a thought through his navis.

I, of course, would need to use the "on" switch.

"Show-off," I jest.

He spreads a toothy grin.

Ordinarily I wouldn't say such a thing to a research participant, but the intimacy of the élan's link tells me it's welcome.

"Just you wait," he adds a wink to the grin, "I haven't even begun to show off." And then he thinks a slew of technical diagrams into the 3V. "The kinetikosonus is every instrument in Mx. Chandiramani's drawers and then some. A lot's electronic, but some sounds you can only get through analogue means, so it has pistons that stream air over reeds, shit like that.

"When I first made it, back in my days traveling around with

Djen, I controlled it with my navis. I imagine the sound; the instrument makes the sound I imagine. But obviously that wasn't going to work in public since I'd be killed for being nauta without a sponsor, and, worse, working as an artist. So I added the 4V interactive projection plates, put a scarf over my head, came up with a dance routine, and acted like my gestures controlled the instrument.

"When I left Djen and went mainstream, I needed to remove my navis so I could pass better. So I put the programming for the kinetikosonus onto the dataslip and used the 4V to control the instrument for real. It's funny, I started out operating the instrument as smoke and mirrors, but it was all on the up by the time I signed with 100 Worlds Music. Well, except for the fact I told everyone it was programmed in a modern Perl dialect, not quantum code."

"You made the instrument when you were fifteen and lived with Djen in the underground community of Freedom?"

"Yeah." The images clear. Caran leans back and folds his arms behind his head, using them for a pillow.

"We'll get in-depth into Freedom later, but could you summarize to frame my notes?"

"Yeah, sure. Freedom was a bunch of connected cells across inhabited space made up of people who knew about the élans. They had a rule that you could only join if one of the élans invited you, except they'd stopped extending invitations. Some folks though, like Djen, were second and third generation members. Freedom was dying out because of the strict rules around joining, and they were letting it. Which was too bad since Freedom used to be the only place nauta could exist outside servitude and not be on the run. A community. Off the grid. Protected by élans. Freedom hated me and Muse. Muse was confusing. We weren't supposed to be there." His good mood snaps off as the 3V goes black.

"What do you mean weren't supposed to be there?"

"I wasn't invited by the élans when Djen brought me in. We broke the rules. Muse didn't know what it was, wasn't a part of it, and the other élans didn't recognize it. They called Muse 'detached' and 'broken' and 'incomplete.' Freedom and the élans thought there was something wrong with us. Story of my fucking life."

"Thanks, that's helpful. So we were at the Studio Six mainfeed show. What happened after that?"

His eyes narrow into angry lines. "It all went to fucking shit."

◊

Ten hours after the interview, one hour after the show: I'm thinking, *never let 'em take your sweet freedom? Yeah, right.*

LaRoque pulled a fast one on me and Mindy both, leading us down the hall after the show and straight into a party zone before we realized it wasn't the way back to the hotel. Now I'm trapped in this opening night party.

I feint toward the bar again but once more hit Mindy's wall of muscle instead. The dark blue lies are metabolizing their way out of me, and if I don't find a socially acceptable excuse to cover my behavior soon, rumors are gonna fly. I need a fucking drink. Don't I deserve a nice fucking drink?

<*noworry* i'll take care of people's perceptions> Muse think/feels, swirling a brew of telempathic <*deception/deflection*> into the party mix.

<but i like being drunk>

The creature's pumped with the power of the show and the fans and the after-party frenzy. It's got enough resonance with the crowd to change perceptual filters, just like that alcohol buzz

Mindy's denying me. If I stop talking, they think I'm basking. If I stop moving, they think I'm relaxed. If I get weird and fidgety, they think I'm still amped from the show. Anything but the truth. Always, anything but the fucking truth.

The fucking truth being in an hour I'm going to feel like I've been lit on fire. And in another two-to-four hours after that, I'll die.

◊

"I'm sorry to keep interrupting. But again, just a little background, in your own words, on the drug. Why were you worried you'd die?"

Pleasure and desire lurches through the link; and also, snarling beast-feelings. But Caran says, mild enough, "Nyquolium-quadrolate. That pap's a class-D illegal, but for normals it's just a mild empathogen like X or, if you want to, a sweet way to suicide."

"But for you?" I probe.

"For me? NQ binds differently to the body's receptors if you've got nauta genes. It's a variant of U4, which was made for nauta. NQ amps verbal-sequential thinking, makes for fluent speech and movement, lets you ignore sensory overload, packs a massive rush—"

He stops, going almost cross-eyed. Breathing, just breathing. When he starts back up, his normally expressive voice falls clipped and flat. "NQ makes nauta pass as normals, no matter where they are on the severity scale."

"And where are you on the severity scale?"

"It's too late for a true read, but probably between Class Nine and Class Eleven out of the twenty levels. Low enough to muddle through without twenty-four-seven assistance, but high enough I can't hope to hide it."

"At a time when it was illegal for nauta to be anything but sponsored programmers, so you'd be killed on the spot for being an artist?"

"Yeah, seven Galaxy Awards notwithstanding. NQ takes about eight hours to metabolize, and the withdrawals kill you, at least if you're doing as much for as long as I was. Four drops every eight hours to stay alive, six to fake normal, eight to rush rush rush."

"And how long since your last dose by the time you got to the party?"

"Maybe six hours? Six and a half? The effects were fading but I wasn't in deep shit yet. Least not earlier in the party."

"All right. Please continue."

◊

Someone's talking to me, so I put a smile on my face like I'm listening. The party sounds have gone too loud to make sense of them, threads of conversation woven into the roar of environmentals no one else can hear.

I slink back, anchor myself against the wall. The environmentals behind it vibrate through me, a bass rumble-hiss, tink-tink, rumble-hiss. The machines sound like they're making words. The rumble-hiss says "overlong overlong overlong" over and over. Tink-tink.

I haven't been able to get in touch with Greene, the only Europan dealer I've still got blackmail on from my Freedom days, for more NQ. That pap's so unpopular it doesn't even have a street name. How many drops left in my crystal vial, thirty? Fifty? More? Less? If I just do six drops each time, will I last till the gigs on Luna, where I've got three more ounces lined up?

Five shows here on Europa, one per day. One down four to go. Greene could still come through.

All these people, smiling, shiny, sycophantic people, would turn and kill me they found out I'm not normal.

Maybe I should let them. NQ's gonna kill me anyway. Ten drops of the pap and I'm dead. I've got maybe another ten years left before the only thing that could keep me alive's a lethal dose.

Fuck you, Djen, this is all your fault. You in your bright red spacer's suit, and tight black curls in an enormous sphere around your head in the zero-g, and your big, round laugh making me love you. Stella and Muse weaving their alien patterns in flash-zaps of electricity as you lied and told us were free. You wanted us to travel with you forever and I—

I sigh because I do not know what I want.

I want that bottle of Cassiopeian red rye whisky casting ruby shadows over the bar.

I pass Mindy a filthy look, but she's looking the other way.

One eternal hour later, half-conscious at the door between my room and the security suite, a tendril of Muse inside me is the only thing keeping me upright. Mindy gives my room an exhaustive search—three times—then mutters, "all clear," and gets the fuck out of my way.

I slip in and Muse's influence slips out of me, taking with it the extra energy.

Flash into blackout from the hours and the exercise and the never-enough-sleep.

I come to before I hit the floor, stumbling back up on aching knees.

"Lights off."

I sway in hissing dark. Everything buzzes. Phosphenes crawl behind my eyelids from visual over-stimulation. Pulse sloshes in my ear canals. Even in the darkness and silence, the world pushes, screams.

Deep breaths.

Opera breaths.

Let the tension out.

Imagine Verani's "Symphony in Twelve Dimensions;" recall it from memory. Play it out with perfect pitch. Let it override the push, the scream, the pain. Vareni is perhaps the best of the 24th century composers. Listen to those bells. Listen to that birdsong. Intricate tones.

For ten minutes, I listen; I breathe.

Then the overstimulation fades enough so I notice heart rate escalating, hands shaking, flash of nerve pain dashing.

"Lights extra-dim," I whisper into a muscle contraction and another flare of nerve pain. For how long did the exhaustion mask the withdrawal symptoms? This is more than playing it close. More than playing it too close. This is playing it like I want to die. Just have to make it to the hotel dresser, reach the platinum-coated lockbox where I keep my pap, align the retinal lock with my eye, stop shaking long enough to grasp the crystal vial, ease out four drops. I can do that. One step at a time.

Remember the steps. Fight through the dysfunction.

Step one, straighten up.

Step two, orient body to dresser by pivoting left.

A woman sits in the high-backed chair next to a bed covered in kilometers of purple satin. She's dressed like an expensive lawyer in an austere gray Vemi business suit and a black bun wound so tight it pulls her skin.

"Hello Dragon," she says. "You've ended up a long way from Freedom." Her vocal tones are superiority and ice, and the light reveals the pale blue sheen of a navis installed beneath the skin of her forehead. She's nauta. She's not from Freedom, but I know her from then.

How did I miss her? I'm not that fucked up yet.

More to the point, how did Mindy miss her?

My platinum-coated lockbox sits in her lap, lid open. In one hand, she holds a slender, closed, golden fan, tendons straining under its uncanny weight. In her other hand, she holds up my vial of NQ so it glitters dark blue, sparkling like stars in the light.

She smiles with the same saccharine snow as her voice. "Are you looking for this?"

Jordis Ansari enters my office at All Worlds Scientific with so much presence it feels like her space, not mine. With an enigmatic smile, she helps herself to the tea she requested I provide, and sits poised in the chair, not the sofa, with the china teacup in one hand and the saucer flat against the palm of the other. Her hair is in a black bun wound as tight as Caran described it. I don't know my designers well enough to say if her suit is Vemi, but it looks expensive. The suit, like her eyes, is dark gray. Her skin is pale and her bone structure angular. The blue flash of her navis across her forehead when the light hits it right, and the blue flag of the Callisto colony pinned to her lapel, are the only spots color on her.

"Good morning," I say.

"Good morning, Doctor Steven Kwon." She smiles and takes a small sip of tea. "How do you prefer to be called?"

"Steven's fine." I smile back, curious about how I will build a rapport with her. "And you?"

Her lips make a subtle upward quirk, but the gesture is too ambiguous to label a smile. "Just Jordis. No titles needed here."

I look at my notes to give myself time to adjust to her presence, rather than to reference them. Her schedule hadn't allowed her to come to Mars with the others earlier in the week. "I understand the élan known as Europa will make the link between us?"

"If Europa will have you." Jordis' expression is a smile now, but I'm still not sure how to interpret it. I've watched a lot of media of Jordis Ansari, but all I've learned is that she's a consummate politician.

"I also understand that you're the only one of my interviewees with perfect recall?"

"During this set of interviews, yes."

"And what does perfect recall mean, exactly? There are a lot of myths."

"Poor memory in humans isn't a storage problem; it's a recall problem. For Operators, nauta, those of us who use a navis, we've programming to build pointers into our storage. It's the 'memory index' function, and we can turn memories on and off like a blink. Noa's memory index was—well, you'll see. And Caran often makes...unorthodox decisions." She sets down the cup and saucer on the table between us with frosty efficiency. Then she looks straight at me with a raised brow and no smiles. "You do understand that there are many things I will not recall for you."

My limbs go cold as I reel my imagination back from what those things might be and cover my unease. "Your participation in this research is entirely voluntary. You do not need to participate in this, or any, research study. You do not have to disclose anything you don't want to. Exactly as written in the consent you signed."

The smile returns, but with a predatory edge. "Exactly as written in the amendments you and All Worlds Scientific signed in the presence of my lawyers, as well."

Jordis Ansari is not like any nauta I have ever met. They're usually easy to pick out, even the less affected ones. There's a slight delay to speech and movements as complex programming struggles to express thoughts and feelings in real-time, and there's a subtle jerkiness or unsettling smoothness as they are, quite literally, marionettes manipulated by the strings of their programming. They have tics, like Caran's hand-shaking and pacing. But if this woman covered her forehead, and I had not known better, I would have assumed she was normal. She's Class 15, though; high on the severity scale.

"All right," I say, "I'm ready to link when you are."

She nods and the air cools. The tiny hairs all over my body stand on end. I'm in the presence of an élan vital, one without any of Muse's playfulness and warmth.

<silverseashimmer hunger hungry roll the dice and play to win dark-soothe heat-food! hungry HUNGRY flying through the cool-blue! have you got a penny give a penny get a penny, penny penny I AM COMING TO EAT YOU NOW>

"Fuck!" I curse, I actually curse as I recoil from something so intensely alien my intestines lurch.

"Oh Europa," Jordis says unphased—perhaps a touch amused—and holds one finger up to something I cannot see. "Surely we can find a common ground. Look at the honors and awards on the wall behind his head."

Before I'm recovered the alien comes at me again and this time with a feeling of <*ambition-defiance-pride*> all bound up in <*risk-thrill!*> THAT *all of that* has driven me, Steven Kwon, to succeed apart from, above my peers!

Hunger breaks over me like someone's smashed an egg on my head.

Not the pressure-cooker hunger of Caran's desire for NQ, but the hunger of a predator.

<to be specific, the hunger of the predatory ecosystem beneath the surface of europa's ice> The words are in Jordis' voice but her

lips have not moved. Such a coherent telepathy has not happened yet with Caran. And, with a chill, I realize Jordis' answer means that she heard the unspoken question in my thoughts.

<remember> Jordis continues, a knowing inside my head <europa-élan spent billions of years unaffected by humanity but very much aligned with the electromagnetic emissions of europa's uniquely hungry sea life. also, you will find i am a good deal more disciplined than caran> Her expression is of amusement, but her eyes crinkle with sympathy for my reaction. She knows this whole business of aligning with alien intelligences is unsettling. But more importantly, this is the first indication she's given that she might possess humanity.

I'm not sure how to think words back rather than having her pick up my thoughts by happenstance, so I say aloud, "What I learned from my sessions with Caran is that the best way to tune the resonance is to just start talking. So, give me a little background on why you went to Europa, what you thought you were getting into, context. Then we'll get deeper into what happened as the resonance strengthens."

"That sounds good." Jordis also speaks aloud, but there's a precognitive echo: her thoughts brush through the link ahead of her voice. So there is a lag with her programming, it's just so small I can't detect it with my eyes and ears alone.

Jordis continues, legs crossed, and hands folded neatly in her lap. "I went to Europa because of the bombing in Hangar 19, the one that got blamed on the Genetic Liberation Front. The Galilean Black Market—my father's syndicate—owned the hangar. The cargo destroyed in the bombing was part of a delicate negotiation between the Galilean Black and the Empire of the Moon—which I represented. The situation was politically unstable and required someone of my rank to investigate and sanitize."

"You were an Enforcer for the mob."

She smiles. "Don't be crass. The Empire of the Moon has a legitimate Corporate Charter."

I don't comment that the Empire of the Moon is a chartered front for the Luna Black Market. "But you were not a legitimate Enforcer."

She taps her nose with her finger. Her eyes still smile. Her <*pleasure/hope*> leaking through the nascent link tells me she likes a game, particularly one of verbal wit, and also that's as close as I'll get her to admitting to criminal acts. "It is true that as nauta, I was not allowed a position as a Corporate Enforcer. However, Madame X, who runs the Empire from Earth's moon, has always been more forward-thinking than the government. She understands the benefit of matching one's occupation with one's talents."

I try not to think too hard about some of Jordis Ansari's talents. "So you were in a leadership role for the Empire, working for Madame X, even though your father led the rival Galilean syndicate?"

"That is correct. However, no one on the Galilean side—including my father—knew I was working for X. Officially, Jordis Ansari was sponsored by ComSat to program communications relays. I was Gala Baudin. Since no one on Europa had seen Jordis since she was twelve years old and pig-tailed, they never equated her with the tall woman I'd become."

"This was your first time back since you were twelve?"

"It was."

"One last piece of information I want to make sure I have clear. Would you say there was special significance to the cargo beyond its role in negotiation between the two largest Sol-system syndicates? I mean, with respect to the Great Changes?"

"Oh, yes, I see where you're going." She takes a final, slow sip of tea, and places the empty cup on the table. "The negotiation involved an exchange of Empire-owned freedomtech for goods and territory agreements from the Galilean Black. The Empire had a monopoly on relations with Freedom at the time. We had an Arrangement whereby they would provide us with their technology in return for our protection."

"Did the Luna syndicate know about the élan vitals?"

"No, only that Freedom held a valuable secret—one that enabled them to bypass all electronic security and access any information they wanted, as well as to create magical-seeming freedomtech, like my fan."

"Fan?"

She laughs a little, as one does at a slightly fond memory. "Ah yes, my fan. It has the ability to adaptively bend electromagnetic and sonic waves around whoever is using it, rendering them undetectable."

"Like a magic shield?"

"No, it provides protection in a bubble, like that popular superhero, who is it?"

"Camo-Man. I think he's a supervillian?"

"Maybe. You know who I mean. We'd tried to get Freedom's secrets for decades, but we couldn't torture them per the Arrangement, and they'd confounded every more oblique attempt. Madame X thought chasing those secrets was a fun game, but I was just frustrated. The two representatives from Freedom who had supplied the freedomtech were also killed in the bombing. This made it a diplomatic incident between three entities—the Empire of the Moon, the Galilean Black, and Freedom—except that Freedom's existence was only known to the Empire. Madame X sent me in to sort it out and clean it up. I was already in the area, in my private shuttle, looking into some interests near Ganymede, so I could get there in about an hour."

"Thank you. Okay, so take me there. Take me into those memories. Show me your Europa."

◊

(the transition to Jordis' memories is instant and complete; the bombing has occurred fifteen minutes before)

The cool, smooth hiss of the private shuttle's environmentals surrounds me. The seat is soft and comfortable; the arms inlaid with smooth wood. Black, star-studded sky fills the window, crisp through the void of space. The pearl of the moon Europa floats in stars, still too far to appear to be getting closer.

I was twelve years old when you sold me to a Nursery on Luna, Daddy, twelve years old when I watched that perfect pearl shrink until it vanished. Twenty-two years of living on memories that will never fade, memory-indexed playback of glitter and grace, undersea wonder, endless ache.

I press my hand to the window, covering Europa. Checking again to see if the moon has swollen past my open palm. No, not yet.

Soon, Europa, I will be in you and your ocean will surround me like a womb.

Madame X sends a signal to my navis, requesting a report.

I accept, connect, and enter the call in her private informationspace at a break in a wrought-iron fence, stepping through a tangle of perfumed orchids and wisteria. A gibbous moon casts soft shadows from a starless sky puffed with lazy clouds. Crickets chirp and the air smells of flowers and dew. The center of my chest glows faintly pink with pride at the level of entry privilege I enjoy. *I am a Key Enforcer now, Daddy. Not because of my skills at programming my behavior but because I am as virtuoso a politician as you. I deserve my birthright, and I will take it from you.*

As I move toward the center of the garden, a gazebo flickers through foliage like white ribs. Madame X sits within. She presents as a fully realized rendering of the subject of Singer-Sargent's painting "Portrait of Madame X," full of hauteur and longing in her black evening dress and up-swept hair. I ascend the gazebo's wooden stairs and bow to my Queen. Not so low as I once had. When our ranks are equal, I will not bow at all.

"Did you speak with your father's Primo Capo?"

"Yes." I take the wicker chair opposite X around the iron table. "He claims my father has no idea what is going on with the freighter bombing on Europa."

"Well. That's disturbing." X twirls a lily between her thumb and forefinger, clouds moving quickly across the sky in response to her thinking.

"What I find more disturbing than my father being on the shut-out"—I smooth the always-perfect creases in my presentation's pants—"is that Freedom's cell on Luna seems to have no idea what's going on with the bombing either—or, if they do, they feel it's important to hide it from us. But their shock seemed genuine, and they've never been good at hiding their feelings."

X nods and her mouth makes a semi-smile, though the moon in the night garden clouds further in response to her concern. "How close are you to port?"

I don't dare switch focus back to the physical world. Europa City mewls at the gates of my desire like it's alive, and I won't be able to keep a neutral face if I let it in.

I split off a thread of consciousness and query the pilot instead.

Through his implanted com, since he is obviously not an Operator, he subvocalizes that we'll make port in fifteen minutes.

"Jordis, are you sure about this? We really can send someone else." Madame X's eyes fix on the center of my chest, watching to see if I betray any of my emotions there.

I keep my center dark. "Absolutely. There are none better for the job."

X exhales but her eyes do not relax. "Remember, you are to investigate the bombing, and nothing else." Thunder rumbles in the landscape.

I meet my mentor's hardness, allowing my chest to glow with blue-gold-silver colors of love, honor, and just an edge of indignation. "I am a Key Enforcer for the Empire of the Moon. And you are far more my parent than my mother-killing father ever was."

A breeze smooths over the thunder and X's eyes soften. "I promise you, someday, you will have your chance at your birthright. But not today. You are a Key Enforcer and they must respect you. You are my talented daughter-in-heart and I trust you. You have abilities they cannot fathom and that amuses me. And you know Ray Ansari better than anyone. I want you to find out why our goods were destroyed and our people killed. And then I want you straight home to Luna."

But Europa is my home. I hold my own surface ice as thick as Europa's crust. "Of course I'll come straight home."

X tilts her head toward me, her pale, beautiful face catching moonlight in an enigmatic half-smile at some unvoiced thought. I rise, kneel, and kiss my Queen's hand.

The night garden warms, plants bending inwards as X takes

my face in her soft, aristocratic hands. "My blessings to you, Key Enforcer, daughter-of-my-heart. May your journey bring the Empire reward."

I walk just far enough from the gazebo to maintain the illusion of reality, as is polite, and cut the connection, switching my focus to the physical world.

While I've been speaking with X, Europa has consumed the star field, filling the window. I barely have time to process that before we hurtle into the black tunnel carved into the surface ice along with dozens of other shuttles flicking toward East Bay Entry Port. I hug the shiver-thrill in with my arms wrapped around my shoulders as green lights flash through blue-white ice.

The shuttle buckles and slows as it hits inky black liquid water. Strands of guide-lights lilt in the boundless sea. At the end of those lights is Europa City. The Dreaming City. Home.

The Europa City torus emerges from the watery darkness, a six-story ring floating around Europa's rock core. My hands tremble in my lap; my breath comes in quick, cool pants. The multi-colored neons of Casino Row glow through the torus' windows. Every night of my exile I have watched a 3V of this approach, trying to quench my homesickness. But this is real.

My skin prickles, like I'm standing in a static field. I touch the window and get zapped. An electromagnetic interaction between the shuttle and the water?

Has the city always felt so conscious, so much like it is screaming through the darkness to me?

Ten minutes later I step into Europa Immigrations. Tourists flow through the vastness. I don't remember the port ever having been so busy, but then, I'd been in my father's company, and he can clear whole sectors of the torus when he wants. *You're good at clearing things away, aren't you Daddy? Your mistake not to clear me away when you had the chance.*

I spot a four-story window and do not stop until my fingertip makes contact with the cold heavy glass. A moon-full of sunless sea flows beyond, lit by the glow from the window and the vanishing strands of guide lights. The air of my homeland smells of brine with a hint of decay's perfume. My pulse flutters against the strap of my Vemi suit-bag. Out there, in the indigo black, is an ecosystem older than Earth's. I am slightly ahead of schedule, so I stop and wait for hope of glimpsing life.

The tourists do not. They bore of black waters and move on for Casino Row, or the All Worlds Scientific Conservatory where they can see Europa's sea life trapped in cages behind glass.

I replay memories from my childhood with perfect recall: standing before windows onto black waters waiting for the flash of life. There! A school of angeltorch. A softly floating colony of wormgrass. And that one time when I watched a filigree jelly envelop and consume its stick-like garber prey.

In the here and now, my patience is rewarded by a school of pale, eel-like quarana arcing past the customs window, their translucent sides flashing in the glow of the port. I feel my own flash of love, hunger, a nostalgia so strong my toes curl inside my shoes. If only I could transmute into a quarana and join them, or become a nightmare filigree, or even a furtive angeltorch, anything to bind more strongly to Europa's first life. I want to crawl inside the soul of the moon.

But I have a job to do.

I pull back. The glass reflects the two-story 2V promo behind me. Scrawled in backwards mirror-script on the window between the worlds: "Caran Watts all week at the Mnemosyne! SOLD OUT!

(flash-flash-flash) Queue up now for cancels!" I couldn't go even if I had a ticket. The entertainment establishments of Europa are "no Operators allowed," and I've no use for costumes.

On the 2V advert, the performer's slender, amber hands open to reveal a mini-supernova against a background blending from indigo to pale tzaddium blue. "Two Shades of Blue" scrawls almost illegibly over the animation. Daring, that; the world is rarely kind to any who give such obvious reminders of humanity's dependence on Operators. But then Watts always rides the edge of acceptable, and always gets away with it, too. Artists can get away with almost as much as Enforcers.

I turn from the window and walk past the long tourist line and the humiliating Operator line to the VIP booth. The Immigrations agent intones "Enjoy your stay on Europa" to the people in front of me. Then I stand before him.

"Gala Baudin," the agent drones as I swipe the webbing of my thumb over the plate and my identifying data appears in his 3V.

I smooth the lines of my suit and the tight black knot of my bun while his slow normal brain processes his display.

He looks up from the splay of color. "Operator Class 15, sponsored by the Empire of the Moon?" His eyes are dull and cold, voice strained, resentful that he has to be polite to me.

I smile at his discomfort and nod. "If you'd like"—I lay on the sweetness of implication—"I can connect you directly with my owner."

"Oh, no, that won't be necessary," the agent replies blandly, but I'm rewarded by his shudder. He knows X. Everyone knows X. The Empire of the Moon has fingers everywhere.

He opens my suit bag and a cloud of hazard-sensors buzz like bluebottles but find nothing of interest. Or rather, report nothing of interest.

The illegal bio-mod wand rolls over my body but manages to "miss" the custom dex-enhancers swarming in my blood.

I don't know how anyone gets by without paying off the authorities to look the other way.

"Enjoy your stay on Europa." He pauses and then adds, under the onus of his bigotry, "And make it brief. Unless you belong to one of the casinos, your kind isn't welcome here."

I give him a small smile, small like the person he is, and make sure he sees it drop before I've turned from him. There are lessons I can teach him about respect, but the flash of the quarana has put me in a forgiving mood.

My heels clack across the gossamer veil of light marking the national boundary. "Welcome to Europa: Nation of Dreams" sprawls in gold inlay on the black-tiled floor and projects in 3V from the gold-tiled ceiling. Two-story banners display the ruby-and-indigo water droplet sigil of the Europan government. Europa has the only independent government amongst the Core worlds of inhabited space, and she's retained that autonomy across all her centuries; I am proud of her for being always herself. I lick sweet-saltiness from my lips as I stride to the yellow tube line.

Six minutes later I board the platform for the Four-Points Express to South Node. The 2V ceiling feed plays an update about the freighter bombing. The landing patterns at South Bay are a mess. Expected operations-back-to-normal in another twelve hours. All indications point to a terrorist action by the Pro-Operator Genetic Liberation Front. *I do not envy your damage control, Daddy. I know how much illicit cargo was on that freighter, splashed now all over the walls of Hangar 19.*

The feed begins a feature on the Genetic Liberation Front. Radical Operators. Terrorists. The Europan government is trying very hard to track down who is responsible for obscene graffiti sprayed in tzaddium-blue on the wall of Heng University.

The whole thing feels off to me. I know most of the real terrorists, and none of them are interested in helping Operators. I have never heard of this "GLF."

I close my eyes and open a channel to the informationspace of the Mem with my navis. It's a simple, reflex thought sent into my programming to tune the receiver to a local node. If one removes the modern frills like dimensional relays, the Mem is no different from the 20th century's internet. Digital signal transmitted on an electromagnetic frequency from infrared to radio depending on how far you need it to travel. The Mem is a sensory layer programmed atop the signals to make it easier and more practical to manipulate. It is a deeper version of the holicons normals use on their 3V and 4V displays.

Yet, no other Operators on Europa could access it as I just have. They are all corporate-owned and restricted by hobbles, limited to only those parts of the Mem pertinent to their work, and never allowed to communicate freely with each other.

I have no hobbles. Madame X gifted me with the programming to break them decades ago. What we Operators could do together if we were all unbound.

I make the most of my tube ride by multitasking in the Mem: catching up on business with a buyer, attending a disciplinary hearing on one of the crews, and ordering new furniture for my home on Luna which I hope never to see again.

Twenty minutes later I walk into dust and ash and death.

The bomb in Hangar 19 of South Port's industrial sector has pulverized the freighter bound for Luna and all of its precious freedomtech cargo, as well as Greene and his crew, Luna's ambassador to the Galilean Black, and all of the members of Freedom's Europan cell.

"Gala! She's over here, come quickly." Primo Capo Som Bliss snatches me from the ruckus of purchased police and bewildered Enforcers. Som was barely past puberty last time I'd seen him in the flesh, one of Daddy's favorites, and now he's tall and handsome. His dark curls sit short and flat in the neo-Roman style, and his muscles flex beneath his tight sweater. He flashes the hands-open palms-out greeting of the Black followed by the hook-fingered gesture of his rank.

I return protocol with the slicing motion of my rank, and he leads me to the far edge of the room. A huddle of medics surround something bloody on the floor. Thick white dreadlocks and the exposed shine of tzaddium where the flesh of the victim's forehead has burned away tell me she is—or perhaps was—Hyperia of Freedom.

"Move." The medics part to let me by.

Hyperia isn't alive, but she's just barely dead too. I open a shortwave band to her navis, hoping there's enough brain function left to get a response. Random noise skitters through the channel, then a ghostlike image a ballerina—the way Hyperia presents herself in the Mem. There's something more though, if I can grab it, something she's placed in machine memory, not committing to her meat, and it's encoded to allow my patterns to access it—

There. A bundle of raw data jetting up toward me like a torpedo—

I catch it.

Random sevens and a rotating ellipse tasting of cream cheese and jam—

It's in Hyperia's private internal language which I will not be able to decode.

But there's a faint common pattern over the unreadable jargon, a ghost of the lingua franca that she may have been building as she died. She'd been hoping someone would pick up on it. If there's enough there I can filter it and I see—

A feathered, winged white dragon presentation I've not seen in years. It belonged to a young man named, unimaginatively, Dragon, who'd run with Djen in the Stella-Maru. He'd been an ass.

More images follow: a snap of musician Caran Watts, the luminous pearl of Europa, a Greek Muse beside a well that I recognize as the corporate sigil for the Mnemosyne Hotel and Theatre, a throb of horror, a word in carefully spelled letters—

"Dragon is Caran Watts, he's on Europa at the Mnemosyne Theatre. Tell him everyone's in trouble. Dividia's behind it; going to kill us all."

"D.i.v.i.d.i.a." in carefully spelled letters. I do not recognize this word.

Som Bliss rocks forward with a worried, hopeful look. "Was she fresh enough to save any of her data? She's only been all the way gone twenty minutes. We kept her alive as long as we could, as you requested."

"Give me that." I snatch a sharp thing from one of the medics faster than he can see and slice away at the rags of flesh on Hyperia's face. I pull out her navis; the micro-filaments connecting it to her brain through the pores of her skull tear with a ripping, squishing sound. I wrap the device in a wad of gauze.

Som stares at the bloody bundle. His dark eyes reflect revulsion over the exposed Operator hardware, but I sense I've gained his respect for my indifference to the gore.

"She's too far gone to get information the easy way, but I might be able to pull something from the hardware." I lie with disinterested superiority so that I can keep the device. There is extra hardware tacked onto Hyperia's navis that warrants a closer look.

I feel red triumph, and my pulse flicks a thrill.

Caran Watts is Dragon, that asshole kid from Freedom.

Nothing in the Arrangement between Freedom and the Empire of the Moon precludes the blackmail, torture, or coercion of former members of Freedom. If Watts is Dragon, he'll be using NQ to function as a normal—"Two Shades of Blue" indeed. How not-clever. *You are as weak and stupid as I remember you, Dragon, always taking the easy way out instead of the higher, harder road to power I took. And if you are so weak and stupid as to get addicted to NQ then it will be no trouble to use NQ to take Freedom's secrets from you. I will then do as you do and slip through the protocols of the Mem to take whatever data I want. I will build magical devices that defy the laws of physics. And I will use it all to take back my Kingdom.*

That night, I cross my legs in the plush chair at the Mnemosyne Hotel and Theatre and smile at the wreckage of Caran Watts. The opulence of the Orpheus Suite evades gaudy by virtue of its dream-like quality, like a painting by Marc Chagall. Red and purple fabric with hints of green drape against cobalt walls. Constellations stud the ceiling in faceted quartz. Conversations I've had with Madame X about lost art enable me to identify a replica of Seon's "Sleeping Orpheus" on one wall, and Khnopff's "The Caress"—a young man cheek-to-cheek with a cheetah with a woman's head—on another. The Orpheus Suite indeed.

"How—" Watts sputters at me, tripping on the plushness of the plum carpet. He is in even worse shape than I'd hoped for upon finding his stash.

I flick open my golden freedomtech fan, its semi-intelligent adaptive EM field rendering me invisible and inaudible. *Soon I'll know how you work your undetectability magic, fan.* He shows no surprise at my disappearance, but plenty of drug-sloppy papper indignation over my possession of the technology in the first place.

"You're not supposed to have that kind of tech—"

"Tsss." I snap the fan shut, reappearing. "Since your day, Freedom's gotten more expansive with what it's willing to trade for our services." The hypocrisy of his horror makes me laugh. I wave his drugs at him. "Oh come now, surely you know the sorts of things people will do when they get desperate."

He makes a grab for the vial, but he's slow from withdrawal and I'm faster than human with my bio-modified reflexes, and he misses me by a quarter meter. He stumbles into the black lacquered dresser behind me, bashing his shins on inlays of neo-Classical youth exploring adventurous sexual positions.

"How—" Watts weaves back, flushed and sweating in a ridiculous leotard that ripples with colors in response to his voice.

"A bomb went off at the space port earlier today." No reaction. "It destroyed a freighter loaded with a fair amount of freedomtech, as well as Hyperia and Jost." A reaction at that, stiffening. "Hyperia had you at the fore of her thoughts when she died, for reasons I cannot fathom. To your credit, I was surprised to learn that Dragon wasn't dead, but instead had become Caran Watts. Or, perhaps better stated, had returned to being Caran Watts. Though after researching your early history it's hardly the sort of past one would want to return to, even to reclaim a given name, so, I fathom you did it because Caran Watts is tagged as normal in the Citizen ID Bank."

He lunges at me again, and I shift my weight to send him crashing into the bed. There's no reason for verbal fencing with one of my own kind so I get to the point. "You're going to slop all of Freedom's secrets, particularly the ones that get me around the Mem's security protocols and into manufacturing items like my fan, and then I'm going to give you back your pap. We'll start," I set down the heavy fan and pull the thin blue rectangle of Hyperia's navis from my pocket, "with you telling me exactly what this extra hardware is for."

"She was torqued up on biomods, what could I do. Couldn't do anything. Nothing besides biomods makes a person move that fast." Caran tells me.

He is still angry even though the event happened four years ago. He takes no measure to hide it, pacing and glaring.

"And then she just spits out about Hyperia and Jost, like they weren't my friends, like she wasn't telling me my friends were fucking dead." He shakes out his hands and then balls them into tight fists. Release, shake, squeeze, again.

I've slipped into the link easily today. In my training, Cami had said: "The more you match frequencies and align with a particular élan, the easier it gets to find resonance, just like getting familiar with a person. At first, you're monitoring to make sure you're not doing or saying something that makes 'em unhappy, but then you fall into easy conversation and all that self-monitoring goes away."

I'm still self-monitoring with Caran, despite my growing comfort with Muse. If anything, the self-consciousness is worse. It's not like I'm shy about his celebrity; it's something else.

As an anthropologist, I'm trained in self-reflection. In my field, we fully acknowledge the researcher as a part of the research; the researcher cannot be separated as an "objective observer." Self-awareness, transparency, disclosure provide defense against error. Until I identify and compensate for my unease, I could ask him the wrong questions, avoid key follow-up probes, or misrepresent his story through the distortion of an unidentified bias.

I feel drawn to him too strongly; I need to keep my distance. Something about his story feels too familiar. While I can identify what I'm experiencing, I can't identify why I am experiencing it.

"Steven?" Caran's voice quivers my name, hesitant and fearful.

"Oh, sorry." I focus on him with the warmth I genuinely feel for him. "Flaky researcher." I point to my head with an embarrassed shrug. "I get distracted by my ideas."

He collapses with visible relief into the sofa and gives me a crooked grin. "Yeah, just like Noa."

"I'm sure my ideas aren't as interesting as Noa's." The link makes his grin contagious. Or maybe I would have grinned at him anyway. I blush because he makes me a little flirty, and I'm doing nothing to hold myself back. This makes me even more uncomfortable because it is my job to hold myself back.

He looks at me from under his lashes, also a little flirty, and laughs. "Yeah, no one's smart as Noa!"

"So back to that moment with Jordis in your hotel room. Did you recognize her?"

Anger flashes again in his shiny black eyes, but the rawness of it has broken and he stays put in his seat. "I recognized her as Gala Baudin of the Luna Black. But I didn't know she was Ray Ansari's daughter. I'd never given thought to Jordis Ansari, didn't know a Jordis Ansari existed. Tried to stay away from that Black Market shit back when I was running with Djen, and never liked Gala anyway. We had history. I'd never met her in the flesh, but her presentation in the Mem looks just like her body in the flesh so I'd seen her before. It's near-impossible to fake someone else's presentation. My presentation's a dragon so she never knew what I looked like in the flesh."

I squint my way through the slightly disjointed monologue and nod. "Can you elaborate on 'history'?"

"Yeah, there was a lot of it and all of it bad. But the worst was when Djen and me had to steal this art for Madame X in return for med supplies for Freedom's Emory cell. The security systems blasted a hole in *Stella-Maru* on the way out, which meant we might not survive our next dimension dive. But Gala—she was our liaison with the Luna Black—wouldn't pay for repairs even though it was her fault for not warning us they had cannon.

"'Should've been faster,' she'd said. But we couldn't be fucking faster, there's a top-limit on real-space engines even for a class 6 exploratory vessel, and we didn't have shit to pay with. We thought to resell the art, but Gala made it clear she'd kill us if we didn't deliver the goods, so we ended up almost dying in a dimension dive to Nerion Station where we could hole up in a pay-for-fuck place to pay for repairs. Everyone wants to have sex with nauta, but no one wants to admit it. Made the money fast but it wasn't good. Wasn't fun. I hate pay-for-fuck. She was a bint, Gala. Hated her."

His seething hisses at me from a deeper place than friction with Jordis.

"Yeah, deeper." The link is strong enough now that it's transmitting my thoughts. "The way normals use us, our bodies and our minds. Pay-for-fuck is what society did to us nauta for the past five hundred years. I said Freedom needed to get out of bed with the Luna Black. The Arrangement was they'd protect us, and we'd sell them exclusive rights to our tech. But we were slaves to them, same way Operators were slaves to normals, more pay-for-fuck. But who listened to me. No one listened to me. I was shit-nothing. I was Djen's breach of protocol."

It takes me a moment to process all of that back around into the story at hand. "Jordis—Gala—had you trapped in that hotel room the same way the Luna Black had Freedom trapped in its trade Arrangement?"

He bares his teeth with a seething, sucking sound. "That's how Freedom played it, yeah—trapped by the Luna Black. No way out. But I didn't buy that the Arrangement was the only way."

He looks down at animated hands, twitching and shaking out a rhythm in his lap. He swallows, breathes, closes his eyes.

His hands quiet and his face clears.

When he opens his eyes to me again, they hold a nervous, desperate-edged light that outshines his darkness. His voice is brighter still: "There's always hope. There's always another way out."

◊

Hyperia and Jost are dead.

Hyperia and Jost

are

dead.

I hadn't seen either of them in ten years, but the words still drop the floor out from under me.

No more Hyperia dancing through Europa City's abandoned back hallways doing back alley ballet with dip-dyed white hair frizzing around her narrow brown face.

No more Jost holding back, watching, showing his maturity as older sibling, hands cupped around the seeds I brought back for him from Arcadia to plant in his beautiful back alley garden—

Oh, shit, I'm the only one left on Europa who knows about the élan vitals.

I reach for Muse, for comfort, for not-being-alone, but the creature is off hanging out with my fans.

"Freedom's secrets." Gala waggles my vial of NQ at me, reeling me back to the now. "A fair trade for your life, jo?"

Brother-fucking how much sarcasm can I drool through my voice—"Oh Gala, you know me so well."

That gets an eye-roll, tip of her fan twitching, slime-ball politician feigning offense so I want to punch her.

Fuck. Fuck this sticky, itching, sweat-soaked leotard I've been wearing since before the show, don't care if I tear it, I don't care how much it fucking costs. Fucking off, get it off, OFF OFF OFF!

Air.

Naked like I like to be, save for the weight of the platinum-coated dataslip on its slender chain around my neck. Breast-bone pressure.

Eyes closing on exhausted tears.

Finding the bed with my fingers, can feel the slip of satin as the sheets slide against each other but can't feel the sheets against the pads of my fingers because of my fucking stupid hyposensitive sense of touch. I hate Gala I hate myself. Cover me over in meters of purple satin sheets, let me sleep.

I cry instead.

Knees hugged to my manic heartbeat, withdrawal pain flares and I welcome it, pull it in. Hurts less than my feelings. Stupid, useless, blown-it-all-for-everyone should never have been born.

I can work this.

I won't be useless if I die defending Freedom.

I'll never give Gala our secrets.

I shiver in satin, squinting through tear-blur. "Tell me about the bombing." I hold my voice almost steady.

"Tell you…" She laughs cold disbelief.

"Were Hyperia and Jost collateral damage, or the target?"

"Oh, no, you don't." She holds up the vial to the light again.

I swallow the agony marching through my flesh. "Oh yes I do. You weren't sent here for me, Gala, you were sent here to investigate the bombing and I can help you out like no one left alive."

"Freedom's secrets and I'll dose it." She sing-songs off-key.

"You're in over your head and you know it." I sing-song back with the voice of Orpheus.

"Over my head? It's only a matter of time before you can't maintain the lie and the card-house falls."

"Yeah. And Madame X wouldn't send an Enforcer into Ray Ansari's territory unless something catastrophic happened with the Arrangement. Hyperia and Jost were all that was left of Freedom on Europa, so it's not like you've got anyone but me. You don't wanna go back to Mommy empty-handed, do you?"

"I won't be empty-handed." Gala twirls my vial again and I salivate.

"I'd rather tell the world I'm nauta than tell you what I ate for breakfast." I wipe spit off my chin with the satin sheets and bare my teeth, but I want the vial bad, so bad. Sweat rolls down my chest and I cough into a flare of agony. Through halos of pain, I see Gala shift and I sense I've unsettled her some way. Good.

"You've just the crap-ass attitude I remember."

"Then you remember I think the Arrangement binding Freedom to Madame X's syndicate is the worst idea since treating depression with trepanation." I dish out a pleasant, mocking smile.

"Your life is worth so little?" She quirks up her own lips, but I wouldn't call it a smile.

"More that keeping you ignorant is worth so much." The only

thing worse than organized crime having unlimited access to human-élan technology, is organized crime manipulating human-élan feedback. Muse does enough damage to my handlers, imagine ethics-free Madame X manipulating élan resonance on an interstellar scale. "You're bound by the Arrangement, and since Freedom was present during the bombing, you've a contractual obligation to tell me about it."

"You're not bound to the Arrangement anymore. When was the last time you were involved with Freedom?"

"One doesn't get uninvolved with Freedom, Gala. You know that or you wouldn't be trying to kill me for its secrets. Now tell me what happened at the bomb site."

She assaults me with a cold stare that goes on too long. I can hold it. I spend half my life with media. She gives. "The bomb went off just as they finished loading the freighter, so we lost max cargo and max lives. Hyperia and Jost from Freedom, Madame's ambassador to Europa—"

"They call grift enforcers 'ambassadors' these days?"

A demure shrug and a glance toward the door. "If you don't want to know..."

"All right, all right. Go on." Hard to play nice with my heart beating its way out my chest.

"We also lost one of Europa's Capos, a man, Greene, who'd been our inside connection to Freedom's cell on Europa for decades."

Fuck. FUCK. So *that's* why Greene didn't show up today with my NQ. Greene's not coming back.

Greene's gone and I've got no other dealer on Europa. There's no hope of getting more pap until Luna.

Wish I could see the vial better with Gala sitting way over there; how much is left? I can live on four drops a dose—six before public appearances where I've got to look normal. That's four more days, twenty-four hours in an earth-standard day here, that's sixteen drops a day, but I shouldn't be totally out in case something goes hinky on Luna—Is there enough for that?

Shit, I can't see. I can't see the vial.

Gala has my vial.

How is it that every part of my life tangled up in that fucking freighter bombing? It delayed *Sonica's* approach, killed my friends, killed my dealer, brought the Curse of Gala down on me, there's got to be a connection here—

"But shadows coming alive makes as much sense as attaching crystal matrix to a navis." Gala's still speaking while I've stopped listening.

"What?" The purple satin sheet's going bright, light reflecting off the sheen, little fluffs of thread floofing up from the glimmer-weave. I see every thread, each one a shimmer-song, scree-scree so softly is the sound of satin rubbing against itself. Gala's words skid away, "our own sa-va-va-ing eye-wit-ten-ness sah, tah, shad-OH-dah-calive."

It's the NQ burning out; I'm returning to my true senses.

My nauta state.

I tug on the platinum-coated dataslip until I can feel the pressure past the numbness of my sense of touch and the screaming of withdrawal pain. I'm not gonna make it. I'm not gonna fucking make it.

◊

"I need to take a break." Caran stands, toppling the coffee table into my shins, and stumble-runs from the room.

The link remains; I feel Muse as a heat on my face, a drumming in my heart. No, that's Caran's pulse drumming, my own trying to match it in the anxiety of his storytelling.

<*noworries*> Muse feels to me.

Something in the link shifts and rebalances.

<to give him some space> Muse injects into my thoughts, answering my question about what's shifted. <no need to break the link but i give some privacy. the link is more you-me than you-he now.>

<is he okay?> I think back reflexively. I am just as astonished today as the last time the alien communicated with me directly. It doesn't feel alien though. It feels as comfortable as my own thoughts—if someone else were thinking them for me.

<he is okay. he is clumsy. he had to pee. and collect his feelings. you push hard. he's learning to release before he pops.>

I rub my shins and laugh at the creature's bluntly mundane explanation—and its joke at the end? Can élan vitals engage in verbal humor, double-meanings?

<if they spend their lives with poets>

"Poets, what?" Caran returns. He's flushed like he might have cried or screamed for thirty seconds, but there's nothing else amiss about him. I sense the link balance shifting back into what Muse called "you-he."

<poets poetry potency productivity pedantry telemetry> Muse rattles off as its influence fades into the background again.

Caran rolls his eyes at the creature, settling back down in the couch.

"You okay?" I ask.

"I had to pee," he answers.

"Since we're stopped, can you explain what was so special about Hyperia's navis? Why was Jordis asking you about it?"

He scoffs. "I'm no expert. Navi might as well be magic to me. I didn't start using one until I was fourteen, when Djen gave me one."

"But you knew how the crystal matrix attachment—the one Jordis was interested in—worked?"

"Yeah, though the attachment is less about navis tech and more about the élan vitals."

"Tell me about that."

"An ordinary navis uses a person's brain for swap and storage. It's got a tiny piece of crystal matrix in it we call the 'hard memory' that's used to store things a person doesn't want to, or can't, have processed by their brain. That's where Hyperia put her dying message."

I nod.

"Well, the attachment isn't the hard memory. It's a separate piece of crystal matrix with hyperdense storage. The élans can put bits of themselves—or a copy of their whole selves—into it."

I wait for more but he's sitting back satisfied. "Can you say a little more?"

"Like what?"

"I think most people who haven't spent a lot of time with the élan vitals are going to be confused by that statement."

"Really?"

"Yes. Really."

He stares at me in a kind of "are you looped" disbelief but shakes himself and indulges. "Some people resonate naturally with an élan. These are your Dieuvéssaus, who work at the magic shops. Before they knew what the fuck, they thought they were chosen by gods. But how many Dieuvéssaus are there? It's less the point-oh-oh-five percent of the population. And most of them can only align with one élan. So how do you communicate with the creatures if you're a member of the unlucky and can't get the services of a Dieuvéssau?

"Well, if you're nauta, you can attach a specially-configured piece of crystal matrix to your navis and then the élans do this fractal thing—create a smaller but exact replica of themselves—and put that fractal-self inside of it. Then the navis' neurotranslator and programming and everything helps calibrate the resonance. The élans leave bits of themselves behind so you can call them back easier. If you spend too much time trying to access the data in an occupied matrix, you might summon an élan vital."

"So if you told Jordis what the crystal matrix was for on Hyperia's navis, she would know Freedom's secret about the élans?"

"Or if she'd triggered it and summoned an élan, she'd know. It wouldn't take her long from there to figure out that cooperation with the élans is how we bypass the security protocols of the Mem, make freedomtech, and stay hidden in the surveillance age. And then organized crime wins the world. That is, if the élans didn't decide humans were just too dangerous and destroy us all. That's why it was such a big deal Djen brought me in without an invite from an élan. The élans weren't happy with humans. We'd already blown our chance of a peaceful co-existence. They felt we'd manipulated them too much. We can change them as much as they can change us, and they don't like most of those changes. Which is an important factor in how they reacted later."

He clears the images and leans back on the sofa, feet up again on the coffee table. "There was a false bottom in my lockbox, under where I kept my stash. My navis was in there. It had the same matrix. A little poking around between mine and Hyperia's, and Jordis would have had all the answers without blackmailing me with my life. Might have even summoned Muse or Stella from it."

"So there was a lot at stake in that hotel room?"

"Fuck yeah. You think I wanted to suffer?"

He winces as the lie comes through the link, and I wince too. But I'm an anthropologist, not a psychologist, and something about the nature of the lie makes me squirm harder than I feel I should. "Shall we get back to the story?"

◊

"...to a navis." Jordis is talking and I'm still not listening.

"Sorry. One more time."

"I said, our only surviving eyewitness said the shadows came alive. Honestly, do you even want to know this?"

"Yes, I do. Sorry. It would be easier if you let me have my pap. At some point I will lose speech, you know."

"And I know you've ways around that since you managed to survive the first fourteen years of your life. Here's what the eyewitness said." Her eyes unfocus as she accesses her memory index. "'They came rolling from the corners and boiling from beneath the freighter and got solid-like enough to pull people—shit! Whole people!—off the ground and jolt 'em full of blue lightning. Goddamn smell, I'm never eating meat again. Then they made the freighter go ka-boom. Wasn't bombs though, you won't find no bombs. It was the shadows, the blue lightning. Ka-boom.'" She focuses back on me, pausing a loaded eight-count.

I hug my shivers tighter, hiding my reactions in withdrawal symptoms.

"Which, as I said twice already, makes as much sense as attaching a second piece of crystal matrix to a navis. Your turn—why did Hyperia have extra crystal matrix attached to her navis?"

"You didn't find any evidence of bombs, did you?"

"No."

Shadows coming alive makes every bit of sense for an élan vital. The creatures control EM from visible light to radio, and they can manipulate current—enough current to kill people and light fires. An élan would explain what happened, though not why. Gala's in over her head, and from the sound of it, so is Freedom. And so am I.

"So what's your theory?" Gala probes like a dental drill.

I try to shrug and shake my head but all that happens is a shivering fit. It's not like I'm going to say, *that "bomb" was probably an alien.* The real mystery is why would an élan want to blow up a freighter?

When the shivering's done, I see Gala frowning at the pale blue sheet of Hyperia's navis. "A human brain is ever-so-much-more efficient at swap and storage, so this attachment doesn't make sense."

"It makes sense if you want to store something without remembering it. Once you use the meat for swap and storage the data's a part of you. Can't un-know things, you know. Like I wish I could un-know you."

"Since what you say is self-evident," Gala pushes, "and there's already a hard memory component for that, I might ask what, exactly, Hyperia would want to keep out of her meat so badly it required a hardware redesign. I looked at it under a quantum imaging 'scope, and the matrix is wired in hard to the neurotranslator. Does it have something to do with how you people get around the security protocols of the Mem?"

I open my mouth to snark but:

roaring blank black emptiness

dash of "aaaahhhhhhh" C-flat forth octave

tumbling fear-anger

Goodbye expressive language. Fucking NQ. Always quits when I need it most.

Air-hiss: sigh.

Tap-tap-tappa-twelve count.

Twentieth century song + echo links by way of rolling rumble from orange oblong edges of justifiable outraged need-to-know—

Song flows where flat speech can no longer follow: "Message in a bottle / message in a bottle—Hyperia's?"

An intake of surprised breath from Gala. "I didn't say she'd a message for you."

Lyrics from a new song by The Rocket Brigade + echo + Mx. Bennet's hit I sing: "Come on, come on, come on baby—a bomb went off in the spaceport today. Hyperia. Give it / give it over / give it to me sweetheart I've a right to know."

A light mocking laugh from Gala. "I don't know about that, actually," she says as she taps the freedomtech fan on the lockbox. It makes a pleasant click-tap but she's got no sense of rhythm.

"You don't know about that"—I echo and point to Hyperia's navis—"*actually*." I want to stop her hand, force the click-tap into steady 3/4 time.

"I do know you're out of time. Tell me what this crystal matrix is for, nice and specific, and I'll give you a few drops to take the edge off."

Language lurches back as a last dreg of NQ burns through my body. I give her a focused stare, mouth full of cranky command—"I can't form a useful theory about the bombing if you don't give me all of the information. Hyperia wouldn't give me up for no reason, Gala. I'm fucked up, not stupid."

Bottom drops out, language lost; I burn. *Are freedom's secrets worth so much pain? What has Freedom done for me lately?*

"All right, but if you don't give me something I can use I'll drop this vial in the reclaimer." Gala stares, relentless. "I retrieved the message posthumously, so it's not like I had a conversation with her. Hyperia said that you were Dragon, and that you were on Europa. Then she said to tell you, more or less, 'Everyone's in trouble. Dividia's behind it; gonna kill us all.' That mean anything to you?"

The word "dividia" hits colder than the oblivion clawing for me. I've never heard it before yet, somehow, I feel like I recognize it. Is it the name of the élan that created the explosion?

Why'd Hyperia slop my identity to get the message out?

She could contact anyone instantly with a thought. If I were her, I would have contacted Fish and Freedom's cell on Ganymede, right next door. Or pointed Gala there.

Why'd she risk everything by revealing me, my weakness, my compromised situation to an enemy?

I'm the only outsider who knows Freedom's secrets and oh fuck is this what death feels like—"More, tell me more, tell me more more more more," lyrics by Ragoon Toons singing out my clenched teeth but I don't care anymore.

Gala's brows converge into a hard, cruel line. "No. We're done here." She leaves Hyperia's navis and my lockbox on the chair and menaces with my vial. It's centimeters from my face but I'm so tensed up I couldn't make a pass for it even if I could bypass her super-speed. Spittle dribbling from clenched teeth, burning up for bitter-sweet drops on my tongue, the sting-song of release.

"Do not assume I'll mourn your loss," she continues, cold breath on my raging-fire face. "You are no longer part of Freedom, you are not bound by the Arrangement, and you've nothing of value to add to my investigation. You can't game me, Caran Watts, not like you game your handlers, your fans, and the whole of the inhabited worlds. The deal stands, you tell me Freedom's secrets and I'll give you what you need to live till morning."

Fuckit.

Done with this burning shaking heart trying to flail itself out of my chest shit. I'm not gonna destroy Freedom tonight. Freedom's doing a good enough job of that all on its own.

Passing the fuck out now, thanks.

◊

The link lurches. Static fills my vision as Caran's consciousness collapses around his pain. The story shifts sideways into a spinning vertigo of alien perspective. The room becomes a glitter-flow of color, rivers of EM frequency beyond the range of visible light twinkling, flickering, defining the hotspots and the secret conversations of environmental-controlling nanites through the walls.

<i come> Muse thinks in my thoughts. <i touch caran; i touch jordis. i story-tell too!>

The creature's personality brushes against my mind, a flutter of dream wings and nightmare oil, insatiable be/longing.

The sensation subsides; the color-spew of EM signal dims and physical objects regain opacity. I experience the hotel room through the double-vision of Muse's and Jordis Ansari's senses as Muse establishes a link with the Enforcer. I cry out in wonder—

◊

—the air sharpens with the smell of an electrical storm.

I, Jordis, flinch from Caran, my hand stinging as I'm zapped with a painful static charge from the satin sheet.

◇

I, Caran, think: a-one and-a-two and
LIGHTS FLARE FULL BRIGHT
crack-zap hiss!
(thirty-second rest)
GO
Muse is in my chest spidering through my limbs lifting me to my knees I scream-think at it <took you fucking long enough> I toss my head back and jeer-laugh, filled with the élan, "Hail, hail, the gang's all here!"

◇

I, Jordis, recoil from the electrical charge flicking over the surface of Caran's skin. The air ionizes. Everything sparks. Caran sings horrible words in his beautiful voice: "I'm on a ghost train to London / packing monsters in my mouth!"
I'm confused.
I'm frightened.
I'm a Key Enforcer; he is a nothing—what is happening?

◇

Muse and I, Caran, form Unity.
<she will be tricky> we think/feel together <*warningEXCIT-INGchallenge*>
We reach out with a tendril of matter/thought, curling fingers/ waves around Gala's arm to make inductive contact. She is the mirrored edges of power and pride. We are jaggedy art and loathing, but beneath that—

<she is like us> Muse-mind rumbles <she has fought and found a way around her fate; she desires/deserves to be free!>

<no, never!> Caran-heart gags <she is not like us, never like us, she is a black market bully no better than the schoolyard gang>

<give in, take her> Muse-mind hisses <there are as many commons as differences. she holds hope *hope!* !>

<fuckit i need the nq>

We soar in on riots of bandwidth, hooking into places of resonance: the trapped-animal snarl of dreams dashed by genetics, the made-for-something-more-than-bondage.

We find the place where thought/feeling matches and bite into it, aligning the rest of her to become like us as resonance forms and holds on with the fury of a starving wolf—

<what's a wolf?> Caran-heart.

<something gala knows; we have her> Muse-mind.

<i will not submit!> Jordis-screams.

Frequency climbs.

<it's time you feel what we feel. its time to eat your own meal>

We fill her.

◊

I, Jordis, spasm a last rebellion but then:

I'm feeling through Caran's skin, choking on his toxins, his thoughts and feelings now mine. Invasion, disorientation, pain beyond imagination.

I stumble back from the bed and vomit onto the thick plum carpet. My heart pounds. I crash to my burning knees and heave again, expelling bile and the never-ending horror of aloneness no matter how many drugs I do or fucks I land or how many mouths scream my name in adoration.

I rise, limbs jerking, vision melting as the invasive presence gains control of my nervous system. I am the burn of Caran's withdrawal and the sour cruelty of his damage. I am a third, unknowable party, a chatter of alien desire. <*fear-love/pressure* STAY! *hope-and-future-bells*>

Inhuman laugher vibrates through the crystals inset in the ceiling.

Caran crawls toward me on the bed in jerking stop-motion.

I stumble toward him, dragging one foot through my vomit as I suck dark blue liquid from the crystal vial into the dropper. I can't stop myself; I have become filled with something else.

Below all of that, I analyze: *well, isn't this interesting?*

A wicked laugh chimes through Caran's throat and echoes in the buzz of the crystals in the ceiling. I reach the edge of the bed and Caran opens his mouth and tips back his head.

The ceiling crystals buzz-hiss their chorus of piezoelectric voices, speaking what I'm also hearing in a direct, telepathic injection: "Your true name is Jordis Ansari." <your true name is jordis ansari>

Three drops, four, five, six, seven eight—<ten will kill me no matter how high my tolerance gets and i can't afford eight, not with greene dead stop, stop, stop, gala/muse, stop, that's enough now!> he/we pleads.

◊

NQ slam-punches me, Caran, with voice and power and I shove Gala away with all my dancer's force. "You're Jordis Ansari! Does Daddy know you're in his territory?"

Muse releases its active control and she crumples off the edge of the bed. She's panting, shaking, her mobster-cool broken like a glass goblet smashed against a brick wall. She wipes bile off her jaw, spits blood from her bitten tongue. She rages through the link.

I point and laugh. "You're nothing but a schoolyard bully!"

◊

The NQ rush spreads in hot, bright salvation from my/his burning tongue. I tip my head up at him and spread my teeth in a violent blood-flecked grin.

He's kneeling on a stage of purple satin. His bare skin glows in light that isn't coming from any source that I can tell, his mouth in a free, open smile. I hear music—the very music playing in his mind's ear—a triumphant recapitulation at the finale of this evening's sonata. I hear his rage of triumph as though it were my own.

And it is my own. We have somehow aligned.

"It's not over yet, Dragon," I say, "it is definitely not over yet." Biomods engage and I'm at his neck before he can see me move. Then I twirl to retrieve my fan and crack it open on my way out.

◊

The fan cracks, its adaptive field bending all waves around Jordis. She appears to disappear. The fan's field bends Muse's frequencies away from Jordis too, severing the link.

I, Caran, touch the nape of my neck, disoriented by emptiness where her mind had been. My fingers come away slicked in blood.

The heat of the rush goes cold.

She's ripped the platinum chain off my neck. She's stolen the only existing copy of the programming for the kinetikosonus. I can't reprogram it, not with my publicity schedule. I can't play the instrument live because I can't use my navis on stage.

I've a show at the Mnemosyne Theatre in front of thirty thousand screaming fans in less than twenty-four hours.

"I ran at max bio-mod speed from the sickness and the pain," Jordis says the next day in my office, "pavement on the soles of my shoes slapping away the bitter rush of NQ on Caran's tongue. I ran from the adrenaline thrill of my theft, and from the deliciousness of identities exposed. I ran, invisible and silent, behind the open, bobbing, oh-so-heavy freedomtech fan until the lights faded and the sounds silenced and the alarms from my bio-mods told me I had to slow down because the repair nanites could no longer keep up the pace, and my muscles were tearing themselves apart."

Jordis' lids are closed as she relates this, but her eyes twitch behind them like she is dreaming as she watches the scene through perfect recall. There is an uncharacteristic poetry to her words, the influence of Caran and Muse leaking through, perhaps. I can understand why that first violent contact with Muse is something she does not wish to share with me. There have been many criticisms made of Jordis Ansari, but self-compromise has never been one.

She opens eyes of grey stone, giving nothing away. If Caran's eyes reflect more light than they should, hers absorb more than they should, flat and unyielding. "We've worked with the élan vitals since then to negotiate boundaries of consent for telempathic contact and control."

"Yes, of course." I shudder, imagining something else taking control of me.

Jordis gives a tight, emotionless semi-smile. Europa makes her invisible presence known as the air cools on my face and the hairs on my arms stand on end. The static field seems a constant in signaling the presence of an élan—I'm told it's the very phenomenon that created the phrase "walked over my grave." But there the similarity with Muse ends. Muse turns up the heat; Europa drains it.

The coldness of my own ambition pulls me in, making common ground with Jordis Ansari. The victory of being awarded these so-important interviews. The desire to do more, be more, stand at the top of every game—

◊

(Casino Row, Europa City, Europa, folds around me and fills me as I turn a one-eighty and look behind me.)

The neons in the heart of the Row glow and spark like distant stars: all the premium pleasures of the Via Aureaus, twinkling bright. The less premium pleasures begin where the Aureus branches into Wymer and Hunan Lanes. I stop there, on the edge of the darkness. Our Lady of the Deep blinks its mermaid blue-green holography onto the line where the golden tiles of the Aureus give way to Eastern Arc's simple blue-and-white floor. Where I stand, just outside the glow, it is very late night on Europa.

I bend to catch my breath; my skin is feverish. Beneath my sharp leather shoes lies the crossroads where Wymer Lane webs into narrow streets lined with establishments that tend to quieter needs. A state-controlled opium house. A tiny café. A grocery store. Residential housing for the people who work the Row. A hotel that costs less than an average month's salary in c's, but, unlike the hotels on the Aureus, has no clever theme or smart-art feature. I snap my cloaking fan shut and put it in a pocket, my hand shaking its relief to be rid of the weight.

This area isn't for Operators. However, the authorities won't bother me as long as I don't call attention to myself. The same would not be true on the Row, where paranoia of Operators influencing the betting machines reaches improbable levels of hysteria. My room at the Filigree Hotel is six blocks away, but I can't go there yet. Not with my bio-mods adrenal-amped and my memory full of Watts' fever. Not with my fist clenched around my stolen treasure; Watts' dataslip will have a tracker.

I smooth my jacket and twitch the cuffs to straighten the sleeves. Then I step softly down Sadie Street, through an alley between a Rounda Waffles and a basic housing unit. Three local crew kids step from the doorway of the unit, faces shadowed by wide-brimmed hats in the dark of Europa's simulated night. One prick of the poison needles implanted in my fingertips is all it would take. Instead, I flash them the x-shaped corporate pin attached to the webbing of my right thumb along with the slicing gesture of Key Enforcer. They recoil, hats bowed, hands up, palms open. Political power is so much more satisfying than physical; I flash my hands in an approval sign. They will remember the gleam of blue across my forehead should I ask them for a future favor.

And what kind of power entered me in Watts' room? I touch my shoulder where current burned through the thick fabric of my Vemi suitcoat. That current had paralyzed my arm with impossible precision. A vertigo-wave of drug-induced euphoria passes through me as though even separated by so much distance I am an echo of the singer's body and mind.

I finger the hard edges of my fan through the fabric of my suit-coat, thinking about the magic of freedomtech. Did Watts have a piece of freedomtech back in his room that enabled him to hack my bio-electrical processes? I can hack my own bio-electric processes to some crude degree with my navis, convincing my body to produce melatonin so I can sleep better for example, so it's not outside of the realm of the possible. However, it seems unlikely. A complete human physiology has significant complexity, even for Freedom's magic.

I replay my memory of the event:

left hand reaching with dropper

right hand clenched around crystal vial

Watts kneeling, head back, mouth open, hair splayed out in static charge

blue electricity crackling—*blue electricity, isn't that what the witness talked about during the bombing?*

my hand stinging with static-electric burn

the dataslip glowing

his jugular throbbing as I lean in—as something not-me leans me in—close to him

his pulse against the platinum chain

not-my fingers squeezing the dropper onto his tongue

the dataslip glowing, full of information roiling—like I can see the interaction of the slip's wireless with the room's ambient signaling in rainbowy loops of wifi and pulses of datapackets. I can see *inside* the datapackets, patterns of black-and-white on-and-off; I could enter inside of them from the very air instead of through the hardware of my navis—what they read like is the sound of pulsars and a melody—

I pull myself out of the memory. It confuses me; it's like I was wearing EM goggles, perceiving spectra far outside of visible light. Only all I had were my naked eyes.

Tell me, Dragon, has your fetid little network of outcasts in Freedom finally cracked telepathy?

I smile at my whimsy in the darkness. Psychic powers are the milieu of fantasy; if nothing else the navis has proven that even when people can share thoughts, they cannot share a common enough thought-language to communicate. Mediation is required.

◊

"Hold on a moment." My desire/intention to break back into the here-and-now of my office shifts the levels, returning me to my own experience without breaking the link.

"Certainly." Jordis sits in the chair, legs neatly crossed in her dark suit, saucer and tea balanced on her knee. Just enough pale amber liquid remains for me to see over the lip of her cup.

"I'd like you speak more to your statement that people can't share a common enough language to understand each other's thoughts. I know it's an important concept for any nauta, but it's not something most normals ever consider."

She shifts now, lifting the saucer and uncrossing and re-crossing her legs in the other direction. A sip of tea. A balance of the saucer on the arm of the chair. "It goes back to why us, why nauta, why are we the only ones who can use a navis, doesn't it?"

I nod. She takes a deep breath and a long, frosty exhale.

"Information is dangerous." Her eyes narrow and warm at the same time; through the link I feel her excitement and pleasure at that truth. "Corporations keep their blueprints secret even though it stifles innovation, else rivals steal the profit. Citizens need to know what is happening in their neighborhood, but free media can breed misinformation. Personal data, credit, medical records—necessities, all, yet weapons in the hands of one's enemies. Some people are cooperators; others are defectors. In an information-based economy, privacy and surveillance is a two-headed snake."

For the first time in our interactions, Jordis is going off on a nauta associative tangent.

"Hence," she concludes, "the importance of encryption."

Ah, not a nauta associative tangent. More a corporate lawyer preparing the frames to jam her point in.

"Encryption is older than the information age; in fact, the need to decrypt radio transmissions helped spur the invention of the first Turing computers. As time passes, every strong encryption code falls to even better decryption methods, like the dance between virus and antibody."

"Secret decoder rings," I smirk, thinking of the silly fad that's recently reemerged in children's toys.

Jordis replies with her semi-smile and a subtle bend of her long neck. "Then comes the large-scale quantum computer."

"The Revolution."

"The Revolution, which mostly refers to a revolution in computing, although its consequences were the near extinction of humanity. Infinite calculations in real-time. The most strongly encrypted data reduced to plain text instantly. Everyone's database became an open book." The same history lesson I was taught in grade school, but without the rhetoric that the crisis was the early natuas' fault.

"Enter a nauta's idioglossia," Jordis says.

"A language known only to one person." I nod.

"A 'symptom' of our genetic condition."

"But everyone has their own language down on the lower levels of cognition, right?"

"True. And that's exactly why telepathy—at least without an élan vital generating resonance—is not possible between humans. Normals like you develop a more seamless integration with common language; in varying degrees we nauta do not. In return, we have better conscious access to the language of our minds—a language too unique, synesthetic, and irrational for even a quantum computer to decode."

"So quantum code is like the mental DNA of the programmer?"

"Very much. And more—it is a window into their soul." She stares at me with politician's cool, but there is a hint of challenge in her emotional tone. Like she is challenging me to accept that in this day and age we could discuss matters of the soul.

<the un-quantifiable, interconnected gestalt of one's singular existence> I accept her challenge and think through the link.

<exactly that, steven, exactly that>

◊

I reach a semi-circular park on the outward-facing curve of the torus and don't stop until my hands press against its three-meter windows to the endless sea. With the darkness of Europa's night mode behind me, the neons of Casino Row glow unimpeded into the black water. The light reveals small changes in the current, reflecting off macroscopic clouds of microorganisms. This is the best time to spot angeltorches, following in the clouds' wake, their fiery sides absorbing the microbes' heat as they devour the tiny creatures in great, hungry gulps.

I am breathing heavily again, my own mouth gulping strangely as though to take the microbes in.

Europa's alien life is neither plant nor animal by Earth standards; it is its own thing. What if the thing that controlled me in Watts' room wasn't freedomtech but a new kind of intelligent life?

I shake my head and back away from the glass. *What are you thinking, Ansari? Every educated person knows the Vanguard Theory holds. Human beings are the first to attain second-order cultural and institutional awareness. Take Europa as an example. Europa's life is older than Earth's, yet all it knows is hunger. We've explored countless regions of the galaxy, and the Vanguard Theory holds.*

I pull away from the window. My bio-mod-amped pulse is almost back to normal. I no longer feel Watts, and it's likely I just imagined his influence in the stew of adrenaline and endorphins following our encounter.

A grouping of empty benches sits three meters back from the windows. I pick a bench, stand before it, and spin slowly, scanning visually for surveillance. Then I close my eyes and open a channel, scanning first for radio signal, then working my way down through the frequencies until the place where infrared meets visible light. Nothing in the park is actively receiving or transmitting. I go giddy with lack of surveillance. Anywhere under Federal Banking control would not be so clean. I am proud of my Europa; she plays by her own rules.

I unclench my fist. The dataslip slithers down its broken platinum chain. I hold it dangling, swinging side-to-side like a metronome.

I enjoy Watts' music. "Grande Echo" sounds like he's singing at the edge of a vast canyon, the wind whistling in tune. "Trilogy-Metro" drowns me in scattered shouts and clicking heels and the rustling of raincoats, revealing the songs the buildings would sing were a city given voice. His music is complex, atmospheric, yet always has a hook, a phrase I can't shake, a lyric and chorus that shines clear and pulls story from sound.

Too bad I know better now, that the artist is just a sad papper who lies about himself. *You'd have done better to take my road, Dragon, even if it meant staying in the shadows. The Empire of the Moon could have helped you.*

I open a shortwave band to the dataslip, only to have it slide off the standard channels. He's mucked with the signaling. I replay my memory of seeing the slip's frequency back in the hotel room with that strange multi-vision. I tune to what I saw, like twirling my fingers on an ancient FM dial, tiny nudges of adjustment in nano-hertz with my mind. The receiver in my navis finds the frequency. The storage opens: no security traps. No tracker either. Only the tampered frequency, fine-tuned to a bandwidth almost impossibly narrow. I never would have found it had I not seen it earlier. Clever. I recognize the encryption layer as, amusingly, an old Black Market hack he must have retained from his Freedom days. I, of course, know its key. I enter the dataslip:

Soundscapes open into vast vistas of logic
trumpets spew ruddy pleasure-pain-pressure
whistles of silver waterfalls and
shards of tears and beauty
a deep corduroy bass clarinet whirling in kaleidoscopes of anger and the scent of a field freshly watered by early morning rain—

I terminate the experience of Watts' idioglossia and sit shivering for a full minute. It is like visiting the art in the Luna Heritage Museum, as though there is only so much elation a body can bear from beauty before it turns to sorrow.

My own language is all image and taste and structure and ice, and, while beautiful to me, does not transcend itself into art. There are Operators I know, cryptography specialists in Madame X's employ, who could crack Watts' code, place a lingua franca over it, make it public. Something so personal and revealing of Watts'— and the proof that he programs his instrument in an Operator's idioglossia instead of normal code—what a fine price I would fetch. But I am not after short-term credit. I am after my birthright, and I like that Watts is perverting the mainstream with his veiled taboos, the irony of his musicality. *I will not take the music from you, Dragon. Your life, yes, that is a clean end. But the music—that is where you and I are the same. Both succeeding at forbidden games. Both made for something the world does not want us to have.*

I frown.

Too much sympathy for my pawns will get me killed. I replay Watts' sweaty face and unapologetic hunger, reminding myself of all the difference between us. *I have never sacrificed my self-respect, Dragon. Yes, my public face is a slave to the Empire, but Primo Capo Som Bliss' face is CFO of Mentist Corp and my father's is owner of the Argus Hotel and Casino. Our lies are the time-honored cost of doing business. Your lies, Dragon, are at the cost of your soul: loathsome, self-injurious lies. I've spent my life fighting for dignity and you've used up yours pretending to be something you are not.*

I coil the broken platinum chain around my fist until it cuts off the blood to my fingers. The chain has no clasp or catch and is too small to slip over his head; it must have been assembled around his neck. The latch connecting the slip to the chain has a tiny needle on the underside; a DNA lock. He'd not wanted that dataslip removed, though he hadn't accounted for someone with my bio-mods.

He'll make the trade; he has to.

Unless he controls my actions again.

Whatever had happened, it stopped when I'd snapped open my freedomtech fan. Does the fan counter it?

I put my thoughts away for now. I will know everything once Caran makes the trade.

I pick up my feet, walking toward the Filigree Hotel at the quiet crook where Sadie Street turns a blind corner. The hotel's siliplas shingle, lit by a dim purplish everbulb, stands stark against its black flank, illuminating the bio-luminescent shape of a Europan filigree jellyfish. Real jellies do not glow, nor are they so small; however it would be impractical to have a shingle large enough to hold one twice the size of a queen sheet. The shingle got the filigree texture of the creature right though—a lace of predatory force.

As I cross from Wyman to Sadie, a cold, wet drop hits the bridge of my nose.

I paw it away and look up. All I see is ceiling, three stories above, glowing with dim blue everbulbs beside the darkened sunsim daylights. I wipe my hand on my trousers, but it leaves no wet mark.

A half-step later, a larger drop hits the dusty tile floor. I bend to touch it, smell it, maybe taste it—but my finger comes away dry.

I look up at the nest of environmental systems' pipe-works and wires along the ceiling. Tourists might live in fear that the Europa torus will spring a leak and let the endless ocean in, but I know better. That doesn't mean something else isn't leaking. I will be very cross if it spoils my sleep; the aftermath of bio-modified activity needs healing time. At minimum, I'll have to report the leak to the concierge.

But I see nothing amiss on the ceiling.

I take two more steps toward the Filigree. At my feet, a splatter of droplets appear in a controlled, directional splash.

You're leading me.

I blink and step back. *"You"—who?*

The droplets form a line of unnatural agency down Sadie Street, past the Filigree Hotel, and into the blind alley. My breastbone hums with golden power that vibrates: <*affinity/kinship/familiarity*> in the direction of the alley.

I pad after the drips and turn the blind curve. The air ionizes, the hairs lifting on the nape of my neck and the tops of my arms. There's a second bend at the end of the tight, curving corridor. Voices whisper, and there's a briny odor, like fresh Europan sea. I lick my lips and taste salt.

The droplets lead me on, leaving only dusty tiles behind.

"Sssst." A sound like many people hissing in harmony, like how the air in Watt's room had hissed my given name. Only now there is no threat, simply a summons by someone I don't remember, but have fond feelings for, nonetheless. Like a lost twin sister.

My face is wet again, only this time it's from my own tears. How strange.

I round the bend.

A pearly glow hovers midway between me and the dead end. It—no, she, a woman—floats above the ground haloed in backlight from a seven-pointed star. Hair the color of ice half-hides her delicate white face, and her black garment refracts light like deep sea water. She runs a hand along her necklace of pale, alien bones.

No, not alien bones. The boron-based bones of quarana, and apogee, and at least three other native European species.

The woman is beautiful—until her torso ends just above the waist and brackish water trails and drips from where the rest of her should be.

No, you are beautiful all the way up and down.

My toes curl.

<*longing/belonging* i want to be a part of the soul of you, moon> Thoughts and feelings mingle and flow through the space between us—whose? I cannot tell. I can tell, though, this is the moon Europa incarnate. I know it in a way neither explicable nor divisible, but as I, Jordis, am myself. Identity needs no proving.

"Hold sssstill," the apparition rasps like dry bones on rusted metal. Then she sing-songs in a high, gibbering pitch with many voices at once, "Be a pretty echo, be a shiny copper coin. Would you like to know my seeeeekkkkretssssss…"

It is not the apparition of the moon, nor what she says, that turns the dream to nightmare. It is the ball of stupefying age, power, and terror accompanying Europa's final hiss that drives me to my knees. Something that old and that strong should never be that afraid. It would be like seeing Madame X afraid—it is worse than seeing Madame X afraid.

I rock up to my feet, a protective, angry growl in the back of my throat, the poison needles in the tips of my fingers extending. *How dare something threaten you, Europa, my home, I will take it down!*

Europa sways and shimmers, light catching her sides then flashing dark like the flanks of the quarana in the torus' lights. "Quietly now, it, they, listennnnnnn."

"Who?" I whisper aloud, retracting my needles, reaching out to the moon as though through physical contact I might regain some vital piece of myself.

But as my fingers brush the space where she was, Europa elongates and dissipates, gathering into form again a meter away at the dead end. Phantom water spatters large, dark letters on the dusty blue-and-white tiles—

D. I. V. I. D. I. A.

—and evaporates.

A complete image of Europa lifts off of herself—a ghost peeling from a ghost—and shoots itself into Watts' platinum-coated dataslip dangling from my cold fingers.

The spirit rasps, "Do not believe me do not believe me do not believe me after today do not believe a thing I say—"

Europa's manic chanting aborts and the dataslip where she's injected—what? herself?—grows so hot the platinum chain smolders and hisses, but I can't unclench my fingers. The spirit is on the move, her beautiful woman's face snarling into a visage of concentric circles around sharp, pointy, white teeth, the deadly maw of the quarana making a grab for prey. "AN-SAR-EEEEEEEE!" Europa screams.

And she is gone, the bolt of blue electrical discharge of her passing driving me once more to my knees, only this time paralyzed and twitching.

◊

"Have you ever been exposed to significant electrical current, Steven?" Jordis breaks the link.

I shake my head negative as I say, "Once there was a live wire in the reclaimer and I touched it by accident—it wasn't too many volts."

"Reclaimers run, what, ten to fifteen volts? That's unpleasant enough," she acknowledges, "but you're right, it's not too many. That's one of the problems with human-élan relations—the fact that they can zap us dead should they have the desire, which happily, most do not. I'm not sure how much current Europa discharged into me with that night as she's no comprehension of our system of measure, but I was out cold for thirteen minutes, and it took me another seventeen to make it back to my hotel room less than twenty meters away."

"A strong electrical discharge to your navis could be disaster," I realize.

"Indeed it could." Her demeanor shifts slightly into maybe a nod of approval. "But none of my circuits fried that night. I got lucky."

"Noa did not," I whisper before I can stop myself, even though we haven't gotten to that part yet.

"Indeed. Noa did not. I want you to keep the élan's potential for destruction in mind when you judge our actions later. The Freedom folk will speak eloquently of feedback loops and how one élan can attune another to be more like itself, or how élans and humans can attune each other to become more similar. They'll speak of the power of human-élan relations to shift paradigms through resonance, and how that can lead to either creative or destructive consequences. But the élans have a more direct capacity for destruction in simply electrocuting us."

"It's not my job to judge anyone's actions." The words sound too flippant. I wince. "I appreciate what you're telling me here. To say, 'the élans could kill us all,' is too big, it becomes meaningless, even if it's true. It's like saying, in the information age, 'nuclear weapons could kill us all.' But you've made it small enough to be personal."

"I try, Steven, indeed I try," Jordis nods once, her lips in a grim, flat line, and restarts the link.

◊

(Time has jumped.)

I sit on the edge of the bed at the Filigree in a stiff white robe, my skin damp from the shower. I work the bun from my hair with aching, shaking fingers, letting it fall in restless auburn strands to the bottom of my shoulder blades. The place where the necklace chain burned into my hand is a stiff, stinging, line of angry red, but a low priority for my overtaxed healing nanites. Logically, rationally, I know I have experienced the impossible and therefore should run a diagnostic on my navis and psyche for glitches. But the rest of me knows Europa like I know my own existence. The moon is alive, and has waited for me all this time, tangled in my dreams. I'd connected with her in my childhood, standing by windows, watching quarana, fingers crossed that I might see a filigree, heart pounding as though I, myself, were a part of the creatures' endless hunts.

I WAS a part of those hunts through you, Europa. Through the you-in-me and me-in-you and us together—

I close my eyes and exhale shakily through a smile.

Your existence, Europa, means there is life here that All Worlds Scientific has yet to discover. Sentient life. Life capable of second-order emergence? Do you have culture? Laws? Self-determination? You have art; I saw the necklace of bones around your throat.

Watts' platinum-coated dataslip is warm like a living thing. It vibrates against my skin with faint electrical discharge. I know what I will find within in, but my Enforcer's training requires data, facts, investigation, confirmation. I open a channel, tune to the default frequency the device has reset to and look inside.

The singer's programming is gone.

Something compressed and feeling like Europa pulses in the crystal matrix, too dense and strange for me to examine with my human mind.

Crystal matrix, like that attached to Hyperia's navis.

My encounter with Europa in the hall had similar tells to my encounter in Watts' room: the static charge, the alien voices. Jealousy flares that Hyperia or Watts might have been intimate with my Europa.

But no, the flavor of what touched me back in the hotel room most certainly was not my moon.

The threads slip away. Either there are clues missing or I'm too tired to see how they all connect.

I rub my eyes with tired hands, everything painful in the aftermath of adrenaline overload and a spirit-induced taser-blast. My stomach complains about hunger, and I need ointment for my burned hand, but I'm too tired to retrieve the items from the room service slot even if I could summon the energy to order them. The healing nanites that keep my muscles from tearing themselves apart during speed-enhanced action demand sleep so they can initiate a deep repair. The looping, exhausted rut of my thoughts needs dreaming to become insight.

I find the opening into the cool covers with my toes and slide my legs in.

A voice whispers inside my thoughts as through someone else were thinking them for me: <three-four-five-nine via fortuna, media-fifty-three, oh-eight-hundred ansari>

Painted above me, on the ceiling, lilts a pale seascape. Three colonial filigree jellies stalk a school of quarana while the quarana approach a spherical colony of wormgrass. Beneath the sheets I push off the bathrobe and imagine I'm suspended in water.

It's an address: 3459 Via Fortuna, Media53 Studios. Media53 owns three of Europa's mainfeed media channels.

The dataslip containing Europa seeps warmth into my chest where I hold it close.

Oh-eight-hundred is a time.

I will be there, but first, I drift.

I'd always strategized sabotage as my first move to retake my birthright. I'd take the temperature of the kingdom and catalogue the weak spots. I'd visit my half-brother Jordan—maybe as Gala but most likely as myself—and convince him to help me. *Jordan's one of your biggest weaknesses, Daddy, more than happy for a reason not to follow in your footsteps.*

But sabotage and strategy are games I'd learned on Luna, old and known and grounded in Earth's culture.

Europa's culture is of a different world entirely. It is chance. It is a gamble to lose all or win the house. It is an alien ecosystem. It is darkness and theatre and bright lights and hunger. *Your games are not the games of Luna, my Europa, but they are the games I most like to play. They are the games I am* most suited *to play.*

I close my eyes to the painted seascape and cup my hands around Europa-in-a-dataslip. I whisper to the dark, "I will protect you with my life."

A peace I've not felt since I last lay beneath Europa's icy crust covers me in a second blanket.

And beneath that: hunger. Hunger for power, yes, but also for the hunt, for the kill, for filling the abyss of my belly. I fall into alignment with the moon.

Dreams slip into the ocean as I catch and consume translucent, eel-like quarana in the deadly net of my filigree form.

"So you had a plan for your missing dataslip?" I ask Caran the next day in my office.

He's humming, clattering his fingers against a degradable cup from the water spigot in the lobby. It's empty, so I'm guessing he's picked it up for its value as a percussion instrument. He ignores my question.

"You're in a cheery mood."

He flashes me his roguish grin followed by a vocalization of the main theme from the Jovian Symphony's Europa Movement. "Origin story," he trills at the end.

The link hasn't formed yet, so I've no idea what he means.

He laughs at the funny look on my face and flops onto the couch, head still bobbing to the beat of his fingers on the empty cup. A tangled lock of black hair falls forward into his face and his speech flows in rhythm to the beat. "It had to be early afternoon. Handler evasion was harder mid-afternoon, and the morning's schedule was too packed. It had taken all my post-bedtime time to come up with the plan and talk Muse into it. Then Mindy made me eat lunch like fifteen times. I love eating, so it took my all-over-everything to hide my impatience or she'd know something was up."

"So you had a plan."

"Yeah. I had a plan." He stops tapping and looks at me, flicking the hair away from his eyes. "Time out."

"But you were surrounded by people, staff, security, fans—"

"Time out."

"Now? You need a time out now?"

"No." He laughs. "Then. They took me serious ever since I called time out, didn't get it, pushed the hair guy off the balcony. Now that was a shitstorm—so much fuss over the guy's broken nail. Just can't take it sometimes, even when I was on the NQ, so I call"—he shrieks; I flinch—"TIMEOUTNOW—and then they take me serious. I was good at giving the slip for short stints. Gotta get alone to dose. Helped that Muse could make me invisible and silent, just like Jordis' fan—that's how freedomtech works, you know. It's got a piece of an élan vital inside of it—they extract bits of themselves, like a residue—not enough for sentience like the Pathfinder ships, and certainly not a whole real élan like what Jordis had in my dataslip, but enough to do a simple trick."

"Ah, the Pathfinder ships. Like the Djen's ship, the *Stella-Maru*, with its resident élan Stella?"

The cup falls though his fingers and hits the carpet in silence. He whispers. "Stella was part of the plan too." His body hunches, bare feet on the carpet, elbows on his knees.

"I want you to tell me about that, but first, what did you mean by 'origin story'?"

His mouth smiles but the black eyes that look up at me through strands of messy hair catch no light. "Jovian Symphony. Europa Movement. This is its origin. Walking out on Europa's streets was when I composed it."

◊

"TIMEOUTNOW!"

YES

I go to my room, pop the corporate identifier pin off my thumb and drop it on the bed, glad for the billionth time that it's the removable type. I slip out the fire exit, Muse unlocking all the e-locks for me.

Outside:

slip-stop-step

the clap of boots snap on the polished tile streets

sweet-sugar sense of freedom.

No disguises, who needs disguises; if it matters Muse'll just blur me, but it doesn't matter, just a fan-boy look-alike; no way real Watts would be out without his handlers.

Glitter-twinkle lights: Europa's Casino Row.

<hey muse, shortest, safest path from the mnemosyne hotel and theatre to the nearest 100 worlds music shop?>

Muse integrates itself into the local information systems and makes a Mesh with the heart-mind of the city. Fragments of raw knowledge pulled from passers-by. Data flowing through airwaves. Local flavor, inspiration. Information.

<could be there in less than 15 on the triple-chance way.>

Voices through the telempathic bond, Muse soaking it like a sponge: *Did-you-know a famous diva was murdered on this street by her lover; last year's Anna Pavlova Ballet Award winner once sex-danced in that bar; 40c's for the cobweb dress in the window; down that alley authorities killed an Operator for being part of the Genetic Liberation Front; look there's the CEO of Merru who comes to Europa every year and spends exactly two million c's but no one knows on what—*

Voices from the people on the street, music in my ears: "Please, do you have a token, I won't slot it, please, I promise, I'm leavin' the probabilities alone, just need to buy a ticket home—"

Songs from the city: tick-tock-clack and the beat of feet on golden-tiled streets echoing off facades and the fake blue ceiling-sky. A brassy rush of laugher and whoots, breaking up the percussive chatter of crowds. Live adverts whistling from corners, actors attempting novelty where recorded promos have become too competitively unique to be distinct.

Memorize the sounds of Casino Row, remix, composing, building phrases and themes for later when I'm off tour and can get them thought out into code for the kinetikosonus to play.

Behind the native noises, my music rises; I test the theme.

No, not that, what about this?

No, too spare, this is a sound-rich space.

But no, needs a quiet spot because of the oceans.

Hungry, shit! This place is hungry.

Is there another élan here?

No, just me, connecting, interacting with the song of the moon. Together with Muse entwined it's like the good old times with Djen, striding to the next new thing, seeking local resonance, making song.

Single cursive "A" projects onto the street. Gold-and-jade feather-and-fan facade motif.

<"a" for argus casino and hotel; "a" for ansari>

Argus belongs to Ray Ansari—Jordis! <*violationRAGE*>

—telempathic backwash from both Muse and me provokes a man to turn and slap his stunned companion.

<sorry, tell them we're sorry!> I think/feel to Muse. Fuck.

In front of every casino the holos glow: NO OPERATORS ALLOWED.

Random input from radio signal: <the casinos of europa's east arc are the largest conglomerate of operator sponsors on the jo-

vian moons, with operators managing all probability machines, smart-arts, and facilities. on io however, where the electromagnetic storms make it impossible for electronic equipment to reliably function, no operators—>

Voice from the street: "Please, just one more token for the probs, I'll win this time I know it, please, please give me this one more chance—"

We reach the glittering facade of the 100 Worlds Music Store. Millions of mirror-treated synthetic diamonds reflect my face or replace it with crystalline shine. The corporate sigil, a golden harp in a circle of red roses, glows from the neon set in the facade. People pause in information hotspots as feed blows at them, adverts, trivia contests about their fav-acts. Answer right and get a discount! Answer right and enter a drawing for a free track! Show your token from Europa's upscale casinos, get a patch!

Some spend all day on the trivia, watching their name jet to the top of the fan charts. I've been forced to endure a painful dinner with more than one of them.

Fanfeed crawls over the 2V inset in the wall, just to the right of the mirror-surfaced doors, tuned to my flow. The 24/7 discussion on Caran Watts scrolls by and hooks me, like a tube wreck or a nightmare.

◊

*->holy fuck did you see cw do 'silence' last night? best sound-orgasm EVS @ min 4:04!

*->haha he was totally drunk in that studio six interview yesterday

(->no way they don't film him when he's drunk

+->how would you know?

(->isn't he always drunk?

*->CARAN HAVE MY BABIES

*->you're all pervs to love an op-lover jacker like that

(->cw's no jacker, doesn't even have a com!

+->yeah, he's a pure

+->everyone knows cw's op and can't subvocalize into a com

—>not true, he's totally pure won't have a single piece of tech in him. total pure!

—>some people just don't use coms, that's what cw said in the m.katx interview

—>he's just a genius is all. fucked-up crazy. best music ever.

*->caran watts is so sexy

(->haha jacker feeble-lover perv

+->shut it or we'll mod you this is fanfeed not bashspace

*->who's got tix? i've got night 3!

(->lucky fuck

(->yeah i've got night 3 too

(->I've got night 2, TONIGHT!

◊

The mirror-surfaced doors open, breaking line-of-sight on the feed, giving relief from the flow. Nothing new or interesting, same old endless speculation and sycophantic drool. No need to worry about the fans' discussion around my genes; give my PR people enough of an alternate narrative and they'll spread it. Give Mindy and LaRoque enough credit and they'd lie to themselves almost as much as I do. We scrub the fans clean of every skin cell that could belong to me after those spacewreck dinners. No one actually wants to think about the truth.

The crowd inside jabs my senses like the pincers of an angry huilda-lobster, sounds of commerce cymbals banging off-key. Cacophony of colors creates vortices of eye-stabbings instead of resolving into signs and faces and goods like it ought. Fucking mobsters, fucking Ansari, and fucking Green. Had to skimp on my afternoon dose to make the NQ last. Best not to appear like myself anyway. I've had enough drops that I can manage if I try.

I try and focus through the mess and see a group of fankids dressed up to look like me. They nod in envy at the prowess of my costuming.

"How may I help you?" The clerk asks.

"I need a dataslip." I modulate my voice into a higher register and add an irritating burr. Put my hand to my throat, calling the clerk's attention to the missing part of my costume. At least I've had enough NQ my words still work. The back of my neck where Jordis tore off my chain itches beneath the synthskin patch; don't pick at it, don't pick.

Clerk's a slender girl, hip with tzaddium-blue powder over her cheek bones and dressed in a "Two Shades of Blue" tunic. She doesn't bat a lash at my resemblance to the face splashed across her chest.

"Sure, over here," she points my attention toward a bin of useless siliplas replicas.

I run my eyes over the lot of them. "I was looking for something a bit more... upscale. Limited edition, maybe?"

I'd signed off on the tour swag and know every item sent to 100 Worlds Music. Might not have perfect recall without my navis but my natural memory's near as good, no matter how many drugs I take to try to kill the fucker.

"Ah." The girl gives me a look-over: fine silk of my white dress, designer cut of the dark gray pants beneath, flush of expensive powders across my cheek bones. I pass the snob test then, or maybe Muse has applied a bit of telempathic pressure, because she nods without asking for a credit scan. "Right this way."

She leads me away from the crowds to the back of the store where the signed 3V stills and fake-unwashed bits of my laundry and other unaffordable things live sequestered in secured cases. Her finger presses a DNA lock and click-snap-schwing—a drawer opens.

"This one's genuine platinum." She holds a chain and dataslip up into the light. "Only five hundred made, and only five sent to our store. Real dataslip too, stores 90p. Best repro ever, exactly like the real thing. Without whatever magic CW puts inside of it of course." She laughs with a dismissive hand.

Except this one has a 100 Worlds Music Corp sigil stamped to it, the harp-in-a-circle-of-roses. It's tastefully engraved, and no color, so if I keep the sigil side against my skin, hopefully no one'll notice.

"Perfect." I maneuver a grin onto my face, cursing my choice of such an irritating fake voice. "I'll take it. You know, I'm CW's number one fan!" I wink.

She smiles indulgently and holds out the credit plate for me to pay.

I swipe my hand over it while Muse takes control of the device and turns the red approval light to green, even though there's been no actual transaction with the Bank.

The clerk smiles more, and I smile more, and the chain passes from her hands to mine.

Back on the Europan streets, I clip the chain around my neck. Relief to feel the weight against my breastbone again, though it doesn't sit all the way right.

One more thing to do before tonight.

Don't want to.

Have to.

Fuck.

She isn't gonna be happy to see me.

Not happy at all.

◊

"I hadn't communicated with her in ten years."

My awareness returns to my office just in time to see a tear to slide down Caran's jaw.

"Who? You mean Stella?"

"Yeah, and Djen. Either of them, hadn't had contact with them for ten years." His brow wrinkles, and he looks at the floor. The tear quivers and falls, the path of it across his cheek drying in the over-warm air. "But I had to tell someone responsible what I'd learned from Jordis about the bombing and the élan named Dividia. Djen's a pathfinder. She's got access to all of human knowledge. She'd suss it if she knew it was happening; I had to get rid of the weight of it. What was I gonna do with it? I'm useless. Better push it off on Djen."

I've seen him dazzling and I've seen him fuming; I've seen flashes of resentment and exultations of artistry. But this is a new thing. He's hunched over like a child waiting for a beating.

I shiver. Memories of hunching over like that myself surface, like I thought they never would again. I push them down. None of this is about me. "Tell me a little bit about Djen."

He brightens and comes out of his hunch a bit. "Everything with her is big," he says. "Big laugh, big shoulders, big appetite for hedonism, big enough to match mine." He gives a big laugh of his own. "There are so many stories I could tell you about Djen and me. About the dumbass shit we used to do. Like that one time we were in Red City and we were so hungry. Shit, we were always so hungry. And Djen cooked up this plan for us to crash this corporate party as the entertainment. We had full run of the banquet table and all their designer drugs, and then we filled our bags with food and ran off. Enough for weeks it was. Half the fun for Djen was the danger; she loves that adrenaline rush. I've never been into the danger, but anything with Djen is so much fun that danger doesn't matter. Shit, we laughed in a back alley in the bad part of town after we ran off, our bellies, our bags, everything full.

"Then this kid showed up; didn't know them. There are always kids in the bad part of town who've fallen off the grid, no corporate identifiers, no citizen id chips, blanks like we were. There's freedom in being blank. You aren't watched all the time and the authorities leave you alone so long as you don't taint the shiny parts of town. But it's not roses either, like you can't buy anything on the up, and if you go to the wrong places or do the wrong things you'll be arrested and rehabilitated or just disappeared. It wasn't so risky to be blank for Djen and me because Stella and Muse could do all sorts of electronics magic, trick citizen id readers, hack the tube systems, that sort of shit.

"Anyway, we were laughing and coming down in that alley, sharing a bottle of whiskey, and this kid shows up and it's clear he's hungry. So Djen just hands him our bags of food. It wasn't even a question.

"Djen's like that. She's the most generous person I've ever known under all that cranky-crust." Caran shakes his head, hunching back to small and sad. "Should've never left her. It was an asshole move. I left her so lonely. But I couldn't spend the rest of my life hidden away on a dimship either, no matter how much I loved her, no matter how much space there was for us to explore. Needed to connect with society to grow my art. Needed an audience, interaction, connection in the light…"

He trails off into silence and then Muse tickles in my thoughts. <we left stella and djen in red city when we signed on with running horses>

<shutup> that's Caran's thought through the link.

<it's important backstory> Muse pushes <*irritatedFirmness* this is my story too>

I'm sure my jaw has fallen on the floor but I'm too amazed to pick it back up. The élans were to provide a telempathic link for me to experience my participants' stories—not to be participants themselves.

<oh yeah?> Caran's cranky tone shoots back at the creature.

<also, people will be interested to learn it about you>

<yeah?> Caran's tone is slightly less cranky. <but they already know i was on the running horses label before 100 worlds music>

<but they don't know what was is like to have been there>

<what, to live through making the worst decision of my life?>

<to live through how we entered the light>

All of Caran's cranky is gone and a bemused laugh rolls through the link. I feel forgotten as they fall into banter. Is this what it's always like between them?

<of course YOU would say that of this total fucking cluster-mess> Caran laughs at the creature.

<of course i would>

Caran bares his teeth at me in something that would have been a grin if it had any warmth behind it. "I'm gonna make you famous."

◇

"I'm gonna make you famous."

The words come at me across the table in Tanzia Talks, Shirring Point, Red City. Didn't even know there was anyone sitting there. Air's blue-brown, thick with darkness but sparkling in side-light off the bar. Drink in my fist, first of the night. Relaxing after my show. His voice has no color. Bland.

"What?" I weave my body back and forth to see enough of the angles of his face to construct an impression. Soft, young, well-dressed. Too expensive for this joint—for this part of town. Kind of linen-weave fabric that makes a rich swish-swash when it moves.

"I'm gonna make you famous," he repeats.

"Yeah, whatever." Guess I'd heard him right. I laugh. Sure, I'm talented like nobody's business but I'm so far outside the outside that I don't even have a real name.

"No, really." He leans forward so that a slanting ray of light from the lav sign falls across his face. He's got pretty cheek bones. "You're amazing. You're, like—you're Orpheus, man!"

"I'm, like, amazingly illegal, too. Man." I flash him my hands. Look, no corporate pins! I slide my hands over the citizen ID reader in the center of the table. See, I'm not even tagged! I flash him a dragon-y grin. Sure he could com the authorities, but it's not like they'd come to this part of town.

"That's OK," Mx. Cheekbones is unfazed. Also, his cadence isn't Red City local. What is it, Luna? Earth maybe? "Talent like yours makes a lot of things possible."

"I don't want to be famous."

"You want to do something special with your voice, right? You want to sing all the time?"

"I already sing all the time." I vocalize a playful, mocking riff off his accent.

"My name's Harold Jones, Running Horses Music Corp. I can get you booking on Europa. Or Emory. I can get you into the feeds, exposure, all the love of a hundred worlds. And people are gonna love you, boy are they gonna love you!"

My skin tingles as Muse hooks interest. <*lovempoweresonate*>

<what, you think this corporate shill's for real?>

Muse sends me a pressure-push <from the wheat field. the wish. we want to be a star>

<you remember that?> ...visions of a wheat field long ago.

"You could draw thousands with that voice of yours. You worked your way over six octaves in that second song, and I bet you cover more, yeah? And the colors, man, the tonal colors of your voice! And that thing you're playing, what is it?"

"Kinetikosonus."

"Yeah? Where'd it come from."

"The reamed-out science lab of the dimship I live on."

"The—you made it?"

"Invented it. Yeah. Made it."

"Amaze-a-fucking-tastic."

"Yeah?"

"Yeah. But you know that, don't you?"

I laugh. Course I know that. But he doesn't know there's a blue shimmer of a navis beneath my scarf, my very best scarf with the twin-dragons twining up the beaded edges. He probably doesn't even consider me a person. I've got no future.

<but what could we accomplish if we could sing to the world?> Muse pushes.

The blue-brown air of the room shivers with the thought—

<we could sing a better future for freedom>

<ta-ting>

"There are mega-theatres on Europa and Emory," I say, looking under my lashes at Harold Jones.

His greed's so strong it puckers his lips. "Yes, there are. And here on Cassiopeia Prime. And Earth and Luna, too"

Muse reaches into me, twitching.

<calm the fuck down, beast>

But it laughs in my mind because it knows me too well.

Of course we're going to sign the contract. Figure out the details later, how to hide, how to keep the secrets. Of course we'll sign...

"You WHAT?" Djen stands on the threshold of the *Stella-Maru*, hands on hips, hair everywhere. Red spacer's jumpsuit, red like her rage.

"Signed a music deal with Running Horses. It'll be good."

Djen's dark brown skin is turning bright beet red. One more pressure-notch and her eyes are gonna pop out of her head. "In what way, exactly, will it be fucking good?"

"It'll get us credit for Freedom, corporate and clean. It's our way out of organized crime. Gets us off Madame X's tit."

Djen's face achieves a perfect match with her jumpsuit. "By you pretending to be something you're not. By swallowing NQ."

How'd she know? How'd she even fucking know that's what I was planning? "Oh come on, don't you try to play pristine. Remember that night we breathed up so much tracer you thought you could levitate spoons with your mind because you didn't know where your hands were!"

"Yeah, that was tracer. This is NQ. You almost died getting off it for fuck's sake. For real, forever, almost fucking died. Stop lying to me, to yourself. This is just your excuse to get back on the pap!"

She is rage in tight black curls. "Even if you don't care about yourself, stop and think a minute about me!"

"I am thinking about you! That's why I have to do this. I can be useful to Freedom; I can get us truly free." Why does no one ever fucking understand me? I hit my head against the wall of the common room in an aggressive four-four march to vent the endless communication frustration.

No one understands me because I'm incompetent, incomprehensible, incoherent. Worthless.

Communication failure.

Com-failure.

"People understand my music," I scream. "This is my chance to be heard, to be understood. To make credit on the up and send it back to you. You watch, I'll get Freedom free of X. Then I'll get all the nauta free, not just Freedom's nauta, the slave Operators too. And then no one will have to suffer like we do again ever, never again!"

"You're abandoning us for a fucking fantasy and an excuse to kill yourself! You stupid, selfish, little boy!" Djen throws her meal tray across the room, once-innocent protein squares looking to maim me.

"At least I'm willing to try!"

Two days later, Djen and Stella leave Red City without me.

One day after that Harold Jones takes me and my secret stash of NQ on a charter flight to a new life.

◇

He's up and pacing, hands shivering like leaves. "It was a mistake. The kind of mistake so big you can't admit it, or it will kill you.

Djen found us and rescued us. She stuck up for us, even though they would've kicked her out of Freedom for bringing us in if she hadn't been the only functional Pathfinder left. They couldn't lose her, or the cells would've had no way to communicate."

"But you and Muse—"

Muse feeds a heat-flash of <*fury*> through the link.

Caran scoffs. "It was that stupid rule in Freedom, that you could only join if you got an invitation directly from an élan. But Muse didn't know about Freedom. Muse didn't even know it was an élan, that there were others of its kind. It was—'detached' is the word they use, but they say it's not quite the right word. They said it was a fragment and not whole. Let's finish this. I'm tired. I hate this part already."

◊

Ten years after Harold Jones and leaving Djen and Stella, I'm in Europa City working my way to the fringes of Casino Row. Next step is to pack the stolen dataslip with a recording of last night's performance. Then I'll have what I need to cover up the fact I can't play the kinetikosonus live because my real dataslip is in Jordis Ansari's mobster hands. After the tour leaves the Sol system, after wherever-it-is I'm playing on Mars and Luna and Earth, after wherever-it-is I'm playing after that, we'll be in a deep dimension dive on *Sonica*. Then I can snag a day to cut down on the NQ and reprogram the fake dataslip for real. And see if there's a way to get rid of the logo. For now, just have to be careful to keep my dancing in synch with the recording. Pissed as shit at Ansari; only bright spot in my day is making fucking music. Only thing that is real and true anymore. At least the singing'll be live.

Digging my nails into my palms so hard it's gonna leave bruises. Bruises Mindy will notice and ask about; she inspects me even more closely than she inspects the stage for threats. Even with the NQ making me close to normal as I'll ever get, I can't properly feel pain.

Trying to remember where there's a safe space to be alone and uninterrupted. <hey muse, isn't there an hvac zone just outside the row?>

<yes, over there>

Feet leave the gold of the Aureus, onto the blue-and-white tiles. Away from the neon glare. Past some hotel with a big filigree jelly-fish sign. Into the deep tunnels, high walls, claustrophobic feel for anyone who doesn't like the reminder that they're in a big air-filled tube under water. Quiet here. Sound-quiet and information-quiet. I need both, but mostly information-quiet. There's nowhere in Europa City where the longwaves won't tangle up in my summoning, but at least the transmissions are just the environmentals talking to each other

  - sorting out whether to warm or cool

  - adjusting O2-ratios

  - regulating scrubber-gills

  - controlling national feed-dust clouds

  - modifying dehumidifier anti-window condensation

  - negotiating com signals, adverts, media feeds, intel exchanges, Mem-flows, info-babble max-density—

<FUCKING-A MUSE WILL YOU STOP TRANSMITTING ALL THAT CRAP!>

The noise in my head goes quiet.

Then: <i don't want to do this> Muse whines.

My fist has hit the wall before I realize I've snapped. I bet it would've hurt if I could feel anything. <I TOLD YOU TO SHUT

UP it's your fault too that we left djen and stella alone, both of us equal parts asshole, so suck it>

<*malcontent*> floats from the beast but nothing else.

I find a dusty corner inside a mostly empty closet and kneel. First deal with the dataslip, then deal with the summoning. Pants pockets: pull out a portable 3V projection plate and a multi-slot slip reader, filched on my way through the Row. Stick the thin rectangle of the platinum-coated dataslip in one slot, and a recording of last night's performance I'd swiped from the media guys in the other. I learned a lot about stealing and hiding during my life of crime with Djen.

<ok, you know what to do?> I ask Muse.

It vibrates <*assent*> Then adds <this isn't the part i don't want to do. i don't like this part, but i want to do it>

<that's right, because i was unclear on the exact dimensions of your discontent, and your clarifying complaints help so much> Access to every human brain in shortwave range, and the élans still don't understand sarcasm.

I flick the 3V switch and amp the playback speed to 30x. Footage of my show plays in quick-time. Rewind with a blink at the holoicon on the lower right and wait.

<i'm in> Muse takes control of the light playing over the 3V.

I engage playback again. This time Muse bends the light and signal to remove me dancing across the stage, remove my voice from the sound layers, strip and patch until all that remains are the colors and shapes playing over the 4Vs and the music of the kinetikosonus. The transformed footage feeds into the empty slip. Like all élan vitals, Muse can manipulate light and datastreams as easy as I can pick up a cup, though typically they've no reason to do so. But there are still limits to how much energy the creatures can control at once, even the ancient, vanished ones, which Muse certainly is not. The creature's too alien to play the instrument with any artistry, but it can play the sound guys' 3V monitors like a lyre. Or rather, a liar. Nothing but dark blue lies.

At least my singing won't be lies. It's still my songs, too.

So why does this feel like a kick in the jaw?

As the data transfers, I pull the summoning objects from my pockets, objects that will resonate with Stella and draw her to me. Things that were I to make a Temple to Stella, to delight and attract her, to build her up into being even more herself, I would include.

A tiny replica of a dimship, a child's toy.

Four steel bolts from the *Stella-Maru*.

A vial of the pale amber liquid that powers her dimension drive.

And, gently now, a tiny white flower, pressed and dried, its six petals spread in the shape of a star.

The playback ends and I put the platinum slip, now containing a feed of my show sans self, back on the chain around my neck. Muse withdraws, its influence shrinking as far as possible while still staying connected enough to act as a dimensional transmitter. Wish I'd filched a bottle of something strong back on the Row. I don't want to do this any more than Muse does.

I circle the 3V with the bolts and place the toy dimship in the center of the plate, balancing it on its stubby back fins so the nose at the end of its elongated oval body points toward the ceiling. Then, taking four tries on account of my shitty fine motor control, I poke the stem of the flower into a small hole at the nose of the dimship, turning the toy into a tiny vase.

The elements of the summoning are in place.

I take twelve deep breaths because I'm scared.

This is the last of Stella's flowers, picked up on that planet with the starfish, and the last of her fluids too. I'd lost the rest along the way with the tours and the transfers from hotel rooms to dimships to a million parties and a thousand blackouts, and I hardly ever know where I am come morning let alone what I'd had in my pockets the night before.

Are Jordis' shadows—Hyperia's Dividia—enough of a crisis to use up this last of Stella's star-flower memories?

I know Muse and I should never have left them. I know they were right, and we were wrong, and we should have listened back then. But in over ten years, Djen and Stella could have at least sent me a sig on my fucking birthday. They obviously don't want anything more to do with me. Why should I care about them?

More deep breaths, quiet humming.

Maybe they'll take me back.

A whimper whines out of me as I shake my hands to release the tension. I relax as much as I ever can.

I begin, softly, to sing.

"You were watching Caran summon Stella, weren't you, Jordis?"

"Yes, I was, but I thought you wanted my story in order."

"Yes, I do." I laugh, a bit nervously, as she reminds me of my own words. "Caran left me on a cliffhanger yesterday."

"Ever the entertainer." Only one side of her mouth quirks its slight smile, but I see a flicker of real warmth for Caran in her stone-colored eyes. "Let me share what I woke up to that morning."

The 3V over the coffee table comes alive and Jordis replays archival footage from Europa Mainfeed News-11. It's from five years ago.

◊

A cheery jingle over bouncing colored dots resolves into the stream identification: "*The Morning Show with Mav and Chad*!"

The two commentators appear in overstuffed chairs before a wall painted with Europa's water-drop flag. Mav, shaved bald but with hair sketched on in matte black paint, wrinkles his brow with concern. "Well, Chad, I think that's a very good question, what would motivate Operators to sacrifice themselves? Their lives are so easy with everything taken care of, and it's not like they have feelings anyway. You'd think it's more evidence of their feeble-mindedness, but I think it's an erosion of basic social decency."

Chad nods, makeup caked on to look like plastic, "I think you're onto something there. Operators are a necessity, but so's a sewage system and we keep those hidden from view." She laughs. "Now Nurseries take their Operators on 'field trips out in the community.' I see little trains of them behind their minders all over the torus. Open a can of worms like that, and this is where we end up, with them wanting the same 'rights' as people. Which, of course, leads to the recent unnecessary violence."

Mav snaps his fingers and footage plays of three Operators, foreheads revealing tzaddium blue, kneeling on the green-and-white tiles of the West Arc. Their heads explode as the Europan authorities shoot them from behind, execution style. Chad stares at the gruesome footage with a bland, slightly interested expression.

◊

Jordis pauses the playback. "*Mav and Chad* would not be my first choice for morning news, given its conservative leanings, but I was looking for worst-case backlash on the bombing. I'd expected to hear them spinning on about the imaginary Genetic Liberation Front, or some other anti-Operator, pro-corporate conspiracy theory about the bombing. Mav and Chad weren't talking about what happened in Hangar 19, so I did a simultaneous lookup on why Operators were being executed in the West Arc."

The Morning Show compresses into a small cube and zooms to the top left of the 3V's display area. A new vista expands over the plate. I have to admit, I'm envious that she can do that without having to blink at an endless series of holicons.

Clips of mainfeed footage spatter in rapid succession, starting with a timestamp three months back from where we are in the timeline.

Two Operators from Europa's CentralCom stand up from their workstations, bite their embedded citizen IDs out of the thumb-webbing of their right hands, and step outside. They kneel on the street, hands behind their heads, and wait to be shot for going rone.

Five Operators from Casino Row's popular Zhavongi Smart Arts Corp do the same.

Then three from Fashionista gash their citizen IDs out with sewing tools from the manufacturing floor and walk outside to die.

Just a handful each time, but with increasing frequency as the timestamps move across three months of Europa's history, until a total of one-hundred and twelve Operators from fifty-six separate corporations have slit their thumbs, removed their CIDs, and knelt to die.

"The story hadn't made it past local Europan mainfeed," Jordis says. There is rancor in her voice beneath her ice-calm control, but her face is its usual politician's cool.

"The start of the uprising," I whisper. Academic shivers crawl all over my spine; I'm an anthropologist who studies social movements. Or maybe that's Europa's presence, preparing to invoke the link.

"I didn't know—Europa didn't know—none of us knew that Europa's Operators had broken their hobbles. It seems so obvious in retrospect. They wouldn't have been able to coordinate that kind of action unless they had communication."

The Morning Show zooms back down and unfolds/expands from the cube back into the archival feed before I can form the round "O" of my lips into some words.

◊

"What I find curious," Mav looks serious beneath the fringe of his painted-on bangs, "is that none of these 'protesting' Operators mentioned the Genetic Liberation Front. We see the GLF graffiti, and there was that bombing yesterday, but the ones that line up to die don't reference the GLF at all?"

Chad shifts primly in her over-stuffed seat. "I'd love to say it was disorganization, but the fear I have—and this is the fear echoed by a lot of folks—is that we might be dealing with two separate terror groups."

"I know corporate law is to shoot rone Operators on sight, so they don't do something terrible like what happened in the Revolution. But I think the police need to tranqgun some of these degenerates. Make them talk." Mav smacks his lips.

Chad snickers. "Because they're all so good at talking, right? But no, I follow your point. If they're trying to make a statement about their 'rights,' they should be clear about what it is."

◊

Jordis terminates the playback and sighs. "Except the Operators in question had, in very clear terms, presented a list of demands to the Europan Office of Operator Affairs six months before the protests started. Primarily—" she ticks off points on her fingers "—physical safety oversight in Operator Housing, limits on aversive Socialization techniques, and a stop to the use of stimulants and other chemicals in nutrient feeds during programming sessions without the Operator's knowledge. They'd made a strong case that Operators on orbitals run by the New Organization of Federal Banking Worlds had such protections, and the fabric of society had not fallen apart."

"This is the first I'm hearing of this. Why didn't they release these issues more publicly?"

"How? They were supposed to be hobbled—where, when, and with whom they could communicate restricted to the finest of lines. Also, Europa had a policy to remove peoples' navi between shifts; they had no way to communicate with anyone outside of work.

"Plus," Jordis twitches, and her grey eyes flash with anger, "even if they had released footage publicly no one would have believed it. There remains to this day a misconception that because we can modify data with our minds any footage we produce is a deep fake. Operator-originated footage is still legally dismissible in court according to corporate law throughout the inhabited worlds."

"Really? Still?"

"Complex, ingrained systems move slowly, you know that, Steven. Europa's Operators weren't thinking big yet and considering the leverage they actually had; they'd spent too long without power. So they'd tried the avenues they thought were open to them, gotten nowhere, and resorted to only real power they knew they had—their bodies as corporate commodities. The normals didn't care about Operator suffering, but they certainly cared about the loss of their financial investments."

I frown, thinking of the research I'd done preparing for these sessions. "Europa employs more Operators per-capita than any other orbital. Not just in the Core, but anywhere."

"That was a big part of why they had so many restrictions." Jordis shifts in her seat, not much, but enough to surprise me. Her posture becomes unselfconscious. "The Operator-to-normal ratio on Europa was one Operator for every fifty normals in terms of tagged residents, as opposed to typical population distribution of one-percent with the K-syndrome mutation."

"I think you might have enjoyed a career in academics." I smile at her as the growing link provides subtle feedback that I'm interpreting her movements correctly.

Her eyes crinkle in guarded wistfulness. "Social analysis is a politician's skill too."

"Of course it is." I lay on just enough mischief to be confident she can feel it through the link. I would fail at my job if I did not find ways to understand the fullness of her, right? "Please, continue your analysis. "

"Europa's economy is driven by the entertainments of Casino Row and the original All Worlds Scientific Center for Europa's Ocean Ecology. Add to that the engineering requirements for life support under water—and the fact that as the only independent nation in the Core, Europa has to protect itself from Federal infiltration—and you're talking about a uniquely high computational demand. From smart art and chance-machine programmers, to presidential encryption specialists, to the Operators who maintain the air filtration code, we are everywhere. That changes the dynamics of oppression.

"They put us in what they called 'storage' between shifts by removing our navi. For many of us, this meant becoming completely helpless and dependent on our minders, unable to communicate or even move to manage basic animal necessities. They took away our assistive technology, and our human dignity. Make no mistake, Steven, as much as I love my Europa, without my father's protection I was far better off for having been exiled."

The air is cold in Europa-élan's current and I feel her influence claiming me.

"The trick is to keep people down enough so that they can't fight back, but comfortable enough that they don't really want to fight back anyway. Europa lost control of that balance. Europa's Operators had nothing left to lose."

◊

(and with that, she takes me in)

I make my way to Media53 and wait outside the door. The hungry feeling in my breastbone, where the dataslip pulses like a second heart, elates me. Everything is alive and alight, new senses opening in the aura of the sleeping moon around my neck. I sample the emotions of strangers—tired, bored, engaged, scared, in love, dreaming of a future conquest—like whiffs of perfume as they pass.

Beneath the invisibility of my fan, I lick the taste of salt from my lips.

A herd of Media53 employees stampede toward me, coffee steaming in their fists. They chatter about nothing, as normals do. They are excited, flushed. I've always been adept at reading normals, but now I don't just read them, I feel them. They flash quickly like quarana, unaware I flank their herd.

I follow their currents—various employees breaking off here and there to their separate offices—into a splicing room paneled floor-to-ceiling with 3V projection plates. While the editors fuss with their coffee on the edges, I stride invisible to the middle of the room, and turn a slow circle on my hunting grounds.

At the far end of the space a lone Operator lies on the large black bed that supports us during long programming sessions. He hasn't initiated the device yet, feeder and waste tubes dormant, the surface cool. I know the temperature of everything. The slight difference between the floor and ceiling. The faint differentials around each person's body heat. Is this the tactile heat-sense of a colonial filigree, or a perception of infrared like an angeltorch?

The Operator watches the editors with distant, resentful gray eyes. His reddish hair twists back into a long, thick braid that falls heavy on his soft brown clothing. No one has acknowledged his presence: he is the feed-tech, part of the equipment. The editors finish fussing with their coffees and one of them—*the lead editor, I know that's who you are*—snaps her fingers at him. He activates the bed and goes lax as his consciousness flows into the room's electronics.

"Bring up the feed-dust from Hangar 19," she says. "Let's get this feature wrapped before the news gets stale."

The smoky waste of the bombing site swirls. Ash falls, sizzling bits of melted metal, and there's a crashing, cracking sound.

This footage is from minutes, or maybe seconds, after the explosion. The torus may have a paucity of the mounted sensorcams used by Federal Banking Worlds to track citizens, but it's full of nanocams—feed-dust—programmed to seek and wake at celebrity arrivals or CEOs behaving foolishly with booze and whores and illegal tech on the Row. But this recording would have come from National's feed-dust, programmed to alert at anything that threatened public safety. *Well, well, do you know mainfeed media has this sensitive footage, Primo Capo Som Bliss?*

There's movement at the edge of the disaster. Hyperia and my eyewitness, the customs fixer Baltus from Greene's crew, emerge from the swirl. Hyperia isn't dead yet, but she's taken her fatal wounds. Baltus is a mess too, flesh black with burn, ribs sticking out. He drags Hyperia, failing to find the exit in the haze. When they reach the wall, Hyperia cries out and goes limp. Unable to support her, Baltus props her against the wall before sliding down next to her, passing out from the effort.

"Perfect, freeze there." The cool soprano of the editor cuts through the smell my memories have overlaid atop the recorded scene.

"Center on the pair, especially the rone Op. I want a close-up, that's gonna be golden."

The lead editor's verbalized stream-of-consciousness is the Operator's command. The 3Vs zoom in on Hyperia's shredded face.

"Yeah, clean that up."

Dust and ash disappear, resolution increases, the iridescent blue of Hyperia's navis becomes a sharp contrast with the ash-soaked blood from her wounds, her long, bleached dreadlocks. Hyperia's blood-slicked fingers curl around the unconscious man's arm, and she gasps, "Dividia. CryCorp. Gonna kill us all."

Consciousness split:

Thread One: Watching the editors, the recording, the feedtech in his bed.

Thread Two: Doing a lookup in the Mem: CryCorp.

Thread Three: Seeking a short-wave frequency on which I might be able use my cutter programs to slip in around the Operator's hobbles and communicate with him.

Lookup in the Mem on Thread Two returns: CryCorp is a Level 3 chartered corporation based on Ganymede. Originally chartered 423 years ago as Cryosprings Corporation for processing cryovolcanic resources, CryCorp is currently chartered for terraforming, cryovolc processing, and associated resources. Key facts:

- #2 in terraforming via All Worlds Business

- One of the "original six" corporations to venture from Earth and into the Ort and Kuiper belts to mine asteroids

- Foundational in the settlement and terraforming of Ganymede

- Has scientific research centers on sixteen worlds

- Employs 200,956 across inhabited space
- Current CEO Ulrich Ellison; list of past CEOs includes...

Cordon off stream and redirect into machine memory for later analysis. New search: CryCorp crossref Ray Ansari OR Galilean Black Market OR organized crime OR syndicate OR Argus Hotel and Casino OR [list of names in any way connected to the bombing]

◊

Thread One, back in the room: "Great, great, OK, rewind and remove the sound between there and there, good," the lead editor says. "And now with the new dialogue."

Hyperia's fingers curl around Baltus' arm, but the splice is uneven, her voice pitched too high. "Just the beginning. Genetic Liberation Front's gonna kill us all."

"Come on you useless feeble!" The editor yells at the Operator. She mutters to her second, "Gods, need to get us a new one of those, this one's broken."

"You mean more broken?" the second rolls her eyes.

The lead snaps back at the Operator, "And replace 'us' with 'you' for fuck's sake. Can't even get a simple pronoun right."

Replay, seamless now, Hyperia's bloody fingers curl around Baltus' arm, her wince of pain reads as a sneer with the snarl in her voice, "This is only the beginning. Genetic Liberation Front's gonna kill you all!"

◊

Thread Three, through the vortex into informationspace, seeking the shortwave lay of the land, find the bright spot where the feed-tech's navis sends signal to the editing machines:

I stand in the specialized program I'm running to map local frequencies; a splay of colors forms a topographical structure where wavelength is visceral. The feed-tech glows in heavy red-oranges, occupying local equipment only. I pull up my cutter program, designed to find a way past an Operator's hobbles, the insidious programming that prevents him from accessing signal not associated with his job. I make a connection with his shortwaves and release the cutter—a shivering silver thread—to infiltrate the standard security package all Operators must to run.

Expecting resistance, the thread instead melts into the feed-tech's stream like a pat of butter on a burner, drawing me into his frequency along with it.

I back out, pulse thumping. It's got to be some sort of a trap.

But a soft sound floats out, a "ping" like an ancient sonar sound in a historical holovid. There's an encrypted message with it.

I pull it in, but I'm not an encryption specialist. I've no idea what it says.

I approach the feed-tech's signal again, take a deep breath, and step in.

I stand before him with the soft blue glow of friendly emotives in my chest, my surprise and suspicion tamped down behind my ice. He presents in the Mem as a more colorful version of himself, emotives expressing through the shifting patches of color and texture on his tunic. Surprise, worry, curiosity—"Who are you? Where did you come from?"

◊

Thread Two, my searching:
Ulrich Ellison, CEO of CryCorp Xref Ray Ansari, CEO of Argus

Hotel and Casino: fifteen reported meetings in the past Earth-standard year.

CryCorp Xref Argus Hotel and Casino: Subcontract #156790b awarded to CryCorp from Argus Hotel and Casino for Landscaping Services and Backroom Access.

Look at that Daddy, you and Ellison have business deals. Now why would you need a terraforming giant to work on the Argus' atrium when an xenoarborist would do, and why would Ellison need a subcontract for premium casino content he's already entitled to as a chartered CEO? What's the Real Deal, Daddy? And does your Primo Capo know?

◊

On Thread One, in the flesh, I walk myself out of the splicing shop and toward the tube station, deactivating my fan and splitting a fourth thread to contact Primo Capo Som Bliss to let him know I'm on my way to his office with new intel about the bombing.

◊

Thread Three, to the feed-tech: "I'm Gala Baudin. I work in Security. I saw what they're making you do. I was going to give you a program to get past your hobbles, but it appears that is not needed, cheers to you." I radiate calm, friendly, so much blue glow that I can see my own aura extending out from my chest.

"Security?"

"Empire of the Moon. Corporate Enforcer." I hand him my full identification in the lingua franca of a gold coin. "The Empire has a long-standing policy of treating Operators as human beings."

"I'm Ammiel," the feed-tech says, reads my identifiers, and frowns. "You're organized crime."

I beam an apologetic yellow along with my friendly blue. "True in some respects, but the Empire has a proper corporate charter too. I've a regular sponsorship with the Empire, as you can see. The Empire has stakes in a stable Europa. I'm here to investigate the corruption behind the lies you were just forced—against your will—to concoct. We both know there's no Genetic Liberation Front."

Ammiel says nothing, and in the silence a shiver runs through me. Could Ammiel's surprise broken hobbles be the—I shiver again at the appropriateness of the metaphor—tip of the iceberg? I take a wild chance and say, "But we both know there's another Operator-led movement on Europa, one that is very real."

His colors flicker fear and suspicion; he has no schooling in how to control the evidence of his emotions.

I project steadiness, and put my hands out, palms up. It is the universal symbol of friendly intent within the syndicate, but others tend to understand it too. "Don't worry; I won't tell anyone." I laugh a little, then give him the deepest bow. "Your movement has my awe, respect, and delight. Not only for having broken the code preventing free Op-to-Op communication, but for keeping that fact from the authorities. Bravo."

Ammiel's emotives relax a bit. "You aren't hobbled either," he whispers.

I laugh. "No, of course not. My 'sponsor,' the Empire of the Moon, knows that we are more effective free than bound."

"We don't want to die."

"The executions?" I follow his associative mind because it flows like mine.

"Yes. But we don't know what else to do. We can't risk someone knowing we can communicate with each other. It's too easy for them to take it from us. Could the Empire help?"

I hide my excitement behind my ice and continue projecting friendly blue. Broken hobbles would explain how the Europan Operators are coordinating their suicide protests. How many are un-hobbled? Could it be all of them? Uncontrollable chills run through my physical body, implications unfolding and unfolding again. "The Empire can certainly help. Perhaps you can connect me with others, and we can begin a dialogue?"

"Perhaps." Ammiel considers with such complex emotions that his tunic shifts into an unreadable mud. "What are you going to do about the lie I was just forced to concoct?"

It's important I answer this right. Perhaps the truth will serve me best. "I'm going to find out what really happened with bombing. And then I am going to expose it."

"Do you have that power?" He crosses his arms, part challenge, part skepticism.

"No." I smile, warm, blue. "But I work with and for those who do." I meet his challenge honestly. I open my hands and let spill a small, safe, subset of names, companies, alliances to which I have access, spies, proxies.

His eyes go wide, his colors freeze. "Really? You are with us?"

I smile. "Of course. The Empire of the Moon has little love for federal law when it comes to Operators. But more to the point, am I not one of you?"

I give Ammiel the means to contact me at any time and cut my connection to him, my heart beating fast over the implications of an unhobbled Europa. I need to focus now in the physical world, where I have reached Primo Capo Som Bliss' office at Mentist Corp.

Just over the threshold, I confront a smart art statue of Orchis raping a priestess. Orchis pauses and appraises me, reading my body language. I presume this is a test. Finetuning my own pro-gramming to hide any cues that I sympathize with the priestess, I tip it an ambiguous smile. Orchis resumes his rape.

"You've affinity for my decor, Gala." Som leans against the edge of his black desk, handsome and grinning in his neo-Ro-man curls and taut muscles. "Orchis stops his rape for most. Or the priestess rescues herself, sometimes quite creatively. You've a stomach for cruelty."

"Well," I return a mirror of his grin, angling myself so my fore-head shine dulls in shadow, "you and I are cut from the same stone, as it were."

He warms further. "I'm so glad you've finally a good, if unfor-tunate, excuse to visit Europa in person. Yesterday at the hangar there was a lot going on; let me more appropriately extend my hos-pitality." He gestures toward the oval table at the edge of the large room. "If you don't mind, I had lunch brought for us." An array of expensive snacks spread over the surface in a rainbow.

I am hungry, though not for food. "I appreciate it, Som, and I, too, am pleased to finally be here in person with you." *But we have spent time in person before, you just do not remember the little girl with pigtails.* "I enjoyed the summit between our regions last year, but as a projection I was unable to sample the Morovian caviar." I add a light laugh and reach for a slender wedge of pale cheese dotted with dark pink roe.

Som reflects my laugh, at full ease now within the rapport I've been building since yesterday. "Between you and me, it was worth your wait. I get my stock from actual Morovia, whereas I can't say the same of the summit's caterers."

"Well—" I flash a sly smile, still keeping my forehead out of the lights, "—they do say good things come to those who wait."

He laughs, then sobers into worry-lines. "You have new intel about our investigation?"

I nod and dust crumbs from my fingers. I check the tightness of my bun. "Are you aware there's feed-dust from the incident?"

Increased heat, revelation, resentment—oh no, clearly, he was not. He answers as though it's no big deal. "No, I'm not. What's it show?"

"The more interesting question what is it being altered to show."

We stare at each other, almost for too long. Then I break the suspense. "The mainfeed is spinning it as a terrorist attack by the Genetic Liberation Front, which you and I both know does not exist."

"Would you rather them spin it as syndicate warfare?" His resentment at not being in the know kindles into an active smoldering; there's a snappy edge to his voice.

"I'd rather them not spin it at all." I hold his eyes captive, slipping the next steps into place. "Since the Argus Hotel owns the hangar, it would have been simple enough to invoke corporate privacy law to destroy the recording and let the incident slide into obscurity. All this will do is direct undue attention toward us—it was our freighter and shipment—making everything more difficult for both the Kingdom and the Empire."

Som sets down the pakafruit he was about to consume. "We've been told to let media do its own thing. No active damage control. Orders from above."

"Orders from above?"

"If you'd like an audience with King Ansari, then—"

I frown and shake my head in a way that communicates my own disapproval of Ray Ansari's orders. "No, not yet. But soon perhaps." I appear to reflect, and then catch my breath. Let it out. Put on my best concerned brow. "The real recording shows Hyperia implicating a company called CryCorp in the bombing. Public records show King Ansari's had some recent dealings with them."

"What are you saying, Gala?"

"I'm just telling you what I learned. Your own enforcers can find the evidence easily enough at Studio 53 on Via Fortuna." I pause again, crafting a fine aura of subtle awkwardness. When the silence gets uncomfortable and Som opens his mouth to speak, I say over his intake of breath. "Although—"

"What?"

Running an embarrassment program, I shake my head and look down, stimulating my blood flow into flushing. "No, nothing."

"Come on, Gala, that was a something."

"Well, it may be inappropriate for me to offer this, but I'm never going to be promoted above Key Enforcer." I shift so that the iridescent blue of my forehead shimmers in the light now, reminding him of what I am. "And if I didn't say something inappropriate once in a while I wouldn't be much of an Operator, now, would I?" Add in a wistful, self-deprecating smile. "But my unique, un-promotable position affords a certain, well, security to those who still have someplace higher to ascend."

Som hardens as I remind him of my otherness, but his voice is soft. "If you've something more to say, say it."

"Well," I let out a little sigh, eyes flicking at my shoes. "Let's just say some felt more secure when you were next in line as Ray Ansari's favorite."

Som's eyebrows rise, and I cover my mouth as though just realizing how terribly socially inappropriate I've been. Som bursts out laughing as though I've told the best joke he's ever heard. "Oh Gala, you are truly one of a kind!" He wipes the corners of his eyes. "Yes, that was very, very inappropriate, but you know they say there's often truth in an idiot's ramblings."

I let the insult go. *Because I will teach you differently later, when I am your Queen.* I laugh with a nervous quiver. "Well, I guess I just proved why I'll never be Queen." What little remained of the tension dissipates.

"I don't think any of us would have picked Jordan Ansari as Prince," Som says, "including Jordan himself. But our King is young and strong, and not only will he be around for a good long while, but he has plenty of time in which to produce more heirs. And who knows, really, what Jordan may become if he stops messing with paints and starts paying attention to business. He may surprise us all."

That is what Som says, but I've planted my subversion. Before my half-brother's birth Ray Ansari had been priming Som for future King. How jealous I'd been of him. But Som turned out solid; he will be a good second when I am in charge.

"Anyway, before I make more of a fool of myself," I stand and give Som a small bow, "I'd better leave you to your business. I'll send you a copy of the feed-dust recording—the original version."

"Thank you. And it was nice to have your company—and your honesty—but yes, I've a busy afternoon."

Pausing at the statue of the rape, which continues graphically, I turn back. "As long as I'm being inappropriate—" I twitch my mouth without resolving the gesture, leaving him to wonder if I've intended a smile or a frown "—your King hates Operators. That puts him at a disadvantage, particularly where Luna is concerned, as we do not have such limitations. Just something which may be to your fortune to consider." I do smile then, Madame X's smile which hides more than it reveals, and close the door behind me. Europa's currents shift.

Many things shift.

One of them is Watts.

I sense his movements as though I were a filigree jelly tracking him as my prey.

◊

"You knew where he was because of the resonance Muse built between you or because of Europa's influence on you?"

"Likely both, and possibly more. It's not like I can track Caran on an ordinary day. Which I imagine," Jordis laughs, "is for the best. But there was quite a confluence of events. Caran and I had recently linked through Muse. I was barely divisible from Europa-élan, aligned as I was with her frequencies, and he and I were thinking about each other because of the stolen dataslip. Also, Caran was contacting Stella, so all of her resonances that amplify sense of location and navigation were in play. All of us were influencing, amplifying, realigning each other; that's why élan resonance is so potentially dangerous."

"So I count then, three élans engaged in the events."

"Four, if you count Dividia."

"So, to be clear, ordinarily, élans don't give humans the ability to track each other."

Jordis laughs and waves a pale, long-fingered hand. "Oh no, of course not. Nothing about these particular events was ordinary."

I tip a finger off my brow and smile. "So, tell me a little about Stella."

She frowns. "Caran or Djen would be a better ask."

"I'm not sitting right now with Caran or Djen."

"Well then, you can learn about her as I did."

◊

Caran Watts kneels in a maintenance closet, singing to a sleeping 3V and a disorienting array of objects: four screws, a child's toy dimship with a dried flower stuck in its nose, and a vial of something amber clutched in his hand. He's performing a ritual to some god that I do not recognize. His face shows anger, love, fear, hurt, longing, resolve. The edges of his emotions enter me as though they are mine, and I wish for the first time I could turn off my newfound senses. He turns on the 3V.

A star field rises, constellations setting the stage for the tiny dimship. Music rises with the stars, atonal and whispery, punctuated by eerie moaning. It's familiar, so I feed it into my memory index: space noise. What stars and big bodies like Jupiter emit at radio and microwave frequencies, transposed into audio. Watts' singing ambles and weaves with the space-sound, until it seems the dimship itself is singing.

The air ionizes and my skin prickles. My chest fills with joy and longing and curiosity unbounded—feelings neither mine nor Europa's.

The stars ripple, flowing as the toy dimship with its star-flower nose speeds through space. Shimmering, spinning, surging, sound climaxes into a melody as the song switches seamlessly from atonal to an evocative major key. The man—musician, magician—crescendos and upends the amber liquid into the circle of stars.

White current cracks through charged air and strikes the flower. The liquid ignites; the flower bursts into live flame, devouring the dimship. The stars on the 3V spark and flare, then dim to glimmer and glitter-dust from which emerge two bright, blue, silver-lidded eyes.

Silence.

The flame burns now without fuel, floating in the air.

The spell of the song releases me. This is not like what had happened to me before in Caran's hotel room, though it had similar tells. Instead of being invaded, I'm being drawn in, like gravity, like magnetism. Watts' face is lit in warm flame, shadowed by cold resentment, and shining with tears.

<*anger* why have you summoned me here?>

The communication comes to me like Europa's had, as though it were a feeling and a thought of my own but created by someone else. The flavor is different. This is a smaller, gentler thing than a moon, but a thing like a moon just the same.

"Stella," Watts whispers with tenderness, wrapping his arms around his knees and gently rocking. "I—"

<you, nothing. nothing for you. nothing from you. *hurtAnger*>

"Fucking listen to me," Watts snaps, voice beautiful even hard with pain. "Hyperia fingered me with her dying thoughts, so you fucking listen to me. Something bad's happening on Europa, something Hyperia thinks threatens us all. I think it could be a destructive élan. Plus that bint Gala Baudin is really Jordis Ansari and she's here, and she's got Hyperia's navis. She could figure out what the spare parts are for. So don't you tell me nothing, there's a whole lot of something. So no lectures, you get Djen in the link. Now."

The blue eyes blink their silver lashes from the center of flame circled by stars.

Then the flames and the glitter-dust, which I had assumed were projections from the 3V plate, rise away the device, twining and twirling into tendrils of fire like the radiation bursts of a star. They enmesh themselves with the singer's skin, hair, entering his eyes and ears and mouth. He jerks, then goes rigid and still. The air becomes dense with signal, information, a communication between Watts and the sun, but none of it is accessible to me; I cannot tune into the frequency.

Forty-nine seconds pass and the aura and the tendrils withdraw and coalesce into a glowing sphere. Blue eyes open in the center of the miniature sun, burning hot above the charred remains of the toy dimship and the small white flower.

<*acknowledgeInformationTransfer* we will consider.>

"Consider? Is that 'consider' like actually think about it, or 'consider' like you said you'd 'consider' dropping by to say hi once in a while, maybe making sure I was all right?" The singer's voice rises, hands flailing in increasing agitation. "And no, I'm not all right, not at all, thanks for not fucking asking!"

<*shameOnYou*>

The eyes and the light wink out. The room smells of burnt offerings and tears. I want to hit Watts, hit him again and again, hit him until his heart stops beating and his face becomes unrecognizable.

This feeling isn't mine; it's his.

I back away, my stomach churning.

I've been dealing with Freedom for nearly two decades, so why had I never witnessed/felt/experienced such a thing as this before? My fingers curl around the warm dataslip.

Perhaps because I've always dealt with Freedom's representatives, not a weak-willed papper who they kicked out of their number. Did I just witness the secret they've been hiding?

Watts emerges, eyes red-rimmed and make-up smudged.

If Europa is the soul of a moon, and the thing Watts summoned above the projection plate is a similar sort of being, what is it? Have I witnessed one of the so-called "gods" that the Dieuvéssaus claim they commune with? No one ever described a Dieuvéssau summoning something anyone could see though; that magic stuff is just cute superstitious nonsense that sometimes seems to work. Djen always was strange about that ship of hers, the *Stella-Maru*. The name means "star-circle." The sun and the silver-lidded blue eyes.

The blue eyes over the projection plate. Europa in the alley. The violent connection with Watts in the hotel room—

"Get Djen in the link," Watts had said.

Link.

I try to think it the rest of the way through but have to concentrate on not losing him as he weaves his way back through the laughing, crying, buying, strutting, hoping masses of Casino Row, dragging himself like a broken doll.

He does not try to contact me when he gets back to his room.

He does not try to contact me after he's dressed, fed, fussed over, and poked some more.

I enter the dataslip around his neck easily and examine its contents. It contains only the 3V A/V feed of last night's performance, sans himself. Yet, he is unconcerned by the lack of real programming within. His technical people are bound to notice the difference, unless... unless what?

Maybe he wants to fail to produce a viable show tonight? He is dangerously self-destructive. No, he comes back to life at mention of the music.

I follow him into the Razor Club, high-end trendy, not Black Market controlled. My wrists are exhausted, tendons twitching, from waving the heavy golden fan. Something is happening here too, something that makes the hairs on my arms stand on end like they had in Watts' hotel room. Like when Europa came to me in the alley behind the Filigree Hotel. Like the moment those blue eyes appeared above the starry 3V. I'd felt that same static charge, that ionized air, at my first sight of Europa a day ago.

You're unconcerned by my threats, Mx. Watts, because you're not alone. An invisible intelligence accompanies you, helps you. Europa, Stella, your shadow—no more the same as you and I, but, as we are both human, so too are these creatures all the same manner of being. Freedom's secret is that it's made contact with second-order intelligent life, and based on everything I've experienced, that life has fine-grained control of the EM. Fine enough control to make a puppet out of me.

I consider that experience in greater depth. I play it back through my memory index, approaching it with the fresh lenses I have just acquired. The creature's influence on me ended the moment I snapped open my fan—my freedomtech device with the adaptive EM field that bends waves around it.

I look back at Watts. I'm guessing if he used my fan, it would mess up his connection with the creature too. What I need is a large-scale version of the fan's EM interference to wrap him in. Like the electromagnetic storms of Io.

I lick my teeth.

I have all the information I need to see his bluff and raise him the house.

"Your invisible friend, Mx. Watts," I say aloud, very close to him, thrilling that neither he nor his invisible friend can detect me behind the safety my fan, "just showed me how to break you. I know, Orpheus, I know how to tear off your head. And you will sing for me."

Caran's entrance into my office segues seamlessly into the first leg of a long, agitated pace. He blows great breaths out as he blurs, a mass of anxiety, back and forth. I wait, thinking it will quiet, but his steps only grow more violent. "Caran? You okay?"

"It's just today," he says. He doesn't break his stride, but he doesn't speed up either. "Just this session today."

"Well, if you don't want to do it, remember—"

"That participating in this study is my choice, blah, blah, I know, you keep saying it. Really good memory here. Just 'cause I want to participate doesn't mean it's pleasant. Just 'cause it's unpleasant doesn't mean it's not useful." The pacing slows but doesn't stop. "You ever do this, Steven?" he asks.

"Do what? Participate in research?"

"Yeah. Do an interview where you have to talk about the really awful shit you've done?"

"Is that what you think? That you've done really awful shit?"

"Well I have, haven't I? All sorts of awful shit." The pacing finally stops. His back is to me as he shakes out his hands. "All I've ever been's a piece of shit."

"And a Galaxy-award winning artist, and an inspiration to billions, and the reason why today we have—"

He stops my mouth with haunted eyes. "We're at the night of

my second show on Europa. The one where Muse was going to trick the tech guys into thinking I was playing the kinetikosonus live when I was really playing prerecorded sound and light."

"Yes, that's where we are in the sequence of events."

"All right then." He balls his fists up so tight I worry he might be hurting himself. His teeth grind across each other. "Muse has trouble with this part, too. This is the night Dividia changed Europa to resonate more like itself."

◊

(I am in Caran's memories without warning.)

I stand on the edge of some posh party place called the Razer Club, somewhere LaRoque and the PR people felt I should Be Seen before the show. But I don't want to party. I don't even want a fucking show.

What had I been expecting of Stella, really? A welcome home with open arms? I'd known before I'd started Djen and Stella wouldn't want me back. I hadn't summoned Stella to ask them to take me back. Hadn't asked for it, hadn't expected it, but yet—

I'd hoped for it.

Hoped.

Hope.

Hope is what they'd given me once. Twenty-six years ago.

School'd been postponed for harvest and I was hoping to drive the hauler because I'm too fuck-all clumsy for all else and none of it matters anyway because oh, look, here's another fuck-it-all-to-hell party by the Nikkoti kids and this party is better than anything on Agrippa's got any right to be. Because I'm buzzing on NQ, the choice drug, the best drug, the one that fries my nerves enough I almost feel like a human drug.

Katie O'Brian'd brought me my first drops two years ago. She'd held up that little vial of dark blue shine, same color as the sky full of stars that jiggle and throb and never stay still, vision all wavy lines.

"I don't want this junk, it's no good," she'd said.

"What is it?"

Katie was three grades older than me and almost major. She had bright orange hair and freckles dense as the stars, and we'd been getting high together for going on year on whatever we could scrounge, lying back in the wheat field under the cacophony of the stars. She told me her theories on human nature and what it had been like when her brother raped her. I sang her song after song after song because she asked me to and because I would have been singing anyway. I didn't understand most of what she said, but she never cared if I said anything back.

"NQ. It's some dumb euphoric. More than a drop or two will kill you. All it did was make me want to love everyone for about an hour. I'm gonna toss it if you don't want it."

"Nah, don't toss. I'll try. How's it work?"

"You put just one drop on your tongue. Then it makes you really friendly. It's stupid."

One drop on the tongue was all it took for the stars to stop shaking.

Katie O'Brian left Agrippa as soon as she hit major. Now I've got a hot boy on either side of me and a cute girl sitting at my feet with her head in my lap. Everyone hates me but loves what I can do for them. Yeah.

"Whatcha doin' at a party without your navis, pretty boy?" The girl slurs at me drunkenly. She's got the tightest black curls, could be siliplas. Could be snakes. On this much NQ, just looks like hair.

"I'm not a feeble, silly," I laugh at her.

"Like hell."

"Like hell? I'm not!"

She brings her volume down so low that no one else is likely to hear it except me. "You're having three separate conversations at the same time, like it was nothing." The girl tips her head to look at me with huge brown eyes. Shit, is that a shimmer of blue beneath the skin of her forehead? "Normals," she says still in that same extra-quiet way, "can't do that."

"It's a B-flat," I tell Hot Boy Number One.

"Nah, my mom doesn't give a flying fuck what I do. All she cares about is her beaus and her beers," I tell Hot Boy Number Two.

"'Course they can." I squint at the girl. They can, can't they?

She laughs and brings her volume back to normal. "Your mom really doesn't pay attention! How old are you? Ten? Eleven? Sing it for him; he doesn't know what a B-flat sounds like."

I sing the B-flat for the boy and snap, "I'm fourteen, thanks," at the girl.

She pushes Hot Boy Number One away from me so she can crawl right up to my ear to whisper even more quietly, "Three conversations, yeah, maybe normals can do that, but an hour ago you were having fifteen simultaneous convos at once. You don't even know it, do you? But then, you're papped out on NQ."

"How'd you—"

"Cuts the sensory overload and amps motors. You'd never be here otherwise. NQ and U4 are the only things that'll do that, and U4 won't make you quite so chatty."

"Fuck you. I'm no feeble." Now I'm whispering back to her at that same volume no one else can hear.

"Fuck you. You're certainly no normal. Wanna see something real?"

"Will it kill me?"

"Maybe." She pushes away from me so we can see each other clearly. Her big brown eyes catch light sharp as stars, and she's not drunk at all as she says clear and loud. "I'm *GEN*. From space. Djen with a D."

"I'm Caran. From shit. Caran with a W-A-T-T-S. Whatcha doin' on this piss-ant backwater, Djen with a D?

"Looking for you."

I laugh, an arpeggio of golden sparks. "You're ridiculous. I'm a piece of shit."

She stands up, eyes walking all over me. "Things grow in shit, farm boy. I'm seeding Freedom."

Hot Boy Number Two's nibbling my ear, but he's not very good at it, and it's kind of annoying. Push him away. Only thing matters is the girl. "I'm into freedom." I say as meet her stare.

"You've no idea what you're saying." She stares back.

"No. But you're cute."

"Yes. But you're high."

"Yes, but I'm crazy."

She chuckles. I like the sound of it, like nut shells rolling in one of the industrial crackers. "No, you're not crazy. Who will notice if you run away?"

"Nobody. Least nobody has when I've run away before."

"Faboo."

"Where are we going?"

She laughs, still with that nut-brown laugh, bright red jump suit. Spacer. Didn't see that before. How old is she? Older than me, but not by much. "Your voice is beautiful," she says. "We're going to the stars. To Freedom."

No idea what's going on. Don't care. Got an eighth of a dram of NQ in my pocket and so long as I don't run out, she can take me wherever she'd like. "Got NQ where you're taking me?"

"No. I've got better." She grins, hauling me outside into the dark night.

Smell of ripe wheat.

Sound of the grasses shush-shush-shush.

Away from the party, away from the light and the sex and the booze.

Muse flares visible, rainbow waves of <*joy/push* go with her, do!>

Djen laughs, draws a finger through its light. Like she expected to see it there.

What the fuck? Thing's never shown itself to anyone but me and the birds.

Muse ripples in time with Djen's laugh, in time with the wind in the wheat, under the stars, and me singing like I might be good for something after all.

I left Agrippa with her that night. She shoved me in her possessed spaceship and cleaned me up and gave me a home. Built me a navis, taught me how to code, how to summon the élan vitals. She'd promised that me, a worthless fuck-up from bum-fuck, could be someone. Could be Dragon, a runner for Freedom, helping Djen Pathfinder and Stella keep the free-side alive. Hope.

We were good together, too. She'd float into my personal space giddy to explore some new planet Stella'd found, and we'd walk ruby beaches and gaze into purple skies and discover new things that grow under strange stars.

But I'm not a Pathfinder like Djen, and Muse isn't a normal élan; it's messy, inexplicable, in some way incomplete or detached, uncomfortably entangled with me, can't do anything right and neither can I. Djen wasn't bringing me into Freedom to keep its population from dying out; she was just lonely.

Today Stella'd been cold and stiff, not added Djen to the link, just sucked up my intel, left me in a pool of shame. All I've ever brought anyone is shame, my mother, Djen, Stella, Mindy too.

No matter. Djen hates me, Stella hates me, everything is awful, so here in this posh-ass Razer Club let Muse take what it wants, gorge on the fervor of the fans, the eight drops on my tongue, what's it matter if I've enough to last the week, rush it up, riding high, my demon and I! Fame-feeding-fame, Muse reinforces its own hysteria, catching and hooking in everything, pushing, PUSH-ING <*fillthevoidfillthevoidfillthevoid*>

I push back at Muse with hate-laced disgust; if only it had hu-man feelings, I could hurt it. All I can do is vaguely ruin its enjoy-ment. Fancy people in fancy clothes standing around just to be seen and reported in the feeds, I didn't even leave home with a change of clothes, if only they could see me then, starving in my own shit while my mother was out with boyfriend-of-the-week painting the town red, washed-out Watts in a confused stupor all the time, and what am I doing flirting with Europan haute couture and pretending I'm like them?

FUCK HOPE

Glass shatters; whatever I'd been holding meets the wall of the Razer Club. Shrapnel and vermouth everywhere.

But the music keeps plugging and the patrons keep dancing and it's just fucked-up Caran Watts, whatever, pay no attention to the god-freak, he's always like that, isn't it the cutest thing ever.

Muse pushes trippy-down-excitement, feeding me thought-streams from the room <*OWOWLOVE**love you, love YOU! MyPop-IdolHeroGod*>

Fuck, Muse's energy feels so wrong tonight. Out of sync, off-beat. Signals scramble: waves degrade. I feel like something is influencing it; something is realigning its energies. Thing reads like bad math. <go away!> I tell it.

But it doesn't go away, it rubs at me, making raw nerves, bleeding brains, nowhere to escape but deeper into the party.

"You're nothing but discord!" I yell. Watch all the good people pretend there isn't an out-of-control man yelling at nothing. Watch Mindy take a step closer, not sure if this is Save-Me-From-Myself or Let-Me-Implode.

I back away; the latter, thanks.

Mindy's hand on my arm, her voice in my ear, "Caran, you have a show, you have got to stop—"

"Fuck off." Fuck her "concern." Fuck all this fucked up shit, Jordis and her ambition, Freedom and its death wish, the public and its insatiable need for me to do something Even More Extreme. Give Muse what it really wants, give the humans what they think they want, and at the end of the long, hollow road of excess, the élan won't be able to reach me and my handlers won't be able to touch me and Jordis won't be able to threaten me and the past can't crawl in to wreck me.

I move into the crowd, wrapping myself in the Special People of Europa, money, jaded hauteur, all they are is ego, fad-processed look-and-feel. Honey to fill me up. Smile for the cameras, see what a good boy I'm being now? Right where Mx. Manager Jonathan La-Roque wants me. Play, play, play!

Bodies press in close, to feel me, to sex me. Wait for the right one, the right ones. Let Mindy fall into the shadows of awareness, the ignorable constant, she'll keep the damage contained.

Music-beat, tribal and old and new. Trash music, no art to it, just pulse, speed, sex. Warm skin against my bare arms, shivers into the excruciating clarity of my senses.

"You up?" Beautiful pale-moon-light man with long gold curls and a dress of ribbons shims the edge of his hip against mine.

"Not enough," I whisper and lean closer.

Beautiful black-as-space woman with tiny sequins across her breasts and hips comes up beside me, takes my hand. Grinds to the beat. "Magic Man." Tiny jewels stud the woman's smile at the center of each of her teeth.

The three of us dance past the side-eyed envy of others, envy that Caran Watts has chosen these two, not them, to bathe in his aura. Maybe they still have a shot at me tonight, this week. Club trash, spoiled royalty, have no idea that all of them, every one, is my salvation. When I'm void inside their egos prop me up. When I've no way out, their doors open into Marketing-Guy-Sanctioned self-destruction that the feeds spin as grand success. "Watts makes splash at Club Snobbery" they'll spin, and I'll laugh bitter irony.

Dancing together past sticky toilets with no doors into the back room where the golden-haired man lays out long pale lines of psychotropic tracer, and we breathe up until there's no more up to go, and drink thousand-year-old port until the up and the down hit a perfect balance and nothing can touch me. I'm free in the between, feeling nothing/everything, beyond even my own legend.

Poor kids have no idea I'm full of NQ and in the bliss-reaction with the tracer I fuck them both, drawing bloody strips across their backs with my nails as the fake dataslip swings wildly and we cry out in the soft shapes of nowhere.

They want to be fucked any/every way they can. I swirl in the empty full silence and breathe more tracer and drink more port till it's time to go, stumbling over the sleeping shapes of the Europan royals like yesterday's clothes.

Lights flash and times change, and the shiny surfaces of transit tubes make unclean transitions.

Hotel room and another dropper full of NQ.

Show call and a few pounds of makeup. I giggle as the brushes tickle my cheeks.

"He can't go on like this! He's entirely too drunk to do the show!" Mindy Ming.

"Shut up you old prude," I giggle.

"Let him be, he can do the show just fine." LaRoque.

"Yeah, let him be." I echo. I haven't been this up in months, gonna be good, yeah, best show ever! That's because I'm not even going to do the show. Well, except the singing part. "He can do the show just fine!" I echo LaRoque. Too korkered to find words of my own even with the NQ, and it's stupid I ever cared about anyone knowing I have trouble with words.

"He's a loose cannon!" Mindy rants. "He could do anything out there! This is not the night for antics, didn't you see the feeds? They've tied that bombing to the Genetic Liberation Front, there's a hunt for rone Operators, and an increasingly wild panic in the torus. There's talk of locking down the ports until they route the terrorists. If he starts making references to technology on stage, any technology, not just the computer stuff, even veiled references—"

"Then what?" LaRoque, scornful. "Then it'll jack the sales even more, right? We've always made bank on transgression, Min. Not just us, the whole industry. People love it when an artist pokes at their taboos. And no one does it like our boy here."

"No, JL! " Mindy snaps. "Have you forgotten about the attack on Emory last tour, that Op-hater with the jerk-gun? That laid me up for a month because I took the bullet for him. Or that mob in Portland we almost didn't escape? Or maybe you forgot that I'm the fucking head of security?"

"He's been like this before and always sobered up when he hit the stage." Make-up guy, quietly.

"He goes on." LaRoque, LaRoque, LaRoque.

Down the tunnel to the stage, all so silly, "Ridiculous!" I modulate my tone to resonate with the walls and amplify obnoxiously back. "Ridiculous!"

Two steps from stage Muse washes through me with a panicky force and shoves itself into the sound systems. I'm so much up and so much down I don't know which way I'm going, but I'm going there, red hot fire-cracker!

Roaring crowd.

Yeah, good!

Hands fumbling around the fake kinetikosonus slip, dropping it on the stage. Out to the crowd, giggling, "Oooops! I dropped the ruse!"

The crowd goes wild even though they have no fucking idea what the joke is.

"I want to tell you. You're going to love this show tonight. You're going to love it best of all my shows, even those who have been to my shows before." The illusion of programming appears over the 4Vs as last night's recording begins to play. "Because after tonight I'm retiring from my excellent career as a pop star and starting my new life as a popped star."

Muse finishes settling in and it's time for go. "Thank you, Europa! Blood Deeps!"

We dream-dive through that song and move on into "Light." Muse manifests right there on the stage in rainbow waves. Guess the audience will think it's a new part of the light show? Or maybe it's the tracer, hallucinogenic lightshow Muse no one else is seeing— world tips sideways into blackout—

Come to awareness two skips down the set list and into "Heaven Is Anyplace I Can Never Go." Yeah, they love me scream scream scream some more—-

Shatter-round falling stardust so fucking fucked up—

We're on "Voice" now. Muse wraps the stage like a slow, heavy fog of terrifying shadows.

No, Muse is waves of rainbow light. This is some kind of other fucked up shit. Was my tracer spiked?

Waves of rainbow light meet the fog of shadows and the two start to undulate together, merging at the edges, becoming one as though they'd always been the same from the start—

Streaks of blue lightening rain down in a haze of sparks—

Next time I'm aware, I'm swaying in the door frame of my hotel room crashing hard. Down down down coming down. Stuff's making sense again which is too bad, but down a little further and I'll be out into five full hours of nightmare-fueled sleep before the withdrawals wake me up again. If I'm in the door frame and Mindy is gone and Muse is gone too, off playing with the fans, and it's dark in my room Mindy must be doing her final-stalker-check. Oh gods hurry it up Min, legs shaking, giving out over here. Come on Mindy, hurry it the fuck up, done for here—

Inside the room: CRASH-SMASH! thud-d-d

Silence.

One foot over the threshold. "Mindy?" I squeak.

"You can come in. It's perfectly safe." A familiar voice. Not Mindy's. Not welcome.

A tentative step in. The light snaps on, shocking, blinding, blinked.

Mindy lies on the floor not moving. Four very thin scratches ooze blood across her cheek.

Jordis Ansari stands above Mindy's prone form, dressed like an expensive lawyer, her perfect black bun tight. "Hello, Dragon."

Fucking, fucking—there is no curse strong enough. Least not one I can find in the swarming sparks of faintness of my vision. "I see you're still working on your daddy issues," I knife at her. There! I hold on long enough to see her smile drop and feel satisfaction that I've hurt her. Then the world tilts full on into oh fuck—

The crash down off the drugs folds over me.

Words gone.

Thought gone.

Blackout.

Nothing.

Then: a nightmare.

The nightmare begins in a fog of darkness. It clears into a dreamland version of a memory that also began in darkness.

Sitting in the old house on Agrippa. Cold floor; lights out. Waiting for someone to hear my cries but the waiting is a hallway in a hallway in a hallway that never ends, and no one makes it out alive because there isn't anything to eat. Can't move. Can't figure all the steps. Wanting, needing, but brain/body dislocate, and volition doesn't mean a thing.

A spark: a presence. Muse.

Waves of rainbow light reaching out to make mind-contact, to touch, to be together, but the dark bits creep from the corners a darker shade of darkness than even the alone.

I SEVER

I SEVER THE CONNECTION TO THE LIGHT

Smudges rear up, scuttle together, combine, merge, become the world—

I AM THE SOUL OF DISLOCATION
THE POTENCY OF NEGLECT AND FEAR
I AM THAT WHICH HAS NO HOME
I AM
YOUR FAULT.

◊

I wake from the nightmare in a chemical sweat and curl fetal. Too terrified to figure out, delirium slippage back into sleep—

—where beating like a metronome an atonal chorus whispers the name: *dividia - dividia - dividia - dividia - dividia -*

◊

I, Steven, wake in the here-and-now from Caran's nightmare in the there-and-then. My awareness of myself returns mid-crawl across my office coffee table toward him.

He's coiled as small as possible, arms around his knees, a snarl of hair over his face, shoulders shivering, shivering, shivering.

I climb onto the couch next to him in a gesture that is as unstoppable as it is professionally forbidden. I wrap myself around him. His body is hard with muscle but feels much smaller and more fragile than it looks.

I remember what he's said so many times about not feeling things properly unless they are extreme, so I squeeze him with all my strength.

He howls, an awful, hopeless sound. My embrace is not enough. Nothing will be.

Nothing fills the void.

PART 2:

SOL SYSTEM,
JUPITER ORBIT: IO

SESSION 8:
CARAN & JORDIS / MUSE

I wake.

(I, Doctor Steven Kwon, am inside the story without preamble, without pleasantries, without a word of warning from Caran. He's said nothing of my transgression of professionalism into intimacy last session. Neither have I. I worry about it infecting the rigor of my methodology, and about ethics. I'm not sure why *he's* uncomfortable.)

Blurred vision slits painfully into a small room. Shabby and peeling. Reminds me of that corporate hostel Djen and I always stayed in at Nerion Station. Not sure if it's clean. Very sure it smells of sulfur and the oxygen content is high; makes me giddy and my head throbs with the ache of hangover shaken over one shot of NQ withdrawal with a finger of sour wine aftertaste.

On my back.

Naked.

On a bed.

Everywhere silent save the soft sound of someone messing with something in a corner as a click-thump-scritch echoes off hard walls. Strange heavy to the quiet, missing something I'm used to.

"How's your hangover?" Jordis' voice. Fuck.

I twitch beneath scratchy sheets. Move my eyes to avoid moving my head until I find the edges of Jordis sitting prim at the end of the bed, my dataslip around her neck.

Something's odd about the slip but my eyes keep blurring out.

"Where's Mindy?" Almost heave with each word.

"At the Mnemosyne. Don't worry about it." All coolness.

"Don't worry about it? What'd you do to her? I need her. She brings me vitamin juice, lunch, dinner, keeps me on schedule, makes sure there's time for sleep, you think, you think—" Words choke out from fear.

"I think your need for more of what's in this vial isn't going to be satisfied by Mindy Ming." She waves the crystal vial of NQ in my eye-line with that mobster smile I want to scream off her face.

Is this some fucking time loop? That tactic isn't going to work any better now.

But no, something's different this time.

I push myself up on an elbow. My eyes slide over the dataslip. My dataslip around her neck, the real one that bint stole from me. When I look at it, I hear the music of Casino Row, the song of Europa that I half-composed while walking there a lifetime ago. The slip resonates with a sense of *Europaness*, and the sketch for the song's bridge enters my mind's ear, brilliant bad timing. The dataslip glows slightly which goes to show how fucked up I am since dataslips don't glow. "Don't you get it, Jordis? Don't you understand that I can't just disappear for an evening? Or for a few minutes? If no one lays eyes on me in twenty, police'll dismember the Europa torus till I'm found."

"What makes you think we're still on Europa? And who do you think owns the police? X's influence is broad." The timbre of Jordis' voice has changed. It used to be flat, but it's full of the colors of Europa. Part of the song.

"And who do you think owns Caran Watts?" I shake away the music, the silence, the strangeness. *Focus, you stupid shit.* "My handlers don't give a filthy fuck about the Galilean Black Market or even the Luna Black. I'm on the All Worlds Charts, Ansari, not the fucking Europan B-circuit. Corporate kings will sacrifice as many pawns as they need to, plus a bunch of bishops, to get their flow of the credit I generate."

"And I thought a man of Freedom wouldn't care about such things." Jordis smiles a thin, annoying line.

"I don't care about such things. Such things care about me! You've no idea the stinking shit-stained trap I'm—it's just—it's complicated." My elbow buckles, sending me flat on the bed, words run out, weariness raging in. "You got anything that goes up?"

"Yes, because exactly what you need right now are more drugs." Jordis laughs sarcastic icicles.

Knock, knock, knuckles on siliplas. Slightly damped; hollow. Siliplas door, lightly soundproofed.

"Excuse me." Jordis rises with a creak of springs and I close my eyes, following her with my ears. She opens the door, steps out, closes it. The soundproofing's a little too good and the voices a little too soft so all I hear are cadences of fear. Jordis Ansari afraid?

And the quiet; something's wrong with the quiet.

Pop-creak of the door, tap-tap of Ansari's feet returning across the floor to me.

My tongue's dry and heavy as the quiet and I realize what I'm missing—"There's no electrical hum here. No electricity. No environmentals. What the fuck?"

"Go back to sleep, Caran."

Pin-prick at my jugular. Nerves screaming icy-fire with whatever she's just poisoned me with.

Blackout.

◊

"Hello." Jordis Ansari enters my office in her version of flushed, which is more like breathing a little hard, and with a single piece of lint on her starched Vemi suit. "Meeting ran late."

Caran's shiny black eyes focus on her with none of the malice of their early interactions. He puts his feet up on the coffee table, arms crossed over his hard stomach, as loose as he ever gets.

She gives him a casual nod, somehow knows the lint is on her shoulder, brushes it off, and sits in the chair with her knees crossed as usual.

I wouldn't call the professional distance between them comfortable, but I wouldn't call it strained either. Relaxed, but apart; "familiar" is the best I can describe the dynamic before Jordis takes a breath.

"I didn't think you were going to need me again until after you interviewed Cami." Jordis speaks with such blandness that I'm unclear if she's communicating regret, simple fact, or something else.

"That's mostly true," I say. "But was I hoping you could fill in what happened on Europa during the next two weeks, before you met back up with Caran. It's always been a bit unclear to everyone."

Caran emits a soft scoff and Jordis flicks her eyes at him sideways.

"As I said," Jordis moves her flat-gray gaze back to me, "there are some things I will not share. Certain aspects of my business dealings being one. Corporate confidence and all."

"She means if she tells you what she was up to on Europa, the mob'll come and kill you."

"Caran. Don't you start with that again." Jordis sighs without malice.

"Sorry," he mutters without apology and fidgets with his fingers.

Jordis takes a deep breath and exhales into speaking. "After I'd gotten Caran isolated behind Io's electromagnetic storms, I had to return very quickly to Europa. I didn't want to leave Caran alone on Europa's sister-moon, especially when I was so close to getting Freedom's secrets from him. But because Dividia had realigned Europa's resonance—we're guessing that happened sometime around Caran's show—to become more like it, everything had escalated to a panic. The mainfeeds amped their misinformation campaign; the Operators their execution-style resistance. The Europan government started scrambling hard over the number of Operators it could lose—which was exactly the point. We're people, it's not like we can be replaced with a new build from the factory floor. I worried I wouldn't be able to return and finish my investigation of the bombing for X before President Nye closed Europan airspace." She pauses the smallest amount. "A destabilized Europa was bad for my father."

"Is that what you were hoping for? A destabilized Europa?"

"Me?" Jordis laughs with monstrous indifference. She sobers, blinks, perhaps considering for the first time. "Maybe, but when I stepped back on Europan ground, that was not my intent. I had my connection to the rebellion via Ammiel and could ally X's forces with the movement and facilitate destabilization. But I also had my pots on the fire with Som Bliss to consider. If I helped quell the uprising by allying Ammiel and the rebels with Som and the Galilean Black I might facilitate a coup against my father without damaging Europa, and also gain wins for the Operators. The path of diplomacy was riskier, but more satisfying. Even though I was also affected by Dividia's influence on Europa, I didn't want to burn down my house before I moved in. Dividia's influence just made it hard to believe peaceful solutions were possible."

"Jordis likes to have her cake and eat it too," Caran pipes in with a succulent smack of his lips. "Stash me on an uninhabitable rad-soaked moon in the morning, take over a criminal empire at noon, torture me for Freedom's secrets before dinner, you know."

"I'm still sorry about all of that." Jordis says quietly.

"Yeah, I know." He looks at his fidgeting hands and then flashes her a grin. "Doesn't mean you don't like to have your cake and eat it too!"

Her eyes crinkle into un-Jordis-like mischief as she flashes back, "And isn't that cake delicious?"

He mimes eating. "Nom-nom!"

"I can tell you, though," Jordis says back to me, "what I learned about CryCorp's role in the unrest."

"That would be helpful." I tell her.

"As soon as I got in range of the Mem again, out of the interference from Io's EM storms, I cross-queried a broad range of current events with Ray Ansari's public dealings with CryCorp and its CEO Ulric Ellison."

"Not just public, surely, you must have had access to more privileged corporate records?"

"Some, yes. I was a Corporate Enforcer after all, we have extended records privilege with the Federal Reserve Citizen Id Bank. But I didn't go any deeper than what I was officially allowed."

I cock a brow at her, wondering if we're stepping on the edge of legality.

"I didn't need to go any deeper." She catches my drift. "There were statistically significant correlations between the interactions of Ellison and my father and the Operator tensions on Europa. Specifically, my father and CryCorp's CEO were working together to create and promote the fake Genetic Liberation Movement and stoke the tensions it generated. It was not clear, however, why."

I whistle softly. "Would you be willing to package up your data and send it to my research assistant?"

"Certainly. Look," she says, "I have to go. But I should be able to swing back a few more times in the next few days. If you'd like."

"I would very much like," I smile at her. "Thank you."

She rises with her usual poise and leaves. Neither she nor Caran acknowledge each other further, but I sense through my link with Caran that this is a nauta thing, not an animosity thing.

I turn to him but he's already plunging me back into his storyline.

◊

I wake. I'm in the same bed, the same sulfur-smelling highly oxygenated room as before.

Jordis is gone.

Her poison is gone too. So is the hangover and the edge of withdrawal.

In their place: hunger, thirst, the vicious need to piss.

I kick off the sheets, torn between needs, and stare at my body which someone has dressed in light gray pants and a sleeveless white dress. Soft cloth. I like it. Next to the bed: soft black ankle-boots, a new version of the scuffed broken-in ones Mindy keeps trying to trick me into discarding. Also: a cream-colored wrap-thing, warm, could go over head, arms, whatever. That fucking bint left me clothes I like.

What else?

Small, square room. Dusty, stinky like an egg. Not much to it, typical low-rent hostel room. Low sink, single scratched drinking cup. Lav hole a meter further down the wall. I take a piss first, then lap at the thin trail of tepid, processed water that comes out of the sink. It's got the recycled flavor of water on a dimship, or on an orbital with nothing potable to tap. No sign of shower or bath, but if this is a place where water is scarce, bathing will happen in communals and with something that isn't wet. Where am I?

I feel strange. Too light, too... strange.

Just the bed, the sink, the lav hole, the boots—something next to the sink, on the floor. A neat arrangement of sealed food rations.

Something in the other corner. A tiny square of black fabric. On it a tiny pyramid of fourteen pills. About a week's supply of U4. U4 is NQ with the teeth taken out, prescription med for nauta to run maintenance on their navi. Sure, it's non-addictive and amps motor sequencing and cuts the sensory noise. But it gives nothing in the way of a kick to verbals and no rush at all, fucking useless. Fucking fucker! FUCKING FUCK

Sobs hurt like food caught in my windpipe.

U4, is that why I feel so strange?

No, something else, something worse.

No environmentals adjusting the air to my body temp, no cameras or monitors, no reclaimer bin, no 3V plate, no information hotspots, no tech of any sort. Too much oxygen, sulfur smell, U4 sure isn't NQ even if it stops the withdrawals, but something deeper's wrong.

Oshit panic propelling me around the room, shaking my hands, got to burn off the fear, got to burn it, got to—

I don't feel bad. I just feel weird. Too good? Too lightweight. So lightweight.

Breathe, okay. In, out, okay? Breathing exercise number forty-nine. In. Out. In. Out. Deep. Out. Okay? Okay.

OH MY FUCKING SHIT WHEN I REACH OUT, I CAN'T FEEL MUSE

No. No, that's not a thing. Not possible. Not a thing. It's normal for Muse to run off for days or weeks or more at a time.

But I can always call it back.

Flashes of memory from within the drugged-up blackout of the show: a fog of black shadows merging with the rainbow light.

Nah, that was nothing. That was NQ and booze and hallucinogens and altered perceptions. Doesn't mean a thing.

Static zaps at every touch, my small hairs prickling. Room's full of the ambient charge that precedes the manifestation of an élan, so my connection to Muse has got to be here, got to. What else is here?

Complex time signature, tap it out, hands and feet, tap-tap-tap. There's a door. Locked from the outside with a mechanical keyhole the like of which I've only seen in history holos. Ceiling, center: a top-quality, full spectrum everbulb showing off the flaking paint and sulfur stains, beaming cheery fake sunlight. Made necessary by there being no windows. Because what would be the fun in windows?

No electrical hum, no electrical appliances, no electricity, NO CONNECTION TO MUSE.

SHITFUCK.

I reach out more deliberately. Think/feel into the ether, to find the resonance, find the bond.

Static hum.

Dead station.

It's gone.

Not gone-to-mingle-with-the-fans gone where I can still feel it licking at me, always someone to come when I'm in trouble.

Choking, tipping, knees giving. Sprawled on the floor. Alone.

Help, I want to whisper, but nothing comes of the wanting. Panicked soundscape of nonverbal thoughts. A thousand days and nights of alone vomit from the abyss of the past, wanting to scream but no sound coming out, screaming out loud but no one near to hear, no one ever cares, never, ever there.

Choking, choking, mouth of black silence, I scramble from the monster called Alone until the back of my head hits the wall and my palm comes crashing down on the tiny pyramid of pills, skittering them across the floor: thunk-skree-skree-rattle plop. Sound of my panting. Pound of my heart. Curling up around fear choking, choking alone fuck fuck fuck.

Okay, rhythm, noise, anything but silence. I can work this. Pick up the beat with my hands, swish-clap in rhythm with my pulse, slide my bare feet slap-pat, fill the silence with sound. Give the panic a voice. Let it have its solo. Swish-clap, pulse-pat, slappa-slappa-flat-plat. Give the fear a background drone.

I have to get out of this room.

Jordis—did she know I'd break if she left me alone? Not death, death is an okay way out of the lies, really, but this, I can't be alone, can't be—

I have to get out of this room.

Not that Jordis-perfectionist-Ansari would leave me an actual way to escape.

Count, tap, think. Had to have been unconscious at least ten hours, with a break for fresh threats from Jordis around hour eight, judging by memories of nerve pain. Takes around ten for the NQ to flush and fact that my thoughts are wordless soundscapes means it has. Could have been out longer though, these are twelve-hour release U4 pills. I've slept. Like really slept. More consecutive hours than I have in years. That's why I feel so light.

Or is it the absence of my shadow that makes me feel so light?

Or is Muse the real me and I am the shadow?

Fear requests another solo. Need more distraction to figure things out. Movement, rhythm, sound. I have to get out of this room.

The room's got neat acoustics; the siliplas walls both reflect and absorb. Bring out the full voice, play with scales. Relate to the space, find the story in the peeling paint and sparseness. Interaction, connection, the place where sound becomes music.

There's an outside to that locked door.

I fill my lungs and vocalize in forte to pass the soundproofing. If only that bint Ansari had left me with some liquor to calm my nerves. What I wouldn't give for a bottle of Cassiopeian red rye whiskey right now—

Red whisky, red whisky,
Red whisky, I cry,
If you don't give me red whisky,
I surely will die.

The old folk song has ten million verses plus as many as I can make up and just as many versions, and I'll sing every one of them till someone shows up.

Oh, whisky, you villain,
You've been my downfall,
You've kicked me, you've cuffed me,
But I love you for all—

A sound at the door.

I rush over and rattle the knob.

A woman's voice, muffled, grumbles, "Shitty locks, I know why we need 'em but they get so gobbed up with the godsdamned plains-dust..." She trails off as her feet trail away.

Don't go don't go don't leave me alone—I panic-pound on the door.

Return sounds. A hissing, scraping, rattling around the lock. Click.

The door opens on a small woman with large muscles and a frizz of black hair in a navy jump suit. "Hi, that's some singing. Are you new at Jeanie's Hope? I'm one of the supers till I go back out for diamond sparkle, welcome to Hostel Six. Sorry about the lock, they're always gumming. I cleaned and oiled it good, and the skeleton key worked, so I don't suspect you'll have trouble for the next week at least."

One knee buckles relief and I let the smile on my mouth answer her as I hold the door so she can only see half my face. Can't speak a fucking word.

She decides my silence deserves the answer, "Unreal, just unreal, your voice is like wow, you gonna be on the ticket later today? I'll come see you for sure and tell everyone I know."

I nod, swallowing.

"Great! Always need something that doesn't stink on Io!"

And she's gone.

I close the door. What made Jordis this sloppy about containing me? Has she forgotten how hard it is to box me in?

Doesn't matter. Someone heard me; someone answered. I'm not alone. And the door's unlocked and I'm on Jupiter's inner moon Io which is right beside my handlers on Europa so all I've got to do is find some way to get signal out and I can sing at Jeanie's Hope and people will love me and I can do this, I've done this before, it'll be just like back when I was running with Djen, and hope indeed and—

There's no mirror in the whole fucking place.

I exhale until I'm dizzy.

I go to the sink, work my fingers through my hair, teasing out the long spikes the hair guy spent six hours making, washing the purple away in a month's ration of water but what choice have I got, water's the only thing that kills the styling nanites. I comb it out with my fingers; there's no brush in the room either. Not that a brush would help; hair's black, and fine, and makes waves that tangle no matter whatever. I dab my face with the corner of the wrap-thing and it comes away clean. No make-up. My whole body's clean, now I notice, clean of sweat and toxins and whatever else would've coated it by the end of that last bender—Jordis must have washed it all away. Fake platinum-coated dataslip's still around my neck; I fumble it off with my stupid clumsy hands and stuff it as far as I can into the lav hole.

Io. Jeanie's Hope. Okay. Never been here before but a bar's a bar. I can work this.

Terrified, really.

Start to pocket the U4 pills then remember I've a habit of losing everything in my pockets. Just take half instead, seven count, three and a half days, just to be safe, no telling when Jordis dosed me last. Put on the soft black boots. I'm still Caran Watts. Music is mine, always has been, always and forever, with or without Muse. Artists can do anything. I've survived worse with less.

Outside: a shabby hall. And outside that a shanty-town sulfur-reeking shit hole, never seen anything quite so seedy, not even on a desperate-for-a-fix bad-part-of-town adventure. High O2-yield ivies grow out of control along the interior of an atmo-dome so dust-covered it shows no hint of sky. People on the street are few and walk with the furtive shuffle-watch that means the Black Market is everywhere.

This place is dangerous, what was Jordis thinking? Hoping

someone'd knife me in the back for fun and profit? Could have done that herself since Muse isn't here to stop her, so what the fuck? The little lines and stacks of food rations and U4, she must really think I'd never make it out that door. Or that I'd be too scared to make it onto the street. Did she forget that I used to be a fucking runner for Freedom? Shit, I've got more streetwise skills than she does. I cover my head with the shawl-thing and turn my stride into a shuffle-slide. Without the styling nanites and the makeup and the self-confident swagger I should be pretty safe. Mindy's warned me a thousand-million times what a pretty ransom I'd make, what a lot of credit 100 Words Music would pay to get me back. Never go out alone. She doesn't know it, but I never have been out alone. Not till now anyway.

Don't think about alone.

Luckily this, this"Milktown"—based on the half-busted holo flickering "Milktown Depot"—is tiny and I don't have to trudge much of it before Jeanie's Hope emerges from the dust, radiating a huge beacon of a half-busted holo for sex, drugs, and rock-n-roll.

I pick up my step as I enter and turn so my eyes catch the light just right. Flash a smile that says show biz all the way. "Jeanie," I demand of the host. Hope "Jeanie" is the name of a real person.

The host nods and vanishes.

Jeanie's Hope is built better than the rest of the shanty town, but it still reeks of sulfur. Must be an Io thing. Bar sounds clink and laugh through the walls, and the thrum-hum chest-feel of dance music makes a counterpoint to the slap-clang of pole dancers. Rough place, but I've handled worse, back before Harold Jones and the contracts and the handlers and the haze. I can work this. But back then, I had Djen.

Back then, I had Muse.

The host returns with an older woman, thick gray hair coiled in a pair of braids, utilitarian garb.

"I'm Jeanie." The woman holds up both hands, palms open, meaning: either of us could be hardwired or wetwired to kill with a touch, so let's be non-hostile, jo?

I return her gesture, grin a warm grin, and sing a lyric from eighteen hundred and three songs, at least that I can remember, "I wanna be a rock and roll star!"

"We're not—"

"You are," I echo and wink.

"I—"

I give her a shy-sly look from beneath my lashes, picking up more verses from the old folk tune I'd started back in the room,

> *Jack o' diamonds, jack o' diamonds,*
> *I know you of old,*
> *You've robbed my poor pockets*
> *Of silver and gold.*

Diamonds, yeah, the only reason for people to be on Io is the diamonds. I don't wear jewelry, but a single five karat beauty sparkles at the heart of every one of my Galaxy Awards. I turn my voice on the rest of the way.

> *I'll tune up my fiddle,*
> *And I'll rosin my bow,*
> *I'll make myself welcome,*
> *Wherever I go.*

Jeanie's jaw drops and her eyes go the greedy shade of credit symbols.

I trail off, inviting her to want more.

She's silent for a twelve-count. Then, "You know you sound almost like Caran W—"

I laugh and shake my head.

"You sure you're not—"

"I'm sure I'm not—"

Laughing Jeanie at the ridiculousness of the thought.

Laughing Caran at the ridiculousness of the thought.

Oh gods get me off this fucking piece of hell-stone—

"What's your name?" She puts her hand out this time for palm-touching, meaning: trust established, extended.

I make contact, trust reciprocated. "Dragon."

"Pleased to have you on docket, Dragon. The dancers break in ten, could you could fill the gap till their next set?"

"Fill the gap. Next set." Smile. Wink.

Ten minutes later I'm live on stage at Jeanie's Hope, covered in the white shawl-thing and no nasty clothes otherwise, sipping a tumbler of cheap red wine, singing old folk tunes into the sulfury-smoke of a half-drunken crowd, and feeling approval like the heat of a binary star on my face at noon. Someone pulls out an acoustic guitar and someone else starts drumming on the tabletop. Then the audience becomes a band and they're teaching me Ionian mining chanties and I become the lead Chantiman:

> Were you ever down the diamond way
> *Down the diamond way!*
> Where auroras ghostlight bright as day
> *Io-Io-fey!*
> Fortune spreads across her ground
> *Fortune on the ground!*
> And in her fires she'll have you drowned

Io-Io-may!
To the plains I go a-rovin'
To the plains we go a-rovin'
Io-Io-lady-hey!

And it's so much better than that fucked-up last show I don't even want to go back to Europa.

◊

Three hours later I sit at a round, sticky table with all the free drink I want and the less-than-fortunate but highly expected news that NQ is not easy to come by in Milktown on Io. NQ? Who the fuck does that shit? It's just a mild, fancy empathogen or a sweet way to suicide.

Yeah, for dims maybe. But I get a lead on a guy with a half-dram.

Also: If I go mining for Ionian diamonds, I will probably die.

And also: Milktown is run by Io Mining Corp, which supplies equipment, room, board, and entertainment to prospectors in return for a 40% cut of any diamonds found.

No. Scratch that.

Milktown is run by Black Marketeers who use it as a base of operations since Io has no citizenship, laws, or interest from Io Mining Corp whatsoever about anything, as Io Mining Corp will turn a profit no matter-fucking-what. So, if I stick around, I'll probably die.

Also: Milktown moves; mine out an area, move out of the dome and set up a new one. Apparently, the region here's almost mined out which would explain why they've been extra-shitty about the upkeep including spraying herbicide on the overzealous O2 ivies.

And also, most importantly: Io is near-completely com-deaf because of the howling electro-magnetic storms from its interaction with Jupiter. However, Milktown houses two enormous devices called cutters that, at times, shove a big enough hole in the EM to send a com signal through. Oh yeah, and if I have anything hard-wired in my body, I'd better not use it because there might be an EM pulse of the wrong sort at any moment with no warning and then, of course, I'll DIE.

At least the EM interference explains Muse's absence. Creature always was better at manipulating people than making small talk with magnetic winds. Gimmie another beer!

Four hours later, I curl up with my buzz for a nap on the soft cot in a back office.

At 19:00 I convince Jeanie to headline me at 20:00 and trade the promise of my night's tips for the promise of a quarter-dram of NQ come morning; I dust glitter over my cheek bones.

20:00 show time. Folk songs turn into sea shanties turn into Ionian mining chanties and the whole of Milktown gathers to hear me sing, to sing with me, until nothing exists for anyone but sound and booze and laughter.

02:55 and I'm swerving back to my room, afraid of nothing in the golden drunk of Cassiopeian red whiskey, so I let myself wonder about the bombing and the dark shadows and the threat of Dividia, and let myself wish that Freedom didn't need me so bad so I could stay here and sing forever, but I have to get near the cutters tomorrow and stand around till Muse or Mindy or someone bloody well notices, and I'm giggling even though it isn't at all funny, calculating how to use the U4 to stretch the NQ in case it takes a while for my handlers to reach me, thinking of all the ways to make Ansari pay pay pay, it's good to be a freak-out-loud multi-tracking genius and—

All the hair on my body stands on end as an élan vital manifests and lays a mess of emotion on me so violent and angry and chaotic that I vomit explosively into the sulfurous air.

I go rigid with electrical shock; unconsciousness follows.

◊

Something covers my eyes and I can't see. My hands and feet are bound.

Through the darkness, voices:

Woman: So this is the guy Ellison wants? Really?

Man: Yeah. Dividia says so anyway.

Woman: He was supposed to have been on Europa. Crap. This is all wrong.

Man: When has anything gone right with this gig?

Woman: I don't know. Your paycheck seems to go all right.

(short pause)

Woman: Let's make Morgan clean him up, I'm not riding in a rover for a day and a half with him reeking of piss and vomit.

(long pause)

Woman: Where the fuck is Morgan? He should've been here an hour ago.

Man: Fuck if I know.

Woman: (growly) He'll come. He hasn't a choice if he wants to see his daughter again. (pause)

Man: Oh hell—

A crack on the back of the head and I'm back in oblivion.

Doctor Noa Oki stands rigid in my office, staring with ferocious intensity over my left shoulder. She's of an average height, a slender build, and a strongly expressed Japanese ancestry. She holds her hair from her face in the circle of her thumb and forefinger. She wears a no-nonsense, matte black shirt, coat, and trousers, all made of the same soft material as her slight black slippers.

I'm blushing.

Caran's celebrity is irrelevant to me and Jordis is not so much different from the high-end corporate CEOs I've interviewed before, but Noa Oki is a giant of science. Meeting her is the contemporary equivalent of meeting Newton, Einstein, Turing, or Cooke.

She remains silent, staring. She is a Class 20 nauta, and there is little about her that, even with her navis fully functional, reads as normal.

I try to clear the awe from my throat first, but the words come out high pitched and funny anyway. "Please, Noa, have a seat. Can I get you anything, a pillow, water, fruit?"

Her body folds onto the sofa as the hinges of her hips, knees, and elbows collapse around the rest of her. I can see how the effect could slide, for some, into the same range of uncanny valley as zombies and human-shaped robots. Without taking her focus from the place behind my shoulder, she speaks. "No. Thank you."

We've met before, but that had been with Caran and Cami, both of whom generate charisma like solar flares. Stripped of the ability to hide in their auras, everything about Noa has become intensified and awkward. My schoolboy fascination isn't helping.

"It's all right, Steven."

I'm so nervous that I jump at her clipped, precise words, uttered without any non-verbal cue she's about to speak. "What's all right?" I look around myself, like I've forgotten something important.

Slowly, Noa smiles. "To be uncomfortable. It's all. Right."

I am blushing so hard I can't look at her; I duck my head even though I know she's actively avoiding visual contact with my face. *Don't try to force her to make eye contact,* my RA briefed me, *she's one of the ones who hates that.* "I'm not—it's just—" What am I, fifteen?

"Ordinarily." Noa pauses, rocks forward and back ever so slightly, just once. "It is my behavior that causes discomfort. It is nice."— she pauses again, as though there is some quota of words-per-sentence that defines her telegraphic speech—"To have respect cause discomfort. However misplaced. It's all right, Steven. Thank you." Her mouth twitches up into a broader smile that appears forced but it's just the limits of what her motor programming can do with all the tiny muscles of her face.

"You invented coaction mechanics!" I blurt wildly, "You created the mirai equations! You're the most important complexologist who ever lived!" I have to get it out. Maybe then I'll stop being distracted by it.

I make myself look back at her, sideways, so as not to trap her in unwanted eye contact.

She's still rigid, staring with ferocious intensity over my left shoulder, a smile of weird whimsy on her face. It's like I've said nothing at all.

A heat wave blows through the room so fast and brutal I can see the temperature distortion of the air. Had the heat sustained, I am sure it would have killed me. But, like running one's finger quickly through a flame, it passed too fast to burn.

Io-élan.

The awkwardness and blushing turns to fear. If I offend Noa, will Io-élan kill me? Have I offended Noa?

Io-élan, in a violence like lava: <flick. flick. flicker. BURST

<make me a, make me a, make me a rich man—

<flame and ice.

<MAKE! make it happen, make/remake, NOW!

<not yet. wait for change. critical points. crisis points. fissures-and-lights.

<flicker. flash!

<rock and sparkle.

<take! take me!>

Io-élan recedes.

<hello steven> It's Noa's voice but her lips do not move.

Correction: it's Noa's thoughts through the link.

<my navis is fully operational these days, but a navis requires a functional nervous system to optimally compensate for nauta neurological differences. my nervous system has sustained irreparable damages. this is easier. do you mind?>

I nod, swallow, shift in my chair to try to re-balance myself mentally, emotionally. Deep breath, remember my training. "I've been asking the others to start by providing some context and framing to their stories, just to get the link established; that seems to not be necessary."

<io-élan is very powerful> Noa understates. <also, you and i share scientific curiosity; this creates natural resonance. you and

I are already aligned. our apologies; io and i sometimes do not recognize our own strength.>

That doesn't feel as reassuring as it's meant to be, but it enables me to pick my adult self back up again. We are both scientists, after all. Peers in a sense. Sure, we work in different fields and I'll never accomplish the groundbreaking work that she has, but there is a culture and a temperament bridging our worlds. "Am I correct that we're starting your story two days before Caran and Jordis arrived on Io?"

I feel the gesture of a nod through the link as her body remains frozen.

"And also, just for the framing, you're my other participant with perfect recall, right? You and Jordis?"

Wince-y shards blast like heat-tipped shrapnel through the link. Is this Io-élan's alien communication, or am I experiencing Noa's synesthesia? <my memory index was active but glitchy. there was a memory leak. the same memory would replay for me given certain triggers. it interfered with things.> Noa says.

<meaning what for our interview?>

<meaning what perfect recall means for any of us—you experience exactly what i experienced, nothing less, nothing more>

<but what you experienced isn't necessarily what was happening?>

<what is that old saying? b-i-n-g-o? it was not lies, not delusions. it was all real, but fragmented. glitched. broken. shorted out. my navis was broken. everything in pieces. i was the demon of the diamond plains.>

Searing air blasts my face from Io-élan.

◊

Clatter-splash light, living, lively chaos bouncing. A yeasty smell, sour where the mop can't reach the spilled beer in the east corner. Smells like baking bread, and hops, and laughter elsewhere.

And sulfur. I know there is sulfur in the air. But I can't smell it.

I am it.

I am the Demon of the Diamond Plains.

Glitch. Glitchy. GODSDAMNIT.

There are five miners at the table next over. Five went out on the Marduk Plain together twelve days ago. Five came back to Milktown together today. But they'd hunted diamonds alone. Always alone on the Diamond Plains. Except for me. Only me to keep them safe. They don't know me. They don't know I'm watching.

I know them, the five at the table.

One: Kendra. Been on Io eight months. Spooked by declining odds, about to take a rotation as super at Hostel 6.

Two: Jett. New kid. Still cocky about his luck. Needs to pay off a regrettable gambling debt.

Three: Old Man Seek, with the thin moustache. Been on Io two years but measures his time on the Plains carefully so as not to push his luck.

Four: Zackery, joker.

Five: Elly, who hopes the Diamond Plains take her. She's come here to die.

Me: hands, thin, olive. Cupped around an empty plate that once held three of Jeanie's sandwiches. Jeanie's bread makes me happy, and Jeanie's soft cheeses. Once a month I rover to Milktown from my dome way out on the Keroessa plain, and I eat as many as I can.

"Nothing to the southeast." Jett remarks and swallows half his amber pint.

"You mean nothing but wisps." Kendra raises her mug in a toast to the invisible. "Saw more fairy-lights this time than ever. Io's restless."

"Wisps!" Jett scoffs. "Kendra's gone loops!"

Old Man Seek leans forward to give the boy a dark look. "You haven't been here long enough is all. You'll see the wisps. They bring you luck or they bring you the grave, just like the chanties say, ain't no tale 't all. You'll hear the ghost radio too, one of these days. And when you do, boy, you'd best listen if you want to live."

My hands flutter like wisps against my mug. That's me, the ghost radio. Not the wisps, the wisps are something else. Yes listen, always listen to the ghost radio. That's how I keep you alive from afar in my dome. Everybody lives. Everybody gets a diamond.

"Anyone who's been here longer than a few months is looped, if you ask me." Jett waves his hand, like he can brush death away. "Comes from snorting the fomori fumes. I'm gonna find my sparkle before the stink gets me, you'll see."

Kendra leans back in her chair; wood creaks and whines with the weight. She puts her arms, thick with muscle, behind her head. "Fomori, eh? Let me tell you about fomori. Back before we left Earth, when we were still living in caves and scratching our fleas—"

"Looks like that hasn't changed," Zachary snickers and points at sad Elly, stupid in her cups.

"Shut up and listen!" Old Man Seek snaps. He nods to Kendra.

Patterns. Patterns of interaction. Conversation exchanges, swirls between people, personalities, a whirl of complex dynamics. The mathematics of communication in delicate silver-pink whirls.

"Way back then," Kendra continues, "fomori didn't mean a sinkhole or a volcano or a steamer. It was a giant with power over nature. Demons of the sea and sky and such. They raided and pillaged anything they could find, loved to hoard treasure. That's why we call sinkholes fomori, demon pirate giants who move the earth to get at us, lure us in with the beauty of the wisps, then—snap!" SLAP Kendra claps her hands together, CRACK front chair legs smacking to the floor. "Will 'o the wisps'll lead you to your death if you follow them. Unless," her teeth flashing a white grin in the dim light," they lead you to a fomori's diamond treasure instead!"

"Nice tale," Jett snarks, but his words fall into the quiet and fail to stick. Zackery and Old Man Seek spit between their fingers to ward off evil.

There is no evil though, just nature. Nature and me. I am a demon, but I am not evil. Not anymore. I am the ghost radio. I help them live. I lead them to their sparkle.

What about what happened at the Dome? That was evil.

NO

I am a good demon now. Only good. I atone. See, they are alive. All alive.

I could walk over to their table and explain the wisps to them. Tell them the myth is real. Lay out the math, share the equations that prove the existence of the Unseen. I could demonstrate the mirai equations' power, should they fail to follow the eloquence of my proofs. Show them how I can predict within a one-to-two percent confidence interval something they can relate to, like when Io will spit her next diamond cache. I could show them how I run the ghost radio that saves their lives, that has increased the probability of survival on the Marduk Plain ten percent in the past twenty years from Keroessa Plain's baseline mortality rate.

But myth and legend protect me from the slap-hands. Protect them from the demon's wrath. I cannot speak well anyway.

The five talk of practical matters: rover maintenance, how to sleep comfortably in a hazard suit, what they'll do with their fortune in Ionian diamonds if they survive the next trip to the plains. They risk a 40-percent chance of death for a 16-percent chance to find a diamond. One small diamond is worth half a million c's, and where one lies another two or three likely scatter, spat in a cluster by Io's restless crust. It is harder to lead the miners to diamonds than it is to keep them alive. There are more hazards on Io than there are diamonds.

Plainsdust on the floor, the table, my cheeks. A film of dust on the surface of my empty plate. How long have I been sitting here?

Flash-broken-shiverlight. There used to be a timer in my mind, where the shiverlight lives. Used to be a clock. No time, no more, rise-and-fall.

There's a clock on the wall. Old-time springs, analog.

Six hours.

I've been sitting in Jeanie's Hope eating sandwiches for six hours.

I have to go home.

Checklist check: Medicines I can't synthesize. Hull patch for rover. New set of black pants and t-shirts. This month's electronics kits for the regular repair on the sensors and transmitters. Update on the lives of the miners, official data and word-of-mouth, listen-in. Everybody lives. Everybody gets a diamond. Trade fruits and vegetables for cheese sandwiches. Jeanie and Harvey at the Depot all stocked up from my gardens.

Click-shift turn motor control functions back on. Conserve, minimize. Expose as little of my navis to the ambient EM as possible. Minimize risk of spikes, shorts, can't take much more, out of the more exotic materials for repairs.

One-by-one fingers unfold from the cup as I work through the small steps toward standing. Mid-way through my navis shivers and shuts down leaving me in a half-stand. I shut my eyes against sensory overload and wait to be able to move again. Automatic navis shutdown means background programming calculated a greater than ninety-percent chance of an EM spike. That's unusually high odds for anywhere inside an EM-shielded dome.

My systems come back online.

A WHOOSH of air lifts my hair.

I stare into the wild blue eyes of a miner who's been out too long on the plains. His filthy brown curls reek of weeks without washing and his standard-issue navy coverall is so dirty I can only tell it's soaked in blood by the smell. It's Cái Morgan. He's been on Io five years. He hunts alone. He rarely comes in from the plains and keeps to himself in town. Has the kind of sadness that keeps people from asking questions. Io likes him though; Io keeps him alive. He doesn't know me, but I know him best of all my miners because he's been here longest. Sometimes, though, he goes dark, and I cannot find him.

Morgan touches my hand. He looks me over. He sees the blue sheen of the navis beneath the skin of my forehead as he angles just right in the light. His face opens in surprise, twists in disgust, indecision, urgency.

If I'd been home today, monitoring telemetry, running my maths, would I have saved him from whatever has made him bleed? Guilty, guilty, guilty.

Morgan reaches his other hand to me, black with grime and blood. His mouth works silent words. Everything stutters in slow-mo. I amp sensory programming and shut down motor. His mouth makes sounds, hoarse and urgent, encoded in patterns of human speech I will never, without translation from my navis, understand. I sink back into the clunky, wooden chair, body not remembering how to stand. Linguistic-translation programs take priority.

"The goddess of luck, Chyte, told me to give you this," Morgan gasps.

My mouth opens but I can't find a path between the acid-smelling redness of what I need to communicate, and speech-sounds he can decode. My jaw flaps open, primed for input that never comes.

Morgan shoves his hand into my chest, mouth working. "Take it! Take it you rutting feeble, Chyte says it's for you!"

A shout from outside my locus of attention: "Call Medic!"

Yes, yes! Those are the words the acid redness connects to. Motor shudders back into play, body jerking itself to take what the man offers. Hands closing over something soft on the outside and hard on the inside, bigger than my fist. Sticky-wet with a paste of human blood and Ionian ash. Blood and ash, mixing of the species, mixing of the worlds. A memory of sulfur clouds and burning flesh rages through Jeanie's Hope, godsdamnit godsdamnit not now, not now with the memory leak, unintended recall!

"For her." Morgan snaps me out of playback to the present. "For my Cami. For my sweet Camilla Morgan." His other hand hits the table hard, releasing a crumpled 2V flatshot and a brass coin.

He slips from the table, thuds on the floor.

From the flatshot, a smiling blue-eyed toddler beams beneath yellow curls. The pixels have burned out where it's folded and creased too many times. I'd tried. I'd tried to find the man his diamonds, I'd tried to help him buy his daughter out of ransom, but I could not. It was as though Io herself had not wanted Cái Morgan to succeed.

The coin has a heads of Chyte, two-faced goddess of luck. I know these coins, sold for five u's at a magic shop. The tails side would be a rabbit. If I'd been doing my job instead of eating Jeanie's sandwiches I could have saved him. If I'd been doing my job that terrible day nineteen years ago, I could have saved them all. It's not supposed to be like this. Everybody lives. Everybody gets a diamond.

◊

"Death's tits, Noa, that was Cami's father?" Noa's perspective is hard to live within, and my heart pounds along with her panic response to the triggering memory leak. I stop her story because I need a break, not because I'm unclear on how Cái Morgan fit into things.

<it was, steven> Her dark brown eyes stare past my shoulder as her words transmit through the telepathy of Io's link.

Up until now I'd thought of Muse as the warm élan, the one that likes to radiate infra-red, but Muse has nothing on Io. Sweat soaks me. I tug at my shirt collar, tearing out the top two buttons in urgency. The environmentals are working; I hear their hum. Which means that Io-élan is generating more heat than the industrial-grade HVAC system and mature environmental nanites of the All Worlds Scientific Building B can handle. Awe-inspiring, terrifying. Noa appears cool, in her soft, matte-black garb.

<i was isolated on io. the electromagnetic storms make it difficult to transmit any real distance for any extended period. i had sensor relays set up across the plains that i used to monitor telemetry and miners, but none of those signaled further than a kilometer or two. it was too dangerous to use my navis to access the mem even when there was a hole in the storms to signal through. i knew only what cái morgan had let slip to jeanie, or to an inquisitive miner. i had no way to follow up on who camilla was in ransom to, or what else cái morgan was up to when he wasn't mining diamonds>

"I didn't mean to imply you should have known—"

<oh, no, i didn't mean to imply that you implied—> Noa's body doesn't laugh but her mind does, twinkling through the link. <i was just thinking aloud. literally!>

She laughs again, inside, and this time I pick it up too and laugh with her.

Noa's lightness closes back up into the tight ball of her intensity. <one of the troubles—from a human-observer standpoint—with hyper-complex systems is that there are too many non-linearities playing out over vast time-scales for a person to recognize which singular variables matter to any given outcome. i knew crycorp had interests on io. i knew cái morgan was looking for diamonds because he had a daughter in ransom named camilla. i knew there were dark spots where my sensors couldn't penetrate and cái entered them more often than most. i knew that there were shady people on io who used milktown as a kind of black market geneva due to the protection of the em storms. but that these things, and then some, were connected? i would have needed to have known to look for the connections. there weren't enough pieces. it wasn't where my focus sat.>

"Some have argued, though, that as a Class Twenty nauta, accomplished complexologist, and resonant with Io, you should have been able to make those associations. That your natural nauta capacity for visual-associative connections should have realized what was happening sooner."

Noa sends the telempathic equivalent of a snort through the link and the sensation of a dismissive hand-wave. <i am nauta not divinity. 'mirai' may mean 'future' but my 'future equations' still need a person to know what question to ask in the first place. a better algorithm for predicting the behavior of a chaotic system is

Blue as his daughter Camilla's eyes, staring from the creased flat-shot like she knows it is my fault.

Motor programming max now, I rise and retreat to the shadows, trembling. The pouch in my hands is warm, fluttering like a living thing. Like holding a fomori mouse, feeling its little heart flicker in its warm body. I can't inspect the pouch here. I can't be here at all. Selfish Noa, selfish to stay here so long eating Jeanie's sandwiches while miners die. The fomori mice will live on without me; I designed them to thrive on Io. But not the miners, no.

I scuff through dusty streets and fallen leaves. The O2 ivies are out of control. Milktown's dome protects the ivies from Io's 100 K temp, sulfur dioxide vapor, rads that kill in less than a minute, but it doesn't protect the ivies from humanity's insensitivity to what it deems lesser beings. It wouldn't be hard to introduce a sulfur-cricket or a naryworm to manage the ivies. *"Who cares about the ivies?" Harvey from Milktown Depot said. "Milktown moves. Mine out, move out. No point in keeping anything up, Noa."*

When Milktown moves again, it might be too far for me to reach. I could use mirai to know when that might happen, but I don't want to know. I don't ever want to know my own future again. Everybody lives.

My rover waits at the far edge of the dome. It is a bright blue shell in a field of other bright blue shells, differentiated by the ringed-planet sigil of CryCorp stamped on its flank and layers of patches on the body. High-tech supratellurium hull and near-frictionless mechanite gears. Low-tech guts of essentially a steam engine. Sextants and star charts standard for navigation. An onboard radio so useless the miners call it the "death rattle." The rovers work because the only part of Io that isn't a raging electromagnetic storm is her sulfur-laced surface. Even then, things happen.

Like whatever happened to Cái Morgan. Things I'm supposed to protect the miners from.

I hadn't protected Morgan.

I hadn't protected my team.

My hands. All that blood is on my hands. Morgan's blood, which saturates the pouch, is all over my hands.

I climb inside the rover and pull the shades. Twist the glo in the ceiling.

Between sticky patches of bloody ash, the sack is green canvas. I fumble the drawstring, hands never working right. Something squirts out and thunks on the floor. I growl low, like a frustrated jacklet, and reach. The thing I touch, it burns.

Recoil; hiss; shake my hand. I peer at it under the light; my flesh is unharmed.

I reach again for the object, this time ready for its heat, risking higher-order motor functions to transfer it swiftly hand-to-hand. It is hot, burning hot.

It's a stout cylinder, a bit bigger than my fist, made of diamonsteel and seamless. I shake it; it rattles. The miners call it a credit-cow. Io Mining Corp's standard issue container for raw diamonds. They are DNA-locked, only opening at a taste of their owners' blood.

Not my blood.

Not necessarily Morgan's blood either; he could have stolen it.

Wait a minute—given the thickness of the diamondsteel walls then—

Shut down motor; shut down linguistics; query memory index for the properties of alloys and the proper calculations—

Whatever is inside that credit-cow is at least 800 K. Hot enough to melt through the rover's tellurium-based hull.

I place the container atop the pouch. My throat convulses with swallows, some remnant of socialization programming maybe. Or maybe it's a reflex motion. My sense of body/mind is too separated to tell.

The container rocks on the bloody canvas, like an egg about to hatch.

The lid pops open and the contents spill onto the floor in a hiss and a blaze and a reek of burning chemicals.

I yelp and recoil, but the fire goes out fast. I huddle with my knees to my chest in dim light and cold.

It is Morgan's credit-cow after all. Stupid Noa. Stupid, stupid to set it down atop a canvas sack saturated with Morgan's fresh, wet blood. For all my maths, I'll never be anything but feeble.

Eleven.

There are eleven raw Ionian diamonds sprayed across the floor of my rover. That's so many c's I could buy my own corporation back in the Core. But I cannot buy redemption, or happiness, or freedom.

One of the diamonds is twice-again as big around as my thumb and just as long, with a chip that creates a natural facet. The super-dense crystal devours the dim light, refracting it back in prismatic brilliance.

I want it.

I want it for me. Not to sell. Not to give to Io Mining Corp. Not to return to the estate of the man who was its rightful owner and get his curly-haired daughter out of hock. But for me. It is mine; it belongs to me.

No—I belong to it.

We are a-kin, a-kind, the same.

I howl the long, low sound of a jacklet protecting its young and reach for the diamond's ever-brightening demon-light.

The rover shivers; restless Io trembles.

A miniature aurora skips along the rover's dash: blue-and-green, violet-gold. The large diamond catches the light and releases it, magnified, glittering prisms. The air distorts with infra-waves of heat. I shut down my navis against the EM storm rising, inexplicably, within the safety of the shielded rover beneath the safety of the shielded Milktown dome. The Io-quake trembles. My memory leak tries to surface in response.

The death-rattle radio turns itself on in a hiss of white noise. It whines, crackle and pitch struggling to organize itself into pattern. My body, unreachable and uncontrolled, pulls itself inwards in an automatic animal terror-response.

The phantom radio squeals, hissing and clicking half-second fragments. Sounds become words, comprised not of human speech but a recombination of frequencies culled and split and spliced from Jupiter's constant, senseless, radio emissions into the sounds of human words.

The radio sizzles and moans. "I AM IO!"

I moan along. It's happening again. The events of that terrible day nineteen years ago. Not a memory leak. Not unwanted playback. Oh gods, oh mathematics, oh sweet soul of science, it is happening again for real. How could I not have known? I'd run mirai today. I'd checked for quakes and storms before I'd left home. Morgan was not supposed to have died.

"I AM IIIIIIOOOOOOOOOHHHHHHHH!" The phantom radio keens. "YOU ARE MIIIIIINE!"

My shriek echoes the alien tones.

The crackle quiets; the shaking stops. In aurora-filled silence, I surge with feelings that aren't mine. <*courage/apology.i-love-you*>

Through the radio, gently now, "Do not believe the shadows. Keep me safe. Bring me to Ganymede, we escape. I am Io and you are mine." Feelings run through me <*iloveu^_.i-want-YOU*> "You are mine."

The radio shuts off.

The auroras vanish and the diamond becomes, again, cold, black stone.

I sit in sweat-soaked stillness. My pulse, throbbing in the pads of my fingers, pulls me into connection with my detached physical form. I bring my navis back online and wrap my hands around the silent radio, hyperventilating absurdly in the oxygen-rich air. I squeeze the device, shake it, like I can bring it back to life. I bring linguistics up. I haven't made human speech sounds in a decade, only the calls of the animals. I write everything for Jeanie and Harvey on a digipage. But the radio can't read. Broken subroutines work around patchwork patches in the hardware of my neurotranslator and the first words I've spoken in a decade croak out of me. "I can't. I can't leave. There will be deaths. More deaths on my hands. Damn you. Io. I can't. I can't leave."

No sound from the radio. No glow from the cold, hard stone.

"Damn you." My voice is sandpaper and anguish. I reach for the stone, rocking it close. The tightness of tears that never come prick around my selfishness. The real reason I don't want to leave Io because this is the only place where I've ever been free.

And I am only free because I let my team die the last time Io came to me, screaming across the diamond plains, and claimed me as her own.

Caran tries to plunge me straight into the story again before he even sits down, but I stop him by blurting, "I'm sorry I overstepped a boundary the other day. I shouldn't have touched you. It's against research ethics protocols. It won't happen again."

He's really just a slight thing; his charisma and presence makes him seem taller and broader than he is. But turn that off and he's nothing but sinew and bone in loose, thin clothing. His head hunches between his shoulders, hands twisting around each other and feet akimbo like a small child worried they have done something bad. "I like you Steven." The words are so soft and breathless I have to strain to hear them. "I don't want you tangled up in my muck."

"What makes you think I don't have muck of my own," I snap, then cover my mouth with both hands, horrified. So much for repair and reset; what is wrong with me?

But Caran laughs, a free, easy sound, and straightens and grows big again. He flashes a look from beneath his lashes that holds the electrical edge of challenge. "I said I like you, Steven, of course you have muck. I don't get on with people who don't. I don't understand a person unless they've been through some kind of fucked up trauma shit."

"I'm the researcher. I need to stay out of your stories; my job is to facilitate only." I'm defensive. I've had some share of unhappiness, sure, but not compared to him. Not compared to any of them.

"And being a researcher means you're not a person?" He arcs a thick, dark eyebrow at me.

"Of course not. It's because I'm a person that I need to examine, quantify, and reveal my biases. It's called reflexivity, and without it I might as well be Bobbie from Studio Six instead of a scientist."

He laughs at my prudish expression and claps me on the shoulder. "You go telling yourself that, yeah!"

How did this interview get all turned around?

Caran pulls back, hugs himself, going small again. His voice quiets to that quivering edge of fear and hope. He looks down. "I never said I didn't like it when you touched me. Just that I don't want to be an asshole. This next part of the story, it's personal. It hurts."

I liked it when I touched him too, but I also don't want to be an asshole. There's a power imbalance between researchers and participants, like that between teachers and students. Physical contact is not allowed. I'm not sure what to do, and in the space of my indecision he exhales and moves to the sofa. I follow his lead and fold into my chair, unbalanced. I'd come in today prepared to correct the transgression I'd made when I'd held him during his Dividia dreams. But nothing is resolved. I'm afraid to put today's exchange into my research notes because then everyone will know I've broken protocol and I'm barely a fraction into the interview sequence. "I'm sorry it hurts," I say.

"If it hurts, you know you're not dead," he says back.

I shiver.

◊

Shaking and moving. Shards like fever dreams. Sharp spike of withdrawals and the sound of my disembodied voice begging for relief/release. Smack on the head. Long space of unconscious. Rumbling and hissing. "Please, please, please." Shit, hit on the head, again.

I'm awake. The ground has stopped moving. The back of my head throbs, and for once I'm glad I lack a proper sense of pain because I'm sure it would hurt like explosive decompression otherwise. Eyes open to blackness. Blindfolded and bound with soft, pliable cloth.

Not in Milktown. Air's too thin, gravity's too low. Lower even than *Stella-Maru* running at .5 G. I'm cold, which means it's near freezing because that's how cold it's got to be before I feel it. Dizzy, tired, lungs can barely suck enough O2 to keep me conscious. I modify my breathing to take in more air, lifetime of singing saving me.

Still on Io. Seems I should be used to the sulfur smell enough not to sense it, but it keeps refreshing itself in new and exciting nuances of rotten egg. Not pleasant, but not repulsive either. Visceral, like the newly fertilized soil of Agrippa's wheat fields in spring.

I don't feel any withdrawal symptoms, so it's either been less than twelve hours since I dosed U4 at Jeanie's Hope, or someone's taken care of it for me, which could mean anything for time. Probably the latter, since begging for pills comprises the more lucid bits of post-abduction memory. Mouth dry and sticky. Need water. How many pills in my pocket?

I work my muscles, joints supple from all the fucking vitamin juice Mindy pours down my throat, until I can slip my hands from the bonds and reach my pockets.

All of the pills are gone.

Dry swallow the panic. Remove the blindfold. No change in the darkness.

Send out a clicking sound; listen for the bounce-back. Move my head, penetrating click, then again, all around, mapping the room with sound. The space is small and bare, like a compact office or a large closet, save the chair I'm in and something large and flat to the right that could be a bed or a desk or a stack of crates. Feet shuffle outside; I go silent.

The feet walk by.

"I'm just saying, it's shit luck that Morgan got killed on the diamond plains. I mean, the man survived five years, and this is when he gets zapped?" It's the voice of the woman who abducted me in Milktown.

"Well, you said it, five years. Morgan was tempting fate. Never understood why he kept going out for sparkle since the whole point of working for us was to pay off Ellison. Guess he was just impatient." The male.

"Well, we've got no one to watch the prisoner now, so what are we going to do? We're due to check in with Ellison in thirty-four hours and it'll take close to thirty to get back to Milktown without weather."

They stop speaking but the small sounds of movement continue to tell their story: a clink of porcelain, a glug-splash of liquid, a crunch. Shuffling feet. Heavy breathing and the hiss of an oxygen tank. Swallowing. Fuck, I'm really fucking thirsty.

"Shit, this coffee's awful." The woman.

The man sounds like he's speaking through a frown. "I think it'll be okay to leave him here alone."

A pause, the clink of porcelain. Coffee mug or teacup. Glug-splash. Chewing sounds.

The man continues, "Seriously, where's he gonna go? There's kilometers of badlands one way and nothing but mined-out plains the other. He's got no map, no survival skills, air's barely breathable without the tanks and we'll take those with us. He can occupy himself by finding the food and water and heaters. By then we'll be back."

"I guess."

"He'll find the stock room quick enough. I barely tied him up."

"The stock room isn't what I'm worried about him finding."

The man sighs. "Stop worrying. Running into Dividia is exactly what Ellison wants. The two of them can have themselves a nice little chat."

"Dividia, Dividia. Why you trust some conjured spook is beyond me," the woman whines, but there's fear in her colors. Yeah lady, I feel it too when someone says Dividia. The élan vital made of shadows. The neglect and fear that ooze through my dreams destroying hope. The "bomb" that went off in Hangar 19. And yeah, I don't like the sound of "conjured" either. The kind of temple space that would summon Dividia would be a lot less pleasant than the star circle I made for Stella, not to mention the implication that someone is willfully engaging with the thing.

"If that's the way you feel what the fuck are you doing here, Mallory?"

"I work for CryCorp, in case you've forgotten. Not that I expect you to understand corporate loyalty." She sniffs. "All right let's get back to Milktown. We need better coffee."

Scraping chairs. Sounds of people leaving.

Quiet.

Alone—no, not alone. Not like back in Milktown. There's a presence here, a kindred spirit. The zappy, staticky feel is less random. The organized presence of an élan or élans have been here. Or are here. Or will be here soon. Hold my breath, listen; silence echoes back.

I've been to enough low-g worlds with Djen to move carefully until I've acclimated. Aim slow for the walls. Explore with my hands, a knob, a door. I open it.

The light adjusts into dusty simsuns in a large office. A stray cubicle divider strikes a random ruin between a chaos of desks and scattered siliplas pages. I pick up a few near my feet: inventory sheets stamped with the diamond sigil of Io Mining Corp. Kilos of foodstuffs, crates of coveralls, repair packs for hazard suits, etcetera. Date at the top reads more than twenty years ago, Earth-standard. The pages flutter in low-g slo-mo back to the ground.

I'm still wearing the sleeveless dress and soft pants Jordis left me. They're wrinkled, torn, stained, and smell and feel like industrial soap and sanitizer. Might as well be wearing nothing at all for all they protect me from the cold. Djen would be screaming I need to dress better for the weather. Reminds me of that time on Ganymede when I lost my coat. How she yelled. Muse kept me warm then. And other company. Wasn't alone.

Don't think about alone.

On a dusty desktop, the wet smudge of coffee rings the bottom of a chipped porcelain cup. I sniff at it, stick my tongue in to lick up the drops, and put it back. The carafe is empty. Two crumb-filled plates. A bottle of wine with two fingers left. I pick up the crumbs with my finger and lick them off. The wine's a better find: a thick, crude red, mostly gone to vinegar, but I'm grateful for wetness in my mouth and the warmth in my throat and the way it calms my nerves. Although I might as well be drinking saltwater for all it'll fix my dehydration. Where's Mindy with a vitamin juice when I need one?

On a broken plate at the edge of the desk lies one tablet of U4.

One pill lasts twelve hours, so fourteen plus-or-minus before things get scary. If there's one pill left, assuming they fed me one each time I complained, that equals thirty-two hours or more since leaving Jeanie's hope. The man said thirty back to Milktown. I feel fine, but I won't make it back to Milktown on just one pill. Why did they think they could leave me here with only one? Do they know I'm nauta? Why would they; how could they know?

Sharp, anxious panic pushes up, so swallow the feeling down with a gulp of wine; pocket the pill. There has to be more U4 here. Or NQ. If they'd meant for me to die, they would've just killed me. "Whatever else he needs," they'd said, they must've meant the pap. No way they'd just let me die.

I feel faint and remember to pull extra air into my lungs. The CO2 levels aren't poison; the O2's just really thin and dry. I need more clothes, water. But first, NQ or U4.

Take the last slosh of vinegary wine, drop the bottle, and follow the subtle sense of *presence*. Out into a corridor, to the left. If it's an élan I can communicate with, it might tell me what I need to know.

Little tendrils of sentient electricity push me away from one hall, poke me toward another. It's not Muse, but it resonates with me, a strange-yet-familiar vibration. I think I've met it before. I arrive at a discolored door, stuck half-open and covered in the crumbling curls of dead O2 ivies. It's dark within.

I pause on the threshold. Dizzy. Like standing on the border between a dream-within-a-dream, or maybe a dream-within-a-nightmare, and the levels are about to shift.

I stumble and my foot goes crunch on a water bottle just outside the room, shiny and out-of-place, blazoned with the name CryCorp and a Saturn-shaped corporate sigil. If CryCorp employs that Mallory woman there could be answers in that room. Or a full bottle of water. Deep breaths, opera breaths. Oxygen to the brain. Vertigo fades. I shake the water bottle into my mouth, but nothing comes out.

The bottle falls pop-thunk next to a sheet of siliplas. Sheet's new and shiny like the water bottle, and I pick it up. It's got a mainfeed schedule on it. Dates are current. There are a few entries that don't read as media. Like Europa PAS-H19 10:20. PAS-H19... PAS...Port Authority South? Hangar 19? Where Dividia exploded a freighter and all my friends on Europa? Or am I just seeing coincidences?

A tendril of infrared caresses my bare arm. There's warmth in the room. Things I need in order to stay alive. I put the siliplas page in my pocket with the pill.

I step through the door into—

Unloved toys, dead pets, forgotten ancestors, a broken childhood dream.

Displacement.

Knocking on doors and nobody answers: dispossession.

So hungry it's too frightening to take a bite of that stolen bread.

Stinker!

Hey Stinker Watts!

Ha ha ha!

What do you have to say about that, Stinker Watts?

The moan of a lone tiger facing its species' extinction.

Cold, filthy, forgotten.

The empty place where grief used to be.

I gasp thin air, clawing at emptiness to keep from falling, hands crashing into mountains of hopeless, unloved things: an armless teddy bear missing an eye, a locket with the picture burned out, a lock of hair disintegrating with time, the sphere of a blue-green

Earth before humanity killed her— someone has gathered this stuff, placed it here. A laboratory for a broken idea. A temple of hopelessness.

This isn't just a room for summoning an élan.

It's a room for nurturing a particular type of feedback with an élan, a resonance of neglect and fear. These are human feelings, human pains. Someone has used this space to pervert an élan, culturing it, twisting it into a weapon. Into the kind of being that would blow up a freighter at a human's bidding.

But—how could the other élans not know about it? Especially since this is exactly the kind of manipulation they most fear. The élans are all connected—all except for Muse.

A flare of static and Dividia becomes visible, dragging a symphony of hurts. Shadows creep together and collapse; there is no center to hold. Memories of playground bullies and the turned back of Belinda Watts, tossing alone and hungry in the still, dead night, no voice with which to speak, no ears to hear my screams.

He don't answer because he's a stink!

Stinks don't talk and neither does Stinker Watts!

Ha ha ha!

Freedom never wanted me. Kicked me out.

Adrift. Alone.

And at the center of loss and things that never were, the cold stare of hate.

YOUR FAULT.

Hate is a home, a place I belong. A place where I don't have to worry about fear ever again. Why fear the inevitable, the truth? Truth is I am the filthy, the forgotten, the dispossessed, doesn't matter how many fans scream my name. I'm alone, no one wants a fucked-up freak. EXCEPT—if I become Dividia's, I won't be alone.

I step to the center of Dividia's temple and close my eyes. The resonance is already there, like we've linked before. I think/feel to the élan, <you can have me. i am yours. i always have been yours>

But before the shadow can take me, a second élan flares visible just outside the temple, its anger burning bright—hot anti-shadow! It dances like music.

I stand between Dividia's darkness and the new élan's fire.

Electricity from the new one cracks into the Temple of Fear and slaps the shadows, whipping them back. The new one's keening screams through the crystals and ceramics in the space. I scream in reflexive harmony, hands clapping to my ringing ears.

The new élan flicker-flashes bright as the heart of a volcano. Uncountable numbers of nearly human hands fly from everywhere, beating at the darkness. The shadows recoil. I reach out my mind to the new élan, but I have no resonance with it. I turn and run as the alien entities crash light-and-darkness in electrified air. I retrace my steps, forgetting until it's too late that nothing lies that way but dead ends, empty plates, and that shitty room I woke up in.

Shins mash against a metal desk next to the chair they'd tied me to. I feel the impact, but not the pain. Never the pain. Anger flares for my stupidity at thinking I could escape, for my hypo-sensitive numbness, can't feel anything unless it's extreme.

The second élan, the bright one, manifests as visible light in front of me: red, yellow, black, white; flicker: on, off; cycling, flashing. Restless.

Fear claws the nape of my neck, curls in my belly, but the flashing-bright élan sparks <*!urgency!dire* come, i am io, come!> Flicker-flash illuminating a little window set high in the wall. My echolocation hadn't noticed it.

I pick up the chair, tripping over my discarded bonds, and set it beneath the window, but I'm too short to reach.

Io-élan flashes and whips around the room, emitting <*impatiencefear*>

<*calm!*> I project at her trying to stop any feedback of panic with my fear, but either there's not enough resonance for her to pick up on my feelings or she's not easily consoled.

I take a running jump onto the desk and spring for the window; my hands catch the sill. Push up, and over the ledge.

The low-G drop is a story and a half into sludgy half-light and silence.

At the bottom of the fall lies a ghost-town, a tattered wraith-world echo of Milktown. Must be a previous incarnation of the mining town. Like they'd said in Jeanie's Hope—Milktown moves. Mine out, move out. I lie flat in the throes of vertigo and lack of oxygen, gasping around the memories of taunts and punches and my fucking mother, all conjured by Dividia. Io-élan zaps me with electricity strong enough to burn.

Skeleton ivies cling to the interior of the abandoned dome in a rictus; the ground crusted with dead, desiccated vegetation. Dome's so covered in dust and death that no light shines through; Io-élan is all that lights the landscape.

Buildings were simply left. Objects abandoned—a sock, a comb, a mug—lying in the dust and dead leaves. These things that had sheltered the miners, cared for them, kept them warm, thrown away as nothing. Tearless sobs like dry heaves shatter against my ribs. I want to collect up these objects, bring them home, clean them up, give them good lives. I never want anything to hurt. It's so cold I don't think I can move, even with Io's scalding prompts.

Silence save for the occasional snap-rustle of shifting/falling dead ivy and the crackle-crunch of caving roofs.

<*!UrgentCOME*> Io-élan, flicker-flash.

An electrical snap and moan from behind: fear crawling on hooks of shadow.

I can't let Dividia reach me again. I'm too weak. I'll choose darkness instead of flame.

Io-élan skips ahead and back in a "follow-me" pattern.

Poor Io-élan, what must it be like for her to have this abomination within her frequencies? How much might Dividia have influenced her? I'm shivering so violently I can barely see, but I make it to my feet and follow her, struggling to pull in oxygen, stumbling on icy limbs. Io-élan radiates infra; I follow her heat.

I follow her and keep my eyes on her like salvation, because if I catch one more glimpse of the deserted buildings and abandoned things I'll lie down and die. The dry sobs complicate movement. The nightmare runs on, Io-élan blinking before me, Dividia whispering behind. Inside, my small flame of anger tries to light itself and burn but doesn't catch. Pity. It might've kept me warm.

I crash to my knees over the broken doorway to a crumbling vehicle pad. A brand-new, bright blue, dust-free rover sits beside the airlock.

Io-élan blinks over to it, though it's not like I need the encouragement. CryCorp's ringed-planet sigil marks the outside and a siliplas key rests in the lock. Propped on the front seat is a hazard suit.

Djen drilled me on the infernal thing endlessly. Two, four, more years together and she'd still give me "pop-quizzes" and "fire drills," putting on the hazard suit and jetting me out into space, pretending like the *Stella-Maru* was breached. Put those fire drills on the "I Really Hate This Most" list. But yeah, I can do the hazard suit. It'll warm me up and the O2 tanks are almost full. If I'm really lucky it'll have food and water in it. The tab of U4's still in my pocket, along with the media schedule. I slide into the bright blue suit, gagging on the disgusting snaky sensation of the feeder and waste tubes invading, waiting for the sensors to get a read on my body temp and equilibrate.

The engine turns with the same key that opened the door. It runs like the tractors on Agrippa. I'm out of the airlock and rovering toward the red-yellow-blue flickering wisp-light of the moon incarnate as she leads me...

Somewhere.

Shit.

Breathe.

Is that music?

Aurora breaks over terrain like the opening chords of Beethoven's 9th, a sky-full of fairy-light in green and violet against a backdrop of Jupiter and starlight. A blue glow, the color of electricity, hazes along the horizon. The land's alive with music.

The flicker-wisp of Io-élan grows, blurs, reforms into an unstable woman-shape flaring with the aurora, glowing with the fire-color of the corrugated lava plains, crackling blue-white live-wire at her core. I glimpse a face, long and lean, not beautiful in any traditional way but seductive all the same. I want her. Badly. Worse than a fix on the bad end of withdrawal. Even knowing that the desires of a hundred million miners have carved her, created her, realigned her from whatever she once was into a spirit of savage human need, I want her.

Io-élan flashes across the dusty, deadly plain for me to follow.

I sing out, voice reaching for the colors of the aurora; she dances.

I will follow her. Certainly. Anywhere.

But she'd better be leading me back to civilization, because someone has weaponized an élan vital. An élan vital whose resonance I cannot resist. If that thing fills me I could do truly terrible things. I need to tell Djen right away.

◊

The link breaks and I'm back in the here now, back on the couch with my arms wrapped round him as he cries joyously, and I don't even know how I got here.

"It was so beautiful." He sobs wetly into my arms. "The music."

"The music?" I whisper into his hair. It's fine and soft and tangled beyond hope again and smells of coconut.

"Yes." His body presses harder against mine as I press back with all my strength. "Io's song. That's when it started. The Io movement of the Jovian Symphony. Her out on the plains. The sound of the rover. The colors of the aurora. Hope and fear."

"Hope and fear," I echo and hold him. Hold in the fear.

"May I ask you an embarrassing question?" I ask Noa.

<embarrassing for whom?> She shoots back telempathically.

"I'm not sure. Me, definitely. You, maybe."

<didn't they tell you we nauta have no social tact?> Noa's lips quirk up at that, where she sits in her otherwise intense stillness on the couch.

I smile back. "All right then. You spent most of your life as property. Tell me a little bit about that."

The thin, high arches of Noa's eyebrows go up. <that is very bold of you, steven.>

"I told you it was embarrassing."

<i would like to know first, why are you asking?> Her head clicks to the side.

"I think it's an important frame for your narrative. I've gotten a bit of early life history from Caran and Jordis, just as a natural part of their interviews, but I haven't gotten that from you yet. So I thought I'd ask directly."

<that's a very different question> Noa's mouth frowns.

I blink, surprised. "I suppose it is."

<how would you like it, steven, if i were to ask you, tell me a bit about what it was like to fail your maths comps?>

I blush. "Now that's an embarrassing question." I try to chuckle the fact away.

But Noa continues. <what about if i asked you instead, tell me a little bit about what it's like to excel in qualitative research while struggling with quantitative work?>

"Well, that's a very different question—" My mouth makes an "O." This is going about as awkwardly as my last session with Caran.

<exactly.> Noa communicates. <i am not a zoo exhibit to satisfy your curiosity about nauta and suffering. i am here to illuminate a series of events which can only be understood from within the context of nauta suffering>

"You'd make a fine qualitative researcher, Noa Oki," I tell her.

<much better than you would make a mathematician> Her lips quirk back up to take the sting from the retort. Then her body sighs and shudders, and she thinks to me. <it's probably useful to know what I was hiding from. what was at stake for operators. like most born on a federal banking world with the k-mutation, i was removed from my family and placed in a nursery at birth. in the nursery, they give us just enough affection so that we don't— don't end up like caran. the nursery discovered my aptitude for science and mathematics early on. they test us repeatedly; corporate sniffers like to reserve those who show promise in their area for sponsorship after we complete socialization and skills training. all worlds scientific reserved me first, i which is where i did my coaction mechanics work. then crycorp bought out my sponsorship for the io terraforming project.>

She switches abruptly to speech; her hair stands on end and blue lightening crackles over the back of the sofa. "But as far as how it felt? Feelings do not help us survive. Feelings do not help us manage the maltreatment, dehumanization, subjugation at levels that you would never allow for yourselves. We turn to diamond, inside and out."

◊

Home again after a day of rovering across badlands from Marduk to Keroessa Plain. Home from Milktown to my ranch in its dome. The ranch is a big, open building, divided by furnishings instead of walls. I use the living room, kitchen, research labs, lav; the rest I ignore. One wall collapsed years ago; the jungle swallows unused rooms. It brings me comfort.

I lie back on the couch in the living room. I wish I had a proper Operator's bed to sustain my body while I work but the electronics would fry.

I close my eyes.

I am a thousand kilometers away, my consciousness spread over Marduk Plain, skipping signal through sensors I placed beneath Io's crust.

Seismographs rumble in my chest.

The pressure changes of Io's atmosphere freezing in Jupiter's shadow pop in my ears.

Complex spectography spreads in my eyes a rainbow-view.

All of my telemetry, I feed on a thread into the lab's stationary systems. There, the mirai equations use the data to run predictions.

Known parameters of eruptions, past and present.

Tabs on all my miners.

Ambient frequencies that shouldn't make a difference but do.

Work the probabilities; 99.9% accuracy within the next hour; falling after that. Accurate within a six-point margin of error up to five hours out.

Small rumbles here. Tiny EM wind there. Panic at the blind spot over there— Ah! There is a sensor out. Put it on the repair list. Swoop back in, collect, monitor, calculate. And then, on the periphery of awareness, a bright, red flashing light and a high-pitched whine that makes my teeth ache.

PERIMETER ALERT

Something approaches my dome, fast.

Pull a thread from distance telemetry; reallocate to local, inhabit the dome's sensors.

Seismic: nominal.

Atmospheric: nominal.

Radiation: nominal.

Visible light: a bright blue speck, twenty K out to the top-diagonal-left.

Dismiss all telemetry but spectral, wavelengths from infra to ultra and zoom: a rover, coming in fast.

I know the location of everyone on the plains today. All forty-eight mining hopefuls. The closest is eight-hundred K away. The stars shine bright on the Marduk and Keroessa plains. There is no getting lost in the dust.

It's CryCorp coming to get me.

No, no, no, it doesn't have to be.

Don't panic—everybody lives.

Sever all threads but visual on the incoming rover.

—and crash back into the ache of my back. The stiffness of my limbs. The proximity alarm wailing in my ears. The scream of the pinched nerve at the base of my spine. The bright blue dot hurtles toward my dome. I could make radio contact with it, warn it away. But given velocity equals speed over time, by the time the communication completes it will already be too late. Four seconds and the rover will see my dome.

Navis resource reallocation: motor ON; linguistics OFF. Hobble from the ranch. The airlock is half a K a way.

My pace picks up as my limbs loosen. I watch the rover's approach in augmented reality over the rush of foliage beneath my feet. Soft black shoes, standard issue so as not to hurt the little flowers. The rover is still at max speed. Damaged rover? Injured miner? Glitch from my navis?

CryCorp sigil on the side of the rover oh no no no no NO.

Stumble. Fall. Skinned palm. Terrified sound of a fomori mouse coming from my throat.

No, no. It would have made sense for CryCorp to come after me in the early months; the corporation was searching for its lost research station then. But now, nineteen years and the station descended into myth? I pick myself up. If they come for me, I will expose myself to Io without a hazard suit. I will die before I go back.

But I have options. I have weapons! Remove a navis thread from motor, reallocate into the dome's defenses, spin the litegun on its gritty dry gears to target the rover. I will blast them from my moon!

But if someone in the rover is injured, even if it is someone come to take my life—

Everybody lives.

EVERYBODY lives.

(but not everybody gets a diamond)

I release control of the litegun, reallocate threads to motor; run again for the airlock. I stomp into a hazard suit, soaked with hot, anxious sweat that leaves me momentarily freezing as the suit sucks the moisture into its hydration system.

I punch the interior door and sprint down the short tunnel of the airlock.

The rover hits my dome in a violence of sulfur ash as I reach the hatch. Motor and sensory on max, drop everything else. Pawing through dust. Hands colliding blind with the vehicle's flank. Feel along the crumpled surface for the door handle and tug.

A flash of cyan hazard suit in a yellow cloud; a body falls against me. Hook under shoulders and pull. We are soon within the airlock's protection. If there's a tear in the suit, rads will kill, even if injuries are superficial. Everybody lives. They can't have my diamond.

The hatch shuts; pressure hisses. I pop the seal of my helmet and pull it off, panting. The stranger's suit looks intact. I wipe dust from the visor with the hem of my t-shirt and sneeze. No blood. No cracks. Helmet seal intact. I press the buttons and latches to release the suit. The helmet falls away. A man's head falls limply back. I fumble around his neck for a pulse that is—there. Too there. Too fast, too strong. Wrong.

I pull off the chest piece and tug the suit away.

He is not a miner. He doesn't look corporate either, not the kind of corporate that would come drag me back to the Core. He's wearing a filthy white dress, gray slacks, and ankle-high boots so soft they wouldn't last a week anywhere on Io except inside my dome. They would not hurt the little flowers. They are scuffed and torn. He is small, composed of corded muscle clutching slender bones, like a starving dancer. Beneath the pallor and a tangle of dirty black hair his tawny face is very soft, and his jaw shows no trace of beard, as though he has received an expensive styling treatment. How could such a creature arrive on Io without me knowing? I monitor the arrival slate. I know who comes and goes.

Pull threads out of motor and sensory. Reallocate into the medical database at the ranch. Open input to vision, sight-scan the man, my eyes a camera. What-do-I-do? The medical database's baby blue cross overlays my vision as its programming activates.

The baby-blue cross swims along the ghosting edges of the past. Memory leak from nineteen years ago trying to play itself again. Smell of burned flesh. Hit myself on the temple as though it will jigger the broken memory index back into place.

DEHYDRATION PRIORITY ONE—followed by a sprawl of feed from the medical database: diagnostic questions; remedies; steps-to-take. I pull my threads out of medical. Reallocate all resources to motor: remove the rest of my hazard suit; hook my arms under the man's shoulders; drag him to the house.

Is he from CryCorp? Is he here for me? I don't want to go back. Everybody lives. Everybody gets a diamond. *I* get a diamond.

I pull him through the shattered wall of the ranch and leave him on the threshold of the jungle while I collect supplies.

Roll him onto the gurney. Crank it up. Memory leak: smell of burning flesh; screams of pain. Ning Ning on the gurney. Dead before I'd put her there. Hands black with blood and sulfur-laced soil.

NO. JUST A GLITCH GODSDAMNIT.

This man is not a memory. His life is in my hands.

But EVERYTHING is triggering the memory leak now. The feel of the gurney against my hip. The bleep of the diagnostic sensors as I hook them up. The weight of the saline bag in my hand. The fact that I am not alone. The stress of the unknown. If only I could turn off my memory index. But I can't without turning off my na-vis. I need my navis to move and think and do and save the man.

I gag on burned flesh but he only smells of Io and detergent and fear.

I clamp my will over the present like the jaws of a jacklet around its prey and begin the injections of chemicals indicated by the medical database into the saline sack. Potassium, bicarbonate, a muscle relaxant—

What?

The medical database does not stop its scrolling for my what-ing. It calmly updates its assessment of the priority problem and offers new solutions. Unlikely, impossible, terrifying as they are.

I can save the man.

I am, perhaps, the only person on all of Io who can save the man because no one else would have the medicine he needs.

But what then? What will I do when he turns on me because I cannot satisfy his hunger? The jacklets won't care. I can save him, but then—

I can walk away, and he will die here, now. I can call it self-defense. Just like when Markus died. That was self-defense.

No. No more blood on my hands. Everybody lives. Figure it out.

Insert the needle. Start the fluid drip. Add enough sedative to keep him under long enough for my memory leak to run its night-mare course. I can't hold the memories back much longer. His tol-erance to the sedative is high, but I can keep him sleepy at least. Maybe I can keep him sleepy enough he will only remember me as a ghost.

I am only a ghost anyway. Demon of the Diamond Plains.

I sink behind the couch. The past takes me as my glitchy mem-ory index brings that day back again in perfect recall—

◊

Caran enters my office, and Io drops the link. He makes straight for Noa and kisses her lightly on the forehead. Their eyes go unfocused and he cocks his head to the side as though listening, then nods. She makes a low, feral growling sound. He sits beside her, holding her hand in his lap. "Hi." He beams at me, his eyes catching all the light. "Sorry I'm late."

I'm still reeling from Noa's story. I excuse myself to the restroom.

I stand with my wrists against the stone sink, letting the coldness of Martian rock damp Io-élan's fire. My pulse pounds; sweat slicks the loose black curls of my hair straight, and, although it's long past lunchtime, I have no appetite. I've sat through a lot of difficult interviews. Like that series on philosophical prisoners arrested for leading anti-government cults. Or my series on serial murderers; that cannibal guy was rough. Or, rough in a different way, my interviews with the survivors of the colony on Xia, who suffered tremendously before they made it back to the Core. But this is different. This is direct. I am within the stories, as though events were happening to me.

I turn the sink on cold and let the water trickle over my hands. I slap some on my neck too. Then lap some up from the tap, like Caran in Hostel Six, ignoring the dispenser of degradable cups.

I must go back out there and see this through. I must honor their stories. That's the whole point, right? To understand the Great Changes through the direct experiences of those who initiated them and opened the crossroads of a new world. I run a dryer over my hands, my hair.

Back in my office my participants have rearranged themselves. Caran has kicked off his shoes and pushed his body into its usual sprawl with his bare feet on the table. Noa has tucked her feet up under herself, placed a pillow on her lap, and rested her head against Caran's shoulder. Caran flashes his flirty smile. Noa regards me like a feral cat.

I clear my throat. "Thanks for trying this experiment of a three-way link."

"Hey, no prob," Caran smiles. "I think it's a super idea!"

Noa's pupils dilate as Io-élan swoops back into our consciousnesses and binds us all together.

"So, where were you?" Caran speaks the words just after his intention to say them echoes through.

"We had gotten to the part where Noa had gotten you stable. What happened next?"

Caran's bright smile glows even brighter. "I woke up."

◊

Whisper-rustle

THRUM-THUMP

Openness to the left: insect noises and small animals, no wind. Echo to the right: something hard and flat.

THRUM-THUMP

Heartbeat.

Thrum-thump. Thrum-thump. Thrum-thump.

Am I still alive?

Thrum-thump.

I open my eyes. Purple and yellow flora spills over a collapsed silifoam wall. Large insects with silver carapaces hum over heavy white flowers on violet stalks. Pale blades of grass poke through ashy soil until they reach the edge of a plush, white carpet.

Pleasant near-death hallucination?

An animal trills. Songs of things with fur and wombs, with cilia and exoskeletons, chirping insect-song.

I draw a full breath, sucking in the musk of fertile earth. The air has the right amount of oxygen and only the faintest sulfur smell. Thrum-thump. Thrum-thump. My heartbeat is normal. My mouth is wet, and my eyelids don't hurt when I blink.

Above the foliage shimmers the arc of a small atmo-dome. Outside, in the sky, auroras skitter. If I'm still alive, I'm still on Io. Fuck.

I turn my head the other way. I look into the interior of a large, flat house divided by function, not walls. A dining area opens into a living area opens into a lab-looking area dense with equipment. An IV drips into my arm. On the dining counter a double-thumb-sized raw Ionian diamond refracts light from one chipped facet, and the heat of an élan within. Io-élan: I know her after following her so many K through hell. What the fuck's she doing inside a diamond?

I start to sit but realize halfway there I feel too awful and sink back down. Too-awful-to-sit is still light years better than I felt before I passed out. Fine to just lie still and breathe. I'm heavy again, a one g generator somewhere beneath the dome.

How long have I been out, when will I need my next dose, shit-fuck-hell I'm out of fucking pills and—

Shutup. SHUT UP.

Prickly wet tears. The pap's just one more responsibility I can't shake. Responsibility to the fans, the handlers, Freedom, to keep myself alive.

TO FUCK WITH RESPONSIBILITY. Give me just one hour of fucking peace. Too much responsibility in being alive.

Close my eyes. Draw the good air into my lungs and hum. Add my voice to the soft song outside, tune into the landscape. Make sonic interaction with the alien garden until I'm sure that I'm alive.

Hesitant feet pitter-skuff toward me, and another breath joins the song; I open my eyes. A woman has crept up, like a mouse. She holds her black hair back in the circle of her thumb and forefinger.

In her other hand, she holds a nasty needle. She's nauta, the blue sheen of tzaddium flashing across her forehead. Her cheekbones intensify the power in her feral gaze, the same power that lies sleeping in the diamond on the counter, that pulsed from Io-élan across the plains. She is claimed by Io, has half-become her. She'd have U4 for doing maintenance on her navis, which would explain why I'm not dead of withdrawals.

The woman gazes past my face intensely. "Hel-lo." Her voice is abrasive from disuse, syllables flat and clipped as though she's turned off most of her speech programming. She swallows and releases her hair to point at her chest, face veiled. "No-ah."

"Caran." The color of my own voice pleases me, but I want to take it back the moment I say it. What the fuck, did I get brain damaged, telling someone who I actually am?

Weirdly, she gives no sign of recognition.

I weave my fingers in the triple-looped signal for Freedom, but she gives no response to that either. She is a slave then. Where are her keepers? Where the fuck am I?

◊

I want to tell him: your voice brought me back to the here-and-now. I want to tell him: you give voice to my jungle. I want to tell him: your voice made me cry for beauty's sake.

But I cannot reach those words, so I simply say my name.

The sheets have come undone and his skin glows golden. My hands twist around the sedative injection.

I click the roof of my mouth in the warning-call of the sulfur-crickets.

Outside, they pick up the call: danger, maybe. Be alert.

The man is sick and weak. If he were a true threat would Io, Storm Giant, have let him come? It has been twenty-five years since I have laid eyes on one of my own kind.

But what if he turns on me for drugs?

What if he is from CryCorp?

◊

She shifts, and behind her I see the CryCorp ringed-planet sigil stamped all over the science equipment, painted huge on the far wall, notice it now on the IV bag dripping into me. CryCorp, Dividia, the ruin of Milktown-lost, alone, displaced, abandoned. Fear and death and hope OH FUCK this isn't anywhere safe after all.

Sliding, slipping off the gurney. Stumbling, falling, fucking feet won't take my weight. Needle slips from my vein, fluid squirting everywhere as I scream rage and weakness and helplessness, clawing the carpet but I can't get away.

◊

I am on top of him; I must get the sedative into his arm. He panics and flails. I lose my grip on the needle; it skitters under the gurney.

◊

I can't, I can't, I can't overpower her, she climbs on top of me, full weight in one G. I sprawl on the white carpet too scared and weak and frustrated to do anything but pant. She plants her palms hard on my shoulders and grinds a knee into my chest, a black silhouette against alien foliage. Black as shadow. Black as Dividia. Black as pain and alone and fear.

"Cry." She rasps in a voice that sounds like she hasn't used it in a century. "Cry. Cry. Cry."

◊

Glitch, glitchy, glitch, come on Noa, speak, speak! "CryCorp!" I clatter my teeth together, sounding the alarm cry now. A forest of sulfur crickets clatter back. Danger, the danger is real!

◊

"CryCorp!" I echo, terror-scream. I need to shake my hands, desperate-full of tension I gotta drain, but she holds me down, holds me fast, crushing. There is no peace, no rest, no release, and there's nothing to do but choke on the tears that roll into my nose and mouth because I've no strength to turn my head.

◊

He's as afraid of CryCorp as I am.
Stunned, I pull away.

◊

She pulls off me. Then she gathers me in her arms, holding me with pressure enough to feel it. Rocking me with a steady beat. Trilling to soothe the animals outside until their warning screams turn to coos and it's like the whole ecosystem is trying to comfort me.

I stop crying, stop breathing. Two beats pass. Then the kindness sinks in and I lose control into screaming, wailing sobs, she doesn't even know who I am, and this is the first kindness since Djen and before that my old music teacher on Agrippa holding me like Noa is now, tight enough to feel it, as I weep not from punches or neglect but from the exquisite, unbearable agony of kindness.

◊

He lies limply against my chest, breath in tatters, eyes empty and confused. He has howled until his voice is gone.

I set him back on the floor, hiding my face in the veil of my hair. His cheek presses against the soft carpet. His breath slows as he slips into spent sleep.

◊

I wake back on the gurney with Noa leaning over me, her hair brushing my shoulders. The warm seep of a strong sedative spreads, delish. No pain, no fear, just a golden-honey glow coating the hard edges of everything, making it shine. Polydorozopam, if I'm not mistaken. If she thinks 'roze will knock me out, she's going to be disappointed. I've functioned on the stuff for weeks on end and all Mindy noticed was that I'd seemed less jumpy. Well, maybe not functioned on this heavy a dose. This is very nice indeed. "Noa." My voice is made warm syrup, filtered through the honey of the 'roze.

She pulls back, eyes tight with tension. "CryCorp. Are you from. CryCorp."

Is she asking because she's part of CryCorp's Dividia conspiracy, or because she's as piss-scared of it as I am? Well, scared of it as I had been. Now I'm just floaty. If Io resonates with Noa, and Io hates Dividia, and a friend of my friend is my enemy—no, wait, that wasn't how it went—"CryCorp—" I shake my head in an attempt at an emphatic no. Hard to be emphatic when I'm made of warm honey.

"What are you doing here," she says, a little shrug-twitch making the flat words into a question.

I sing from an ancient hit by The Louies with vibrato, "Something terrible / Something wrong / There's been an accident / I don't belong."

Noa stares, annoyed, like she's expecting more. She knows I'm a nauta without a navis, for fuck's sake, and she's given me nothing useful to echo. How does she expect me to communicate?

Okay, there's that number from Joanie and the Hyperstations—"There's been people killed in the hard light of dawn / I was investigating till you came along / Hard on the street and alive with the beat / I was investigating till you came along / Yeah, I was investigating till you came along." No, that wasn't remotely right, was it? Not the song, the song was right. The meaning, the idea of "investigating" is a bit thin, though not exactly wrong. Well, no need to get into the whole truth.

"Investigating." Again, the little shrug again to indicate a question.

"Investigating."

She stops breathing, staring at me sideways. "Me?"

I shake my head. "CryCorp."

Noa exhales for a hundred years, then rapid-fires monotone sentences like darts. "Lab owned by CryCorp. Me owned by CryCorp. Terraforming experiment. Invented ecosystems, dynamic equilibria. Flora and fauna adapted to an environment. Co-evolution. Symbiotic geology. Complexologist. Me. Interdependencies, nonlinearities: my spec-i-al-it-ties." She gazes into my left shoulder violently.

I'm so fuzzy against her sharpness. "Was owned?"

"Was owned. Sponsors gone. CryCorp gone."

"CryCorp gone." This time I'm the one exhaling forever. But—"Dividia?" I whisper.

She shakes her head.

"Mallory?"

Head shake again.

"Ellison?"

A distanced nod. "CEO. CryCorp."

"How long / how long / how long do I wait for thee?" I sing.

"How long?"

"Sponsors gone."

"Nineteen years. No one finds me. Demon of the Diamond Plains. No one comes here. I have weapons." She clicks her teeth together, and an animal outside echoes the sound.

"Nineteen gone, no CryCorp?" I need her to give me more words to use, but she's not running full linguistics. Or full anything else. Though if she's been alone on this hell-moon for nineteen years, she's probably loopy as a pulsar. Pulsars sure are pretty, like that time me and Djen had been loopy on 'roze and parked outside that nebula with the—

"Nineteen gone. No CryCorp." Noa repeats and nods.

And now we're stuck endlessly echoing each other. Good thing I'm too stoned to care how frustrating that is. "What happened to the rest of the people who used to live here?" I ask.

That was too many words, too fast, and not a one of them an echo or a line from a song, which means—"Hey Noa, you got NQ?"

Noa clicks her teeth, strikes a defensive pose.

"I'm not gonna hurt you Noa. Don't want to. Couldn't even if I did, even if I'd the strength. Even if you hadn't shot me full of 'rozo-pam. Io'd stop me before I could finish the thought." 'Roze is sweet dope, but spontaneous words can only mean NQ.

Noa pulls her hair back with one hand. "Lots of maintenance." She taps her forehead. "Lots of EM. Shorts. In my navis. Repairs. U4: controlled. Only sponsors give it. No sponsors. I am free." She glares, haughty and proud. "I am not like you."

"Yeah? Good. It's super-shitty to be me. But how much NQ you got? Can I see?"

"Not much. No."

"I was about to nip a quarter dram back in Milktown before—" no way I'm going to upset the glow by mentioning Dividia's shadows. "A little more love, a little more of the pap."

She shakes her head. "Small amount. In the drip. Drug dosage titration. Adaptive regulation to reduce, eliminate dependency."

"But I don't want to reduce, eliminate dependency," I spin my voice up with a whine, but it has no bite and it's not just because of how sick I am or the honey. It's that if I'm clean enough to use my navis when I get back to Europa, I can upload my intel to the Mesh and warn Freedom about what's going on.

Noa rocks in gentle rhythm with her sentences. "Current dosage: .2 to .25 drops per hour. After the drip, dynamic release derms. Titration to prevent receptor crisis, dangerous withdrawal. Free of dependence: five days."

Not sure how I feel about that.

"Which is good." Noa takes a shaky breath. "Because that is all the NQ I have."

Very sure how I feel about that. "Shit, that sucks." I can get as high as I want afterwards, right? But I need to get the information about Dividia to Freedom.

So how much NQ does she have? If the dosage amounts are what she says and the time span is five days, then assuming the weaning doses will come in increments, and I can be off NQ in five days, she said five days—

FUCK the only reason ditching NQ seems like a good idea is because I'm stoned out of my fucking mind on animal tranquilizer but that's okay, I'll take it. "Can I stay here? With you? Till it's over?"

"Yes," she says, and shoots even more 'roze into the IV.

"Deal," I slur, sinking into the honey-glow. The Io-song needs a few lyrics, maybe: the volcano she will keep you warm / when shadow's turned you cold / when nothing else can thaw the burn / she'll storm away your...

After we break for lunch, I rub damp palms on my pants. "So who's going to start?"

"Well, Noa was doing her miner-rescue-thing, so that'll be boring. I should start." Caran says.

"Ah, yes, the miner-rescue-thing." I clear my throat—and confusing giddiness over the sight of Caran—and direct my focus toward Noa. "Actually, I'd love to hear more about how you rescued the miners. I don't think that would be boring at all. Particularly, I'd like a deeper understanding of your mirai equations. Remember, easy on the math."

Caran raises a brow.

Noa answers, aloud. "Steven failed his maths-comps. A test science-track students take. He is their best score-er on qual-comps. Best ever, in all of time. They couldn't kick him out."

Caran chuckles, low and warm. "Then he has more in common with us genetic freaks than maybe he'd like."

A grin that does not entirely respect social norms spreads over my teeth. "I understand a little about uneven skills. But what makes you think I *wouldn't* want to have something in common with nauta? It's all a continuum of human experience, after all."

Caran laughs hugely and slaps Noa on the back, which moves her as much as it would a solid steel beam. "See, I told you Steven was one of the good ones!"

"Steven is an anthropologist." Noa clips without expression. "He is interested in analyzing culture."

"He is still a person," Caran shrugs.

"I am still in the room," I add. Gods help me, All Worlds Scientific is going to regret handing me this assignment.

"Then he knows even more what it feels like to be nauta." Noa's flat voice might almost sound sour.

"Mirai?" I raise a brow at her.

"Of course, mirai."

The light comes on over the 3V surface of the coffee table, and Caran pulls his feet out of the glow. The first few images are introductory frames to a 101 lecture in nonlinear dynamics. They scroll fast, then slow and stop on an animation of a ball rolling down a funnel.

"Consider a simple nonlinear system with a point attractor. It doesn't matter where the ball starts; it always ends up down the hole." Noa's voice comes from the 3V speakers. "I place the ball on the near edge of the rim, it goes down the hole. I place it on the far edge of the rim, it goes down the hole.

"I can describe this ball-and-funnel system with a set of differential equations, involving well-defined variables and parameters such as incline and friction. With these equations, I can predict that for any initial conditions—for any starting place of the ball—the ball will end down the hole."

I may not be able to grasp the equations that sprawl across the 3V, but I can grasp the idea a predicable outcome. It's a funnel, after all. I nod.

Noa continues. "Contrast this with a complex nonlinear system with a chaos attractor."

A swirling electromagnetic storm on Io replaces the funnel.

It's beautiful—auroras and forks of electric-light. "In this system, the first challenge is in defining the variables and parameters involved. Some, like proximity to Jupiter, clearly matter. But others—does the plume of dust kicked up by a miner's rover have an impact?

"Worse, in chaotic systems like storms, stock markets, and ecologies, the initial conditions matter. Recall in our funnel system, the trajectory was predicable and outcome the same, no matter where the ball began. For an EM storm on Io, the trajectory and outcome of the storm will vary greatly depending on where it started.

"In all these centuries and us having populated the stars, we still can't tell with certainty if it will rain more than a few days out. Not even coaction mechanics can give us that, although it has improved our accuracy."

Caran pipes up. "Noa got an award for creating coaction mechanics. New branch of mathematics, right next to dynamical systems. Cuts wicked problems like storms on Io or impacts of policy change on the judicial system down to almost manageable."

I'm quite sure he's speaking more from pride than interest.

Noa stares into the swirling EM storms on the 3V. "Coaction mechanics helps with variables. But it does nothing to address the problem of initial conditions. We still need to know where things start in order to predict where they end. And we still will never know where they started, or even what at the start will matter further along. This is the proverbial butterfly effect."

"Your miner's dust plume being the proverbial butterfly?" I raise a brow and smile at Noa's adaptation of the old chaos theory metaphor.

"One needs to know when and where the miner's dust plume occurs to predict the course of the storm—including whether or not the miner's plume matters at all. Coaction mechanics is an approximator, not a crystal ball."

"But mirai is." My throat goes dry with awe.

The playback pauses. "Not. Quite." Noa's voice grinds out of her mouth. There is a long pause, and then it emits fluently from the speakers again. "Coaction mechanics came from my imaginings of ways to approximate unknown variables in nonlinear systems."

She's reciting from her lecture "Three Perspectives on Modern Dynamics" now; I watched it during my interview prep.

She continues, "I wondered, is there a way to approximate initial conditions by regressing a sequence of states with an approach similar to coaction mechanics? What I discovered, however, was that I didn't need to know initial conditions to predict the system behavior. I only needed to know current conditions—if—and this is the surprise!—if I added an expression to the equations for the influence of an invisible consciousness. A deus ex machina, right there in my maths."

"And your deus ex machina ended up being the élan vitals." I whistle softly through my teeth, stopping as I see Caran wince. I never claimed to have a sense of pitch.

"You know the implications of the mathematics. Everybody knows the implications of the mathematics." Noa's voice comes from her mouth again. "Questions?"

"Yes," I say, "how does this relate to what your miner-rescue-thing?"

Noa remains an intense living statue, but Caran looks at her with worry all over his body.

She twitch-shrugs, as if to dismiss his attention, and says aloud, "I used mirai. To predict dangers. To predict diamonds. I gathered all the real-time data so I could make further-out predictions. Less margin-of-error. I ran mirai on the lab's stationary quantum systems. Augmented with my navis. If I knew when disaster was likely. I could open a channel to the miner's radio. I would warn them away. From disaster." It's the most words I've ever heard her utter in a single stint, and she's not done. "Back then, mirai only worked on Io because I didn't understand. That my parameters were for Io-élan. But they worked. Like magic. But I am a scientist. So myth encroached on fact and I became the Demon of the Diamond Plains."

Noa goes silent, like her batteries have run out. Caran takes her hand and holds it; her fingers twitch around his and go white-knuckled.

All of the records I've read on Noa say she's healed of her various traumas, other than some nerve damage that can't be compensated for with her navis' programming. But that's the thing about trauma, isn't it? It doesn't ever heal, not really.

"That's really helpful, Noa, thank you. Caran, are you ready to begin?"

◇

I wake to the new composition ringing across the threshold of sleep. Aurora-bells tinkle over the broody bass of hard lava. Fragile flutes and analogue synths float wisps of ash, repeat, sustain, until it becomes predictable and then! The brass shimmer of a diamond's spark. It's Io's song.

I'm not restrained. I don't feel sick.

Except for the dark creep of shadows. The cold, hard promise of Dividia's dreams.

No, no, no you don't, don't you summon that thing here. Io's song, sing it again, sing it now.

I hum the new composition and the room feels brighter.

Whatever dose of NQ she's got me on is pretty sweet; I've got everything but the rush. There's a plate of food and a medi-derm patch on a stool next to my gurney. The sunsim lights are dark and the drip bag's almost empty. Noa's on her back on a long black couch, her face and arms reflecting the aurora's half-light as it flickers through the holes in the ceiling. The colored light undulates, making her look like she's underwater. She's got busy eyes beneath her closed lids; REM or deep in her navis, who knows. She stays still when I slide off the bed.

Fuck it's quiet here. I miss Muse. I stare at the diamond on the counter and think hard at it to keep me company, but it gives nothing back. If I've got to be alone, I can't well be sober for it; Noa's got to have some booze around here somewhere. Or more tranqs.

I eat the soft magenta and yellow food. It's weird but tasty. The nutrients make my blood buzz like they always do when I've gone too long without eating, like Mx. Chanderamani's food bars. The drip bag's empty so I take out the needle and stick on the derm. House is full of shadows. Have a hum for courage, Io's song, yeah. Figure out where the fuck I am.

It's a wide, low, ranch house. Place is big enough to house twenty, but I don't find a single personal item—clothing, flatshots, ornaments. Most of the building's consumed by jungle.

There's a big box of rations beneath the double-wide kitchen sink and I salivate because I can't get at the meal bars fast enough. Delicious. I'd pocket a few but fuck clothes. Instead, I eat three and stash a few in the chair cushions for later.

In the lab area, a stationary system hums, first normal electrical sound I've heard on Io. I turn on the 3V to see what it's up to and get some complicated weather-and-earthquake report based on real-time telemetry.

Harmonize with the hum, yeah, good. Vials of liquids, jars of seeds, coils of wires, I don't fucking know what this shit is. Djen would probably know. She's the better detective. Gotta get what I know about Dividia to her soon as possible.

Past the lab lie the remains of a windowed walkway, wall-and-ceiling shattered long ago; only beams remain sticking from shattered glass.

And past that's a shed.

And in the shed's the skeletons in Noa's closet.

Boxes of clothing from at least fifteen different people. Flatshots of families. Paintings of lily pads. Collections of jewelry. Boxes of shipment records, employee rosters, gardening schedules. Invoice lists of food and seeds and fertilizer, protein baths, gene splicers, broken dolls, monster parts, and dead things in jars.

What? Back that right the fuck up.

Yeah, inventory lists of broken dolls and monster parts and dead things in jars, taboo technology, a locket with a picture burned out, a lock of hair disintegrating with time, the sphere of a blue-green Earth before humanity destroyed her... This is an inventory of the ill-used, abandoned things that filled Dividia's temple. They shipped in through HERE.

Oh no way, no-fucking-way.

Noa was lying about knowing Mallory, lying about knowing Dividia, this is a trap, a nightmare on nightmare so I can never rest, never a moment's peace with CryCorp's sigil stamped on every incriminating invoice, every bar of food, every piece of equipment, every—

Shit, calm down. CALM THE FUCK DOWN

Opera breaths.

Okay? Okay.

The invoice is dated from twenty years ago, Earth-standard. Twenty *years*. Signed off by "Markus Ravi, Project Director," who's not here anymore. All these records, personnel files, all dated between twenty and twenty-two years ago. Scratched in the corner of each employee file with an awl or the point of a knife is a date from nineteen years ago. Everything's cracked and pitted, portions unreadable, like they've been through a disaster. Only Noa's record has no date, but someone's used the tool to scratch out all her information. To scratch out her eyes.

What had she said? "Nineteen years alone, no CryCorp." Cracks in the ceiling of the shed. Fissure in the ranch's roof. Shattered walkway, crumbled wall, encroaching jungle. Disaster. Humming louder, yeah, gotta keep away the darkness.

A point of light appears, dancing flicker-flash, red-and-gold. Io-élan is back, trying to communicate with me here in the shed.

I sing my Io song to her, but she doesn't hook my frequency so I must not have the melody right yet. She dips and sparks and disappears.

I go to where she was and brush aside the debris.

Inside an orange box, a blood-stained siliplas map shows Io's Keroessa Plain and sites for Lab1, Lab2, and Milktown 11. Lab2's scratched out; an arrow shows Lab1's moved. Beyond Keroessa, beyond the badlands, on the Marduk Plain, the map-updater has scratched an atmo-dome symbol labeled "Milktown 12." I put my finger on Milktown 12: the living Milktown where Jordis abandoned me. I put my other finger on Milktown 11. The dead Milktown where Mallory and the thug brought me. Lab1—I move my first finger to follow the etched arrow—is here, where I am. Scratched out, moved, cracks in the wall, disaster...

Underneath the map rests colorful clothing, beautiful silks. They look like they'd fit Noa.

Below that, siliplas pages of maths. Djen taught me just enough for background programming, and I picked up what I needed for the kinetikosonus, but otherwise never cared. This is advanced dynamical systems stuff; I only know the basics.

Near the bottom of the box is a worn cloth mouse. I cradle it against the hole in my chest and keep digging.

Fuck—there must have been a huge Io-quake. Plates moving, Lab2 destroyed, Lab1 moved. Everybody died.

Except Noa.

<what happened here io-élan?> I think/feel as hard as I can, but the moon doesn't answer. Does Noa know about Io-élan? Does she know there's a compressed fractal piece of an ancient alien curled in the hunk of raw diamond on her kitchen counter? Why did Io want me to see Noa's things?

I sift through more maths and frustrated scratching in shorthand.

I clutch the worn cloth mouse tighter, tight enough to feel it.

At the bottom of the pile, I find the luminous sphere of a Cooke Award.

◊

"How did you deal with the fame?" Caran asks.

I, Noa, jerk out of the Marduk sensor network. The simsun lights are warm on my face. Ghosting through the plain so far away, I hadn't sensed the dome shift from night into day. Pull threads from telemetry, stationary systems. Reallocate into: linguistics, sensory, motor control. Open eyes.

"How?" He stands two meters from me, naked, holding Mousie

by the paw. Longing catches my breath in my throat. He is beautiful. I have been so lonely.

He raises my Cooke Award into the faux daylight, igniting the asterism at its center into a starburst of light. "How," he arches his neck, "did you deal with the fame?"

Belatedly I realize, "You. Went through. My things."

"Yeah, sorry." He looks down, plays with the pile on the carpet with his toes. "I'm—I didn't mean to. Io showed them to me. Something terrible's happening. I was investigating. CryCorp trapped me at the old Keroessa Milktown. I escaped and Io brought me here, to Lab1. This is Lab1, right? She showed me where to find the map, in your things. How good's your communication with her? I need to ask her some stuff."

The tiny hairs on my arms raise in ionized air at mention of Io. I look at the diamond on the counter.

He swerves topics again in a way that would get him hit in Socialization. "This is yours, right?" His shiny black eyes flash between me, the Cooke, me again. "Coaction mechanics, that was you. Fucking useful shit that math, know a lotta nauta who use it. I've used it. You're famous back in the Core. Not as famous as—"

◇

I don't want her to know.

But I do want her to know.

I want her to understand me, and if she got a top award too, she might.

But if she doesn't it'll kill me.

I stare into the Cooke like it's a crystal ball. I never thought I'd meet anyone who could understand me these ten fucking pent-up years, because who else is nauta with a big famous award?

My jaw clenches until my teeth squeak. Fuck I hate that sound. "How did you deal with the fame? Did you love the fans loving you? What did you do when they hated you? What's your hole, Noa, you got a hole? Did they fill you up? Are you lost without them?"

◊

Loving? Lost?

No, no, squirming, exposed, stuttering on the feeds, embarrassment burning bright. I hid like Mousie.

"No. No love. No fans. Just mainfeed. Sell adverts. Why."

He drops to the floor in physical poetry and folds his legs. "You really don't know who I am, do you?" His face contorts, conflicts.

I want to tell him all pasts are burned away in Io's fire, but my neurotranslator is too damaged to express such a complicated thought.

I want to touch him. He calls to me like a diamond, dangerous and rich. I don't care that he went through my things; it is time to let the past go. I am lonely. I am not Mousie. The last time I was intimate with one of my own kind was more than twenty-five years ago. I want him inside me.

◊

She slides onto the floor, crawls over, places her hands on my knees, hard, so I can feel it.

Under pressure of her kindness I tremble. Fuck don't cry again. Don't cry. Don't cry. Too many feelings. Can't handle it gonna explode.

◊

I want to know if the rest of his skin is as warm as his knees.

I want to know if his caresses are as expressive as his voice.

I want, I want, I want like the miners want a diamond. His skin is soft and trembling, now I'm trembling, we tremble like fomori mice. Mousie is trembling in his hand.

Why would he ever want a monster, a demon like me?

BUT I WANT

◊

"I'm—" fuck. No.

Yes.

I'm gusting out a huge, stressed breath. It's just like back on the *Stella-Maru* with Djen, I've got a good thing going, I can stay here, get clean, forget about the shadows, the nightmares, the dark blue lies.

Smear that fucking tear off your cheek, asshole, and confess who you are. See if she still wants anything to do with you after that.

She smells of earth and sweat and she's coming on to me. If I were smart, I'd shut up and kiss her, but I'm not smart, I'm terrified. Okay. Okay.

"Galaxy Awards, Noa, you know what those are?"

"All Worlds Music Consortium. Top prize."

"Seven. I have seven Galaxy Awards. One for every set release I've made. Everyone loves me, all the inhabited worlds, and they've no fucking idea that I'm a—"

Ten years of silence explode in a wordless scream.

◊

I hide my face, hide my guts, static in my hair, no, NO, Markus screaming and winging plates like frisbees at my chest and motor controls too slow to duck they hit, hit, hit and hit—

Glitch, glitchy, GODSDAMNIT. Good for nothing feeble retard Noa. "I AM NOT LIKE YOU."

◊

Not like you. There it is. The judging.

"Well fuck you too!" I hurl the Cooke Award across the room where it hits the sofa and stills, momentum damped like a life-unlived on the thick, white carpet.

◊

I slap him.
I can't speak.
I can only hit.

◊

The world stops as the bullies smack me in the jaw.

◊

I curl away to protect my soft places.

◊

"Fuck you, noa, fuck you to eternity in the hell i came from."

◊

He leaves so fast i feel his wind on my neck.

◊

"I'm so sorry," Jordis Ansari breaks the link, "I know I'm interrupting, but this is the only time I have."

It's like walking in on a terrible fight because that's exactly what it is.

Jordis' eyes flick to Noa and Caran. They're still pressed against each other, but Noa's face is red and angry, and Caran snarls at Jordis from the past before his eyes clear into the present. They're still holding hands, but Noa's clenching so hard Caran's fingers have gone white. She emits a low, soft growl and her fingers relax.

Despite Io-élan's silent heat I feel icy-cold and a little faint at the deeply personal nature of what they're sharing. The very first thing I need to do after this session is compose a message to the ethics board about updating our protocols for telempathic or élan-assisted interviews, particularly with individuals who have perfect recall. I know they are sharing willingly and signed the consent forms, but this is not a normal level of disclosure for an interview.

"Hey, boss," Caran smiles at Jordis.

She straightens her already-straight seams, checks her bun, and makes for the chair with her tall, business-like grace. "I brought you some cake," Jordis says to him, "seeing as we were talking about cake."

Caran takes the small, wrapped package from Jordis, looks inside, and grins. He shovels confection into his mouth, spraying crumbs all over my couch.

For Noa, Jordis extends a digipage.

Noa takes it and cocks her head sideways at it, hair swishing to veil half her face. "Very good. This is very good."

I look at Jordis, who shrugs.

"Personnel and equipment orders." Jordis takes a deep breath, brushes invisible dust off her sleeve, and focuses on me. "I've been thinking about what else I can fill in about Europa while Caran was on Io, without violating any laws and agreements."

"Thanks, I appreciate it." As before, Io-élan does not pull Jordis into the link. Cami told me during the training that Jordis and Io-élan have no natural resonance so it's not a surprise, but it makes me eager for the all-way connection Cami says will be possible when Muse holds the link. "*Muse resonates with everybody*," I hear Cami's cheery voice in my memories.

Jordis crosses her legs and wraps her hands around a knee. "After I realized my father and Ellison were behind the anti-Operator Genetic Liberation Front propaganda, I gave Som and Ammiel the evidence."

"Did you take any direct action, or just provide information?" I ask Jordis.

"Just information. I was an enforcer, not an advisor. Could you imagine a corporate enforcer telling a CFO what to do? No, that wasn't my place with Som. As far as Ammiel, I wasn't sure yet what action I wanted him and his revolutionaries to take."

"What was Som's reaction?"

Jordis laughs, not her usual polite, ambiguous sound, but the rumble of a fond memory. "He was quite displeased that my father and Ellison were inciting tensions. It hurt business, badly." She sobers and regards me with the ice of her gaze. "To understand my father, you need to understand that he was the k-mutation carrier. He's the reason I was born nauta and my half-brother Jordan barely qualifies as normal. Killing my mother may have made him feel better, but it did nothing to address the problem. My father's hatred of Operators ran deep and personal. Even the most bigoted of his inner circle didn't hate Operators the way he did, and many of them secretly railed against it. Everyone knows one of the reasons for Madame X's domination is her leniency toward Operators. A dog is more likely to obey its master if it is treated with kindness and respect."

Jordis says this off-handedly, as though she doesn't realize the vulgarity of the comparison of a dog to a nauta such as herself. Noa realizes it though, her mouth going into a hard, sad line and her shoulders twitching. Caran just licks frosting off his fingers.

Without inflection Jordis continues. "Then came the bombing of the Embassy Building, two days after I returned from Io."

The 3V over my coffee table explodes into a million billion shards of mirror-glass from the iconic structure. Slivers pierce suits and flesh, murder men and women from the Europan government, foreign dignitaries from the New Organization of Federal Banking Worlds, natives, tourists, diplomats, children, all equal now; their world ends in shivering glass.

The brutal image is gone in seconds. "The Genetic Liberation Front, of course, 'claimed responsibility.'" Jordis' gray eyes watch me carefully. "That's what decided me."

"'That?" I ask.

"'That' being the Europan government choosing a hundred innocent Operators by lottery and tearing their navi out of their heads as a 'lesson' regarding further terrorist activity. I decided to actively help Ammiel."

Jordis' emotionless stare, my knowledge of the history that follows this point, the cold realization of who I'm sitting in this room with, not just her but Caran and Noa as well, and Io-élan with the power to destroy us all—I stop breathing and the blood rushes to my extremities.

"Got any more cake?" Caran asks.

Is he oblivious to the tension, or breaking it on purpose? Fear banished in four words and Jordis' soft half-laugh. "Eat it slower and it will seem like more."

"But it's cake," he gripes like a small child and rubs sticky fingers on my couch.

Jordis rises. "I've got to run. But I'll be here on Mars for a little bit so I'll check back in when I can."

"Thanks," I rise and shake her hand on the way out.

On the sofa, Noa has tilted her head onto Caran's shoulder as though it's become too heavy to hold up, and they've laced their fingers together.

"Are you two okay?" I ask. "This is heavy stuff; do you need a break? You know you don't have to tell me anything you don't want to."

Caran's shiny black eyes flash at me and he pokes himself in the head. "Excellent memory here, and Noa's got perfect recall. You don't need to repeat-o about informed consent; it's boring. I told you before, this story needs to come out. It's time. It has to. I don't care. People are gonna love or hate, doesn't matter what I do or say or feel, media'll spin it however they want. But it's time the whole story come out. I want to tell it."

"We all want. To tell it." Noa says in her clipped way. As Io-élan's link folds over us again in a wave of heat she completes her thought <there is healing in the telling too, steven, healing along with lava and tears>

◊

Stupid Noa. Stupid-feeble-retard Noa. Stupid to think I can be anything but a monster, a terror, a demon of the diamond plains. Broke, broken, glitchy GLITCH. He's going to come after me and try to hurt me for the rest of the NQ and I'm going to hurt him worse because I'm a monster and—

Flashing orange light in my side-vision: alert, alarm. He needs a new derm patch of NQ. Everybody lives.

I drip dark blue liquid onto the derm. I wish I was like him. I wish I could lose myself in the rush of the drug. Forget the volcano inside. But I only made the mistake of taking a rush-dose once. Never again. The miners need me.

Reallocate threads to motor and narrow perceptual filters to near-in focus: max-processing. Turn off linguistics.

I grab the derm and throw some vegetables and bread in a bag for lunch in case this takes a while and track him into the jungle. He's left broken branches and squashed grasses. Good for the foot-pollinating iron-clover. Bad for the crushed sulfur-cricket. Need to rebalance dome parameters to accommodate another person. Can't reallocate threads yet. Fifteen minutes in, he gives me music instead of destruction to track.

He is just past the obsidian boulder two clicks from the ranch. I approach low, like a jacklet. He stands in the small grove of prometheus laurels, jungle stuck to his naked skin: magenta seed pod, blade of pale grass. Mousie clutched in his hand as he vocalizes long off-key moans and eerie howls strung thinly between fragments of melody that collapse before they can become. The laurel leaves shiver silver and violet. The su-bees whisper a dissonance of need. It's a lonely, broken song that feels like it's calling to the moon. Like Io's diamonds, beauty forged in rage.

The melody-fragments come together into full-fledged song.

Atonality into harmony. Need into hope. The melody reaches into the shivering laurels; the su-bee's hum resolves to counterpoint.

Caran clicks his tongue in the warning-sound of the sulfur-crickets. The crickets return the chorus. The chirp of the pyromantis, the rustle of a fomori mouse—the whole jungle an orchestra.

I click back, creep closer so he can see me in the bushes. The music has freed his face of pain; his eyes invite me in.

I step out. He reaches a hand.

I tap a soft beat against his warm skin. He taps back. I drum-slap-clap against his palm, and he complicates the rhythm until I can't keep up and then he laughs and brings it back down where I can follow. I click and trill, demonstrating the full range of the sulfur-crickets' song. He leads them in a round with the melody. The whole moon joins in, the hairs on my arms lifting in a unified electrical hum.

At the end, silence completes the song.

The sense of Io's electricity retreats, but the spark between Caran and me remains. He loves my wilderness. Loves it as I do, enough to bring it into song. To acknowledge the su-bees and the jacklets that purred softly, once, in the underbrush.

He draws a new breath, opens his mouth, then closes it again. He shivers, frowns, and jerks away from me, with a twitch and wince.

I take his hand, press it, show him the inside of my pack. I expect him to go for the derm; that is nerve pain. But he reaches for my lunch instead, wild like a starving man. He mops up the crumbs of his devouring from the ground with the tip of his finger.

He smiles, makes an unapologetic half-shrug, and applies the derm. Then he worries at the patch, probably wondering if it is strong enough for his words to come back.

It is. For the next two days at least, until the weening dose goes below the threshold of effect.

I take his hands, wishing the motor program that made a smile still worked. I squeeze instead. He tries, not hard, to twist away, but I don't let him go. I pull him closer in and press my cheek to his. I say, "I understand. You couldn't do. The music. If they knew. You hid. Masked. Music is life." I stop, waiting for my glitchy neurotranslator to catch up with my thoughts. "I want you to know. If I couldn't do. The math. Math is life. I would too. Have hid. Myself. The same as you."

He weeps. Not the desperate, panicked tears of yesterday, but the silent, shuddering of relief.

◊

I slip out of the link before Io-élan drops it.

Caran curls in Noa's lap, her arms around him, face buried in his tangled hair.

I exit, leaving only the click of the office door behind me.

I arrive early the next day.

Everything is how it always is: sofa, chair, table. My chair on the other side of the table. I push aside the curtains on the windows to reveal the dusty Martian plains, desperate to make something appear different because it's *just not right* that everything should look the same when everything is different.

Different like I woke up this morning grinning wildly and hard as an adolescent, my heart thumping because in mere hours I'd be seeing Caran.

Different like curling up on my side two seconds later in terror, as my selfsame heart tried to thump its way out of my mouth, because in mere hours I'd been seeing Caran.

Different like having feelings at all because I've done my best to avoid the type of interactions with people that would have given me feelings and I'm not used to them.

Thin light filters in through the windows. The sky is clear of the wispy clouds that skitter through the atmosphere—unimaginable amounts of greenhouse gasses and terraforming magic. We can do anything it seems. We can turn Mars into a more livable planet than Earth. We can create a novel ecosystem that thrives on the hell-moon on Io.

But we can't stop hurting people who are different from our-selves.

Can there be a world in which children who are different aren't abused? Could there be a world where I—

Where I don't understand some part of Caran's pain.

My hand twitches against the cream-colored curtain. Outside a dust-devil eddies around a potted plant on the walkway leading toward the Geology Complex next door. The Researcher. I like being The Researcher.

"Steven?" Caran's voice behind me, the tones of a dream. My pulse quickens and my knees go weak. "What's out there?"

I swallow compulsively, still looking out on the Martian land-scape. The dust-devil teases the edges of the walkway as though it has motive. I feel the heat of Caran's body coming through his thin white dress. I smell his sweat; perhaps he's been dancing. "Noth-ing," I say. " A dust-devil. Just opened the curtains to let in some natural light."

He moves closer and puts a hand on my arm, the edge of his hip brushing my thigh. He lacks any subtlety; he's coming on to me. In another setting I would let him. Maybe I am letting him.

He sings, "The light is thin and not-our-home but it'll do / it'll do for hearts and bones."

I've never heard this song. Between its quirky meandering and how well I've gotten to know him, I sense he's just made it up to express his complicated feelings. The heat off his hip is so warm.

The door swishes open and Noa comes in. "Dust devil. Can be modeled with fluid dynamics. That is. A large one."

I startle and flush, but I haven't done anything wrong, really, I'm still the researcher, I can pull myself together. They're both here now and I can feel someone else's feelings instead of my own.

Caran in-and-exhales one of his large opera-breaths and shakes out his hands before walking Noa to the couch. He takes both of her hands in his and puts all of the hands on his lap. Her hands are larger and poke out between his thin fingers. She is stiff as always, but as the influence of Io-élan enters me I can feel her heart flutter. I feel her fear like choking.

"To have all evidence and not see solution." Noa says, staring in her intensity over my left shoulder. "You know how that is, Steven? When you have all data, have completed analysis, but cannot interpret?"

My laugh of solidarity comes out more nervous than I'd like. "Every scientist worth their salt knows how that is."

"Mirai," Noa says, "Future equations. My maths weren't working. I couldn't find the solution. I got frustrated and added an expression describing the strange ambient energy that built up around me sometimes on Io, as though it had conscious intention. Complex waveforms signifying resonant or dampening dynamics, strength of signal, exact bandwidths—I thought it was just noise. Didn't expect accurate prediction. Predicted currents in a cup of hot tea. Predicted how dust blows across the Keroessa Plain twenty-four hours in advance. Predicted electrical storms a half-day's range from the lab. Every time. But only things on Io. As though this ambient energy prickling around me were influencing the behavior of the whole moon. And then—"

The link establishes itself with Io-élan's hot flash and chaos.

<—then there was io-élan inside cái morgan's diamond, sitting on my counter. io-élan guiding me to the miners on the diamond plains. io-élan wrapped up in everything i lived and breathed and was—> Noa's telempathic voice cuts off. Her remaining breath releases in a small, hot exhale.

◊

"You really, truly, totally, for real have no booze in this whole dome? Even though you could ferment any of these fruits and vegetables? None? None at all?"

I offer him another shot of polydorozopam instead. Whatever he's going through can't be easy. Who am I to deny some small relief?

He sighs and quiets on the soft white carpet where we sit. I think he might sleep now, but instead he pushes himself up with his back against my sofa. He curls his arms around his knees. Voice blurred with sedative, he asks, "How much do you know about Io?"

"I live here." I don't know how to explain that, as a complexologist working on terraforming a new ecosystem, I know Io better than anyone.

"Not Io-the-moon," he says, eyes closed, "Io-the-alien-who-appears-like-light-and-need."

The bottom drops out of me. The memory leak starts to trigger into the smell of burning flesh.

NO. Stop. I am in the here-now.

"Know anything about Dividia? The other alien that lives here, not so friendly with Io?"

I bite my tongue and taste blood. Everybody dies. "No."

"Io-the-alien's attracted to you. You and she are really similar. You talk to her at all?"

Demon on the hillside. Demon in my blood. Phantom radio in my rover and the death-heat of the diamond on the counter. "Not." I stutter. "Not. Not on my terms."

"You know about resonance, Noa? Between you and Io, between us humans and the élan vitals?"

NO (burning flesh), NO (demon on the hillside), NO (Io), NO (me)! "No." I say. The recall subsides.

◊

"I was five years old," I tell Noa, "when I met my first élan. It was night. She was gone, my mother, out to a bar or something. Whatever. Didn't matter. Something more important than me. I was scared. Always scared."

(We are inside Caran's childhood memory, naked, confused, thoughts in whistling soundscapes of fear—)

scrape-creak / shadow-creep

it's gonna get me gonna get me oh no oh no oh oh

no moons, two suns, no moons, shadows from the streetlight help, help, help me

help

"ba-ba-ba" sound bounce, cover it up, cover it over, finger-twitch under sheet screet-scrape screet-scrape the sound is coming it's coming

don't want to cry please no cry please, please, it hurts my face, burns my eyes, hurts my lungs, please don't cry

if only I could move help me please

no! "RAAAAAAAAAAAAAAR!" NO TEARS

wobble-breath, scrape-tap the sheets make a song with the scrapes and the creaks and the monsters and give a voice to the shadows "LA! LA!" scritch-pat "LA!" scritch-patta-pat "LA!"

THE SHADOWS MOVE

animalpanicvisioneyesblur

THE SHADOWS MOVE

too scared to scream

glow.
too scared to breathe
glow.
too scared to—
glow.
?
GLOW.
there is a ball of glow?
PULSE-GLOW! Bursting into light. <*greeting!* i am *glow* i reveal in light:>
- scrape-creak = branches against window
- shadow-creep = shirt, chair, boot
- screet-scrape = a finger against the sheet
<will you have me will you hope me will you be my friend?>
"La, lah?"
PULSE-GLOW!
"Tra-la?"
PLUSE-GLOW-COLOR!
"Haha," I'm laughing; it's making me into laughter.
It breaks into waves of rainbow light.
"When I got old enough to have the concept of names, I called it Muse," I tell Noa as the 'roze blurs over the hole in my heart where the creature should be. "It was an alien, an élan vital, like the spirit haunting Io, like CryCorp's Dividia. I had no clue, so I called it Muse. My Muse. My shadow-killer, standing between me and darkness. But it isn't like the other élans, around forever talking to stars. Instead it—it was new. Maybe? The other élans, they called it 'detached.' They said it was incomplete. Made them nervous."
Train of thought drains off; she gave me a fine hit. I could just fall asleep...but the Dividia nightmare can't come true. "Resonance,

Noa. Know what that is?"

"Oscillations with similar frequencies amplifying each other. Celestial bodies locked in a periodic ratio of revolution; example: Io, Europa, Ganymede. Super-excited, transient subatomic particles. Linked, high energy chemical structures. A heartbeat."

I sing the low note Noa said vibrates her temple bones. "Intensification of vocal tones. Amplification of sound from sympathetic vibrations. Invocation of emotions. Significance." I imagine rainbow waves of light in the air, trace them with my finger smiling at memory. "The aliens, they're sensitive to slow-wave EM signal, including our thoughts, our feelings, the heat of our bodies. Name one Muse and it aligns itself to act the part. Call one Io and it's gonna feed off the storms, the moon, and the miners, and you—it loves you best of all. Gonna align themselves to become more like what we are, in a way. Gonna align us into more of what they are, in a way. We shape each other. They don't die, but we can change them, and they can change each other. They fear changing through resonance the way we humans fear death. It's like a loss of identity."

◊

On the floor of my ranch, he opens his eyes and catches mine in their too-bright gaze before I flinch away. "We control each other, Muse and I." His tone goes aloof. "Events, they simply warp around us. Everything aligns itself to us. We are too big, Noa, too linked. Like Io's orbital resonance, locked in. There's no boundary of influence between us, and we step all over the world. And the world steps all over us."

I am shivering. I am not cold; I am on the edge of discovery. I am on the edge of memory leak triggers, too. If what he says is true, then I truly am to blame for killing everyone. "Danger," I click the danger-sound of the sulfur crickets. "Your Muse, you—"

"It doesn't always want what's best for me, no." Caran's laugh is bitter. "But then, neither do I. The point, Noa, is that resonance can reinforce something good or it can reinforce something terrible, and lucky for everyone all Muse and I want is art, and that's dangerous enough. But in the wreckage of abandoned Milktown humans have constructed a space to amplify and attract ideas of fear and hate, and there's an élan they've aligned with it named Dividia."

"Trouble," I say, "trouble."

"Yes, it's trouble. It's a weapon. If the rest of the élans find out about it, they're going to make a lot of trouble too. We promised them we wouldn't do shit like weaponize them."

But I mean the word. *Dividia*—it's a Latin word; it means trouble. Trouble trouble trouble. Name a thing and it acts the part he says. It's my fault. It's all my fault. Everybody dies. Screams on the hill, a jag of light.

Caran continues, "CryCorp's been nurturing Dividia since you first got here. Maybe longer. I don't know how they found the élan, if they caught one and stopped it from communicating with the rest somehow or if it's 'detached' like Muse. But I found the inventories for Dividia's temple in your shed, I found the plans for Lab2—that's what Lab2 was for, right—but then something happened? An Io-quake. A disaster. CryCorp wants to use Dividia and me for some reason I don't understand, but I'm sure it's bad. You understand? You gotta help me understand because Dividia resonates with me, Noa, me, this thing they fed and coaxed and turned into a hate-machine wants to fill me."

MEMORY LEAK PLAYBACK I CAN'T HOLD BACK:

The ground tilts, toppling me into perfect recall—

"I need readings, Noa, now. Do you hear me? Do you un-der-stand?" Markus' deep voice, patronizing, frustrated, shatters my concentration again.

If only I could tell him to shut up, I need to concentrate, I'm juggling thousands of variables trying to find a hole in this EM storm. But if I do, he'll hit me for backtalk. To him all I am is a broken machine.

"Noa!" Markus bellows and hits me anyway.

"Nrgh." I lose the last thread of focus. Markus has a handsome face, bronzed skin and shiny curls. But he's mean, not just to me but to the whole science team. He knows my life is at risk every time I reach outside the dome to pull telemetry. I'm at risk every time I run the programming that keeps me talking and walking and tracking the complex interpersonal interactions of the team well enough to act like a normal. My cheek smarts. I wish Markus would get zapped by an EM spike.

"What is going on, No-ah?" Markus snips. "Do you understand what is hap-pen-ing? I need those readings. Yes-ter-day."

"I'm trying to find an eye in the storm." I pull my hair back in the circle of my thumb and forefinger and open a shortwave band to the 3V projection plate to show Markus and Joe, standing by with the drill and the last of the geotherm lines, what the storm looks like. It's beautiful enough in visible light, and even more-so when I add spectra. It's deadly, though. The currents in the EM storm are chaotic, unpredictable even with the tools of modern complexology. The telemetry instruments outside the dome's shielding have, rightly, shut themselves off, but Markus demands a manual reset and read. If I get my signal crossed with the storm, the damage to my nervous system could be—

"We're three months behind schedule, No-ah. Do you un-der-stand? What good is your award-winning," he spits sarcasm, "co-action mechanics if I can't get my line laid? Good-for-nothing feeble retard." Markus kicks up the sulpherphiliac thistle seeds Ning Ning laid in the ground last week. I anticipate another slap, but this time he turns away, disgusted by my presence.

Joe shrugs helplessly behind Markus' back. He's the only person on the research team with less power than me and the only one who is remotely kind. He's a very good botanist, but he's working off a sentence for growing tracer weed without a corporate charter. "No money in the science," he grinned when we first met. He always got the worst jobs, shoveling fertilizer, working out the microbial balance in the lav holes. Today, drilling wells in the hard, sulfurous soil and laying piping. I've seen him scrawling his own notes on siliplas sheets; he is at least as good a botanist as Ning Ning.

Markus is right. What good am I, really? My maths are not predictive enough to navigate the storms. I need the initial conditions. I wish I trusted the mirai equations. But this morning they predicted a magnitude 9 quake, which is clearly wrong. All other data and models set the probability of anything above mag 2 so slim, in fact, that the only way mag 9 would occur is if the hand of a god really does reach down—or more accurately, up—from Io's core. That's the whole reason we'd decided to work on the geothermal system today.

"No-ah," Markus is shaking me, and it feels like shards of glass in my skin. I'd never known how badly slaps stung until I got here; I'd always been able to program them out with all of the other Markuses.

"Time, time, time." Markus shoves me. He can't keep his hands off me; it's only a matter of time before he violates me. "I can have you replaced you know. Do you un-der-stand?"

My eyes prick tears. As mean as Markus is, as hard as it is to function with all the storms, I love being here. I love the project, the dome, the fragile life poking through the sulfurous soil, the violent beauty of the aurora, the time to work on my own research. No housemom, no people controlling my schedule, no hobbles around my access to data—If Markus and the team were gone, I would be free.

I hope there is a mag-9 event today. I hope a crack will open and swallow everyone but me. Let the violent crust of Io take them all.

I turn to Markus, words rupturing from my mouth like liquid sulfur from Io's core. "No. I am irreplaceable. You will not call me names. You will never hit me again. You need me. Do you un-der-stand that I can turn the dome's defense systems on you any time I want." I swivel the nearest exterior litegun and fire three laser-white pulses of warning shots into the sky. "I can trap you without oxygen in the airlock, I can break your rover and I can flood your room with toxic gas without leaving my bunk. I am the ghost in the mechanicals of the dome, Mar-kus. I am the only one who can predict the perils of the land and I can lie to you about what I find. I can let you fall into a storm or a sinkhole or kill you with a thought as you dream. So no, I will not risk my life for your deadline today. Not now. Not ever." The air ionizes, raising all the tiny hair on my arms.

The ground rumbles; Markus stumbles back.

Electrical current shorts my navis; I fall.

Reprogram, reroute around damage. Reboot.

Electricity smears the air, crackles over the ground; the arc of the dome aflame with tendrils of blue lightning. A thick band of current strikes Markus and he explodes into chunks of wet meat. Joe freezes, eyes round, suspended by current before collapsing on the ground, smoking. The smell of burning flesh.

I stumble up, blood soaking my knees from the fall, bile in my throat. I try to scramble back to the ranch where there's better EM shielding, but can't figure out how to walk. Reboot. Again. Fast-patch surge-corrupted motor programming; run for the ranch where the rest of the team will be—

As I approach, I gag on the smell of cooked meat and the iron of blood, so much blood, so much, so much, no one here escaped the surge—

I wheel from the ranch and run, just run, deep as I can into the dome, smashing spouts, crushing eggs, trying to escape the smell of sulfur and iron and worse, reaching the rise at the center of the dome—

Where a woman-shape manifests in a rain of sparks.

Fire blows like fabric; parts of her flash in-and-out like aurora. Colored light all flicker-flash, a violence of the blacks and yellows of the diamond plains, a balm of the violets and greens of the sky. A face emerges, long and lean, not beautiful in any traditional way, but I want her. I want her with a violent, greedy desperation that is sexual but not sensual. I want to grab her, to lick her. To possess her. Devour her. Become her.

"No-ah-Oak-ie." The sound hisses from everywhere. "I am Eye-Oh."

The aftershock takes me to the ground.

"I am Io." The phantom wails. "And you are mine. They will hurt us no more!"

Current floods my navis. Electricity discharges into my brain, damaging soft tissue.

Darkness.

Something is bothering me. Someone is singing.

But that isn't right. I'm alone. I've been alone since the storm. Since the quake. Since the dome shifted nearly 100 kilometers on Io's unstable plates and became lost to navigation. Since I needed to use all of my spare tzaddium and all of my U4 on navis repairs.

Those things, they were all long ago. Something has changed since then. Someone is here with me, in the present. I am not alone.

No, I am alone. Everybody dies. It's my fault. I wished it and Io made it happen. I buried the team on the hill at the center of the dome.

But no, that was in the past.

In the present I'm shaking in Caran's arms. My throat is hoarse; I think I might have been speaking. My fault. Everybody dies. No-body gets a diamond. And now he knows. I am a monster.

I try, not hard, to twist away. He doesn't let me go any more than I had let him go back in the forest, when he was the one aching for absolution. He presses his cheek to mine. His voice vibrates in my bones. "Io needed to protect herself from Dividia. You couldn't have known what would happen, and even if you had, even if you'd understood the resonance between you and the moon, you couldn't have stopped Io-élan. They act on their own too, as do we, no matter how tightly linked."

◊

Noa has curled her expressionless, tear-streaked face into the heat of Caran's chest. His arms are around her, his face in her hair. It is role-reversed image of where they ended the last session.

Again, I leave them to be with each other.

As I close the office door, my own worst memories stutter into a lump of misery in my belly, into that place I usually fill with work to keep the misery out. I'm ashamed of my feelings; I have no right to them. I didn't go through anything nearly as horrible as they have.

Outside, I walk out into the thin light of the Martian plain. The dust-devil is gone.

The three of them enter together: Caran, Jordis, and Noa. Noa wears a bright silk sash with abstract designs. I watch their masks slip as they enter my space—small relaxations of muscle groups, less careful distance in their proximity to each other.

"Thank you for agreeing to meet a little early to accommodate Jordis' schedule," I say as they settle themselves into the usual spaces. They stare in silence, bringing to mind an image I've seen of the jacklets in Noa's dome—small, fierce, catlike creatures with round, staring gazes that could mean anything.

"Jordis, you were going to tell me a little more about what you were doing on Europa while Caran was at Noa's dome?"

"Ah, yes," Jordis crosses her legs and folds her hands over her knee, "I was still building the case that my father was behind the Genetic Liberation Front ruse. I needed more than just good statistical correlations of public data if I was going to convince the rest of the Galilean Black that their king no longer had their interests in mind. So I visited my little brother, Jordan."

"As you, or as Gala?"

Jordis' lips twitch up into a smile I would like to unsee. "As myself. I put a fair number of cards on the table and told him, 'Jordan, if you help me, you don't have to become Daddy.' He was rather interested."

"You convinced him you'd be able to do that, get him out of the line of succession?" She has a knack for sounding like she's answered a question when, in reality, the lack of detail is so complete it's like she's said nothing at all.

"My ability to slip undetected into his bedroom and my role as Key Enforcer for Madame X were both fairly convincing." She arcs a brow at me.

I stare back, arcing my own brow.

She laughs a little. "You're a hard man, Steven. No, I didn't torture Jordan or anything like that, if that's what you're wondering. My brother never wanted to lead the Galilean Black; he's ill-suited, un-motivated, and has real talent as a painter. All he needed was a sliver of hope and he handed me the encryption patterns to my father's personal datastores."

A whistle escapes my lips despite my best attempts at professionalism. No wonder she refused to tell this part through the link; the syndicate secrets her mind must contain!

"I found all the hard evidence I could ever want. My house! Dirtied by this foulness."

It's as close as I've seen her to displaying an unguarded emotion—her face tight and hands twitching as she spits the sentences with a disgusted tongue.

"Did you know Dividia had corrupted Europa-élan?"

The muscles in her neck twitch. "I should have, but no."

"Should have, why?"

"Because when I got back to Europa after dropping Caran on Io, Europa felt so different. *I* felt so different. Everyone was running on a kind of cornered urgency that didn't make logical sense. It was a fight-or-flight response on a societal level. I *had* to light the fire under Ammiel's unhobbled rebels. I *had* to oust my father. I *had* to make a chaos so great that only I could stop it, and if I couldn't, then total destruction was no less than everyone deserved. Europa was a sea of fear, and I was no more immune to it than anyone else."

"Europa the nation or Europa the élan?"

"Both. Look," she says, "I knew something was wrong, but I had no way to identify what. I was ignorant of our feedback with the élans, and of theirs with each other. I didn't know I could communicate intentionally with Europa. And I certainly didn't understand that a stronger, mobile élan like Dividia could realign her to become more like itself. I had no idea that the version of Europa-élan living inside Caran's dataslip had become, functionally, a different entity from the one resonating with me in the torus."

I take a few breaths around the terrifying implications of that. "So, at this point in the story, Ray Ansari and Ellison were stirring up civil unrest with GLF propaganda. Dividia had mutated Europa-élan into a hybrid Europa-Dividia entity, and an untainted fractal duplicate—Europa-élan prime for lack of a better term—lay compressed inside Caran's dataslip. You had no understanding of what Dividia was or the connection between Dividia and Ellison."

"Correct." Jordis stands and stretches, then sits back down.

"All right," I turn my focus on Caran and Noa. "But the two of you did understand that connection, right? "

"Yeah," Caran yawns. "We knew Noa's terraforming lab was originally just a front by Ellison's company CryCorp—"

"Not just! The terraforming was useful!" Noa insists.

"—to hide the secret temple-lab where they planned to tune Dividia's resonance, turning it into the fear-monster they wanted it to be. Io-élan wasn't up with that, though, so she destroyed the project with the Io-quake Noa survived. Didn't matter in the end, 'cause CryCorp set up the temple space for Dividia in old Milktown.

We also knew CryCorp wanted me, specifically, for some reason."

"So you knew Dividia was a weaponized élan, that you were possibly some sort of fuse, and that CryCorp was behind its creation."

"And I knew Dividia was responsible for that fucking freighter bombing that set this whole thing a-tinder."

Noa stares with her singular intensity over my right shoulder. "And we knew Io-élan had placed a fractal of herself in Cái Morgan's diamond."

"And Cái Morgan—" I begin my prompt but Caran cuts me off like he can read my mind even without an élan now.

"We didn't realize Cái mattered. I didn't tell Noa he was one of CryCorp's lackies, and she didn't tell me he was the one who gave her the diamond. Wouldn't be clear until we met Cami why Io-élan picked him to carry her back to Noa. Why he was there working for CryCorp."

"Why I had Cami's face on a flatshot and a good-luck coin in my pocket." Noa reminds us of Cái Morgan's dying gifts to her.

"All right," I say. "We can get more into that when Cami arrives. Is there anything else I'm missing?"

"The Puccini Roundup." Jordis says. "The environmental systems failed inside the Puccini Building in North Arc of Europa City and twenty-five died. It was a tragic accident from a shabby mechanical inspection. However, after my father's meddling in the media, the public believed it was a terrorist act by the GLF. Europan police rounded up the Operators who worked in the building and executed them out front. It drew a crowd of over five-hundred, craning and cheering like a medieval hanging."

"I'd been wondering how much that factored into things." I remember the sequence of events all too well. One of our junior faculty lost a sister.

"It factored in perhaps more than you realize." Jordis gives me a cool stare. "Ammiel said to me, 'If they want to play that game, by all means, we will.' He and his rebels proceeded to take over Europa's environmental systems for real. No one knew. They didn't take action—yet. But they were in control."

"All right, thanks. All of that was helpful," I say, to cover my shudders. "I want to be respectful of your time. Anything else you'd like to add?"

Jordis gives me the tiniest of headshakes. "Just a personal request be careful, Steven, when you analyze our stories. There are no heroes and villains in this or any real-life story; there are only people each thinking they are right from their own perspective."

This comment strikes me as curious coming from her, so I ask, "Even your father?"

Jordis stands to go, brushing non-existent dust off the tops of her trousers. She gives me a sad version of her small smile. "Yes. I hate the man, don't get me wrong. But, like anyone, he is a product of his experiences. He had only ever known power—either its passive benefit, or its active application. He'd experienced few negative consequences for his behaviors. You've interviewed high-end corporate CEOs. You know how it is. They fear nothing except that which can take away their power, and that they fear most terribly."

We stare at each other, her tall, slender form made harsh by the angles of her business suit blocking the light from the window. She isn't wrong. But I wonder if it should bother her more. "Thank you. Let me know when you're back on Mars."

"Most certainly. As always, it is a pleasure speaking with you."

I stand. She leaves.

"So, the two of you." I turn to Caran and Noa. "Take me back to Noa's dome." I say this but Io-élan doesn't flash open the link.

"I woke with a detox dose of NQ and nothing else." Caran's voice is sullen.

"That was the plan, though, right?" I prompt, unsure of where this is going or why they're staring at me instead of linking with me.

"The problem with being clean," Caran sighs, possibly answering my question, possibly meandering off, "is that it upsets the delicate balance of denial and spit that holds all the broken bits of yourself together." Tenderly, he takes Noa's hand.

Inappropriately, I wonder if this means our brief flirtation is over. Even more inappropriately the idea makes me dizzy with panic.

He lets out one of his vast sighs and smiles now to Noa, "That was a good day."

"Yes," Noa affirms, her mouth making the wistful smile which, through the quirks of her programming and neurological damage from Io, is one of her few expressions that makes it to her face.

"Everyone always wanted a piece of me." Caran twitches. "A piece to worship or a piece to hate, usually both, but not you, Noa. You just wanted—" He closes his eyes. "Every living thing in your dome, every stone, every clod of dirt, you loved it. Cared for it." His voice cracks.

He takes deep breaths and gets himself back under control while Noa waits. He finishes breathing and continues. "Fomori mice trilling their positions on the frequency the cat-like jacklets can't hear. Aurora dancing through the gash in the roof. Wanted to stay with you, sing at Jeanie's Hope. Vanish in the EM noise. Poof."

Noa closes her eyes and leans on Caran's shoulder. "You cupped my cheek and stroked my hair. It had been almost twenty years. Since I was around others. Since anyone had touched. Me. I wanted. You. To touch me."

"I couldn't think past one minute without falling back apart, so

I stayed in the now. Took up the harmony of your breath and the rustling jungle. Sound beyond the shattered wall."

"Singing. Coaxing the jacklets out."

"They came with huge eyes and soft muzzles."

"I sang." Noa smiles.

"Nice not to have to carry the melody alone." Caran smiles too.

"I showed you my proofs."

"I explained why they worked, because the ambient frequencies you'd added were Io's. You glowed!"

"I showed you where the flora and fauna crept beyond the dome. Transforming Io to life," Noa says.

"Napping on the grass." Caran hums.

"You ate too many meal bars, made yourself sick."

"We made love twice."

"Once wild, once soft."

"That was a good day." Caran finishes.

My face burns. I know now why they had not initiated the link. I do not want to take these memories from them.

"And then." Noa says.

"And then—" Caran echoes.

Io-élan's heat flashes through the room and flattens me into the story, reeling into Caran's perspective, sensory perception, cognition, altered entirely from how it has been before—

◊

I wake screaming at the same frequency as the terror-wail of a siren louder than bombs. Slam hands-over-ears, stumble-crawl into the ranch.

Blinking away tear-streaked pain at OH MY FUCKING SHIT

TOO MUCH SOUND seeing Noa on the couch, spine stiff, eyes wide, not responding as I fall into her line-of-sight.

Make it stop, I want to say, but I can't say anymore, too fucking clean for that, sing out instead against the sonic stabbing, "stop-stop-stop me Mercy / stop me Mercy you're killing me!"

She stays stiff, eyes looking in.

Have to let go of my ears to grab her shoulders; sound shakes loose tears.

"Nrg," Noa moans. Not sure if she said something or just making noise but she focuses on my face. "Proximity alarm." She breathes heavy, eyes white all the way round. Flashes of vision through shards of sound.

"Stop-stop-stop me—" I pant. How come she's not incapacitated from noise as well?

Because she's got sensory programming in her navis and your dose of NQ has gone below the threshold of effect, stupid.

Screeeeeeeee—she tears fabric from the hem of her t-shirt, shoves it into my ears.

Doesn't do much to damp the sound but gods I love her.

"Proximity alarm." She catapults from the couch, dragging me to the 3V plate in the lab, flash, scream, FUCKING IGNORE IT SHE'S TRYING TO SHOW YOU SOMETHING.

Projection, statistics above the plate. Twenty rovers jetting straight for us from the direction of Milktown, blazing with Cry-Corp's corporate sigil. Five prickling with weapons, battery power enough to take down the wall of an atmo-dome. Our atmo-dome. Blackness boiling around them as Dividia swallows the light. Loneliness and hate calling across the distance—I grip Noa in defiance: I AM NOT ALONE!

But it's an empty echo. I'll link with Dividia when it comes. It's too aligned with me.

How'd Dividia discover this place? Io-élan kept Noa's dome hidden for two decades. Something had changed, something.

Me.

I've brought Dividia to Noa's door.

"I have weapons." Noa clicks her teeth and the sulfur-crickets pick up the warning call. "Liteguns atop the dome. Landmines in the plain."

She could take out every one of those rovers and Dividia will still get me. I point at the darkness on the 3V and shake my head.

No time to find lines from songs, I pull a bag from beneath the counter.

"Ten minutes," Noa blinks at the 3V. "Ten minutes before we can't escape."

Can't concentrate with the screaming siren, got to stuff the bag full of food bars, schedule sheet from Dividia's temple, papers and evidence about Lab2—if I make it back to Djen she'll need to know—poor Mousie who can't be left here for Dividia to ravage WHY CAN'T YOU FUCKING TURN OFF THAT SOUND

Flash of shimmer-blue. That's NQ; Noa's put it in the side pocket.

"Caran. Put on clothes."

In my arms—a coverall, pair of socks, work boots. Coverall's scratchy, too big, what happened to the nice, soft things Jordis gave me? Work boots are terrible and there's no way I'll wear socks ever even if—

"Caran. Clothes. Now." Noa's hands pushing, prompting motions. Like Mindy. Like misery.

Fuck. How many minutes did I just waste unable to figure out how to move. If only I could have a few more drops of NQ—

I dress. Slow and clumsy, constantly forgetting what I'm doing.

Grab water, rations, evidence, blood-curdling riot of proximity alarm. Got to get away from the sound. Got to get away—

"Airlock." Noa pushing me. Jagged gash of the break in the wall, opening into jungle. "Airlock."

Running. Sounds grinding from above, white laser flashes in the sky. She's in the liteguns. Warning shots? Or fatal ones?

Fragments of green and slap of branches. Crash of dirt beneath my feet.

At the airlock she faces me with eyes looking elsewhere. "Put this on." Hazard suit in my hands. Her shrugging herself into hers.

Push, prompt, FUCKING ALARM WAIL, piling into Noa's old, beat-up rover, we've taken too long. I've cost us too much time. My fucking drug-less useless unable-to-do-anything-right fault. My fault Dividia's come to destroy us all. No way to outrun them now; can see CryCorp's fleet burning the distance across the violent yellow ground.

Laser-flash, proximity howl.

"You drive. Get me close. To the rovers. I will. Take care of. Cry-Corp. Dividia. We will. Noa-and-Io together. Move Earth. Scramble signal. You drive."

◊

Io's diamond is hot and glowing inside the suit with me.

(I, Steven, am plunged into a human-élan unity like Caran and Muse back in his hotel room, when they took over Jordis' mind. It is not Noa's point of view, not Io-élan's but some merger of the two.)

FRACTURE

I am the ground and the heat. I am the cold crust and the electricity in the sky. I am want and fire.

Flicker-flash!

YOU WILL NOT HAVE ME

NOBODY LIVES

NOBODY GETS A DIAMOND

I/we spin across the Keroessa plain, ballistic, racing toward the CryCorp rovers, racing toward the blackness. Close enough now to act.

They turn their weapons on my dome, my home, my reason for being.

My electricity falls from the sky, hot, bright light. Falling rain of rage. Destroying them! They are destroyed!

They open fire.

I/we scream.

We just obliterated them, how are they firing?

Dividia has tricked us, changed the landscape, made us see them as further away than they really are so we miss.

We miss!

The wall of the dome falls in shattered, slow-motion pieces outside the grav generator's influence. Purple and pale-yellow foliage. Red leaves. The fur of the jacklets. The blood of the fomori mice. Ivies floating through space, untethered, upended roots, firing into the dome firing on my home.

We know where they are now.

We pull fire from the ground; we pull fire from the sky.

We kill them.

We kill them all.

No one lives.

No one gets a diamond.

Watch them melt.

Watch them die.

We have killed them all.

The shadows don't die though. The shadows meet our light and vibrate, pulling our frequencies closer to theirs, changing us, re-aligning us to be more like them. Removing the hope. Removing the joy. Leaving an Io-élan who knows only fear and anger.

<no io, no, no, do not let the darkness win>

but it is too late. I, Noa, feel the warm rush of blood from my nostril where something's burst inside, taste it as it curls around my upper lip and into my mouth, feel the warm rush of hate take me, take Io, take us all into the shadows because everything we'd ever nurtured in the light is gone

gone.

"Caran," my voice rasps as Io slips out of my mind and body and slinks away. New shorts and broken places inside my navis flicker. I can't move my limbs at all. My vision returns to my eyes through the red mist of broken blood vessels. The rover is racing past its max recommended speed. Ground heaves and rumbles. Put everything I have left of navis capacity into motor. My limbs move. Tap on his helmet. He stares ahead, frozen by panic. Pull up on his foot. Off the pedal. Off. Off. Off the accelerator. Finally he comes unfrozen and lifts his foot up. Reallocate everything into linguistics. "Shuttles. To Ganymede. Two today. In twelve hours. In fourteen. From Milktown. Go." Everything into motor. Point at the sky. Point at the star charts on the dash. Everything into linguistics. "Big blue star. Keep center. Stay course."

Wavering unconscious. Hope gone. Still. We. Go. On.

"Dividia has changed Io. To resonate its frequencies. All that's left of home is me."

blackout

◊

Ohfuckohfuckohfuck just keep breathing keep breathing bad to hyperventilate in a hazard suit oh-fuck fuck calming the fuck down.

Deep breaths. Opera breaths. Let the tension out.

The rover rumbles to a stop. I lean back and close my eyes until I can hear myself think above the beat of my heart.

Noa!

Her nose is bleeding and she's out cold, but the hazard suit's crude sensors show that she's stable, so I let her be. Star charts. Shuttles to Ganymede. Keep the blue star center and we'll make it to Milktown. Okay. I can do this. Breathe. In. Out.

I point the rover toward the big blue star and turn the autopilot on as we start moving. Dust off the analogue clock. Never would've been able to read it if backwards-ass Agrippa hadn't been so full of technophobes I'd learned to tell time on one. Thing's got four dials, one for an Earth Standard twenty-four-hour day and three more that I don't know what the fuck. Probably one's Io local, but that doesn't mean shit to me, so I focus on the ES one and breathe. Get familiar with the rover. Check our bags. Make sure Noa's still just sleeping. Fiddle with the knobs. Make sure the autopilot's still set for the star. Try to finish up that Io song. Try not to feel the fear licking at my back.

Hour two. Could wake Noa.

Can't face her.

What just happened, it was my fault. Shit. Useless piece of shit. Stinker Watts.

I pull my arms out of the suit's sleeves, but I can't hug myself tightly enough past the tubes and wires to get any comfort.

Four hours from Milktown. Four hours from my old life, only

now I don't remotely pass for normal.

Mindy demanding where I've been, who to punish for it. Lies I'll need to tell her.

LaRoque pushing me back into media fast as he can. Lies I'll need to tell him.

The roaring, screaming, intolerable pressure of the world's sounds shredding my senses whenever I step outside. Lies I'll have to tell about why I can't say anything besides memorized scripts, song lyrics, and echoes. Lies to avoid a medical exam. We'd already stretched the plausible deniability of "artists are like that" too thin, even with the abilities NQ gave me. Going back in the state I'm in is gonna break me, like Dividia at my back.

What options do I have? Tell the hair and make-up guys to get bent, put my navis back in, and wear a hat for the rest of my life? Unrealistic.

Beg Freedom to take me back? They never wanted me in the first place.

Drop out, hide? I can't. Especially not once Muse hooks back into me, both of us bigger than gods.

And Dividia, Dividia, chasing me across the skies as if I need another monkey on my back.

Ten thousand screaming fans crashing into hyper-acute, un-protected nauta senses. I'll overload in under four seconds.

Fear crawling through the seams of the hazard suit, icy-flutter.

What's on the radio?

White noise hiss punctuated by the weird keening of the magne-tosphere: wails and pseudo-surf sounds and the click-hiss of unnat-ural fire. Can't pull music from the noise. What if my creativity was just an artifact of the drugs? What if all I am is an empty voice, child-hood talent sucked clean by need and the public's parasitic greed?

Broadcast hisses through the headset; I tune a thin bandwidth.

"...Europan authorities have corralled all Operators in the Technician Corridor. Ports remain closed to inter-orbital traffic, with the terrorist crisis estimated at costing the Europan government 800 trillion c's per day. No Operators have come forward with information regarding the incident that claimed the lives of 509 citizens and 21 tourists at the Embassy, nor have there been any leads on the Ganymedian threat. Authorities warn that this tragedy is likely one of many planned by the Genetic Liberation Front, starting with the South Port freighter bomb—"

Broadcast hisses out.

I remember Jordis talking in the hallway of Hostel 6, voice out of character with that frightened cadence, her leaving me alone.

CryCorp's schedule. Europa EXP 13:15:10:00. Explosion? Expo Center? Some scary shit even a crime boss can't fix.

If Europa's quarantined and rounding up Operators, what's that mean for me? Maybe I can't get back to Mindy at all. Or, I get back and sent straight to the head of an execution line.

If I'm exposed now, with Operators blamed for some kind of terrorist act, then who knows what extreme fear-reaction I'll set off.

Air leaves my lungs and I can't seem to refill them even though the suit says I've plenty of clean oxygen.

That must have been the plan all along, Dividia's plan, CryCorp's plan. Dividia isn't the élan vital of neglect and dispossession and alone. Those are just *my* fears. Dividia is the spirit of fear itself. And what do normals fear most, at least right now on Europa?

Sweat covers me faster than the hazard suit can reclaim and I'm stripping my helmet, unclipping my gloves, reaching into the side pocket of Noa's bag. I can't do it. Can't pass as normal; I'll ruin everything for everyone if I try. If I'm unmasked, I'll be the death of all the enslaved nauta on Europa. I can hear the commentary now, "If someone like CW can fool us for so long, who else could be fooling us?" I can see the resonance between me and Dividia turning that betrayal and fear into hate. Expanding, picking up more fear and hate. And more. And more. Until Operators everywhere are sacrificed—I can't do it, can't fake it clean.

My fingers curl around the test-tube of dark blue lies. There can't be more than eight drops left, but it's enough. Four hours to Milktown, pick up that half-dram that waits for me there, stretch it with the remaining U4 back in the hostel room, will be enough to see me through the conversations with Mindy and LaRoque, enough to get back to my room and the rest of my stash—

Noa stirs but does not wake.

I upend the entire container into my mouth, tears riding the hot rush that crushes the fear and I weep ecstatically into the fog of shadows rising from the floor as Dividia enters the rover to tell me everything will be okay.

◊

I am awake and tinkering with my programming. Have to work-around, adapt. Again. Don't even remember baseline function anymore. Hard-memory's fried. Just the meat left. I can run linguistics and motor one-at-a-time or both-at-a-deficit. Sensory's gone. Mostly. Rig two modes, concurrent motor-lingual, and sequential motor-then-lingual. Something's wrong with me, too, this time. Meat-me. Nerve damage deeper, further. Short in my head. Fried meat. Assess later. Open eyes.

"Where are we." I twist toward the front window to dust. Darkness.

"Don't know."

Dim light of the glo in the ceiling. I see him. "Where is helmet. Gloves." Pause. Motor-only. Flick hair from my face. Better, but still too dark. Pause. Motor-lingual. "Where are stars."

"Don't know. Sky's full of dust. Been following sonar."

"No sonar. Stop rover when stars go out." Motor-only. I reach for the rover key. We could be klicks off-course. Stupid. Stupid Noa. Should have supervised better.

He bats my hand away. "No. We gotta get to Milktown, four hours, max."

"No. Always stop, wait out ashfall. Bad to travel at wrong angles." I make another swipe for the key. "We're okay."

"We are not okay!" Caran shoves me from the dash.

The air flashes static as I ricochet off the door in the low g.

"I—we have to get to Milktown. Heard a broadcast. They're killing us on Europa, killing nauta, and I don't want to die, I thought I did but I really don't, I don't want to die here either and we're out of time, everyone is out of time so no! No, we're not okay, and I'm not okay either, thank-you Djen and your self-righteous priss-of-a-dimship Stella for not-ever-fucking-asking me!" He screams and shakes his hands and howls again.

I stare at him through my helmet's glass "You're high."

He smashes his fist into the dash. "If you cared about me you'd understand. But you don't, and you can't, so mind your own fucking business."

"You're reacting to. Dividia." That's why it's so dark inside. The monster. The monster has come inside. "The darkness. Out there. Is in here. Didn't make it. Didn't outrun. Darkness."

"Yeah, and Dividia's gonna get its fucking way if I step back into the spotlight with all my nauta self hanging out for all to see, you've no idea the fucking—"

"Shh." I push him from the controls and squint at the sky while he sucks on split knuckles. I find the telescope in the back seat and adjust the lenses into the murk. Consult my maps. Run calculations. Can't find any of my telemetry sensors. Don't know if we're outside their range or I'm just too broken to connect. The rover crunches to a stop over silica and sulfur spew. Everything takes forever because I can only do one thing at a time. "Maybe Dividia wants you to show the world you're an Operator." I say to Caran. "But maybe it wants something else. Later. We learn. Now. When did you dose. How much time."

"Four hours." He's shaking.

Motor-only. I unlatch my suit and grab him. Press him hard enough so he can feel it. He clutches me like the last breath of a drowning man.

Linguistics-only. "If we're going to get to Milktown in time," I breathe in his ear, "we have got to banish. Dividia. We have got to. Stop being. Afraid."

Motor-only. My breath becomes a nip, a trickle of kisses down his neck. Our love-making this time is brutal, Io's unquenchable desire and the frenzy of the NQ threading us together, burning everything small and human away. When we finish, fear dispelled, fumbling back into hazard suits we never should have removed, the darkness is gone.

I point the rover toward the bright blue star.

◊

We drive in silence for hours, swallowed small by the rumble-wub of the wheels over corrugated landscape. Milktown appears, a glow on the horizon, as the leading edge of withdrawal breaks with a twitch and a promise of pain.

"I got some U4 back at Hostel 6," I tell Noa. "If we take the second Ganymedian shuttle we can get it. If we take the first—not sure if..." If I'll make it. Hope I sound casual.

"We'll. Try." Noa grinds out after a long pause. She's off. Can't tell if it's the loss of her dome or something physical. Maybe both. She won't tell me. It's all my fault.

The rover's wheels go from rumble-wub to tick-tick-tick as they hit the landing pad. The airlock doors swoosh and do their thing. Inner one opens; Noa swerves into a parking spot.

We shuck our hazard suits back in Earth-norm g, and step out into Milktown's overly oxygenated, sulfurous air. I check the bag with the evidence in it—the inventory, the media schedule, all the Dividia stuff to give to Djen.

But they're waiting for us as we step out, a six-foot bruiser and an army of thugs with knives, jackets blazing CryCorp's ringed-planet sigil. Dividia boiling a smog of shadows at their ankles.

I drop the bag of evidence, yellow dust billowing from the *thunk* where it lands.

Can't escape.

Can't escape the sound of my own soul, which is what Dividia is always singing.

Shadows curl like a fast neap-tide fog from the oceans of Emory, like a scuttling childhood fear, spelling out YOUR FAULT. I can't out-run it; it's already here.

We deserve each other. A monster for a monster, two of a kind.

Then Noa's wrenching me around, grabbing the dropped bag, brown eyes catching the scant light like diamonds. Nose caked in a cement of blood and sulfur dust and body haloed in the faint smell of my semen and her sweat, glow in her breast pocket where Io-in-the-diamond lives. Shit.

SHIT

Mind snaps clear as my focus turns more to her than to Dividia, and she's a reason not to give in to it.

Resonance between me and Dividia breaks and Noa and I are running, running, running, away from the thugs, yes, but also away from the U4 in Hostel 6, out into Milktown's ugly streets with her hand burning my arm. None of the shadows are stable.

DON'T LOOK AT THE SHADOWS

We run through fallen leaves and bits of trash unloved, alone.

DON'T THINK ABOUT ALONE

To the spaceport on the other side of town where I'm going to die in pain and cold sweat.

CAN'T DIE YET

Where the shuttle for Ganymede's departing and Djen and Freedom wait beyond the electromagnetic storm.

MUST TELL THEM ABOUT DIVIDIA

Across the scorched concrete floor that echoes the sound of Cry-Corp's thugs closing the distance.

NOT YET

Through the shuttle's cargo doors as they slide shut, nipping the cuff of my sleeve, sound of tearing fabric like the end of the world in the absolute dark of the belly of the ship.

Heart beating fast, too fast. Nerve-pain spasm rend. Precursor to the inevitable, ultimate heart failure that awaits me.

But not yet. NOT THE FUCK YET.

Pressurizers and environmentals hiss.

I see the sparkles of passing out. Not yet, not yet you fucking bag of meat, not-the-fuck-yet. It's just the over-extension. I'm not that far into withdrawal yet. Breathe. In. Out. Opera breaths. Cling to consciousness until the sparkles fade. I'm okay. For now, okay.

I flail until I come into contact with Noa's warmth.

"Noa, you listen to me," I press her shoulders. "When we get to Ganymede, no matter what else happens, you get to Grizwald Squat in Level One North East, Iron City, Number Eight. Looks like an abandoned tenement, but you'll be stopped inside the door. I'll give you the pass-sign. Once you're in, go to the top floor and ask for Fish. You give Fish the CryCorp schedule, the papers from Lab2, tell him everything. Everything. About you and Io, about me and Dividia, that you know about the élan vitals, and demand asylum in Freedom. Say, 'by the resonance between me and Io-élan, I invoke my right to Freedom.' You got that? All right? All right?"

Noa moans and struggles against my grip but I'm not ready to let her go.

"You promise me Noa, you promise on the soul of the moon you've got in your pocket, there's better things that need saving than me. You kish?"

I feel her moving, maybe nodding, and she finally lets out a terse, "I promise."

I let her shoulders go to find her hands. Teach her the finger-sign for Freedom, guiding her in the dark until I feel her get it right. "'Course if you've a bit of time after that, any bit at all, please do try to save my space-wrecked ass." I flash her my trademark grin.

But she can't see it in the darkness.

◊

When Io-élan's influence recedes, and the link is gone, I find myself alone with Caran. This time it is Noa, not me, who has left the office.

He is across from me, on the sofa, feet on the ground, hands in his lap. His shiny black eyes stare at me, unblinking.

I know the wall of will that prevents his feelings from overwhelming him. I know that's a nauta thing, why they sometimes melt down, go catatonic. Everything is heightened, crossed, co-mingled: senses, feelings, language-less thought. He lives with all that, and the atrocities done to him, and he is still sitting here, open, caring.

It took courage for him to make it off Agrippa with the capacity to love anything at all. It took courage for him to have survived a world hostile to every aspect of his neurobiology.

I have nothing but respect for him.

He shifts, lines softening. The tension of the awkward sex in the rover lingers in the afternoon light, teasing my own attraction. I make no move to cover the evidence of my arousal. He makes no move to cover his own.

He says in a rush, eyes crinkled in the almost-panic of anticipated rejection, "you could follow me home."

We stare at each other for a good twenty seconds longer.

We leave my office together.

PART 3:

SOL SYSTEM,
JUPITER ORBIT: GANYMEDE

SESSION 15:
CARAN & CAMI / GANYMEDE

Caran slouches with his feet on the table looking at me with a half-flirt, half-challenge I can't interpret, and I can't look away from. We've been like this for two minutes and twelve seconds according to the clock in my com.

If the Research Dean or the Ethics Board finds out what I just did, my career could well be over. Well, maybe not my whole career, but certainly my engagement with this very important, very interesting project.

Because I'm compromised. Not just that—I am *gleefully* compromised. I regret nothing about the past twenty-four hours, and in fact want more of what we just did.

It's Caran, it's me—but it's also a giddy sense of self-destruction I'm a little ashamed to admit I've indulged in more often than just this time. I try to swallow it, but I can't shake it. Flirting with the edge. Wanting to be destroyed.

"I really can't figure out how to start—"

"How do you want to start—"

Our voices run over themselves and we laugh.

"Where's Muse when you need it, right?" He passes me that rakish sideways grin and a flash of his eyes.

"Yeah, where is Muse?" I ask in seriousness now.

He shrugs. "Doesn't like this part. Hard for it to separate its experiences from mine.”

I try not to think of how hard it is to separate my personal life from my professional life, and how I shouldn't even be sitting here. And how I don't care. “I'm interested in Muse's experiences too.”

Caran shudders. “You'll get them. Later. More than you'll want.”

My door squeaks open and Camilla Morgan bounds in, curls sproinging around her heart-shaped face and up-turned nose, pale gold against her light brown skin. With a delighted squeal, she jumps on Caran and gives him a big hug. He starts to tickle her and she squeals again and flees toward me, bonking my nose in another, less exuberant, embrace. “I'm so happy to be back, and to see you again, Steven!”

Cami is eighteen, Earth-standard, and somehow events haven't tamped her childish glee. She glows with her youth and genuine happiness to see us. Cami's the only one of my interviewees who is a normal, without the nauta k-mutation, like me—although I'm starting to wonder if anyone is truly “normal.” Cami's relationship with the élans certainly isn't typical.

My skin prickles with the advent of an élan vital. I recognize this one, because we practiced with him: the alien consciousness that inhabits the magnetosphere of Ganymede.

“I missed you too,” I tell Cami as she settles into the chair Jordis usually occupies, sprawling askew so that her legs dangle over the arm. She's wearing jeans and a striped sweater, casual and relaxed. She kicks off her clunky boots and stretches out her feet in mismatched toe-socks.

“What about me?” Caran says, sliding closer to her on the couch. “You miss me?”

Cami stretches out a stocking foot to poke him with a toe, “Of course I missed you, silliness.” She turns back to me, head nearly upside-down in her sprawl across the chair. "Jordis had to go back for a while and Noa's got a thing at the Physics Building. Or the Complexology Lab. Some science thing, they've got her doing a bunch of science things while she's here on Mars. But we're at my part anyway, right?"

"I think so," I nod. "We left off during the flight from Io to Ganymede."

"Okay, right." She swivels back around, elbows on knees. "I'll let Caran tell his part, then we'll go back for mine. I'll stay here for the link, to make the bridge with Ganymede. Ganymede likes Caran but not enough to link with him without me. Muse doesn't want to do this part." She blinks at Caran. "Ready?"

He nods.

◊

(Flowing into the link with Ganymede-élan is as I remember it from our practice sessions: a smell of iron and sensation like the sound of metal-on-metal or big gears shifting, a slight cooling, and a dusty weight. Curiosity, ingenuity, inventiveness, survival, originality—these are the parts of myself Cami taught me to focus on in order to create resonance with the élan vital of the largest Galilean moon. Ganymede was the first outer orbital colonized by the New Organization of Federal Banking Worlds nearly five hundred years ago, and its élan the most influenced by humans.

Cami's Ganymede.

But not Cami's consciousness.

A toxic flash of agony and a swirl of thin, dry snow—I am, again, Caran—)

Streets undifferentiated from sky, sky/planet/city all one mess, isn't anything to do but keep tracing a line along the edges of the buildings. Noa told me to wait here, going to get someone. Mindy will find me, she always does. Noa will come back. Someone will find me. Someone has to recog—

Feet hitting pavement, blunted slivers of hearing/vision. Distraction/pain/fascination as undifferentiated as the scenery, in between stop-and-listen-entranced and cover-ears-and-hide. Is this where Noa asked me to wait, or have I wandered off? What is here? Hear?

Push-back as someone slams into me; don't feel the impact just the stumble. Focus into eyes/lips, squint/frown. Female. Mindy?

"You know, you look just like—"

Want to respond but fall back against the hard wall of a building instead. Or is it the ground?

"On second thought—" the woman shakes her head "—maybe not. I was going to say you look just like Caran Watts, but obviously you're not." She adds in nervous-flutter voice, "Sorry to have bumped you."

Blurry, she runs off. Face in hands I laugh, but my hands come away wet so maybe I'm crying. All she saw was some pathetic papper on the street.

Well, that's really all I am, isn't it?

Someone's attacking me, has my forearms in their hands, squeezing—

No. Holding. Holding hard enough for me to feel it. Holding me up as I shiver, and Ganymede is very cold, did I remember to put on clothes?

"Caran. Caran! Track me! Track me, you ass."

"Stella would take me back, she would, if she would just listen a cracking moment." What the fuck am I saying? A familiar smell, but old-familiar, like one I smelled a lot but a long time ago.

"Beloved Zaos, Caran, don't you dare close your eyes!"

"I love you Stella, and you love me and..." Stella—Djen? Someone's holding onto me, and I push my fingers into him/her—her—and smell the scent of salvation as my hands find a mess of long, tight, black curls—"Djen!"

"Yeah. Don't get too excited. You gotta walk with me a little ways."

I am crying now for sure and I grab onto her and let her lead me away into darkness.

◊

Soft bed, soft sheets, soft sounds from somewhere a ways away—a street. People-sounds reflecting from walls and disappearing in air, moving, above and below—a building? A hill? A shout, unintelligible. Normal city-sounds. Big city sounds. Atmosphere sounds—an orbital with atmosphere, not domed. Not Io. Not submerged, not Europa. Soft scuffle within, outside my room. Not alone. I'm on Ganymede and I am not alone.

I hold my breath in anticipation of pain, test-move a finger—doesn't hurt. Let the breath out silently. Trap the air in my lungs again as I remember Djen. She must've come in response to the bombing after all.

Oh shit, is Noa safe? Did she get the evidence about CryCorp and Dividia to Fish? Oh shit, I was such an ass to leave all that to her. And worse, I brought CryCorp down on her.

I open my eyes.

Small room, shabby but homey. Clean, threadbare throw on the floor, intricate Martian geometric design. Flatshot posters on the walls of dimships and shuttles and space, flowered curtains closed over a window to the right. Blooming O2 plants over-spill their boxes along the sill, orange and red. I'm at the Grizwald, Ganymede's freespace. Back in Freedom's territory. Room hasn't changed in the decade since I last slept here.

The small hairs on my arms raise with the arrival of an élan and the door clicks open and there's two-meter-tall Djen in her red spacer's suit, scowling from the depths of her soul. She's holding a can of Aprís All-Day Vitamin drink and I stretch out a hand, though fuck me if I know which I want more, the vitamin juice or a friend.

She gives me neither.

"I swear, Caran. You were in heart failure by the time we got you back here. Noa told me what happened. Typical. Still can't manage your bio-chemistry responsibly." She shakes her head like it weighs a thousand kilos.

Well, at least I know she still cares about me. Stella's frequencies nose at me and I let her synch in. She doesn't add her personality to the link though; just transmits my thoughts to Djen because my speech is gone. <noa! is noa okay?>

"Noa's in medic now, and as okay as nineteen years alone on that hell moon and you being an ass to her will allow. She'll be down for a while." Djen answers aloud instead of through the link, a deliberate slight.

Her vocal tone gives me no comfort, but I exhale in relief anyway to know Noa's still alive. <noa told you everything, about dividia and crycorp and all of it?>

"Yup. She shared all the evidence you two lugged back." Djen sighs then, and tosses a hard, black box onto my bed.

I pick it up and run my fingertips along the polished blackwood. I flip the lid. Haven't seen this thing in over a decade. <i can't believe you kept my old navis>

"Haven't needed to disassemble it for the tzaddium."

I pull out the navis I'd abandoned almost twenty years ago when Megi built me a better one, the one hidden in my platinum lockbox back on Europa. Most of the programming'll be useless without patches. <i seal up the opening in my skin where it slots in when i'm on tour; i can't wear it>

"We took care of that," Djen scowls, distant in the doorway.

<well, the nq then>

"You're on U4. We've kept you asleep for three days so you wouldn't blow the detox again. We'd've kept you under longer but, unfortunately, we need you awake now. Noa showed me how she'd been weaning you off before you threw all that hard work in her face. Play it right and you'll be dependence-free in another two days. Not that I expect you to play anything right." She pauses, sour-faced. "Come find me after you've dealt with yourself." Djen sets the vitamin juice just inside the threshold and slams the door. Stella's presence poofs out along with her.

I stumble after the juice, nutrient-rich, all those buzzing calories, sweet sugars, oh fuck yes! Just sit back a while, glad of food. Heartbeat. Breath.

I find the clothes on my way back to the blackwood box on the bed. Furry, fleecy things, bulkier than I like, but at least they're soft, and Ganymede is cold as a bad review. Neutral grays and whites, nice. Synthfurr vest's a laugh. Fluffy synthfurr boots to match; Djen knows better than to leave me socks. I slide into the clothes, then take the thin, iridescent blue rectangle of my old navis out of the blackwood box. It shimmers in the light: the pale blue truth.

I like a navis for talking to normals and helping with sequencing. But otherwise, I kinda prefer my plain old nauta self without it. Back when I ran with Djen, I mostly I used the navis for making music—translating sounds in my head to the kinetikosonus. Also, amping sensory filters when the edges of things got too confusing and bright. A little bit of sensory goes a long way for me.

Freedom's take has always been that the tech is an extension of us. Hybrid humans: meat-and-machine symbiosis. But out in the real world, the tech's a symbol of dysfunction.

Sat in on plenty of conversations in Freedom about how to reconcile the tech's ability to normalize us with the autonomy to behave as our true nauta selves. Where's the line between using tech to appear like something we're not and using it to do all the fabulous things that only nauta can do? Difference is in who's making the choices about how to use it, I've always thought.

I slide the navis into the surgical opening in my forehead. It's cold and slippery beneath my skin. There are no nerves to feel the AI-driven nanothreads entering my brain through the pores in my skull—just the abrupt presence of a thought that isn't mine whistling gold-and-red. Machine query: initiate device?

Imagine: a French horn, clear through high mountain air in morning.

Soundscapes unfold: textured noise mapping program groups, golden horns for linguistics, red drums for motor, the complicated synth-simmer of sensory segments, purple bass for internals and diagnostics—

I can't fucking move and my thoughts go all skew-wise.

Machine notification: It has been 7496 days since last initialization. Neurobiological synchronization out of date.

No fucking shit.

Machine query: Update systems now?

Think a pink fluted command at it: list systems that need updating.

Machine notification: neuro-translational, motor integration, brain-pattern-mapping sensory regulators, sense-organ baseline readings, memory index from—

Yellow cymbal crash: STOP. Run linguistics update, everything related to sensory. Erase everything else.

Machine warning: Erasing motor control functions will significantly impact capacity for day-to-day functioning; memory index is required for some systems functions such as—

Yellow-cymbal-override-FUCK! Erase everything but linguistics and sensory, okay, already, thanks.

Machine notification: Begin linguistics update. Please start with a brief history of the colonization of Agrippa—

The thing asks me a million questions to rebuild the translation library between my thoughts and machine language, and between my thoughts and the normals' language, because language is not a static thing, even a language as unique as a nauta's. Ambient noise levels damp down and the fragments of the room lock into an image of a whole as sensory filters flutter on.

I can manage motor control and sequencing as long as I don't have to manage sensory integration and communication at the same time and I'm too piss-poor out of practice to write the necessary code to patch motor anyway.

Fuck the memory index. Not worth the time and processing cycles to index twenty years of meat-memories. My natural recall's too good anyway. Wish I could forget stuff. Plus, perfect recall fucks up my performing; there's no art in hammering out notes the same way over and over like a machine.

While it's all updating and bits and pieces of my surroundings are coming into focus, I go to the mirror and take a hard, sober stare.

I look way too young, way younger than thirty-five, without the circles of interrupted sleep beneath my eyes. Days and days of not dancing makes me feel like I've lost muscle mass; too skinny. Maybe I always was too skinny. Haven't seen my hair in its natural state since 100 Worlds Music got a hold of it, tangled waves down to my collar bones. Never thought I was all that sexy but the billion screaming fans beg to differ, so whatever. Just too much personality I don't know how to turn off. Black hair and amber skin bring out the iridescent blue shine of the navis across my forehead. And the fluffy white furr vest—well it's certainly nothing my handlers would put me in.

I make a promo-shot pose and laugh at how much the furr-fluff looks like feathers. Like the feathers of my dragon presentation in the Mem. Bet Djen did that on purpose; maybe she doesn't hate me after all.

I look like myself from the past.

Inside the extra brain I've inserted into my head, there's an out-of-tune box holding miscellaneous scraps of programming; I rummage till I find my old Mem presentation. I lurch into the lithe, winged body of the feathered white dragon. Arc my neck, stretch my wings, wait for the programming to update, adapt to this older me. The bending and stretching feels real. So does the flying. I land and blow open a channel out; listen for signal.

Djen's frequency comes in first, broadcasting strong like she's amping it so I can't miss.

Below that, other frequencies. The soft, deep tone of Fish; Stella's alien hum; a sharper baritone that permeates everything, but I can't name it.

Further out, I sense shortwave devices, 3V projection plates, stationary systems, odds-and-ends. And further still, the feeds, the Mem, the commerce of innumerable transmissions bouncing off stratosphere, reaching for stars. One directed thought and I'll link into them. Find out what the fanfeeds are saying. Indulge in the love-hate bitch-slap of bashspace. Slip into the Mesh held open by Stella and let it blow me into the secret frequencies held by LaRoque and Mindy, find out what they're saying about me, about my disappearance.

But I don't want to know.

Not yet.

Not until I have my bearings.

And a shot of whiskey.

There's a lot of signal, sure, but not as much as there should be. Ganymede's a Core world; there should be more communications background noise. I intuit a query into the Mesh, but my thought is like opening a favorite book and finding the pages blank. Where is the Mesh? Stella's in the next fucking room, there shouldn't be any difficulty scanning it.

I reach for Muse. It should be here; we should be able to connect now that I'm away from Io.

Something reaches back along my summons. Something hungry. Something full of abandonment and ache and clawing emptiness.

I drop my connection to the broader informationsphere and link into Stella's telempathic frequency. Humming a tune to still the tweak of panic as I reach for the doorknob to the next room <where's all the signal? what the fuck is going on?>

◊

"Did you realize—" I have to break the story, "—did you realize what was going on. With Muse I mean? It doesn't seem like you tried very hard—"

"To contact it?" He finishes my sentence. "No."

Cami is sideways the other way in the chair, kicking her feet over the arm as she plays a game on a portable 3V. "He means, 'No, I didn't try very hard,' not 'no, I didn't realize what was going on.'" She clarifies Caran's ambiguous statement even though it looks like she's not paying attention. "Ganymede, bring up the mainfeed Djen had me compile for when he woke up."

The 3V over my coffee table lights up again, but this time it's no nauta operating it. Nor is Cami running it by blinking at holicons like I would need to. This time an alien intelligence controls it: Ganymede inside the circuitry.

◇

Bobbie from Studio Six Entertainment, the day after my show on Europa: "But don't you think Watts' bizarre performance makes more sense in wake of LaRoque's announcement? He says the artist is suffering from exhaustion."

Commentator: "No, I don't think, Bobbie. I'll grant you Watts was suffering from more than just inebriation at that show, but that's not what made his performance so bizarre."

◇

Caran stands at the edge of the stage, belting out the last note to "Light." Rainbow waves manifest from his chest, flowing and tangling around the audience. His knees buckle and he almost falls, but he maintains the note, loud and clear and pure as "Light" melts into the ticking time-bomb that is "Heaven Is Anyplace I Can Never Go"—

◇

Bobbie: "Yes, well, we've speculated for some time that there's no connection between the 4V and the kinetikosonus."

Commentator: "The lack of synch between Watts' movements and the 4V display was indeed bizarre, but, again, it was more than that. I'm thinking of those creepy lighting effects. The weird waves coming from his chest? The thing that happened after that? No one from the Watts' coterie is willing to comment on any of it."

◊

The finale, "Voice," is up and Caran sings, rainbow waves radiating all around. "Echo me / echo me / echo me ever."

The audience returns the words, faces bright in the rainbow sine waves washing over them, threading into them. "Echo me / echo me / echo me ever!"

Darkness enters from the theatre exits in a slow, heavy fog.

"Echo me / echo me / echo me ever—" Caran sings.

"Echo me / echo me / echo me ever!" The audience returns.

The rainbow waves stutter and shiver, coiling away from the encroaching darkness.

"Echo me / echo me / echo me!" Caran sings.

"Echo…" The audience falters as the dark shadows meet the rainbow light and the edges fray together.

All the rapport sucks from the room.

Nervous shuffles.

In the theatre streaks of blue lightening rain from above and the amplifiers melt down in a haze of sparks. The darkness has control.

Someone screams.

◊

Fanfeed:
*->holy fuck did you see that weird show?
(-> o_0
(-> i can't tell if i liked it?
(-> haha he was totally drunk at that show
+-> how would you know?
—> isn't he always drunk?
(-> yeah, what was with the creepy lights and sparks at the end? i felt like they were killing my soul lol
+-> /me felt that way too
(-> i've felt dead ever since. like cw died at the end and took my me with him. like those creepy lights were death. i'm scared.
+-> think they're lying about him just being sick?
—> gods i hope not :-(:-(:-(
—> wouldn't they tell us if he was dead?
=->?

◊

"He knew, even before we showed him that," Cami says, still playing her game, dangling her feet. "He knew there wasn't a Muse like he remembered anymore. He knew that the finale belonged to Dividia. He just wasn't ready to face it yet."

There's no accusation in Cami's tone, and Caran does not mind her speaking for him; I feel a whiff of relief through the link.

"That's why he didn't try very hard to contact Muse."

"Okay. Thank you."

◊

I open the door into the common room of the Ganymedian freespace, simsuns from outside streaming in the windows. Light spreads over mis-matched comfy furniture atop mis-matched carpets piled so high stepping on them makes no sound. Doors all around into rooms where people could stay, an archway to a kitchen. I catch more of a look than I want at the people in the room then flick my eyes down into the mosaic of carpet, as if it could dampen my feelings like it does sound.

I feel everyone through Stella's presence. Fish's dismissal, Djen's hurt and shame, Stella's anger.

But fuck that. I flick my gaze back up to meet them directly. I've done shitty things. But shitty things were done to me, too. When I fuck up on stage, I don't get all weepy. I pretend I meant to do whatever-it-was and keep right on singing. Any performer knows that's how to play it. <since djen's woken me from my pleasant nap, i presume you're planning to tell me what's fucking going on>

Djen lies limp on the ugly orange couch, the small, dense cube of Stella's dimension drive beside her on the scuffed coffee table. <europa's shut its borders; the angry townspeople have gathered on io with torches and pitchforks to hunt operators; dividia's re-aligned the fixed-domain élans around europa and io to resonate with its foul frequencies, and you, as usual,> she flops over on her side as though weighing 500 kilos <are a total korkered mess>

Stella manifests into the visible over her dimdrive, silver-lidded eyes narrow and sunsparks testy.

I spear Djen with a sweet, sarcastic smile <and you, as usual, are a self-righteous bitch-mouthed diva>

<takes one to know one> she spouts back.

<kids let's not fight> Fish looks like he's about twenty,

Earth-standard, but he's looked that way the whole time I've known him so he must be pushing fifty at least. He's still big as a planet, spread in his bean chair in a white tee and purple kilt.

<she started it *resentment*> I fold my arms and lean back on my heels.

<djen *peace*> Fish projects feelings. <dragon-man *welcome/ greet* as djen says, a lot of heavy's going on. you sit. we unpack.>

Fish's transmission is diplomatic, but he can't hide his disapproval of me through Stella's link. Man hadn't thought I belonged in Freedom back when Djen dragged me in, and he sure as fuck doesn't think I belong now. Tough shit, Fish-man. <i'll sit when i fucking well feel like it.>

Telempathic equivalent of a loaded stare passes between Djen and Fish and then an apocalypse of mainfeed clips about my show and current events, plus some fanfeed, flood the frequencies.

"Okay," I feel my throat compulsively swallowing in response to the disturbing update and footage, "I'm in trouble and things are really bad in Galilean space, but what the fuck happened to the Mesh? Why can't I intuit anything into the shared élan-human informationspace?"

Djen and Fish stare at each other with such flash-point rage I almost forget that both of them are also pissy at me.

<remember in the runner wars, when the bad guys captured an élan and weaponized it by changing its frequencies? killed almost everyone and we hadda take the nuclear option to survive?> Fish stares at Djen because he knows she remembers full well and has decided to keep lobbing knives.

<yeah i remember you sitting here safe and pretty on ganymede too while i lived through it> Djen stabs back.

<right, i was sitting real pretty when the élans protecting us de-

cided they were, therefore, done with humanity because we were just too dangerous to them and packed up, leaving us exposed to the authorities>

"Look," I interrupt their dagger-fest that's apparently lost no animosity over the years. "I know full well that humans broke élan trust and pretty much all of them packed up and left except Zaos, which who the fuck knows why it sticks around to protect us, but—where was I?"

<in the middle of a protracted rant?> Djen supplies unhelpfully.

Fish stabs back at both of us <i think you were at the part where the élans said they'd only protect us if we protected them—meaning we don't let random trash like you in, a point defeatists like djen fail to appreciate>

<i did not fail to appreciate the point> Djen raises her middle finger to Fish to punctuate her telempathically delivered rage. <i just don't agree. sure, defeatist djen, call me that all you want, i own it. i don't believe there's any way we'll ever come up winning, freedom died decades ago, but there's no reason we gotta be sad and lonely and bitter on the way out>

"PEOPLE!" I yell and also yell <*PEOPLE!!*> "I don't fucking care about Freedom's internal protectionist versus defeatist politics right now, what the fuck is wrong with the Mesh? Is it Dividia?"

Fish looks at me like he's just woken from sleep surprised to find me standing there. <yes, dividia—the exact kind of enslaved, weaponized élan that got us in trouble during the runner wars. and it just realigned europa and io—the exact kinda harm we promised to prevent. so now even zaos has left us and along with it the Mesh. dividia made the élan's worst nightmares come true and we'll be lucky if they don't come back and kill us all>

"That's because Dividia IS nightmare, some fuck named Ellison from CryCorp's turned an élan into nightmares." I explain but no one pays attention.

Fish's thoughts tumble over my words. <where'd dividia come from? the other élans don't know it, can't track it.>

Djen: <stella knows it>

Stella: <*affirm* it is the dancing darkness counterpoint to the dancing light>

Fish: <and stella gets even more incoherent every day, good job djen, spending all your spare time drifting in uninhabited space away from humans>

<people> I think/feel into the link, half to get them to shut up so I can hear my own thoughts and half because if I think them out loud, the burning intuition that's starting to well up in my back-brain might organize into an actual idea, <shut it a sec i have to tell you something>

Djen keeps right on arguing with Fish: <you have no idea the pressures i've been under my whole life, the responsibilities of being the only pathfinder, if it wasn't for me, you and everyone here would have died out years ago and—>

Fish: <blah blah blah djen's little pity-party, don't you think what's going on is a bit more important than your feelings>

"People," I say aloud with enough volume to hurt everyone's delicate nauta ears.

They shut up and turn to me.

"Jordis Ansari," I say.

Djen rolls her eyes. "Is the least of our worries now, and that should scare you."

"No," I say. "Jordis Ansari stole my dataslip and put it around her neck, but there was something odd about it, something I couldn't put my finger on at the time, something *singing* inside. It was singing the songs of Europa, of Casino Row. Noa show you her diamond? Noa's diamond's got a fractal of Io-élan inside. One that holds her original resonance, not the Dividia-tainted Io-élan."

A snort from Fish and a tear leaks from one of Djen's closed eyes like she's finding me so insufferable she's weeping. Stuff it to both to them, this is important. "Io *knew* that Dividia would change her. She knew it. Why else put a piece of herself inside a dense crystal matrix and give it to her favorite human? It's not a stretch to think Europa-élan knew it too and gave an untainted duplicate of herself to Jordis Ansari for whatever fucking reason. If Ansari's got an uncorrupted Europa-élan dangling around her neck and Noa's go an uncorrupted Io-élan in her diamond, then that means... that means... um. Important things, right?"

Djen and Fish stare at me.

Did I just do something really dumb? Again?

<djen, go get cami> Fish folds his big hands in his big lap.

Djen scowls toward Fish and sighs her "I hate gravity" sigh. <you go get cami. i've been forced to endure your heavy g for six days now.>

<exactly why the exercise is good for you>

Djen scoffs and answers in feelings more than words. <*wtf-coming-from-u?*>

She's got a point; I have never known the man to get up from the bean chair either. But then, I also know Djen exercises plenty enough on the *Stella-Maru* to handle one G. <if someone doesn't go get cami fucking right now i'm going to piss on both of you> I think/feel through the link. <also, who's cami?>

<magnet> Fish projects. <not for any élan in particular but all of them. a universal magnet. she's got something you'll find interesting in light of your ansari observations>

Djen adds, <she's also the daughter of cái morgan, the one who gave noa io-élan's diamond. and who, if your addled version of history that noa told us can be believed, was working for crycorp and dividia>

<wait, what>

<go on djen, go get cami> Fish pokes.

<fine> Djen rolls onto the floor and claws herself to a stand using the sofa. <she hates me though>

Djen returns from an adjacent room with a thin slip of a normal so quick I can't imagine why no one simply called for her.

Girl's shaggy yellow curls and pale blue eyes radiate defiance as she clomps in huge furr boots and blue jeans. Knit fingerless gloves run up to her elbows up in multicolored stripes. She can't be much over the age of major, if at all.

"Omygods you're Caran Watts!" the girl shrieks so high and loud even my newly updated sensory programming can't deal, and I cover my ears.

"Yeah. You're Cami?"

"You know who I am!" More overload-inducing shrieks.

I keep my hands near my ears in case she shrieks again. "Sort of. Djen—Cami please don't screech again—Djen told me the élan vitals like you?"

"I guess!" She doesn't quite shriek, but it's not a well-contained squeal. "Can you sing that note for me the one at the end of 'Picture Me' where it goes on so dreamy for ever and ever and—"

Best get it out of her system so we can have a conversation. I sigh and start "Picture Me" from the beginning. She closes her eyes and beams. It's nice. I close my own eyes and let myself get into it, get inside that long note and the miracle of sound that never gets old.

I open my eyes, expecting a smile, but Cami's frowning and

squinting at me with a Serious Weird Look that kills the warm. "You don't glow like you did at your last show here." Cami says. She pulls something out of a jeans pocket with a grubby-gloved hand. Credit slip. "It looks like Noa's diamond. On the inside. What is it?"

That baritone hum thumps, the music in my head churning industrial clank and ringing forge and the hiss of escaping air and there can be only one answer to that question. "Ganymede-élan."

"Huh?"

<you didn't tell her?> I send glares at Djen.

<*shrug* i told you, she doesn't like me.>

<sourpuss> I shoot at Djen and hold out a finger to touch Cami's credit slip. "It's the soul of the moon."

"Oh shit, that's me," Caran says, out of nowhere, and breaks the link. He stands and shakes his hands.

Cami blinks her big blue eyes like she's coming out of a dream.

"Alarm," he says into our silence. He pokes a finger at his temple. "In my head. Oh, come on, I have that thing? I have to prepare."

Cami's eyes go big with memory. "Oh, yeah. At the Heritage Auditorium."

Then I remember too. "The musical lecture with the Humanities Department. Making the most of your time on Mars, like Noa." I grin, though it's hard to put real emotion behind it.

"You could come," Caran says in a shy almost-whisper.

"Of course I can't come." The reason for my lackluster feelings. "That lecture hall only has five hundred seats."

"And I am in charge of whose butt goes in ten of them."

"Me?"

He rolls his eyes, shyness gone now that he's fingered my desire. "For a smart person, you're kinda dumb." He turns on his heel and exits with a sniff.

"Music and talk's at nine," Cami says. "And no, my butt wasn't invited to fill any of those seats."

Great. Now Cami knows something's going on. Not that we'll be able to hide it forever with her in the link.

"Be careful," she says. "He runs deeper than he lets on."

I swallow and deflect. "Let's take a lunch break and then you can tell me how you ended up at the Grizwald Squat."

An hour and a half later I'm alone in my office with Camilla Morgan and Ganymede. I might be in the presence of other unseen entities too—one or two or thousands of them—but they are not making themselves known to me. They might be making themselves known to Cami. And then I'm picturing the air crowded with creatures whose presence is dipping in and out of slow-wave spectra all around me, bouncing off me, interacting with the signals emitting from my own bio-electrical processes and I have to close my eyes, focus on the feeling of my own toes, get my bearings again.

It's a uniquely modern malaise we experience as individuals, as a society. The sense of violation without direction, tempered with wonder and desire for connection. *Verletzanziehung*, they call it, *violation-attraction*. It doesn't affect me much but putting myself into Cami's context triggers it.

"Steven? You okay?" She blinks her big eyes at me.

"Yes, I'm fine. I was thinking about your..." I laugh and decide to let her in on the funny thought, "...your magnetism!"

She laughs back, though it's the tired laugh of a joke she's heard too many times. "It's just the three of us right now, if that's what you're wondering."

"Yes, that's what I was wondering. So you were fifteen when this all happened?"

"Yup, I'd just hit the age of major!" Cami puffs out her chest, with the pride-in-age only someone who's still below thirty would have.

I hide the fact that I have to count on my fingers in my lap. Six years between the story and...twenty-one. She's twenty-one now.

"I was a blank," Cami continues. "No citizen id chip. No one could track me or hold me. Downside was I couldn't ride the public tubes, had to avoid the blues, you know. But it was all right. I was all right."

She makes the statement with the casual flippancy common to people who've grown up under untenable conditions. She may be a normal with as different a story from Caran's or Noa's as there is to get, but she still has that armor.

I ask, "How long had you been living alone in Iron City as a blank?"

Cami shrugs. "Oh, let's see, I ran away from Ellison when I was eight, so it'd been seven years I guess? Long time. I wasn't alone though; I had the friendbots. I made 'em, I'm a tinker, you know. Or I was before I ended up an ambassador."

"Tell me a little more about that." I fall back on my normal interviewing protocol. Cami might be an unusual normal in her relationship with the élans, but she processes language like most people do.

"I'd always had the knack. I could figure out mechanical things. I took to normie-style programming like that," she snaps her fingers. "I was doing it before Ellison got a hold of me, back when I was a kid with Mom and Dad. My favorite was little robots. They were pretty complex by the time I hit the streets of Iron City. Got a job right quick with Mx. Blue—he was a tinker too. He didn't have to report the employee overhead, and he paid me in credit to so I could get food, clothes, whatevs. It was good, good." She beams at me. "And I made the friendbots to be friends to me."

"All this at eight?" I am having a hard time wrapping my mind around some of her story.

"Well, Margaret helped me too."

"Margaret the Dieuvéssau from Freedom?"

"Yeah. But I didn't know about Freedom. She was just Margaret the nice Dieuvéssau who helped me, you know."

"All right. So take me back to the events directly leading up to that moment at Grizwald Squat, that moment when Caran named the being in your dataslip. Tell me the story of how you got there."

◊

BlackJack's pale as a ghost. He's standing on the other side of the street as I tap down the stairs between the Madame Shane's magic supply and the Rockie's Pizza. I hope whatevs is wrong with him's got nothing to do with me. I pause and push the hood of my parka down till the synthfurr tickles my cheeks. Crowd's moving fast past the once-colorful-now-dusty storefronts, streaming down Kiev Ave. Ganymede equals dusty. End of the workday equals crowded. Crowded equals no one pays attention to Cami. Good, good.

I blow breath out and watch it fog.

BlackJack hasn't seen me yet. I click the smooth, hard dataslips between my fingers and zigzag through the crowd.

"Hey kid." BlackJack leans against the side of the Always C-Store, smack-dab in the middle of its dusty blue-and-yellow lightening-flash sigil. He should be dark as the always-night sky of Iron City, but he's paler than Jupiter's crescent. Bad, bad.

"I'm not a kid. I'm fifteen, bozo. Major and everything." I click the dataslips faster. They flash in the simsun lights, blurring into arcs.

"Yeah, whatevs, kid. You got no Citizen ID Bank account, you're blank, so who's gonna know or care." He sounds like BlackJack but with the voice-colors all run out.

I toss him a frown, flick furr outta my eyes. Click the slips in a different rhythm.

"You got what I want?" BlackJack finally gets down to business.

"Yeah," I thrust the slips at him, but when he makes the grab, I dart my hand away, fast, fast. "You got what I want?"

"Yeah." BlackJack reaches into his parka pocket and pulls out another dataslip. This one's green and stamped as credit. He hands it to me like it was burning his fingertips.

"Slick." I slip him my slips, and snatch up his slip, and it's done, done. And also—ouch! His slip actually is hot; it buzzes like it's juiced, what the? I drop it in my front pocket to cool down in the Ganymede air. Blow on my fingers. Sometimes things just go all electric on me for no reason, no big. Got to get the credit to Mx. Blue and I'm done for the day. Good work. Good job. Backing away from BlackJack's fear-smell. "See ya."

"Yeah. See ya."

I sidle past him between the Always-C and the Motel Millions. Someone's dusted off the Motel Millions making it silver-black with glints of light. I have to blink a bunch to sort out if it's real. Well, not "real" exactly, but if it's normal light or EM frequencies human eyes aren't supposed to see. My eyes are pure human, brain too, and my blood's got only the same old nanites everyone breathes in and nothing more. But that doesn't stop me from sometimes seeing electricity. Seeing into the spirit-air.

At the end of the alley, my feet find the stairs leading into the backways.

Iron City's built on cliffs and canyons, so the ground floor of a building on this side of Marion Hill ends up being the fifth floor on the other side. Some of the switchbacks carved up the cliffs rise and fall a thousand meters at a shot. I know Iron City's hidden scaffolding of stairs, tunnels, skybridges, and caverns that get me up and over and down and around like I know my own skin. Citizens use the heated tubes and skytrams, but my work requires unconventional routes. Plus blanks can't ride the transit. Once Mx. Blue told me about these dumb tourists—who vacations on Ganymede?—who got lost and starved to death in the backways.

But not me.

I'm self-sufficient.

I'm feeling proud of that, too, when I pop out of the backways and into Mx. Blue's tinker shop and see him lying there dead.

The workshop looks like it always does. All over everywhere gizmos and wires and sheeting and the guts of dismembered machines. Except Mx. Blue's tipped over backwards in his swively chair, lips all black and open.

The run had been the usual. Steal stuff for Mx. Blue and deliver it to BlackJack. Come back with the credit. Then Mx. Blue buys me food and clothes and stuff to build friendbots and everyone wins. But Mx. Blue can't bank the credit from BlackJack if he's dead. And I've got this hinkey credit slip, and what's going to happen tomorrow when I come to run or tinker for Mx. Blue and he's still lying there dead.

"Hey kid."

I'm the one pale as a ghost now. The shop's empty, the door hasn't opened, but there's a boy standing there. "Who're you? How'd you get in? What happened to Mx. Blue?"

He's my age, with dust-colored curls cut in a nuevo-roman style. He's wearing a crinkly metal-colored coat that goes down to the floor and then just keeps going down, crumpling into piles on the ground. Not practical. He's pretty though, pretty enough it might not matter. I can't see his hands, stuffed in his pockets like that. I know him but can't make out how and where. What the juice?

"They're after you," he says. "That's why they killed Mx. Blue. But you never told him where you live." His voice vibrates off my teeth, vibrates off the equipment in the room. No—vibrates *from* the equipment in the room. Piezo-electric buzz. Creepy, jo. And also, huh?

Jasper's gang had been after me for a while when I palmed that stuff from Mx. Taylor, but that was forever ago, and all cleared up now. No one else is after me except—well, it better not be Ellison. "Who's after me?"

"Keep me safe." The boy says.

I'm totally sure he means the credit slip I just got from Black-Jack but can't explain why. I just know it, like big know, like I know I'm alive.

<*-imeanit-*>

He's gone.

What the cracking juice?

I look at the big brass bell above the door, still and silent. My eyes slide into frequencies I'm not supposed to be able to see. There are haloes and shines off the credit slip in my hand and it zap-cracks like a livewire. I yip and drop it to the ground.

It wasn't starting to electrocute me though—it was just making lights.

But, well, making lights is never good.

Seeing frequencies I'm not supposed to see is never good, even if it's sometimes useful.

I want to leave the credit slip right then, right there, leave it right on the ground. Done, done. But the boy reminds me of a friend I never had and oh, I don't know—what am I going to do about dead Mx. Blue?

The bell chimes, scaring me out of my skin.

Four corper thugs, slick in black biz-wear enter the shop. Pointing. At me. Bad, bad.

I scoop the credit slip back into my pocket. One of them catches the sleeve of my parka as I duck between them. At the same time, my other hand catches the removable corporate pin on the person's thumb and pulls it off. I break the sleeve-grip with a little twist and slither by.

"Get her," another hisses, but I'm way past them all. Feet fast on the stairs up to what's fourth story here, and onto the catwalk between Refinery Q and a tenement.

Heavy-person noises follow me, but that's about the only thing that can follow as I flip over the catwalk, onto a maintenance platform, and through a door into Refinery Q's basement. I contort my way up the vent shaft and peer out the spy hole looking to where I'd just left.

Their corporate style is dark and smooth; their hair's in sharp, black bobs. They spin, confused and clumsy, 'round corners and into doorways, but none of them'd seen where I went. They're too big to follow anyway, and nowhere near double-jointed enough to fit into the vent.

After a bit, they go away. I ooze out, down onto the basement floor.

What've I got? I uncurl my fingers from the corporate pin I swiped. Ringed planet sigil. CryCorp.

I crush it with broken concrete: end transmit.

So it is Ellison who's after me.

Ellison who killed Mx. Blue because of me.

How did he find me? It's been seven years! Bad, bad.

I'm hot but I pull up my hood anyway to squeeze my face in furr like a hug. Self-sufficient Cami, yeah, but sometimes I wish I still had parents. Sometimes it would be nice not to be the one who has to come up with the plan.

Plan, plan. Planning the plan…

Okay, well, I'll need some things if I'm escaping Ellison again. Laundered credit and access to machine parts for building new friendbots. Ones with shocker-guns. Mx. Taylor always has extra running work, that'll help with the credit till I find a tinker with a line on parts. Then there's the gang at the Grizwald Squat, they've always got access to black market tech, sometimes they even give it to me free, who-knows-why.

But maybe Margaret's best since she's the only one who knows anything about Ellison. Or at least that I'm on the run from Ellison. Because I need to make sure she hasn't also turned up dead. Plus, if she's still alive, she can pull the c's off BlackJack's credit slip and butter up the folks at the Grizwald for me.

I clomp off down the dusty-dark basement to the stairs back down to what's the first floor here, third floor on the other side. At the mouth of the long tunnel to South East, I step over a stinky pool of something dark. Whether the gunk's a chem spill from processing asteroid and Kupier belt resources or human waste who knows. I don't wear Tuff-sole boots just because of the cold.

◊

<wait a minute> I think/feel to Cami-in-the-now through the link.

<sure> She responds. The sub-communication, or link-within-a-link, is smooth as normal conversation.

<you were already part of freedom? you knew the cell at the grizwald squat?>

<no and yes but no> The sensation of Cami's bright laughter through our shared connection. <i didn't know anything about freedom. but margaret is who i owe everything to and she's one of their cantors—that's what freedom calls dieuvéssaus—so i'd met the entire cell years before. but i blocked the élans from communicating with me so they never invited me to freedom which was totally frustrating for poor margaret, but she wouldn't go against freedom's protectionist rules>

I let my confusion flow through the link between us.

<sorry, let me unpack that a little more>

A landscape shimmers around me. Cami's there, and I am, and pulses of light like glowing coals, and a smell of copper and cold. It's a different flavor of perspective than I've felt before in any of these sessions.

<it's a little bit of all three of us contributing to this space> Cami explains in response to my wondering of what I'm experiencing. <how you see us, how i see us, how ganymede sees us. i could break the link and have a normal conversation or retell it in story, but i thought you might like to experience what a cantor can do. no offense to caran, jordis, and noa, but they aren't a conduit for the élans like i am>

Cami calls herself "cantor" with Freedom's terminology, but to the rest of the world she would be a Dieuvéssau—a priest or sorcerer in a relationship with an élan vital. Though "relationship" is putting it too blandly. They are ordinary non-nauta humans who élans like to get inside of in order to—well, I've never been too clear, actually, on why they like to fill us.

I take a few breaths to adjust to the new type of space. <okay, unpack your history with margaret>

The shimmery Cami doesn't become more solid, but sensations

spill into the air to illustrate her words. <i was eight when i made the great escape from ellison. he'd been making me play with the spirit in the bottle, so my eyes were all confused about what was matter and what was energy so i followed the flashes like bread-crumbs in the snow>

My heart beats like a frightened child. There's a gust of cold, an image of buildings and streets and people and flashes in the sky, and flashes skittering across the ground, an undulating rainbow of shortwaves in the air, radio streaking through the sky, city sounds, a path in flashing light.

<it was ganymede, leading me to margaret. i was cold, and hun-gry, and when the fear and the fragments cleared there was a sign>

It shines in neon splendor: "MAGIC SHOPPE: OPEN - INFOR-MATIONAL ZAOS."

<i figured a dieuvéssau's shop had to be somewhat safe—it would be non-corporate at any rate—and i was at the end of my end so i went inside>

I smell more copper, and now chocolate, and other metals, and the crispness of ionized air.

<margaret didn't ask questions, she just gave me food, and a bath, and a bed, and let me sleep off who-knows-how-many days running from who-knows-where. and in the morning, she gave me breakfast and started asking questions to help me sort out what i was seeing so i could focus on things in the visible spectrum only>

<so margaret knew what you were?>

<a magnet for all of the élans, yeah. that's like being a dieuvés-sau for every god, not just the one that chooses you. margaret was chosen by zaos. she's been in resonance with it for over a century and it invited her to freedom. it's not like she could look at me and know i'm a magnet any more than you can, but zaos told her about

me and how much all the élans wanted to climb inside me. zaos told her i was coming even, because ganymede told zaos, and a lot of the great escape hinged on ganymede breaking me out of ellison's castle>

(I'm inside Cami's memories, fragmented and dream-like, lacking the movie-like sharpness of nauta memories.)

SEARING WIND OF LIGHT

—flash-pulse-jabber

mumble of a thousand million trillion voices whistling in languages that are almost but not quite known—

There's a peanut butter and jelly sandwich.

Oh Camilla, oh what have you done you've made a mess, don't worry, Nannie will clean it up before Ellison comes home.

"No, Albia, NO!"

...cascade into a hundred million zillion lights and patterns, voices, pushings, pressings, wantings—

"Hello Camilla. Are you ready to talk to the spirit in the bottle?"

never never never

"Here is a hobby horse."

Nannie gave me machine parts, I like to play robots, can I see Mommy now?

(memories end)

We shiver out of memory and back into empty telempathic space. <before ellison got to us, my dad—caí morgan who gave noa the io-diamond—told me that i might see flashes beyond visible light. he was like me, a magnet, only not as strong.>

The boundaries between Cami, Ganymede, and I separate again, and harden. Cami shifts in my primary focus, inside the smell of copper and dust.

Cami shrugs. <so they all knew, the freedom cell at the grizwald

squat. they knew i was a magnet because margaret knew, and she was one of them. but she taught me too well how to block the élans out, and time makes forgetting, especially when you're a street kid trying to survive, and i mostly forgot about the spirits. but i kept up a friendship with margaret. and i was part of the street scene which included the freedom folk. the only difference between them and me is that they had community>

<thanks> I inhale irritation/resentment/relief from Cami around her history with Freedom. <so you were on your way to margaret's...>

◊

Half hour later, I'm on the fourth floor of quadrant South East, ducking down the narrow stairs chiseled into Priyansh Hill to a door set in stone. Teeth made of dataslips grin from the glass head holding the door ajar. Thing gives me creeps because one time I swear I heard it speak. Flashes of electricity come from the crust of copper wires around the holosign, flashes no one but me can see. "MAGIC SHOPPE: OPEN - INFORMATIONAL ZAOS." Holos projected over a busted 2V playing static and streaming white noise.

My palms go all to sweat because just because the sign's lit doesn't mean Margaret's alive in there.

The glass head just stares.

Inside is a hard-to-focus mess of candles and string-lights sparking off walls dense with glitter, beads, crystals, coins, unreadable languages traced in glowing paints—same things that're in any magic shop. But since Margaret's god is Zaos, she's also got tech, 2Vs and 3Vs tuned to noise, fractals, dolls dressed up as Mel Cooke and Trixie Borgeault who invented the first navis, a pool of mercury, ancient transit tokens, black bird-feathers that blow in the cave's cool drafts, piles of dirt, crossroads stuff—

"You look like you seen a ghost, Camilla. Come in, there's nothing to spook you here." Margaret's got the voice of old people, rusty like the hills of Iron City. She's alive, good, good.

"Hey." I say casual-like, blinking at the lights. Everything in here's juiced but none of it's wired, so none of the 2Vs and 3Vs should be working. But they're full of electricity anyway. I trouble it till I'm looped every time; where's the power coming from?

Margaret's holding a cup of steaming cocoa and I fancy it's for me.

Margaret looks younger than she sounds, but she still looks ancient. Brown skin, grey hair, laugh-lines like etches on a silicon chip. She's wearing her working clothes, thick white robes of synthwool; she says Zaos likes white robes, but I think they're kind of silly. I'd laugh if I was Zaos. Maybe Zaos likes them 'cause they makes him laugh. Dunno.

Margaret sets my cocoa on the Tarot table and bends her old self into a chair. "Zaos told me you were comin'. You got the soul-cold, Camilla. That drink'll put some warm in you."

"Thanks." I sit and un-zip, but don't dare de-coat. Gotta run quick, quick if things get hinky. "I see flashes in this credit slip," I skip the slip over the table to her and sip my cocoa. "Also, I need you to wash the credit from it for me, bad. The people chasing me when I first got here, they're back after me." Proud to get that all out without sounding like I'm out-of-my-skin afraid.

Margaret picks up the slip in her thumb and finger like it's hot— maybe it is again, who knows—and holds it at arm's length, turning it over. She half-rises toward her credit reader, changes direction, and shuffles to the altar instead. "Drink your heat, Camilla. I'll figure the slip."

I take another sip, the spike of rum warming my toes.

Margaret sticks the slip into a datareader on the altar. Reader's not connected to anything, but four of the 3Vs go from white noise to flicker-fast patterns, pretty colors and sounds that speak a code I can't 'cypher. The air smells of cold and dust, and whisky, cinnamon, and copper pipe.

I'm bored because my cocoa's done.

Margaret pulls the slip from the reader and turns back around.

"You keep this slip safe, Camilla." Her laugh-lines have all run down like the joy's drained outta her. Like BlackJack. Pale as a ghost. "Don't you use this in no credit reader, either, and don't you give it to no one, you hear? It's a gift for you, Camilla. Don't you let anyone take it from you, not even from your cold, dead hands."

"Okay." I'm not at all into the sound of that. "But I kind of still need credit if I'm gonna stay on the down-low."

Margaret shakes her head and presses the slip hard into my palm. It's warmer than the cocoa, warmer than the rum. "You don't need no credit, Camilla. You need to get your tail right-fast to Grizwald Squat. You tail it there and tell Fish everything you ain't tellin' me. Fish'll keep you safe from your troubles."

"But the credit? I really, really need the credit!" Fish keep me safe from Ellison? A rone Operator? Yeah, right, he's like a million-billion times less able to run and hide from bad guys than I am.

Margaret purses her lips at me, a long straight line of disapproval.

Whatevs. "Your god got anything useful to say about my troubles?"

"That you got 'em!" Margaret's disapproval-lips go to anger, but not at me. It's a kind of general-angry at the world; she's got a whole different look for when she's angry at me. "You listen to Zaos, you listen to me, and you get your tail to Grizwald and show this credit slip to Fish. Today! Now! Scram!"

Forty-five minutes of catwalks-and-ladders later, I enter the abandoned basement of Refinery J where the equipment long ago got too old to fix. I say hi to the friendbots so they know it's just Cami-come-home and unlock the closet door with the e-key on the chain around my neck.

The friendbots click and whirr—tiny drone ones and little floor ones clacking their tiny pincers. No one's ever found me, but the friendbots sure find plenty of vermin. The big kind that would've eaten all my chocolate. The friendbots take care of them, snicker-snack.

Inside my closet, I kick off my furr boots, flop on the mattress, and shiver in the cold and pitch-dark, thinking nothing.

Feeling freaked.

Like, totally screamy-bad freaked.

Screamy-bad, yeah, screamy, scream—

Before I know what I'm doing, I'm coiled in a tight ball, my knees up under my chin, arms around my knees, screaming, screaming, SCREAMING AS LOUD AS I CAN HELP HELP HELP ME SOMEONE!

But I'm deep in and underground.

No one's here to hear me scream.

Which is the only reason why I'm doing it.

Scream, scream, and scream.

And cry.

A soft purring body brushes my hand and it's Jumbo, my biggest friendbot, rubbing up against me like I programmed him to do when he hears me cry. Good old Jumbo. Synthfurr and heat. Pry my fingers off of my knees and thread them into his warmth. Jumbo doesn't do protection or surveillance; he just keeps me company. Well, except for when he's in defense mode where he can snap off a body's thumb with his extra-large pincers.

I'm achy and hungry now that all the screams and cries are gone. I crack on a glo and say, "Jumbo, chocolate bar."

With one more hard lean on my leg as I sniffle, he whirrs and clicks off to the food stash in the wall. He skitters back on bug legs to hand me the bar with a purr.

I chew and look around at the Jasmine Flowers and Flowers Powers Show flatshots on the walls and my clothes all in a mess everywhere. Good, good. Turn on the space heater. It'll get better.

"Music, comfort mix, quiet. 1V mode," I tell MuseBot. The soft pink cube wakes with an audio-only of Caran Watts' new track "Silence." Atmospheric and dreamy, like I'm floating in space among galaxies. Insignificant. Peaceful. I mouth along, "you are there in silence / you are there in stars / you are there in my dreaming / in everything better than I ever was…"

I sigh without sound. Silence is good. I flick a switch to put the song on repeat.

I know CW's a big celeb, and everyone knows his name, but his music makes me think he knows what it's like to be a non-person like me. And also, like he knows what it's like to see deep into the EM where human eyes aren't supposed to be, like the second verse of "Electricity Alive" about the lights in the electrical fields, and the whole third set release that tells a little story about a telempathic fugitive from the future.

I'm de-freaked enough to de-coat now, and stuff my parka next to my bed. Crack off the glow. Pull the blankets up around my chin.

Jumbo makes a *bruppt* noise and noses me to let him under the covers. He presses close and trills, heaters warming up his furr. I bury my face and hands inside his softness and wait to de-freak enough to sleep. Always easier to think after sleep. Figure out what to do then. See if I can get credit somewhere. See if...

I wake with a cool hand across my mouth.

The room's not dark but it's not proper-lit either. The person hunched over me's glowing, or maybe something behind them's glowing, everything in a blur-smear of un-focus—

Why didn't the friendbots wake up and—

"Shhh, I'm a friend."

I don't recognize the voice as anything but female.

"Just don't—don't bolt, 'k? It's okay if you scream, just don't—don't bolt." The hand comes away from my mouth. "Name's Djen. Margaret sent me. I'm a friend, 'k, friend."

My heart's a million-billion beats of way-too-panic-fast. No way anyone can get past my friendbots except me, no way—

Relax Cami, enough to breathe. You gotta breathe if you're gonna slip her, she's not holding you down well, but if you wanna bolt you gotta breathe—

Djen continues in a funny not-accent, sort of slurred like a drunk person, but not quite. "Ice it Cami, okay? We're just not a threat is all."

I break her hold and scramble back against the wall, switching Jumbo into combat mode. Still can't focus; there's this weird glow bridging between normal light and energy zapping around the room and all the tiny hairs on my arms are on end like I'm in a static-electric field—

A wave of <*greeting-calm*> spreads warm though me. I'm quite sure that feeling's not mine.

"That's Stella." Djen says, like she can read my mind.

My vision clears all the zappings so I'm just seeing the visible spectrum.

The woman's wearing a red jumpsuit, spacer-style. Tzaddium-blue shimmers across her dark forehead in the weird light. Tight coils of hair go down past her butt, and that's a lot of hair 'cause she's like two meters tall. "What's Stella?" I squeak out some words.

"My dimensionship. I'm a Pathfinder. It's not important."

She makes no sense. But then, she's an Operator, and they basically never make sense. An Operator being in my closet also makes no sense, but I let it pass for more pressing business. "How'd you find me?"

Djen shrugs. "Mesh."

"Uh—"

"Margaret told me you were ignoring her advice to see Fish. The three of us had a bit of a discuss about how to handle you in light of that." Djen relaxes onto her haunches, but her hands keep busy with each other and she's wound tight as a clockwork. "It's the gravity. Makes me feel like I'm on fire." She twitches, or maybe shrugs, and grins hugely, "You're a real clever girl, Cami."

"Not clever enough to keep up with you leaving out every other sentence." I pull my head up, proud. "No one does anything with me. Not Margaret, not Fish, and not you. I'm the boss of me."

"'Course you are. But it's not all about you, now, is it. You're not the boss of it all, are you."

That logic's no logic at all.

Djen purses her lips into Adult Face. "You're in a dung of trouble, Cami. I'd be taking you away with me on *Stella-Maru* faster than starlight, except Ganymede wants you here."

I'm done with this, done, done. "Yeah, so, Djen? You seem nice enough and all, but I don't know what you're talking about, like, at all, and now I have to move and stuff since you fingered my locale, so excuse me while I start packing." I slip out of the blankets, Jumbo clacking distress. How am I gonna pack up this stuff, and where am I gonna move it? There aren't that many abandoned buildings even in the slummy parts of Iron City. Maybe the basement of the old North East Bazaar? Hardly anyone goes there since they opened the new Plaza—

"You'll be safe at the Grizwald. I'll protect you." Djen says.

"You? An Operator? Protect me? Yeah, right." I laugh.

Djen narrows her eyes, and I swear I can taste her displeasure bitter on my tongue. What the juice?

She points her finger toward the ceiling, and every one of my security friendbots line up to follow it. How is she controlling them? That's shouldn't even be possible.

"You have no idea what an Operator can do," she says. And traces out shapes in the air.

My security friendbots follow in a neatly flowing line to spell out "I will protect you."

"What the cracking juice?"

Djen's still and silent as the walls, eyes narrow and face masked by the loose blankness of an Operator's stare. "You follow me to where it's safe," she says, and leaves without saying anything more just like the weird Operator person she is.

That afternoon I show up at Fish's door on the top floor of the Grizwald Squat with my things strapped around me and wheeled behind me, swarms of security friendbots at my back and Jumbo clicking along at my side.

The folks on guard let me in.

Fish is in his bean chair sipping a soda, eyes lost in some Operator-realm.

"If you and Djen are gonna make decisions about what's to happen with me," I say, "I'm moving in. You can keep all the bad away from me, since you think you know so much. But don't say I didn't warn you when y'all turn up dead. Mx. Blue wasn't the first, you know. There's a mega-corp after me and anyone who's ever cared for me except Margaret has turned up dead."

Fish doesn't respond, so I stomp off into the divided-up old penthouse looking for a room to set up squat. If they wanna boss me around, least-ways I can make it easier to see the bossiness coming. Plus, it is true that there are always people with big knives guarding the door.

"No fun, Jumbo," I say as he clicks around the edges of the empty room, making a map of the space. "No fun at all."

◊

"And that's," Cami announces as the link fades, "how I got to Grizwald Squat. Now you have to go clean up before Caran's lecture. That I'm not invited to."

SESSION 17:
CARAN & CAMI / GANYMEDE

Caran and I walk into my office after breakfasting together—after spending all night together and waking up together. After attending the most stimulating concert and talk I have had the privilege of engaging in. I've always enjoyed Caran's music—always enjoyed music in general in a scientific way. I study humans and human cultures, and art is part of the triangulation of understanding. Art, science, politics, spirituality—all of our second-order institutions give different windows into culture past, present, and future.

But last night—I have never before felt music connect with my feelings. I've before never gotten chills from it the way that some people do.

Was it my resonance with Muse? The creature was most certainly there, blatant, manifesting visibly and vibrating piezoelectric sound through the crowd.

Was it my resonance with Caran?

I get shivers again and shut down that chain of thought. I don't want to reflect on how compromised I am. On how much Caran is influencing me when I need to be clear-headed, cognizant of bias, aloof, alone. On how badly on some level I hope everything blows up. If I don't think about it, I can pretend it isn't happening for a little bit longer.

But I also learned things about art at the lecture that enrich my research, like about theoretical models of creativity and its stages of problem identification, immersion, incubation, insight, and confirmation. Science and other disciplines use that process just as much as art does, which deepens my understanding of Noa, Jordis, Cami, myself.

"You've got to get out, Steven," Caran is telling me, "be a part of the world. See the glow in your face from just one night outside the box!"

He's glowing too, and gods help us both. I think my skin is of a tone to hide the blush, if not the glow, but I'm not sure. The blush may be too much, may be out of control.

Also, I learned Caran can see through me.

I am terrified, uncomfortable in my squirming skin, but I also want him to see through me. I want to become transparent. To be known. To become a *person* instead of The Researcher.

But isn't a desire to remain aloof, aloft, outside the system, to have my person-ness removed why I became The Researcher?

"It's your music that makes me glow," I say to Caran, "my box is just fine otherwise."

"Um-hm." He captures all the teasing disbelief there ever was in his tone. "And weren't you listening last night?"

"That creativity requires new information and new experiences."

"Um-hm."

Cami is already in my office, playing her 3V game with her legs tossed over the arm of the chair.

"Oh, hey there," She blinks off her game. "I guess the sing-and-talk thing I wasn't invited to went well?"

"Did you know Steven has no friends?" Caran says to Cami.

"I have friends!" The words tumble out in defensive reflex.

"No, you have *colleagues* and *collaborators*."

Cami sighs. "Don't tease Steven. He's enough a fish out of water."

Caran's lightness vanishes like a flame blown out and he fixes Cami with an intense stare. "Aren't we all?"

In the stormy silence he's created, we settle into our usual places. Caran and Cami track each other with their eyes, as though communicating. Perhaps they are, perhaps there is an élan-generated link between them that leaves me outside, The Researcher once more.

"So," I clear my throat, "Noa was unconscious in a Black Market medical, having the electrical damage she sustained on Io repaired. Jordis was on Europa connecting with Ammiel and the Operators and gathering evidence against her father. And the two of you were with Freedom's cell on Ganymede. You'd figured out that the fixed-domain élans attached to Europa, Io, and Ganymede had placed uncorrupted versions of themselves into your safe-keeping—likely because they knew Dividia was coming for them. Do I have that right?"

Cami nods, giving me her full attention now. Caran worries at his hands.

"All right. Ready to take me there?"

Ganymede raises the hairs on my arms, and we are inside Caran's memories.

◊

Cami swings her legs off the edge of the roof who-knows-how-many stories up, and I curl away, chin on my knees. Looking over the edge makes me dizzy like I want to hurl.

"Haven't you been on this rooftop before?" Cami asks, like she can read my mind.

Well, if she's in resonance with the moon, maybe she can. "Not really."

"But you know Fish? He said you got your old room."

"Fish exaggerates. Most I ever saw of Ganymede outside a performance hall was that weird night the InteliCorp theft went bad and I almost froze to death, and most of that was in the dark."

"Ha!" Cami shout-laughs, startling me again with the loud-random-pierce of her sounds. "I knew from the music you knew some of what it's like to be me! I'm a thief too!" She tries to fist bump me, but of course I miss because it takes forever to figure out the gesture since I don't have motor running through my navis. Nothing's ever good as the drugs.

"I was a terrible thief." I tell her. "Hated it. Hated everything about it."

"Really? I love swiping stuff." Cami smacks her lips. "See that sticking-out bit over there?" She points at a crag across the abyss, switching subjects like confusion. "That's Fox Head Cropping, see the eyes? Fifteen meters, straight up. One time I got dared to climb it for fifty c's."

Looking over's not as bad as looking down. City lights strung at angles across skybridges and staggering up cliff-sides to intersect the horizontals of lit windows. The simsuns are dark so people can sleep, but who sleeps all at the same time in a city? Everything's done in shifts, crowds on the ground in the semi-twilight of the streetlamps and Jupiter's crescent. "Did you do the dare?" I ask Cami and squint up at thin, dry clouds.

"'Course I did!" Cami laughs. "Easiest fifty I ever made. Iron City's got strong hills if you know where to put your hands. I always know where the soft stuff is and where it's solid rock."

"That's your connection to Ganymede," I tell her. And now I'm missing Muse, hole near as deep as the hole of my missing drugs. The hole where all the me is supposed to be.

"Hey." Cami jabs a finger in my ribs, hard enough I can feel it. "You wanna see?"

Swallow the hole. Pretend to be whole. "See what?"

"See Ganymede!"

"Iron City?"

"Yeah! One of my fave squares is on the other side of that hill." She stands and steps off the edge of the roof like it isn't a bone-crushing drop to the abyss, and just as I choke on my heart, I hear the clang-rang of her boots on rusty metal.

Crawl to the edge, pulse pounding.

Cami smiles up like a monster from a catwalk strung between the Grizwald and the building across the way.

"Oh c'mon, we can't."

"Why not?" Hands on her hips. "You scared of heights or something?"

"No, it's just the fact that—" That what? First time in a decade, I'm free of handlers, fans, and branding. Fresh patch on my arm means I'm free of worry about my next fix. Navis in my head means I'm free of the more annoying limits of my nauta wiring. It's like being Dragon again. I can walk the streets like a nobody. Have some fun.

My own boots clang-rang on the catwalk beside Cami. I love that sound; stomp and make it again. Clang-rang, clang-rang. Wind whistling through railing rungs. Patter-pat hands on cables, vibrations coming up through the bottoms of my feet as we run, like a sub-woof, yeah! Pure industrial magic! "All right Cami-cam-cam-illa, show me your city!"

◊

Ohmygods I'm running across the grizwald catwalk with Caran-cracking-Watts singing behind me and making music with his feet and everything is amazing!

That is, till I swing the railing, slide the meter down the cliff face, land on the ledge jutting down from Marion Hill, head into the cave, and look back and he's not there.

I go all the way round back to the mouth of the cave to find him a meter still outside, shaking his hands, pale as a ghost like Black-Jack had been—only they told me BlackJack was probably scared because he'd been there when Ganymede had put a piece of himself into the credit slip. "C'mon, what are you, scared?" I laugh at him.

"Yeah, of course I'm scared," he snaps. "And you should be too. You were there when we talked about Dividia. And you want me to walk into the fucking shadows?"

I shrug and release a handful of light-bot friendbots in a sparkle around me.

He reaches forward to try to catch a light-bot like it was a firefly in Flowers Powers' Fairy Grove. Eeeee!

"What are they?" He makes another swipe, his face projecting total delight—OHMYGODS CARAN WATTS IS DELIGHTED BECAUSE OF SOMETHING I MADE—I'm so proud of myself.

"Friendbots! You like them! Little machines with light up parts. I tinkered them myself—I'm a tinker, did you know?—each one alone isn't worth much but together they're way more fun than a glow. Look, they follow my finger to make patterns! C'mon, I want to show you the ice fountain in Kafele Square."

I think everything's fine as we smile, and he takes a few steps in and I turn back and he's still following me. But then he says, "So, we need to talk about the élans."

"No we don't." I swirl my finger to make the light-bots dance.

"Yeah, we do. Djen says we do and this time I agree with her. That's how come I followed you up onto the roof. This is a dangerous time to be a magnet, Cami, a dangerous time to be in the dark, to be in the shadows—Hey, do that again."

"What?"

"Kick that rock. Thonk it against the wall."

I'm kind of mad at him for bringing up stuff I don't want to talk about, but I squeal anyway. "Is this how you make up songs? Am I helping you make up a song?"

"Some parts of songs, yeah. Don't scream again."

I hold in the glee-scream as I find the rock and kick it. It goes tong-ping; I can hear why he likes it. I do it again.

"So the first thing you need to understand about the élans is they're not remotely like us," he says.

"No shit, Thelma Savvy Girl Detective."

"No, I mean it. You can't assume anything. It's easy to fool yourself because they're meta-intelligent like us, they have laws, culture, social structures. They form telempathic links, share our feelings, bridge our thoughts—"

"—tell me where to put my hands on the cliffs." *...lead me to safety from Ellison's castle.* I shiver even though my parka's good quality. "But can't we just enjoy the day?"

He ignores me and keeps talking, making a complicated beat on his thighs with his hands as we walk. He might be the greatest singer ever but right now he's acting like a boring old adult.

"Élans aren't born, they don't die, they split and mutate into new identities, or split and explore and merge back into one. They talk to stars. Some seem attached to a specific location, like Ganymede; others roam the galaxy and who knows, maybe even beyond. They've near-zero grasp of mortality, human frailty. We've yet to invent the tech to detect most of whatever-and-wherever they are. Slow end of the EM's our one-and-only common ground, and they control it hella better than we do. And they've almost killed us all before for changing them against their will with our thoughts and feelings without anyone even knowing."

"You mean the stuff about Freedom Fish explained? About how Freedom's founders got sucked into the élans' debate over whether humans were something to talk to or something to destroy, and then the élans decided to be our friends. But then we betrayed them by weaponizing one of them, so most of them left, and now we have to be careful not to piss them off again or they'll stop protecting Freedom and also might want to kill everyone, except with Dividia that's exactly what just happened?" I ask despite not wanting to be talking about it at all.

"Yeah."

"Why do we even have anything to do with them at all then! Just leave each other be." I'm scared because now I know that the spirit in the bottle Ellison wanted me to talk to was Dividia. I'm also angry because being scared makes me angry—there's no room for fear, fear means mistakes, and mistakes mean not eating, and getting caught, and everything bad. I wish he'd shut up.

"Well, that was the idea," Caran says. "Most of the mobile élans got as far the fuck away from us as possible. Zaos stuck around, probably because it's interested in information and humans generate an ass-ton of fucking data. Some of the other ones would pop in from time to time to fill their chosen Dieuvéssaus, but they never stayed long. With this recent Dividia thing, though, they've all vanished completely except those attached to fixed domains, like

Ganymede. Margaret hasn't been able to contact Zaos for days. Every legit Dieuvéssau's gods've just left 'em. They don't know what the fuck they've been communicating with, but they feel the shift."

I put my hood up; it's colder in the middle of the cave than at the ends. The idea of most of them being gone seems a relief. Less sparks in the air I'm not looking for, less chance of alien voices in my head.

Caran ruins my hopeful thoughts. "Just because they're gone doesn't mean they're having nothing to do with us. They could be plotting a way to kill us all. They could be plotting a way to protect the fixed domain élans like Ganymede from Dividia's resonance—which, again, could involve killing us all. Or maybe plotting some way to change Dividia back to whatever it was before Ellison got a hold of it, which could be messy even if they don't go after humans directly."

Whatevs. Don't see why it's gotta be my job to fix this. It's all aliens and adults and nix that.

"Which is why you need to talk to Ganymede and find out what the fuck is going on and maybe stop Dividia from realigning him too because if all the élans in the Jovian system start resonating fear that would be very, very bad. But a conversation's not going to happen unless you loosen up and let Ganymede in. So how about you tell me your story with Ellison and Dividia that's caused you to shut the élans out because you should be able to talk to them just as easy as opening your mouth to me right now. Slop it Cami, what's your story?"

◊

Could I have done that any more painfully?
Cami stops kicking the rock, and stops moving, goes silent.

"Who says I've got a story?"

"Sorry." I'm sorry to make her hurt, sorry to lose another chance for a friend, everyone hates me in the end. Might as well be a prick up front and get it over with. "Sorry but Stella's empathic, Cami, she can feel your walls. We know your dad was working for Cry-Corp on Io, and Margaret knows you were running from Ellison. It's not like you can keep your story all to yourself because it's half-out already. Slop the rest and then get over it right the fuck fast so you can have a sit-down with Ganymede and fix the fucking world."

I see the edge of her face in the trembling glow of her tiny robots as she looks away. I don't deserve friends anyway.

We walk a long time in silence, save her feet going spoot-spoot in a sad-angry trudge.

When we get near enough the exit there's a sliver of light, she turns back, older-looking under the weight of a pained half-smile. "Well, maybe I'll tell you my story. After all, you came from shit like me."

Well, there is that. Guess Djen and Fish have been telling her stories about me too. I draw breath but I've got nothing to say so I let it out.

Cami twitches back into fan-girl mode, grinning and glowing and gesturing with a thumb. "C'mon. You haven't been to Ganymede till you've had Bean's Hot Pockets in Kafele Square at the Ice Fountain!"

She takes off at a sprint toward the light ahead and I follow easily, the exercise feeling good.

We squeeze through a slender crevice to—

—to somewhere magical on Ganymede.

Castles of ice rise from the dusty concrete, shimmering in the half-light, strung with ropes of stardust. Hard to tell if they're human-made or a natural event, cascades and spires occupying an ambiguity between geometric and organic. Water flows over them. Shaping and polishing, spouting mists that crystallize into flakes in the icy air to float down to children who try, squealing, to catch them on their tongues.

The fountain's kinetic.

Water powers turbines and belts carrying polished stones, shooting them at chimes. Back-hum motor water-tinkle over ice, pressure-pipes whistling, clamor of water over xylophone keys, black beads over corrugated segments putt-putt rhythm—

"Do you like it?" Cami tugs my sleeve, face worried. "'Cause I thought you might, because—"

It's kinetic and it's sonic and it's like the kinetikosonus, only entirely analogue and I'm laugh-exploding so loud I hurt my own ears, and I can't come up with a thing to say even with linguistics programming, so I sing an accompaniment to the ice until Cami relaxes. I keep singing, joining Cami's laugh to the sound of the fountain, making a connection with the cold until we're both laughing so hard, I can't hold a note anymore. "Yeah I like it!" I shout when I have some control of myself again.

Cami lets loose one of her screeches and grabs my hand before I can cover my ears and pulls me away from the margin and into the crowds. It's a blur of colored parkas and fluffy boots, hoots and yells and children giggling. Smells from vendors; my stomach whines.

Cami swipes the hot pockets so fast I don't know she's stolen them till she's dragged me back across the square, back to the fountain, to perch on its edge. Then she holds a steaming pastry in front of my face.

"No idea what's inside," she giggles. "Unpredictable, always delightful. Pairs with the fountain."

I bite into soft crust to tender, savory deliciousness. Water babbles over loose stone. So good. All of it, so, so good—

"Okay," Cami swallows a bite of pie and takes a deep breath. "Dad sold me and Mom to Ellison when I was three."

But of course, nothing good's ever gonna last.

◊

"That was kind of a crap convo." Cami doesn't break the link, but she pulls us out of the memories. "I've told you parts of it already, when I showed you what it was like escaping Ellison's castle. Can I just summarize?"

"Sure," I say. "Remember, participation in research is voluntary. You don't need to tell me anything you don't want—"

"—to tell, yeah, yeah, how many times you going to recite that, Steven." Caran sighs. "I think you're hoping we won't tell the hard stuff, so then you don't have to deal with how it makes you feel."

"Dear gods, you know Cami's story and you still say that? If anyone needs to feel comfortable that the research is voluntary, it's Cami!"

"Yeah, you tell yourself that."

"Boys!" Cami says and a pulse of <*intense++displeasure*> throws itself through the link. "Save your bicker for later. I'm fine with telling, just don't particularly want to go real-time on a tormented hour of Caran dragging the past outta me. It won't be any more engaging to Steven than it was for us, and neither me nor Caran have perfect recall anyway."

"Dad sold me and Mom to Ellison when I was three because of credit debt. Ellison'd been watching him from before I was born 'cause he knew Dad was a magnet for the élan vitals. We think someone from Freedom might've tipped Ellison off in the build-up to the Runner Wars when Freedom was slopping its secrets everywhere. Ellison wanted Dad for the Dividia project because Ellison was having a hard time manipulating the thing's resonance in exactly the way he wanted it to go. He maneuvered Dad into a bunch of bad business deals that put him into credit debit so he could indenture him. But then I was born."

"And you were a much stronger magnet than Cái Morgan," I say her thoughts aloud, the boundaries between us mushy through the link.

Cami's big blue eyes lock into mine, serious and unblinking. "Much. Stronger."

Caran provides, "Élans liked to hang around Cái, brush up against his biofeedbacks. Sniff his feelings. But they liked to talk to Cami. She was catnip to them."

"Whatever that means." Cami shrugs. "Someday you gotta teach me what all the animals in the sayings are, you said you would get to it. But yeah, they liked to talk to me, direct.

"The deal was, Dad would work for Ellison on Io by aligning Dividia's resonance in its temple there, and Ellison'd keep me and Mom for collateral. There's some part of the standard Federal Banking Worlds corporate charter that allows for that, all on the up. Jordis says most corps don't invoke it 'cause there's ways to get the same result with happier workers, but Ellison wasn't interested in Dad's debt, even though till the last I guess Dad thought he could pay it off in diamonds. It was all just a set-up to get Dad working with Dividia on Io and me into…into the lab." Cami shivers a thread of panic through the link. But she holds steady and keeps going.

"Mom was still with me for a while. And then there was also

Nannie, this weird old woman who took care of me. I still dunno if Nannie ever had a real person name, even Abia the security woman called her Nannie. Abia was awful; Nannie was nice. Bad-cop good-cop games, I guess. If I was good, I could see Mom. Today I would've known neither of them was my friend, but back they were like a nice and a mean grannie. Nannie and Abia sometimes taught me things, letters, numbers, school things. Nannie'd gone a little daft so her teachings didn't always make sense.

"Anyway, Ellison did a lot of stuff to open me up to resonance with the élans, drugs, meditation, punishment, ritual magic, till all the borders between worlds were mush.

"Then he'd bring out the spirit in the bottle.

"The bottom of the 'bottle' was a crystal matrix, the disc-shaped expensive kind that stores zettabytes of data. And around it this... well it read as a tall glass cylinder, only it was really microwaves woven in a force-field that held the spirit inside with a holo of glass thrown up around so no one would put their hand through it and fry.

"Ellison would put current under the crystal matrix and it would make the spirit come out in dark wisps like a reverse ghost. That's what I called it: the reverse ghost. I was supposed to talk to it, but it never said anything back. Then Ellison would get angry."

"Dividia," I say.

"Dividia," Cami nods.

A shudder moves through the link, raw hands clawing for purchase and slipping, flailing, and me not caring if I fall—

"Wait, were there two of it? One on Io and one in the matrix on Ganymede?"

Caran shrugs, "Yeah, we think maybe for a little while. We think Ellison may have gotten it to do the fractal thing so he could run experiments in two places at once and then let them join back together."

"Anyway, I slopped all that to Caran, though I certainly made him work for it."

"It was okay," Caran shrugs. Neither of them appears affected by the disturbing, short shift of Dividia energies inside our link. "Thought you were going to hate me forever for it, though."

"I was spun at the time, but it felt good to get it out too. I hadn't even told Margaret most of that stuff. The harder the story is to tell, the better it feels to come out sometimes."

"So then we went back before the others could realize we were gone." Caran says and draws me into his memories.

◊

"Do you think you could find it again?" I ask Cami as we step back out of the cave.

"What? Ellison's castle?"

"Yeah. You remember anything of where it was, a landmark?"

"Nil. When I escaped, Ganymede had filled me. He was inside me, controlling me. I wasn't conscious of how we got to Margaret's."

"Ganymede can help you find the way back then. Open up, let him in, you know how, you talked to him at Mx. Blue's the other day."

"*He* talked to *me*. He's not talking to me now. I can't do it."

"Try to remember back. How'd you do it then? Recapture it."

"I can't. I was eight years old and terrified."

"Then go back to eight years old and terrified. Get into it, wear it like a coat, be it again."

Cami does open it up then, right up into a spit of fury. "Shut-the-fuck-up! You of all people should know some stuff can't be fixed just by wishing it!"

Tears freeze in the subzero Ganymedean air. *Sorry, Djen, I'm done pushing. If you want me to be more of an ass, you'll need to give me better drugs.* "Sorry."

We tromp back across the skybridge in silence and I'm thinking she must be done with me for good. But she stops in a patch of shadow beneath the edge of the roof with a frightened face, throat moving as though she's swallowing all the dry in her mouth. "There's reasons I don't want to open up to it, okay? I'm not just protecting me, I'm protecting everyone. Ellison and CryCorp are still looking for me, and they kill anyone they think knows how to get to me. Torture and kill. Like they did to Mx. Blue."

I reach toward her, but she shies away.

Her next words are colored with panic-rush. "If I let them find me though, they'd probably take me straight back to Ellison and then I won't be a danger to you."

Well now. "Guess that makes one more thing you and I have in common. They're looking for me too." Memories of Milktown-lost and the thugs waiting for me in the rover bay—the shadows we stand in feel alive. My voice makes almost no sound as I force the air in my lungs to say, "Wonder—if we got caught—if they'd take us both back to Ellison?"

We climb back onto the Grizwald's rooftop in silence; I'm not keen on making the idea any more real, and I'm guessing she's not either.

Back on the rooftop, Cami disappears into the hatch and emerges again with an ice cream for herself and a vitamin juice for me. "'S good," she says. "They'd no clue we were gone."

I crack the juice, take big, buzzing gulps. Maybe turning ourselves in to Ellison is a bad idea, but it seems like a good one even though I'm sober. It's probably the best chance we'll have to find out what's going on, and we can prep for it, smuggle in some freedomtech, have a plan to stay in contact and get out. Better than waiting and wondering and guessing at any rate. Better than letting Dividia realign more élans into engines of fear. There's got to be some way the two of us can influence Dividia's resonance. Turn things around.

"Do you want to tell the others that we can infiltrate Ellison's plans?" Cami settles back in on the cold edge of the roof, feet dangling.

"Probably should, yeah." I still can't get close to the edge, though the chasm is beautiful now with the music of the catwalk and the cave and the fountain's clamoring overlaid on the shimmer of city lights. Composing Ganymede's song. "Dividia, when you met it, did you feel afraid of it?"

"Not really." Cami kicks her feet. "I was afraid of Ellison, and of the castle, the experiments… I was a little afraid of the security woman Abia; she was mean. But Dividia was just…lonely feeling. Like it was missing parts of itself. By the way, Noa's awake."

◊

"Hello, Steven." The link breaks and I'm back in my office with Noa standing in the doorway. The air vibrates with the static charge of an élan, but it's complicated and unpleasant; there's dissonance. Like there's more than one élan in the frequency, and they don't get along. "I'm sorry," Noa says in her clipped monotone, "about what happens next."

My office vanishes into Caran's and Noa's memories.

◊

Noa's awake, Cami tells me and I'm pushing through the hatch, running down the staircase, feeling for Noa's signal but she isn't open to broadcast, so I crash into the room where they put her after she got out of medical.

◊

I am on the floor. My back is to the corner of the wall. Mousie is on my lap and Io's diamond cupped in my hands. I need to feel pressure on all sides. Weight. Something to hold me down because I am floating away. All away. Everything away.

He crashes in.

◊

"I'm an ass." I reach for her shortwave signal, but I can't find it. Her navis should be working—"I ruined everything for you."

◊

I don't move. I can't move. Everything is flicker-snap-flash. No points connect. My new, not-broken navis works, but I do not. I don't want to turn on, to connect. Then the bigness will come in and I will float away.

But I do turn on. I do connect. Because my discomfort is his fault. Io's diamond between my hands flares hot.

◊

It's like pushing against a locked door that suddenly gives and I'm falling through, into a searing telempathic link <*sorrysorrysorrysorry*>

◊

The burning diamond in my hands makes a link between Caran and me. My feelings surge through and into him or maybe it's his into me, I am too angry to know. <*fear/rage* so much has changed in nineteen years and you just left me YOU JUST LEFT ME and the world has changed haschangedHASCHANGED—>

// —- - +#wallofBIGNESS BIGNESS! &*fear* <theworldissobig they fixed my navis and everythingis SOBIG! YOULEFTME! *ANGER*!>

<i'm sorry noa hatemeideserveit>

◊

We return to normal communication in Memspace as Io's telempathic link dissolves. We face each other in coded presentations that are more than body and less than mind.

She presents as sketchy approximation of herself, clothed

in a kimono of red-and-gold butterflies. Their wings shiver like knife-edges, emotives sparking fury-fear, her body a glowing coal. She lunges with both fists punching, butterflies igniting into flame, burning my feathers black.

"Go on," I dig my claws into the imaginary nothing of the Mem, flapping wings burned to the bone. "Go on I deserve it."

Noa releases a violence of thoughts roiling too fast to decode, filling the space, filling me, becoming the world, the signal getting tighter, tighter, pushing me, *that's right, fill up my emptiness with your pain, hurt me, hurt me until I'm free—*

◊

I cut the connection, leaving us hard on the floor of the physical room. I haven't moved in days, haven't been able to move in days, but something clicks, snaps over, some piece of biology routing itself around the brain injury, or my navis finally working out the right algorithm—*I AM COMING FOR YOU*

◊

Noa, teeth bared, snarling, rages toward me across the floor of the Grizwald squat.

She contacts me like a catapult, all fists and teeth and hair. I close my eyes as she lets loose everything terrible I've done to her, everything I deserve. It wasn't enough to betray her, sabotage her, destroy her paradise, her freedom, make her leave Io. No, I'd left her to deal with the shout and babble of the Core after spending nineteen years isolated from signal with a broken navis on a hell moon. I was too busy wandering in half-dead papped-out delirium. Blood fills my mouth. Her fists beat my chest, drumming the hate in my heart until she's spent, and withdrawn, and I'm exactly where I deserve to be.

Signal licks at me.

I open a channel, dragon bruised and burnt on the black floor of the Mem's nowhere.

She stands in her kimono of red-and-gold butterflies, their knife-wings limp.

"I'm sorry Noa."

Noa's butterflies shiver. "I'm sorry too. You only deserved. Some of that." She turns away.

Now's the time to make excuses, talk my way back into her good graces. But I'm not drunk, and I'm not high, I'm just sad, so I fold my broken wings over my cracked claws and wait for her to say her piece.

"Time." She looks back at me, the emotives in the butterfly wings whispering remorse. "It's an irreversible process. Life has too many nonlinearities. It is not possible to un-wind events. Not possible to un-know something."

"That holds for love as well as pain," I say quietly, burying my nose beneath my wings.

Noa breaks the channel.

I crack open my physical eyes, blinking through a haze of blood.

Noa's demeanor is different from how it had been on Io. Her wildness is gone from everywhere except her battered fists, her eyes; she is stiff, symmetrical, controlled. "No one in your Freedom has spent enough time in the mainstream to help me interpret the current system-state. I need you to help me understand the feeds. The flows. The news. What the world has become. What the world is."

"Yes. Of course. Does this mean we—"

She puts a finger to my lips to stop me from asking if we can make up. Her voice hisses with a thousand volcanoes as she strokes Io's diamond with bloody fingers. "It means you will help me make CryCorp pay for what it did to my Io."

◊

I break the link with Noa and Caran. I just can't hold the resonance. There is nothing there I resonate *with*.

"More than you wanted to know about us?" Caran's voice sneers at me. "The reason you keep reminding us we don't have to tell you anything we don't want to tell?"

"No, it's not that, it's—I—it's—I'm sorry."

Cami lets out a long, loud, hissing sigh. "Like there's not enough bickering in this part of the story. Let's not feed the feedback loop."

All the heat drains out of me into my toes. I should have realized that's what was happening. Their whole story, in a way, is about the élan-human feedback effect, and the way people and élans amplify each other's thoughts and feelings. But until this moment, on a personal level at least, it was all just academic. "We really are connected," I gasp. "The élans and us. The élans, our actions, their reactions, the simultaneous impact we have on each other." I am aware that I am gasping. Gasping is trite, and yet, it is exactly what I am doing.

"No shit, Thelma Savvy Girl Detective," Caran echoes Cami's scoffing comment from years ago in the Marion Hill cave.

Cami nods. "Caran and Noa bicker, Ganymede in the link picks it up, gets irritated, makes dissonance in the link. Then you and Caran start to bicker, I'm sitting here thinking about bickering because the next part of the story involves even more bickering and before you know it—"

"Everyone's killing each other." Noa's deadpan severs Cami's rant. "Which is what was happening with the Dividia-tainted moon-élans and the humans who lived on them. Including me, at the time."

I can't find my voice for the first little while. "How are any of us even still alive?" I direct my whisper towards Cami.

The edges of her lips twitch up. "Because bickering isn't all there is. Allow me to demonstrate."

(Cami takes me with her this time.)

◊

"There's no one left in Freedom who can get here fast enough." Djen sits heavy on the couch like she weighs a thousand kilos, feet planted solid, glaring at Fish. "Do you even know what the population of Freedom was before Dividia killed Hyperia and Jost? One hundred sixty-three. In the whole of the inhabited universe."

"Hey, this Dividia thing's the real problem. Arguments about recruitment policies can wait," Fish says.

They're talking aloud for the benefit of me and Margaret. Djen glares. "What can't wait is that—because of recruitment policies— we've got no one competent to send to CryCorp with Cami on such short notice."

Margaret rolls her eyes, but I don't know at what part. Maybe at all the parts. She kneads her old-person knuckles. "You should've hid the rum."

"Hello. Standing right here." Caran takes a step towards the center of the room, stumbles, and stays put on the floor where he falls.

"This is why we can't trust you not to fuck things up." Djen's eyes flash to Caran.

I can't make all their bicker make sense. It's people who have known each other longer than I've been alive leaving out all the bits I wasn't around for.

"Oh come on, when have I ever not pulled through when it mattered?" Caran rolls his eyes.

"When you prioritized your busted ego over your friends and responsibilities and ran off with that music producer?" Djen's bitterness rips the air.

"And maybe I would've prioritized my 'friends' if they'd made me feel the slightest bit fuckin' welcome." Caran's so drunk he can't hold his voice steady. "All I ever was to any of you was a tool in your bicker over Freedom's recruitment. Recruit new members, don't recruit new members. 'If we tell anyone the élans will leave us,' Fish whines. 'But we let Caran in and the élans didn't leave us,' Djen whines. News flash—the élans left you decades ago. Maybe you should've been thinking more about how you were gonna lure 'em back. But who listens to weird Caran and his weird élan. No one. Well fuck you all. Go ahead, die out like you've been tryin' to. I can't stop you. You're as fuckin' bad as Jonathan LaRoque of 100 Worlds Music Corp. All I was to you is a fuckin' tool."

"The cards say bad times for you, always have," Margaret clicks her tongue at Caran. "Say you've got wicked demons gonna get us all. Last thing we need is you dragging Dividia around like a bad blanket."

"We need someone to go to CryCorp with Cami," Fish rumbles disgust. "Caran couldn't even make it two days clean. Djen, what do you think about bringing Ansari here?"

"But Ansari hasn't been invited to know about us according to your rod-ass rules," Caran slurs.

Fish shrugs. "Close enough for crisis. She's got Europa around her neck."

"And I'm plenty clean, no NQ left in me." Caran jabs the bottle of rum at Fish, slopping it everywhere. He licks the spill off his hand. "I'm jus' not sober. Who could make it two days sober livin' with the likes of you. But Ellison and Dividia are better company, so I shouldn't need so much drink to survive the run."

"Hush." Noa grabs his arm. To the others: "Probability of success drops from ninety-six percent to twelve percent if Ansari goes in."

"I'm not so drunk I can't see your idea is stupid anyway." Caran pulls himself from Noa's grasp to knock back more of the bottle. "Remind me again what's wrong with just turnin' ourselves in?"

I'm sick of listening to them, but they won't tune out. I finger Ganymede's credit slip on the chain around my neck, nestled there right along with the key to my old squat in Refinery J. Weird, weird how I'd worn the key on the chain like that so I could be like CW with his kinetikosonus dataslip only to meet him after someone else had swiped it so he's not wearing it anymore. Whatevs.

He's right. Why couldn't they just go along with our getting-caught plan? Probably because they were more keen on rehashing dusty-old arguments that didn't matter anymore anyhow. Or because the plan came from the kid and the drunk. If they cared about Caran getting drunk, they should've ditched the drink. Leaving it out was like setting a shiny, new Rebo-7000 sensor pack out and expecting me not to swipe it.

Weird, weird how I used to daydream about being friends with CW, but that was the faked-up mainfeed version of him. I like the real him better, even if he's a space wreck. They need to be nicer to him if he's to learn to be a proper person. I've seen it all over the street; when a kid doesn't get enough love they bite and yell and destroy everything until someone holds onto them long enough for the hate to burn away, and then the fear under that. I'm lucky; I had parents once and they loved me. I miss them.

I stand, the credit slip hot between my fingers. Inside is the boy with the stupid-long coat.

<*wearyMomentum*> Heaviness, weight, grinding continuation. Dust and cold. <they are trapped in cycles. gears grind out of place, ruining the teeth.>

Huh?

He's standing beside me. Neo-Roman curls touching his long, soft lashes, perfect nose. He slouches in the endless metal coat, hands in his pockets. He's a lump of super-dense metal in a stream of colored noise.

<machines break when not properly oiled>

It's nice that I still have my own thoughts even though I'm thinking his too. <yeah, ok, so let's stop the machine>

He smiles, prettier than super-star José Adonis. He pulls his hands out of his pockets, cupping them into a goblet. The goblet fills with liquid gold and the smell of dust and ice. He tips the cup to my lips.

My mouth goes dry; he wavers like he's going to disappear. I remember what Caran said about opening myself up to talk to him, finding the resonances. Instead of being afraid, I remember climbing the cliffs of Su Hill just for fun, the bite of stone beneath my fingers and the icy air on my cheeks. I press my lips to Ganymede's cup.

I drink electric. Sensations of multitudes, sniffing and interest and tendrils of connection from alien strands, tasting me—

Ganymede bats them away <*annoyed/later*> He replaces their probing with himself, the fluid of his past-present-future filling me. <recalibrate-the-engines>

Ganymede fills me.

Combined-thought-form more than Cami, other than Ganymede, some kind of Cami-mede: Voice in two tones at once: "Hey everybody, lay off!"

They stop all right. Even Stella goes still. I see her, a miniature sun with big silver-blue eyes and a thin string of thought/felt <*subservience*>

We, Cami-mede, rumble in multi-frequency: "Ganymede doesn't care about the rum. Cami doesn't care about the dumb argument y'all started before she was born. You," we point to Djen and Margaret and Fish, "could show Caran a little more support. And you—" we swing to Caran "—could let the argument go until the important shit's done. For a bunch of smart people, none of you've half a clue between you. If you want to steal Ellison's secrets so you can stop him, shut the fuck up about the rum and listen to the thief. Who also happens to be the only person in the room who's escaped Ellison before. When she was eight by the way, and I've learned a trick or two since then." We look down at our glowing hands.

The weird glow surprises me back into myself, Ganymede gone, poof, the world clamping down onto a small, squeaky, and strangled yip that makes Caran put his hands over his ears.

All eyes on me. Their feelings project as one through Stella's resonance <*-not-that-simple-*>

I start laughing, drunker than Caran on the rush of power from Ganymede's cup. "You poots have got to be kidding me! Noa can predict the future, Caran can move Hades to tears, and I can talk to gods. That's not even counting the rest of you being able to slip through the Mem's security protocols and whatever all a top-end mob Enforcer like Jordis Ansari can do for us. None of you've the faintest what you're worth, do you? You're so used to living on the margin you don't see you've the power to take the center. There's not a place in the inhabited worlds that can hold us. Seems pretty simple to me."

Sad Noa starts laughing first.

I don't feel so powerful ten hours later when I still can't figure out how to call Ganymede back. I've tried everything, even thinking the exact same thoughts of how much I wish people were nicer to Caran, but nothing works and I run back to my room so no one'll see me cry. Sure we're the closest things to superheroes this side of reality, but now that the plan to get caught's a go I realize anew I don't want to see Ellison again. Ever. Or mean Abia or daft Nannie or Ellison's awful castle. Plus since Ellison's got Dividia on his side, what's that do to our edge? No wonder Ganymede won't come back.

Well, at least we've got a plan. And, even without Ganymede, we've got Caran's voice and Noa's math and my fast fingers. But I'm not used to working with a team. And Caran's still kind of drunk and Noa's dangerous-angry and I don't ever want to see Ellison again!

A tap on the door. "May I come in?"

It's Djen's voice but not Djen's MO. She's more about barging in with no respect for a body's privacy. "Okay."

She drags across the threshold like she's got her magboots turned on and the floor's made of super-steel. Her face is blank as ever as she closes the door, but her eyes say worry. Sparkly tendrils fall around her from Stella, who's not a real élan but not-not an élan either. It's confusing. I blink a few times and don't see Stella anymore.

Djen frowns. And sighs. And looks put-upon. Then sways a little and her face relaxes into a weird, sad smile that doesn't look right on her face because I didn't know she could feel so tender. "Wasn't always like this," she says, "me and Caran." Her smile brightens and she closes her eyes.

"Used to sail the stars together, the four of us—me and him, Stella and Muse. Saw so many new planets, the stuff of nightmare and dream. He was sixteen and I was twenty-one when he built his instrument. Must've been working on it the whole two years since I picked him up, working alone in his bedroom. Never said a word. But when he finished, when he was sure it worked and everything perfect, he called me in.

"What a machine! All brass and glass and wire with a ghost of colored light hovering over a 4V plate beneath his bare feet. He couldn't look at me. Thought he was gonna piss himself he was so scared of what I'd say. Stood there, waited for him to pull himself together. He poked a finger into the light. And there was sound. He plucked the air and tiny hammers hit strings in the mess of the machine. And he was dancing, music spurting from his fingers, spreading from his spinning, his singing weaving a landscape of— you know what he can do with sound. He could always do that with sound. It's where he lives.

"He stopped and stood there, shaking. His voice was so small if I wasn't nauta I wouldn't't've heard it. 'Do you like it?' He asked. 'I wanted an instrument I could play, so I could—I just wanted to share—do you like it?'"

Tears run down Djen's face, she's sad-laughing and joy-crying but she's still standing solid like she's locked onto the ground.

"I'm the first person to hear his music. Not the singing, but the whole of what's in his head. He was so small and fragile in that mess of wires, so scared I wouldn't like it. I remember thinking how ridiculous that was, but he needed me to say it out loud. So I said, 'I love it, shit yeah, I love it!' He convulsed with relief and grinned like a demon and clapped with the snapping k-sounds, 'I call it the kinetikosonus.'

"Gods, I burst out laughing. 'Get out!' I couldn't believe it.

"'No, really!' he insisted.

"'That's the silliest name I've ever heard! Sounds like a dinosaur! It's cracking ancient Greek!'

"'Yeah, so culturally appropriate and all!'

"'Culturally appropriate!' We chased each other all over the ship till neither of us could breathe and then I made him play it again and again and again and neither of us felt near so lonely."

Djen wipes her eyes, opens them, and fixes me with a stare so fierce I think she's going to hit me. "You haven't seen us at our best. But I want you to know I love that ass. Love him a lot more than is good for either of us. He is—he can be really sweet. Really special. He can't really." She stops like she's gotten stuck. Then she shivers back to life a few seconds later. "He can't really manage on his own so I'm counting on you to take care of him. Keep him safe. Even if it's from himself. Swear it."

I'm so astonished all I can do is nod.

◊

"So then we did the run." Cami says as the link breaks.

Caran and Noa look as uncomfortable as when we started, curled up on their opposite ends of the sofa. Cami's trying not to notice. It is awkward, all these personal things leaking over personal boundaries. I wonder if it would have been wiser to have interviewed them alone for some of these parts. I stifle the urge to remind them this is voluntary.

Noa says, "And I planned, with assistance from Fish, to steal a shuttle and take it back to Io. Dividia had realigned Io to amplify fear. I resonated with Io. I reacted to the fear, lashed out, with hate and vengeance."

Everyone sits quietly, looking at their hands.

Noa takes a deep breath and exhales, a banishing sound. "I have to return to Callisto for a few days," she says. "I'll be back with Jordis though. For the final together parts."

I nod. My research assistant had put these details on my calendar. We'd planned the next few sessions to focus on Caran and Cami.

Noa stands with a reversal of the eerie automation with which she had sat. She pauses, turning her head to focus on the air between Caran and me. "Be gentle with each other," Noa says. "Things will get rough."

I'm not sure if it's a reference to their stories, or a reference to whatever is going on between Caran and me in the here-now, or maybe between me and the Ethics board if I finally fess up about whatever is going on between Caran and me.

Noa leaves and Cami and Caran relax; the room lightens. "This next part was fun," Cami says.

"Speak for yourself," Caran huffs at her, but there's a warmth to his voice that I'd missed during all the bickering.

"Oh c'mon, you liked it. You always like a rush."

"I'd rather a dosage-controlled rush in the safety of my own room, not a life-or-death-for-real rush like you and Djen."

"Right, whatever gets you through the night."

They've fallen back into their teasing brother-sister banter, but it has an urgent edge. I am certain they are trying to wash away the bad feelings from a moment ago, to wash away Noa's hungry vengeance, to clear the plate for all the awful that's to come. But not now. Not quite yet—

(I am feeling what they are feeling because the link with Ganymede has reopened, and I've slipped into to Cami-mede)

◊

It's extra-cold on level eight in northwest Iron City. We're higher than where Grizwald sits, and according to a thermometer it's warmer 'cause it's where all the fancy rich-person buildings live with their heated awnings. But it *feels* colder because Caran and I've been sitting here forever swinging our legs over the edge of this catwalk, waiting for Djen and Stella to crack the CryCorp building security encryption patterns.

The CryCorp building sits a half-story below. It doesn't go up tall, but it goes in deep into Pyrinos hill. It's got a cold marble facade and a Saturn-shaped sigil that shines like ice. I pull the drawstring of my hood till the furr tickles my cheeks and finger the friend-bots in my pockets.

"Djen says keep waiting." Caran's eyes are out of focus as he communicates in the Mem with Djen. In the cold even Orpheus sounds thin. The chill doesn't seem to bother him though; he's already lost the scarf Djen wrapped him in, and his hood's fallen back.

I think maybe I should pull it up because of what Djen made me promise, but let it be. He's not going to freeze to death in that big furr coat, plus he's got that knitted hat literally glued over his brows to hide the blue across his forehead. Weird, weird that CW is an Operator. Or nauta I guess I'm supposed to call it now. But it doesn't change the music any. Or the fact that he's the dodgiest thing since sliced cheese and the big bang combined and he's my friend!

A tiny ice-flake tickles my nose. The air's too dry to snow proper but sometimes the flimsy clouds flick a flake or two. What's weird is that CryCorp did most of the terraforming of Ganymede back in the day, and Ganymede's the whole reason CryCorp got so mega, but right now CryCorp is trying to turn Ganymede into an evil monster. What's up with that?

<things change> the moon's answer floats to me. <i am more than a sum of my parts>

My fingers curl over Ganymede's credit slip, on a chain now around my neck, keeping it safe like the moon asked. Yeah, things change.

Then Ganymede's next to me. He swings his feet off the catwalk in synch with mine. His crinkle-metal coat goes down and down and down until it disappears into the ground below.

<how come you only talk to me when YOU feel like it?> I frown over at Caran but he's not noticing Ganymede at all; his closed eyes move beneath the lids, like he's reading stuff on them. <we need to talk> I think/feel to Ganymede. <there's stuff we've gotta know. don't go disappeary on me>

<my sisters io and europa make things difficult> Ganymede thinks/feels back, which has nothing to do with what I've said. <they have changed, and we can no longer negotiate influences>

We both look down where the midday crowds thread between the street and the public tube-holes. Those going in-and-out of CryCorp's doors wear high-end parkas. I can tell the natives from the visitors by how bundled they are; living here makes the cold feel normal.

"Djen's ready," Caran says at the same time Ganymede emotes <*satisfaction*>

I eye Caran sideways to see if he's picked up Ganymede's transmit, but he's just bunched small and scared and staring at his hands like he's never seen them before.

"Hey," I poke him in the ribs, hard so I know he can feel it. "What about you? You ready? I'm ready. Let's do this thing!"

He shakes his head no in quick, stiff jerks.

Great. Maybe I should've brought some rum.

<sing to him> Ganymede says.

<i can't carry a tune he'll die of bad sound>

<it's not the tune you need to carry>

I turn towards Ganymede but he's not there again. Whatevs. I don't need a cryptic alien to pull off a heist. I sing the first verse of the "Hymn to Ganymede," thinking maybe if I sing him something he's never heard before he won't mind the off-key so much.

> *O icy moon, how like my heart*
> *When I had come to thee*
> *Both beat and broke I begged a drink*
> *Your cup eternity.*

He reacts to the bad notes like I've stabbed him in the eye, and I guess I was wrong about him never having heard it before because he takes the song from me and makes it come out right.

> *O Ganymede, your beauty true,*
> *You lifted me on high;*
> *You slacked my thirst and calmed my fear*
> *My head a place to lie.*

> *From belt-to-belt your praises ring*
> *Your offering be strong*
> *To guide my way in night-of-day*
> *Ganymede be my song!*

He grabs my arm and slips us both off the catwalk and straight down to the enemy's domain.

◊

"See?" Cami grins at me, Steven, as the link breaks. "There's stuff beyond bickering."

I'm aware of how young she is. The hope in her face. The brightness of her smile.

But my thoughts are dark with fear. *If only it were so simple,* I think.

I hadn't meant my thought to broadcast, but I hear in my consciousness, in a fluty dual-tone of Caran's and Muse's mind-voices meshed together, <ah, but nothing ever is so simple, is it?>

The shadows beneath the sofa shift out of synch with the light. Tendrils reach toward Cami's ankles like the monster under the bed. I squish my eyes shut in brief terror, but when I open them the light is normal. My imagination must be overactive with all this talk of moving shadows.

Cami sighs, and shrugs, and brushes her hand through the air. "I think that's enough for today," she says. "I think you two should go have a nice dinner, celebrate all the things that're good." I see in a flicker, a split-second waver in her voice, that Cami's bright light is just her way to hide the darkness.

I look at Caran. His head is to the side in a listening pose, a posture of hesitant vulnerability. A cloud of anger moves across his face. He gusts air from his lungs and swipes his hands in a banishing gesture.

I don't understand what's happening; the past few sessions have been odd-feeling. Dissonant. Not the sessions or the stories exactly, but the air in which they've occurred. The influence of the élans, perhaps, feeling uncomfortable because of how Dividia had violated them. At any rate, the feeling is now gone.

"I am hungry" Caran says. " Maybe we can go to your place after dinner. I've never been to Trewal, one of the only inhabited worlds I haven't, so you can tell me about it, stop being my mystery man."

Except he shouldn't know so much about me. The more he knows me, the more it will bias the stories he tells me. The more he likes me the more he will take actions to please me. The more I will take actions to please him. The more the feedback spirals into compromised methods, compromised data, a compromised project.

But I say: "Sure. I'd love to tell you about Trewal."

But I feel: Terrified. Because very little happened to me on Trewal that I want to remember well enough to retell. Because I'm falling in love and I don't know how to say it and I don't know how to stop it and I can't imagine any world in which he'd feel the same about me.

SESSION 19
CARAN & CAMI / GANYMEDE

"So you two just walked right into the CryCorp building?" I ask be-cause I need some way to transition my mind off that last kiss and onto doing actual work.

"CryCorp's got a public lobby." Caran shrugs. "Why not."

"It's really dodgy, too," Cami perches over the edge of the chair, "see?"

An image of the lobby appears over the 3V surface of the coffee table, presumably from a directive she's given Ganymede.

The scale shows the lobby at a hangar-like 100 meters square and three stories up. A floating sculpture, reminiscent of a cloud of delicate white islands spurting plumes of crystalline ice that shim-mer away as they drop towards the floor, dominates the space.

"CryCorp's glossies say the sculpture is 'a reminder of our past with a gleam toward the future'," Cami recites.

"Yeah, right, a future with way less nauta," Caran scoffs. "You're right though, it is a fun lobby!"

"A bit too fun," Cami returns the scoff. "I had to keep pulling you on, you kept getting stuck."

"Well, that sculpture was very engaging. And my sensory pro-gramming was still out of synch."

"You were even worse in the showroom."

"Ohh," he sighs, "yes, the showroom was very nice, too."

The image over the 3V changes to a big room of tiny terrariums in floating bubbles. A cold desert-world colonized by coiling succulents and miniature brown mammals. A bubble of diminutive wheat fields shimmering in an impossible breeze. A jungle-sphere, a water-world—samples of worlds that people might want.

"Yes, that people might want," Cami says. Can Cami pick up my thoughts without an active link like that? Is it something in her special magnet-ness? "Focus, Steven, because this is important," she continues. "Just because you're sleeping with Caran doesn't mean you have to be distractible like him."

"Some things are worth getting distracted by!" Caran leans toward the table, poking into the hologram with his finger, moving the little orbs around. "When you get close to those globes you can hear sounds in them, what each world might sound like. Like, if there are little bird-things in the globe, you put your ear near and hear little bird sounds."

I say to Cami, to let her know I'm paying attention after all, "The power to want a world, and to know you could obtain it." I'm thinking back to the big project I did with corporate CEOs; all the themes about power: economic, political, sexual, emotional. And also Jordis' observations about her father.

"Yes power," Cami says. "CryCorp had a lot of it, and for a long time. The people who CryCorp sold planets to did too. It's all power bound up in power bound up in power."

"Bound up in Operators," I say.

"Yes. Bound up in Operators," Cami nods. "Without them, there would be none of this." She splays her fingers out into the holographic show room and the image disappears. Caran looks disappointed. "You wouldn't be living on Mars. There would be no on life on Earth, even such as it is. Imagine if Operators decided to do their own thing instead of what the normals ordered?" She smiles as she says it, mischief in the crinkles around her eyes. "Imagine if Operators *charged credit* for their services?"

"Yes, imagine that," Caran winks at her.

They both laugh.

I'm not amused though, because the horrible facts of history are too fresh. I want to share the snark, but I don't. I'm not allowed. Everything bad for Operators is the fault of normals, of people like me. I am the researcher, outside, apart. "So you two just walked right into the CryCorp building, I presume with Djen and Stella in the Mem to confound the cameras?"

"Yes. And then we got to the door in the back of the showroom," Cami's mischief ratchets up a notch.

◊

"It's a mechanical lock," Caran says to me like it isn't totally obvious. Like it's some sort of a problem.

"Yeah, so? It's not a fancy one."

He looks pale.

I poke an elbow hard into his ribs. "I thought you used to be some kinda thief when you were running with Djen?"

"I didn't say I was a good thief," he mumbles.

"Well, at least stop acting like a suspicious character. You're all slouched down and shifty. First rule of thieving's to act like you belong." I turn away though because I've got no more time for him right now; only for the lock.

I pull the little box holding my intrusion swarm out of my pocket and set a couple of switches on the main frendbot controller. I open the box and tiny robots flow out onto my palm, over the bridge I've made of my fingers, and into the keyhole. A thin line of smoke curls from where they're going to work with tiny drills and sacs of acid.

The lock opens: click-clack.

I make the finger-bridge again, calling the friendbots back.

The door opens, slick-slack.

I pull Caran out of the showroom and into the hall.

He says, thankfully not-loud, "Djen says we're clear of security sensors all the way to the data room if we go fast and now. She says we've nineteen minutes and forty-five seconds before the security encryption patterns cycle and she and Stella gotta hack them all again. You remember the way?"

That's a dumb question; unlike Caran, I'm a very good thief. I've already got us moving, turning left down the industrial-lit hall. Into the service door. Down the emergency stairs. Djen and I coordinate through Caran with her cracking the encryption patterns on electrical locks and me and the friendbots handling the mechanicals. I could get used to working with an Operator!

Then we're at the door to the room on sub-level five, where the data systems live, staring at the thick, metal door to the vault. My sensor tells me it's twenty centimeters of pure, Iron City-made steel. Uh-oh. "My friendbots don't have enough acid left to punch through and bypass any of the locks," I whisper to Caran. "I don't think they even have enough for the tumblers on the mechanical one. We're gonna have to work this door the old-fashioned way."

Caran looks like he's gonna puke all over the place. Too bad stomach acid's not strong enough to refuel my friendbots' sacs. "Look, see," I point trying to take the scary out of it for him, "there's a mechanical lock here and a citizen ID reader here. I'll pick the lock—the tumblers don't look so bad—but I need you—and Djen and Stella or whatevs—to work on the reader, right?"

I watch him blink himself out of whatever fear-freeze he's gotten himself into, miles of long lashes flicking over those eyes. He's got way too much presence to be a good thief. Even if he wanted to be hidey, he'd stick out like a neon holo-sign. Good thing we wanna get caught.

Just not yet.

"Okay." His eyes go unfocused again, communicating with Djen.

I pull out the wires and tiny hooks I'd brought for this kind of just-in-case.

My hands sweat; bad, bad. Slippery hands make slipping on the swiping.

I lied a little about what my sensor showed on the tumblers; they're big and complicated.

"What's our countdown on Djen's control of the cameras," I jerk my shoulder toward the sensor cam staring down at us but hopefully not seeing us.

"Three minutes fifteen seconds," Caran intones, flat and distracted.

Bad, bad. *Okay Cami, you're the most juiced tinker that ever lived, even more than Tinker Special on the Flowers Powers show, you can do this.*

I block out thoughts of the countdown, the corridor, the fact that right now's not the right time to get caught because we need stuff from the other side of that door. *Make it happen, Cami.*

I'm spliffy-good with mechanicals, but one of the tumblers is in too deep in for my tools to reach. Uh-oh.

"Hey," Caran pokes me. He's so distracted there's drool in the corner of his mouth and I almost bust out laughing but it's just all the stress. "Djen says to set your intrusion bots loose in the lock."

I feel the tiny hairs on my arms stand on end.

I think of asking what-and-why, but we don't have time, so I pull out the box and let the friendbots climb over my finger-bridge into the lock.

I wipe my sweaty hands on my jeans and get to work on the parts of the lock I can reach. Think about what to do about the deep tumbler while I tinker. Maybe I can rig something by pulling a wire out of somewhere else, extend my picks, if I can do it fast enough—

But I don't need to because I see on the sensor that Djen and Stella are controlling the friendbots, like back in my closet in Refinery J. They're climbing into the hard-to-reach spot and going into a configuration I could never program, strong enough together to press the tumbler open. We just might make it through this and—

CLICK.

The big door opens, SLICK!

I take Caran's hand and pull him in.

We slide inside to the hum of electricity and heat swirling off the flanks of big machines. The stationary systems are huge and black, and covered in blinking lights. Everything's so juiced I have to close my eyes a sec because it's too much and makes no sense.

When I open my eyes again, I see racks of crystal matrix towers, standing half-a-story tall. Their shiny black casings protect the delicate crystal storage and tzaddium-coated processors within. This is the data storage for CryCorp HQ's operations. Not the sensitive research and development stuff I'd love to get my hands on, but the admin stuff we need. Well, the admin stuff Ellison is most likely to most believe we need, plus the security stuff we *actually* need but hope he doesn't realize we've swiped.

I pull us into the shade of a big fan, out of sight of the cameras because I'm pretty sure the countdown on Djen's control of the security systems has hit zero.

"Which one has the crystal matrix with the files about you?" I ask Caran.

He's unfocused, frozen, and still hasn't wiped that drool off his face. After like forty long-ass seconds—and for every one of them I wonder if I should interrupt him—he shakes himself awake and points a finger toward a cluster of black towers. It's about as far away as a thing could be. Bad, bad.

I look up at the security sensors. Too high to reach. Coverage is just about everywhere. High-quality; they've got the Merrick Security sigil stamped to them, more bad. "How long till Djen and Stella can crack the security system again?"

A blink of a pause from Caran. "She and Stella can crack into the cameras in about ten min, but the rest of the sensors are a separate system. We're shit out of time for cracking both, and the anti-intrusion security on the motion and heat sensors is tough. No time."

"No big." I put my hands in my pockets. "Tell Djen and Stella to do the cameras again. I've got bots for the rest." We've got no time for fear, so I grin.

Caran, on the other hand, looks scared to all kinds of death.

"Aw, don't worry," I tell him, "this part's gonna be fun!" I pull out a blink-bot, the kind I made for when Mx. Blue wanted me to swipe that blueprint from Fancy-Nancy's Trinkets. It's a tiny drone with silvery whirly-wings. I show it to Caran.

"We've got another problem," he says. "Stella says there's a maintenance crew around the cooling unit, between us and were we've gotta be."

Okay. We can make this work. Just gotta think. I've got skills. I can do anything, as long as it's tinkering or stealing.

I close my eyes and take a big-ass breath. Usually I'm trying to turn off my vision of energy, not turn it on, but whatevs. Seeing the juice in everything's sometimes good for things besides annoying the teeth outta me. I open my eyes into the shimmers of frequencies I'm not supposed to see.

There's a frayed connection in a big, thick cable west-ways. Good, good.

I blink a bunch of times, until my eyes go back to seeing just normal light.

I crouch Caran down below the flash-pass of the big fan blades so if he twitches no one'll see.

I pull Clipper-bot out of my pocket. Clipper's big, almost the size of my clenched fist with his pincers extended and now I'm glad I gave up so much pocket space to bring him. I hate to lose him, but the other option's to do the deed with my own hands and there's no way I could do it and get away in time not to be seen. I put Clipper on the floor and he unfurls from a sphere into a bot with six pointy legs. Now he's exposed his belly. I lift him over and poke the pins underneath with a needle to set the settings. Flip that switch on, that switch off, these three to—all right. Set the rest with the controller. Good, good. Kiss his gray hull for luck. Set him down, *go, go, Clipper, go.*

Clipper furls back into a ball and sets off on a roll in the direction of the fritzing wire. Good job, good, good. I run circles around the fancy thieves with their fancy gizmos because hi-tech-sec never protects itself from tinkers. All the big security companies can think of is rogue Operators and high-tech jammers. But they've got no imagination. And no one's got friend-bots like mine.

"How long till Djen cracks the cameras again?" I ask Caran.

"Should be about four, five minutes now. Tops." He intones, eyes closed. Gods I wanna wipe that drool off his chin.

Okay. Should work. I grab Caran's hand. "Soon as she's got them and the techs are gone, we're gonna run for the stationary with your data on it. You follow me fast and keep your head down. Like, literally down. And do everything I do. Everything. 'Echo, echo, echo me ever,' just like your song says, right? Like you were me, every movement, only a half-step behind. Okay?"

Caran nods, eyes flashing in-and-out of worlds. He's in a funny kind of mood, not making any of those performer-poses or fidgets he falls into when he's not sure what to do with himself. He arches his neck and shivers in a slow, controlled way, like something sleek and deadly. He must be experiencing a different kind of being in the Mem, or the Mesh, or wherever-it-is that he is. "Dragon" the Freedom-folks call him. He gives me a toothy grin. He does look like a Dragon. For sure.

A crackle-hiss-flash from Clipper's direction.

"Shit! I told you we needed to fix that cable last week!"

"It's not like anything was going to make it fray more, and we have to move the XY-7's to get to it."

"Well, something did make it fray more. Fray and break!"

"Shutthefuckup, there's live current squirting. Kill the fucking breaker at sector nine."

The maintenance peeps turn toward the sparking wire, shouting nice and loud and scraping their toolkits along the ground to cover our sounds. I squeeze Caran's hand and prep my blink-bots to get us gone. "Where's Djen at?" I whisper to him.

"Thirty-eight seconds."

I start counting.

The key to timing a blink-bot is to toss it just far enough ahead that it'll blank a sensor as I streak past, but not so far ahead that the blink'll be done before the all-clear. I've got that timing in my bones, but I haven't ever done it dragging someone else along with me. I've reprogrammed the delay, but still.

Djen better have the cameras under control because there's no time left.

I flick my wrist and the first tiny blink-bot flies into the sensor like a moth to a flame. Whatever a moth is. Trust in hands and feet and tinkering and MOVE!

Caran follows with speed and grace that almost makes me trip. But why should it, really? He dances his music, moves to make the kinetikosonus sing. He found a beat in the sounds of the street. Everything must be music to him. Even the blink-bots. Especially the blink-bots!

Timing. Timing is everything. The two of us keeping a beat. I flick a blink-bot at the next sensor and we duck by. Perfect-on-time timing.

Keep flowing, keep dancing, keep being alive.

Six blink-bots later, we reach the cluster of stationaries where CryCorp's data on Caran lives. Only two blink-bots left. Good thing we won't be needing them for the way out.

"OK, which one are we aiming for?" I whisper, now that we're closer to the cluster of machines. Each tower's big and black and taller than me, and polished sharp. "'C'mon. It's only gonna take them like fifteen min to fix that fritzing wire, probably less."

"Give us a sec," Caran's words hiss out. It's a sound of concentration though, not exertion. Other than acting shady, he is turning out to be a pretty good thief. If we live through this maybe he'll take up thieving with me, that would be the dodgiest!

"I told you—" his teeth grind, and he winces at the sound "—I was never any good at this cloak-and-daggery stuff." Then he punches his finger at one of the towers. "That one. Stella says that one's got my data all over its crystal matrix. Third disc from the bottom."

"Right." I put my hand in my pocket. Just one more friend-bot left to use. "You gonna be okay? Stay quiet? None of that flappy-pacey humming stuff you do when you're trying to keep a beat or just 'cause you're bored?"

"Don't worry Cami. I won't fuck up until it's time." He grins that dragon-y grin again and reaches into a graceful stretch. "I've got plenty of room to flap around in the Mem with Djen."

◊

I stretch my clawed wings to hear the feathers rustle. If nothing else, Noa shredding my presentation's code gave an excuse to rebuild the thing with more sound and grace. Still not as good as the newer version in my navis back on Europa. Doesn't matter. Won't last anyway.

"Talk to me, Dragon, what's going on?" Djen's mind-voice flows into me.

Focus over to her, merged with Stella streaming in the flickering wave-spaces of the human-élan Mesh. She's never called me Caran; back when we met, I was done with that person. I was Dragon.

Djen hasn't changed her presentation in the last decade, least not in any way my badly programmed sensory inputs can detect. She presents as a 16th century sea captain merged with a horror-holo tentacled-sea-monster. Stella's enmeshed arms undulate from the ridge of her spine, merging into the fabric of our hybrid human-élan virtual reality crackling like a star's plasma.

I glance back into the material world, make sure nothing meaningful's changed. Cami's still working at the hard, black surface of the tower.

Focus back on Djen in the Mem. "Cami's extracting the crystal matrix. If luck holds, Ellison'll think that's why we came here. So get fast with finding Ellison's encryption patterns." My emotives wince around me as I hear myself falling back into ease with her like there aren't ten years and so much shit between us. But there is so I add, "Get it the fuck done, I want you outta my head."

"Hey," she punches me in the side, floppy feather of her tri-corner hat bobbing in the not-air. "It's not gonna get the fuck done without your help. You said it wasn't a mistake to send you in, so stop your grumble; prove it. Help us out here."

I puff a hiss through my nostrils and open up to let Stella in. Tentacles branch around me, nosing at the edges of my programmatic skin. Deep opera breath. They penetrate with tingles of electricity and settle. If someone had the right kind of sensors back in the server room, they'd see a static field building around me, increased electrical presence not accounted for in the room's infrastructure, the electromagnetic evidence of an incursion from another world. But no one's got those kinds of sensors except maybe Cami with her enhanced cantor senses.

Djen and Stella and I link in, forming a human-élan-data Mesh to access all of locally accessible knowledge.

We intuit a question into Meshspace: location of Ellison's encryption patterns?

Response received: question under-specified; more constraints required.

Us: fuck.

All-of-locally-accessible knowledge: shrug.

Us: okay, locations of densest encryption / business plans / CFO

reporting / after-hours access / human access / CEO-related terminology / higher-level decision-paths—We rattle off everything we
can think of to triangulate which encryption patterns throughout
the CryCorp systems might be Ellison's.

Split thread: I, Caran/Dragon, blink back into the server room
to check on Cami's progress.

She's standing in front of the black server box. The shiny surface crawls with more tiny robots than I thought could fit in her
pockets. Miniature pincers snap at the casing, flit in swarms over
security sensors, form trails into the place Cami's digging at with
a slender, hook-shaped tool. No idea what she's doing but it looks
impressive.

"You're glowing," Cami whispers over her shoulder.

"Glowing?"

"Yeah. Margaret says that sometimes I can sort of see the élans
I guess. You glowed when I snuck into your show, too. You glowed
brighter than the stage lights then. Guess that was Muse? That's
why I was surprised when we met at Grizwald and you didn't glow.
Everything going okay with finding Ellison's encryption patterns?"
Cami's tone is bright but her inflection's distracted.

"Sure. Need anything from us?"

"Nope. I'll have the crystal matrix out of the stationary in less
than five. It's sticky-labeled 'Mozart's True Name,' which might
amuse. The maintenance crew'll be done with the wire in about
the same. So what I need from you and Djen is, um, hurry?"

"Do we want the maintenance crew to see us?"

Cami shrugs, back to me. "Whatevs. As long as I've got the matrix and you've got Ellison's encryption patterns, sure. As they say,
don't look a gift horse in the mouth." She twists around to show
me the wicked grin on her face. "Whatever a horse is!"

I focus my primary thread back Mesh-side.

All-of-locally-accessible-knowledge: searching…

Djen twitches impatiently in her oiled leather coat and poet shirt.

In material reality, I finger the hard edges of the dataslip around my neck. Platinum-coated, on a platinum chain, the most top-spot replica of my kinetikosonus slip ever made, just like the one I'd left in the lav hole on Io—"*Course I swiped one,*" *Cami said when she handed it over, 'I used to keep the e-key patterns to my room on it but then everyone wanted to steal it off me so I had to leave it home.*" She'd even filed off the 100 Worlds Music Sigil.

All-of-locally-accessible-knowledge: PATTERNS FOUND

All right. Open a shortwave channel to the fake kinetikosonus dataslip.

Us: transfer Ellison's encryption patterns.

A pillar of sensations erupt from the fabric of the Mesh-space and vomit into my dataslip.

I grin with all my dragon-teeth at Djen, tip of my tail shivering. Grin at Cami too, and say in both places at once, "We've got Ellison's personal encryption patterns. We can access all his shit and escape his castle when we're ready. Time for phase two."

"Good." Cami fishes a heavy crystalline disc from the eviscerated stationary system. "'Cause here they come."

We intuit into the Mesh: Where?

Mesh answers: Four at the south, two where you came in, twenty behind the security wall.

Us: Okay, thanks.

Wait, twenty behind the—

"Cami? What the fuck's a 'security wa—'"

A click of a switch releasing; a slight pressure-change.

The back wall of the room clatters to the ground spilling a posse of corporate muscle. Black suits, black bobs, golden CryCorp sigil-pins sparkling on lapels and thumbs. Sound-dampening armor, surreal in silence.

Mesh falls apart as Djen cuts her channel to me; Stella's gone, poof.

Cami shoves the crystal matrix under her arm and yells, "Run!"

◊

"There wasn't anywhere to run to, of course," Caran says with a satisfied smack of his lips. "There never had been."

"But we sure put on a good get-away show!" Cami laughs. "I made it all the way back to the showroom before they tackled me. Well—" she beams, chest puffed out "—before I let them tackle me. I could've slipped 'em if I wanted!"

"After that it was restraints, blindfolds, walk, walk, walk, and then we were on a slip-slide of moving surfaces, maybe tubes, maybe elevators, almost hurled. Then traveling for a long time by private shuttle in the dark suffocation of that hood, couldn't draw a proper breath or talk to Cami, so I made rhythms, hummed scales. Could tell Cami was next to me by her sounds. Everyone makes their own flavor of sounds, you know. You make good sounds, Steven, sounds I like."

Cami stretches in the chair. "Every now and then they'd separate us and ask us questions."

Caran puts on an authoritative, booming voice. "What were you after in the data room?"

Then switches back to his own voice. "Information about why CryCorp was after me."

And again, playing both sides of the conversation:

"How do you know Camilla?

"Drug contacts on the street.

"Why didn't you contact 100 Worlds Music?

"Because I didn't know what the fuck-all was going on, for all I knew Mindy and JL were behind the abduction on Io as some fucked-up publicity stunt, blah blah."

Caran shrugs and ends his simulated dialogue. "Cami and I'd worked it all out, had our answers straight."

"After the last round of questioning," Cami says, "Caran and I weren't put back together."

"But you could still talk to each other?" I prompt around the public version of the story. I know there are certain secrets still guarded, but—

"Yeah, we had the freedomtech com rings," Caran says. "Heavy gold ring, etched out with maker's flows, piece of an élan inside."

Cami rubs her ring finger. "You talk into them and listen from them, but no one else can hear. The piece of the élan inside can bend perceptions of sound, like Jordis' fan. 'Course anyone watching would still see a person holding the ring up to their face and muttering so it was kinda impractical." Cami's sour look makes it clear what she thinks of such engineering inelegance. "I mean, if you're going to make a secret alien-hybrid com ring, and you *can* make it so that you're stealth about it too, why not?"

"The Red City cell liked its irony," Caran shrugs, "plus, helps the device not to be too powerful if it falls into the wrong hands."

"The wrong hands?" Cami blinks. "Y'all were shipping these to Madame X's syndicate!"

"Exactly. The wrong hands."

"But—so how does it *work*?" I ask.

Caran laughs at me. "You're as bad as Jordis on Europa, trying to get Freedom's secrets out of me."

"You *are* Freedom's secrets," I laugh back.

"Touché!" He stands and paces back and forth a few times behind the sofa, fast. He stops and plants his palms on the back of the furniture, pushing forward against it, stretching. The oblique light from the windows draws definition in the muscles in his bare arms. Dancer arms. Artist arms. I don't think he notices me noticing because he's looking at his hands. I remember his tongue running up my arms.

"Right, okay," he says. "The way it works is, basically, this. You've got a human in resonance with their favorite élan, and they decide together to make some device. The élan breaks off a non-sentient piece of itself and sticks it inside the device to manage the fine-tuning of the EM. This is called a Mesh. Mesh is what we call a weaving between élans and technology, could be a permanent Mesh like freedomtech devices or how Stella's woven into the *Stella-Maru's* dimension drive. Or it could be a temporary Mesh which is what happens when an élan links up into informationspace, makes it possible to intuit into all of human knowledge. Reason the devices are so heavy is because of what they're made of although I don't know what that is. The human crafts the device to support the device's function, plus the artistry to make it look pretty. Freedomtech's made by nauta, so its physical design always has a bit of poetry."

"Jordis' fan," I say, "that keeps you invisible and inaudible as long as you're fanning with it but not otherwise. That's a bit of poetry?"

"That and just the general look of the thing." Caran launches himself over the back of the sofa and back into a sit with a gesture somewhere between an elite athlete's vault and a wild animal's disregard for propriety. "It's all gold-metal lace that burns with fire along the maker's flows when it's active."

"I saw it inside Jordis' story."

"Hey," Cami says, bored. "Can we get on with it? I'm hungry."

"How about," I stand and also stretch, "we just break here. Back in three hours?"

Cami pops off the chair like the cushion just turned to acid. "Sure thing bye."

I'm attuned enough now so that I can tell, too, when Ganymede is gone. My skin prickles though; there's still an élan in the room.

I think I see the shadows beneath the chair moving again, but startle as a warm, solid body collides with mine. Caran's come up beside me, fast in my distraction. I feel his breath on my neck.

"We have to talk about this," I say without looking at him. Trying to keep myself from leaning into his warmth. "I have to tell you something about this."

"You normals with your words, words, words, and talk, talk, talk," he says, but his tone is soft and teasing, not annoyed. He shoves his hand under my shirt and walks his fingers up my spine.

"No." I try to step back but have no room to maneuver with the chair behind me. "I should have said something sooner, I should have—I'm a terrible person."

"Yeah, probably, but aren't we all."

We're facing each other. The top of his head comes up to about my brow, but he stands on tip toes to even us out. I look at our feet. My comfortable shoes; his bare toes. "No, really." I put my fingers to his chest and push, trying to get clear of the chair, make some distance between us. "I should have told you sooner but this—this isn't allowed. We can't be doing this." *Come on Steven, you can be at least a tenth as strong as the rest of them.* "It's got to do with research ethics. With professional responsibilities. I should have said so from the start—I'm not allowed to have intimate relationships with my research participants."

He pushes me in the chest this time, lip curled in a sneer. "Except you don't care."

"I do, I do care, I could be pulled from the project, I could be—"

"Except"—he pushes again, fingers to my chest, pushing me down back into my chair with his wiry strength—"except you don't fucking care."

He's right.

I really don't.

I grab him in both hands and pull him into me.

He falls against me; we bounce on the springs of the chair. We flip, my body pressing down onto his, hard enough for him to feel. Someone could walk in and see us at any moment. We're on the floor now, in the shadows, the shadows curling around us, not caring about anything but each other at all. Not caring about the fear. Not caring about anything but filling up the void.

This is hardly the first time an anthropologist had gone native. I'm hardly the first anthropologist to fall in love with someone in the community of study. There's precedent. There are reasons to let it slide.

His bright, black eyes hold all the light in the universe. They arouse me. I shift around in the chair.

Shadows shift behind the curtains; shadows collect in motes that make no sense beneath the sofa, in the corners of my office. I'm terrified and sweating, but also excited, welcoming.

Cami is sweating. I see the beads of sweat on her nose in a preternatural awareness of sensation that feels like a fever.

Caran is relaxed. He slouches on the couch, bare feet on the coffee table, mouth twitching the edges of a grin. He does not seem affected by the strangeness.

I want to shake out my hands the same way he does, to relieve some of the emotion, sensation, pent-up expression, so I sit on them. Quiet. Quiet hands. Sex has done nothing to reduce the dissonance I feel. And yet—it's not dissonance, is it? It's resonance. It's the next stage of resonance, starting. It's me being changed by the élans, by the humans; me being realigned.

When prepping for these interviews, I'd watched a demonstration of resonance in an oscillator. In the demo, a wavelength—

peaks and troughs—was exposed to an interference signal close to its own amplitude. For a time, as the interference signal acted upon the wave, their combined frequency changed shape and became uneven, and increasingly amplified. And then the tipping point arrived as the two signals synched up. The frequency amplified more, and more, again, peaks and troughs climbing, exponential, approaching infinite heights if not stopped by the constraints of the physical world—

This same synching up and amplification is happening to me; they're changing me, reshaping my identity. I want it. I want the shapes of these new frequencies to swallow me. I want to become one of them. All of us one. I want to be a part of Callisto's colony, to be a part of Caran's life, to be—to be nauta too. I can do that through the link in ways forbidden me by my biology.

"Ellison's castle," I say. My voice sounds rich, alive. I am perceiving it the way Caran perceives it. He likes my voice, my sounds. My senses are in stereo.

Caran grins. The link reels me in.

◊

I'm alone in a posh suite. Still on Ganymede but not Iron City—moon's barren surface undulates beyond a large, clear window. Jupiter's just a sliver on the horizon, not throwing enough light to matter, but the outside's lit an ambient eerie twilight. Probably some kind of floating lighting rig outside my line of sight. The hat Djen glue-clipped to my hair still covers my forehead, and I'm sweating like the end of a gig in the furr coat. Air blasts from the environmentals—probably cold as the surface of Ganymede—as the room struggles to respond to my bio-stats. I feel for signal, sensors I'm expecting will be monitoring every action, but the room is clean.

I strip down to the hat and my pants, get rid of all that fucking nasty fabric, hate it against my fucking skin. The environmentals calm down.

Room's big, not cavernous. Cozy, not claustrophobic. Sleeping area and waking area. Bathroom's mostly a sunken tub with fun-looking attachments. Everything furnished in white fabric and colored glass by someone with unlimited credit.

There's a personal waste reclaimer inset into the wall. Device'll break everything tossed inside down into its basic chemical components. That makes one of the things I've got to do next a whole lot easier.

I finger the freedomtech com ring on my middle finger. It's heavy and irritating; hate jewelry, always hated jewelry, hate it more even than clothes. "Cami?" Always feels weird talking to my hand. "I'm in a posh bedroom suite alone and it's clean."

◊

Caran starts talking to me through the magic alien comring, and I hope what everyone told me is right and no one else can hear it. I've got to get it near my mouth to respond though, and my hands are behind my back. So I take advantage of my double-shoulder-joints to get my hands near enough to my face because electronic restraints are the one thing I can't outright slip. The pin jammed in my wrists would be easy enough to lose with a rough tug, but it'll zap me to fried meat if I do. And there's no way to tinker it since I can't move my fingers much without getting less spectacularly, but still painfully, shocked.

"I'm somewhere smelly," I say into the com ring through my hood. "They haven't taken my credit slip with Ganymede in it so that's good at least. Think we're near each other?"

◊

I feel for signal again, this time seeking the com ring frequency. "Not close enough to find your signal on the shortwaves. I'll search a broader band."

"Uh-oh," Cami says on the ring, "someone's outside. Later."

Good point; someone could be outside my room, too. Every second I keep my navis is a second I can blow the plan. Best take care of the ugly business with the reclaimer before I'm somewhere with a less irreversible way to hide the evidence.

◊

A door screeches and someone comes in. The hood comes off and I get my first good look at where I'm at. And who Ellison's sicced on me for starters.

"Hello Camilla." The long, square face of Abia Bennett, nasty piece of personal security, unhappy as usual. Bad-cop Bennett.

"I'd've thought you'd've been fired on account of me escaping." I try to toss curls out of my eyes, but they're stuck to my skin with sweat. "Demoted at least. They still let you carry weapons?"

"I can still zap your smart ass into oblivion, if that's what you mean." The security woman hasn't changed in eight years. The kind of lank brown hair that looks always dirty, and hard blue eyes that look always like I've done something wrong. "You've led Ellison on a mighty chase, you know."

"Last I checked I was over the age of major and Ellison's got no legal hold on me. Never did anyway. You people are criminals."

Abia laughs, a condescending sound with no fun in it at all. "And that's why you went straight to law enforcement to report us so many times these past eight years, right Camilla?"

"What do I need LE for? I can take care of myself. Plus, they don't like my business practices." So strange sitting in front of this woman now. How scared I'd been of her back in the day, but now she's just a puffed-up bully. I did grow at least a foot since then, maybe more. I square my shoulders, ignore Abia, and take a look around.

They'd put me in worse rooms before, but not much worse. I'm on a nasty mattress atop a mangled box spring. Someone's peed on it and it stinks. Probably because there isn't any lav hole. Couldn't they have used the corner though? Whatevs. No windows either, air has the cold-dank of underground. I can't see the floor well through the murk of the dim greenish everbulb. There isn't any-thing to tinker into something else in the room, which is more dis-appointing than the mattress. Even the worst of the places they'd put me during the experiments at least had a vidcam. The lack of surveillance means something. "I'm guessing I'm considered in trouble." I wave my hand at the room.

"I'm guessing you are." Abia passes her own hand over the re-straint and the device withdraws.

I rotate my wrists.

"What were you thinking trying to steal data for Caran Watts?" Abia asks.

"It's all about him now is it?" I flex my hands, stretch big. Yawn. "And here I thought you missed me. Where's Ellison? I wanna talk to Ellison."

"Just answer the question, Camilla."

"If you must know, I was thinking gobs of credit." I smack my lips, unzip my parka, and check my pockets. Empty of course.

"Gobs of credit?"

"Yeah, gobs of credit. He's a megastar. Promised me gobs of credit. Untagged. Hey, when I got to go, you want me to use that spot on the mattress?"

Abia smacks me across the cheek. "Stay on topic, Camilla."

I close my wide-open jaw. All those years trapped with Ellison and Abia and the others, no one ever laid a hand on me. I touch my face, heat of hurt radiating from the point of impact.

"Since you're major now and can take care of yourself and are all tough on the street, you must be ready for the big-girl games." Abia's voice is colder than rime on a windowpane. "Now, there are two things here that don't factor right. One, we don't think you'd risk getting caught for any gobs of money. It's not your MO. Don't forget how well we know you. Two is this." She pulls something out of her pocket that glints silver in the light.

I blink until the halos of tears are gone. I'm major. Fifteen-years-old, that's major. I don't take shit from anyone on the street so I sure as cold nights am not going to take shit from Abia Bennett here in this room. The object rocks pendulum-like, until it slows enough so I can see it right. CW's platinum-coated dataslip. Uh-oh.

"Go on." Bennett pokes it at me.

I take the thing, turn it over. Exhale with relief I can't hold in when I see the 100 Worlds Music harp-in-roses sigil etched on the side. It isn't the one Caran had around his neck during the run, with Ellison's encryption patterns on it. The one we need to infiltrate the rest of the way into Ellison's castle, and finish up the recon on what all's going on, and then use to get the juice outta here.

"That's right. It's not the one around his neck right now, but it was around his neck once. It's got a recording of his current show on it with himself edited out. But that's not the really interesting bit."

The dataslip glitters in the green light as I twirl it. Good thing I've no idea what Abia's going on about so there's no way it can get me into any trouble. I palm-and-unpalm it just for something to do, there-and-gone-again. To Abia I say, "The really interesting bit is that you've seen enough mainfeed to know what it is?"

"The really interesting bit—" Abia snatches the slip away faster than even I could have done "—is that we found it stuffed in the lav hole of a room on Io that the Syndicate rented to stash him in. In the room, we also found tabs of U4. That drug's only given to Operators. Makes 'em able to function a little without their—" her throat goes hoarse with disgust "—technology. Why do you think we found that?"

"Because you were looking?"

The smack comes so hard and so fast this time that I don't know it's happened until the sting spreads heat on the other side of my face, twin bruises. Tears stinging. Abia Bennett has dexterity-enhancing biomods. Doesn't matter how fast or contortionist I am, no way to beat that. Abia wins.

"Ellison raised you to be a lady." The security woman is at the door faster than I can see her move.

"Maybe I'd be more of a lady if I were in a proper room and had a fancy gown." I swing my head side-to-side to shake out the pain.

"Act more like a lady and maybe that can be arranged," Abia snaps and slaps the door shut behind her. The light winks out.

I frown into piss-smelling darkness.

Well, this isn't how it was supposed to go down. We were supposed to have been taken to Ellison. And then we were supposed to have gotten intel. And then I was supposed to escape back to the

Grizwald and hook back up with Noa, and Caran was supposed to go to Europa and get his other navis and hook up with Jordis. And then we were all together supposed to come up with a plan to defeat Dividia.

Right.

I cup my throbbing face in my palms and whisper into my com, "Caran, are you there?"

Silence follows.

◊

Heart's fluttering like the edge of withdrawal, only this time it's just nerves. Haven't had stage-fright this bad in decades. But then, haven't had a performance this difficult or this high stakes ever. This is my chance to not let Djen down. To make up a bit for what I've done to Noa. To be a friend to Cami. Really, what I'm doing, this is just a show.

Close my eyes, open my lungs, conjure the "Ride of the Valkyries" with my voice. In the sounds, huge Viking women with swords slay the five-headed monster of apprehension.

I imagine the thunking flat notes at my navis that cause it to turn off and disengage.

Can't feel the tiny threads of connection leaving my brain, but I feel everything else. The small, isolated claustrophobia of being alone in the bright synaesthetic soundscapes of thought that no one else will ever understand. The loneliness; if I reach out, I'll touch nothing. Not even thin radio transmits. Sensory filters gone; a roar and hiss of sound fills all sensation-spaces. Figure-ground become slow to resolve, the unreliability of vision as terrifying as the radio-silence. It's been so long since I've been in my completely natural state that I've forgotten what it's like. Terrifying in some ways, yeah, but beautiful too. A relief. A wonderment. The twinkling light with each ping from the uneven blade in the near-silent fan hidden in the ceiling, the flow of conversation from the environmentals humming beyond.

Above it all, the Valkyries ride. Cami and Noa and Djen, my demi-gods, leading me to Valhalla. Can't let them down. Jordis too. Europa saw something worthy in Jordis, and the élans don't choose their humans at random; they choose them because they resonate on similar frequencies. Jordis is my Valkyrie too.

I peel the dead med-derm off my arm: the last, Noa said. *After this one, you are free.* Scares me more than my naked mind, so box the feelings away.

I shove the navis and the derm into the reclaimer and listen to the last of my life support crunch and crush and vanish, decomposed into chemical components like they had never been an intricate computer.

Well, not the last of my life support. It comes without rush, speech, or dependence, but the tab of U4 I work out of the hem of the furr vest'll sort and dull my senses and enhance motor sequencing for the next 24. By then I'd better be back on *Sonica* with access to my navis or nothing else in this plan is going to work either.

Swallow the 24-hour tab. Sit on the floor, the room a mess of broken image and splintered sound, and smile at the ridiculousness of Viking operas until the noise fades. U4 still gives me more abilities than I'd had the first 14 years of my life. I can do this. I can pull this performance off.

A long count later and more piss-nervous than I've ever been before, a silent man in a black suit-coat comes knocking to lead me out. We pass through richly furnished hallways and foyers to a room created in the improbable afterbirth of a business office and spa. Steam rises from the burbling pool at the far end. The rectangular table's polished to a mirror-shine, reflecting the Ganymedian stars from a whole-ceiling sky-light. It's occupied by one man, two rock-crystal tumblers, and a flared decanter glittering with the ruby glow of Cassiopeian red rye whisky.

"Privacy, sir?" Black-suit asks CEO-man with a subservient twitch.

"Yes, thanks." Ulric Ellison dismisses the muscle. To me, "Please, sit. Cassiopeian red?" He tilts the whisky. Shimmers the color of blood in the easy light. "It's the '19, good stuff."

"Yeah, thanks." Thanks indeed. I sit in the chair. It's more comfortable than it looks. I down the shot in one, warm burn stilling some small corner of panic. With enough of the red I might be able to pull off this impossible performance.

"First, I want to say—please, before anything else—I regret how everything escalated, especially on Io. The intention was never to spook you. Mallory and Dave can be—well. Totally unnecessary. Please, let me to make it up to you." Ellison's face, etched with time and scrubbed over by cosmetic surgery, reflects the warm light in cold angles as he adjusts the cuffs of his casual sweater. "You're just a very difficult person to reach, Mx. Watts. I tried everything, even to book you for a special event, but your people wouldn't let me anywhere near you at any price. I'd intended to speak with you at the Dreaming City Afterburn party, but then—" Ellison squints into the rich red whisky.

But then Jordis-fucking-Ansari abducted me, too bad for you. I nudge my empty tumbler. Ellison refills it with a condescending smirk that I want to smack off his face. So much easier to tolerate condescension on a few drops of NQ.

"So why *did* the Syndicate take you to Io?"

I mean to sip slowly, really, but my hand shakes and all the whisky ends up in my mouth again. "I'm a hard person to reach," I echo Ellison's words back at him with a grin-shrug, wiping my chin on the back of my hand where the dribble of whisky tickles. "Syndicate tried to book me for a special event, but my people wouldn't let 'em." Collage together bits of someone else's speech. A little lyric might not be too strange here, so I sing, "didn't stay to find out / didn't stay long / took myself out of dodge and scram I ran on."

Ellison laughs and pours me a third shot. "So you forgive me?"

"Cassiopeian red? I forgive you. Mallory and Dave—well."

Ellison settles back with the same smarmy ease that sweats off the admin-types LaRoque drags into 100 Worlds Music with binders for me to sign. "Good. Since, really, I wanted to speak with you because we have so much in common."

I barely cover my choke with a cough, which turns into an excuse to wet my throat on that third shot. One or two more and I might even start to feel it.

"I don't mean that we're both men of credit and power—though that is true. Nor do I mean that we've both a deep appreciation for the arts, though that's true as well. But that we both have similar things at stake with respect to Operators."

Inhale, exhale, tap my foot on the polished marble floor to keep up the beat.

"I see you're surprised." Ellison's smile spreads like a rash over perfect teeth. "I know I don't look like a man who follows media trends, but I have been following your career. See, I maintain my position as CEO of the oldest and most accomplished terraforming corporation because I control a not-inconsequential number of the creatures. You're held in your position as the brightest and most accomplished popular artist because society loathes and fears them.

"Never kid yourself about the power of transgression Mx. Watts. All your considerable musical talent wouldn't be enough to make you as big as you are without the way you brush up against, and tease the edges of, society's deepest taboos. Performers have been pushing at taboos since the dawn of culture.

"Never kid yourself about the importance of controlling your own assets, either. I'm one of the few who knows you've refused to release the rights to any of your music. Everything else in your corporate charter is game—you don't even own your own feces—but somewhere between drug-soaked orgies you realized the songs themselves had to remain under your control. You're not so dazed and confused as you'd like them to believe, are you?"

This is nowhere I'd expected the conversation with Ellison to go. Is he misreading me as a normal, or am I being played? If only I was smarter, better at this kind of game maybe I could see the difference. Or drunker maybe. But I don't want to ask for another shot just yet. That would be inappropriately excessive, even for me.

"Now I want you to imagine a world, Mx. Watts, in which feebles are not taboo. Nothing to be ashamed of, nothing to be transgressed. What happens to your power, to the privileged position you've crafted for yourself? How much do you think your handlers will look the other way when it comes to your behavior? Imagine a world where feebles have rights. Where they are no longer assets we control. What have they done to earn rights? Nothing. We have fed, sheltered, and kept them alive and healthy, and in return all we ask is that they manage our data—a task for which they are uniquely bred and which they enjoy performing. You and I have worked hard to earn our places. But what happens to the bedrock of society, the weave of social structure, when the weak and impaired are allowed in to ruin all we have built?"

The tiny hairs on my skin tickle. There's an élan in here with us. For how long? The whole time? A buzz in my chest, a resonance in the hollow of my throat. A feeling that *fits*. Dividia is here, passive now, unconcerned with connection, like Muse confident in its ability to reach out and link into me whenever it wishes. A laugh colored by fear's vibrato escapes my lungs at a distance, like a sound made by another man.

"Exactly," Ellison continues. "Imagine a world in which Operators are no longer under our control. Where the line between the natural and the defective upon which you dance, ceases to exist. Where you and I no longer control the assets we need to retain our well-earned privilege. Where creatures that have not earned their privilege swarm in and are allowed to take what is ours."

My teeth chatter and, propriety be fucked, I reach for the whisky and gulp straight from bottle until I feel warm again. I sing with a fake slur so Ellison'll think I'm drunker than I am and maybe the weird signing which is all I've got for communication won't seem so weird. "That's not the world we live in, man / it's not the world you understand."

"Ah, but it will be, if we don't do something to stop it. Already the fabric of society has loosened. Did you know, here on Ganymede, they've started letting Operators out without their minders? But, more to the point for why I've wanted to speak with you," Ellison reveals his pink gums in smile that makes Jordis at her worst look friendly, "I know a very special secret, very special indeed. If used correctly, it could keep us—and everyone like us—in the positions which we have rightly earned."

"A very special secret indeed." I scoff, mocking his words back at him.

"It is a very special secret indeed." Ellison's eyes are slits of seriousness, red tongue licking over pink lips. He pulls his chair in and leans close until I can hear the intensity of his breathing. "What would you say if I told you I'd found a way to capture, nurture, and transform one idea into another—say hope for Operator civil rights into fear that Operators will destroy society—and then release these ideas into the world to influence events? Not in the age-old propaganda sense, but directly into minds and hearts via something akin to telepathy."

I vocalize a nervous, dubious laugh-sound. Maybe it's for the best I've no words of my own, because otherwise I'd be screaming *how dare you mind-rape and murder-change the only meta-intelligent species we've ever met and abuse us, your power, everything that could have been right and good, no wonder the élans abandoned freedom and left the mesh for good fuck you fucker you fucking—*

"Ideas with which we could control the inhabited worlds." Ellison spreads his thin lips in a hungry smile. "Or rather, maintain our existing control of the inhabited worlds. Because ideas are alive, and they are dangerous, and with warming views regarding Operators throughout inhabited space, they are increasingly not in our camp."

I put the decanter back down on the table. Stomach's too sour for another sip.

"I see you may need a little more convincing. I admit, it is, unlike Cassiopeian red whiskey, difficult to swallow—" Ellison chuckles with a nod to the whiskey and continues into my silence "—like some poetic preaching by a Dieuvéssau. But I will show you exactly what I mean so there will be no question. A full demonstration.

First though, let me give you one more piece of information and my proposition.

"I am assuming you've not had time to catch up on recent events, with Europa shutting its borders due to its surge of Operator-related terrorism? And, of course, your regrettable side-trip into petty thievery with the effervescent Mx. Morgan."

I make myself nod.

"Apparently, some feel you crossed the line of transgression just a little too far at your most recent show. " A 3V flickers to life above the surface of the table; whole table's a projection plate beneath its mirror gloss.

A video feed springs up, showing ratty Jonathan LaRoque in Mindy's security suite. "All Worlds says if we can't produce him in the next three days, it's going to dissolve the contract."

Mindy, face palled with fear. "Just because the Genetic Liberation Front says he's one of their secret leaders, doesn't mean it's true. Has anything from the GLF been corroborated? Anything? Even responsibility for the bombings? I don't think there's even such a thing as the GLF at all. It's all just fake news propaganda."

LaRoque: "Does it matter, Min? It's a revolution in the making out there. How many serious death threats against him today alone? You're over a thousand count aren't you, and at least a hundred need looking into? You've worked in the media as long as I have. When has truth ever mattered even a little? If we don't get him back and demonstrate conclusively he's not a k-dromer like the GLF says he is, it's end of game."

The 3V flickers off. Ellison gazes across the void of the table, pale eyes relentless with greed. "It seems if you want to keep your position of privilege, you'll need to do a little extra convincing that you're on the correct side of the transgression line.

"Which leads me to how these circumstances offer us an un-precedented opportunity to work together.

"Specifically, you'll do a benefit show to raise chartering funds for my new humanitarian org, RealsOlutions. We're in the business of protecting the rights of normals. It's a perfect platform for a public announcement to re-establish the Caran Watts brand on the correct side of the transgression line, neatly dealing with your problem. Win-win.

"And then, there's my special secret. You'll use it during the show to generate enough fear that people will start culling the Operator population. We need it down to a number that no longer risks a large-scale uprising. Just exactly how that works will be clear after my demonstration."

Ellison smiles up into the stars, poisoning their light. "I think this partnership will work out well for both of us."

The room spins and I wonder whether there's more than whisky in that bottle or it's Dividia trying to find its way inside me from where it coils, steaming, in the corner. Is this really what Ellison wants from me? We'd assumed he wanted to use my nauta status against the Operators. That exposing my secret would add to the trumped-up anti-Operator sentiment. But Ellison seems to sincerely think I would want to protect my own position at such human cost—

Unless it's bait to drag my loyalties into the open. Bait, maybe, to get me to admit I'm nauta—

"It's okay," Ellison laughs, slapping my knee with a locker-room familiarity that makes the Cassiopeian red almost come back up. "I knew you'd need time to digest all of this. I'll have one of my boys see you back to your room where you can relax. My boy can get you whatever makes you comfortable. Including more boys. And some girls. And some cute little toys who are both or neither. I know you like them all, gender doesn't matter to you, does it. Whatever you want. Take the Cassiopeian red with you. We'll have dinner in two hours, and then I'll give you that demonstration so you can understand the resources at our disposal." He claps and a youth dressed like Ganymede appears beneath the lintel of the oaken doors to take me, staggering, away.

◊

The light snaps on and it takes a moment to adjust and identify the stooped shape of Nannie at the doorway. I could slip past Nannie no problem, no way that old arse is going to get dex-enhancing bio-mods. But I rather fancy Abia Bennett is standing just outside my line of sight. "Time for good cop now?" I shield my eyes with my fingers.

"Abia told me you'd gone bratty." Unlike Bennett, Nannie's aged plenty in eight years. I'd never known her to be young, but she's so cracked and bent and pink now it doesn't seem possible she can even still be alive.

"Abia's gone bratty herself." I touch my throbbing cheekbones.

"Rickie wants to see you." The crone comes close enough I can see the bundle in her arms, a pile of fabric and little shoes dangling from a fingertip.

Rickie. Ulric, Ric, Rickie. I'd never been clear on if Nannie had been Ellison's nanny too. He's so old, but then Nannie's so impossibly ancient that maybe—

Good, good. A convo with Ellison is what I'm here for, not sitting in a stinking cell waiting for Meanie Bennett to slap me on the face for no reason at all. The plan's getting back where it's supposed to be.

I take the bundle of soft crinkling fabric.

A strapless party gown, black or copper or silver depending on the light. A matching bow on a clip for my hair. Delicate slipper-boots with little heels that sparkle like ice crystals on pavement. Pristine gloves. Princess clothes.

I run my grubby hands over my jeans and parka, look down at the furr of my boots. It's been a long time since I've dressed in something I can't move in, or something that could tangle up in pipes or catch on a door latch as I'm scooting my escape. Anything that can't cut the Ganymedean cold. Been since I'd lived in Ellison's castle, in fact. Hope that's where I am.

Nannie pulls a bucket and sponge out of nowhere and tries to fumble my parka off.

I push her away and undress. Evaluate the dirt on me from the run in CryCorp's headquarters two thousand years ago, and then use the bucket to wash my hands and face.

"You used to like your sponge bath," the daft old woman whines, tears quivering in the corners of her eyes.

"I used to like a teething ring too." The new clothes fit so well something must've taken my measurements during the trip.

"Sparkle and rime, you do clean up so pretty! Have a cookie."

I blink around the dank piss-stained cell and the woman offering me a chocolate chip cookie with fingers hooked like Monster Witch on *The Flowers Powers Show*. Or she would look like Monster Witch if she wasn't so old and sad and senile. If I didn't remember her as the only person who was ever consistently nice to me, no tricks, in all of Ellison's castle. I'm not sure she's clear-headed enough to be capable of deceit. "You're taking me to Ellison now?"

"Yes, yes, Rickie wants to see you. Wants to see how you've grown up. Have a cookie. They're your favorite, the kind with the two kinds of chips. I made them fresh when I heard you were back. Milk to go with when we get to Rickie. I missed you so much." Nannie starts to cry.

Whatever. I'm hungry. Nannie's cookies are delicious.

◊

When we come out of the link, I'm hungry. I'm hungry. I'm hungry and the cookie is indeed delicious.

It's dark outside; the Martian landscape full of shadows.

The shadows are a part of the room. A part of us. Curling and colliding. I'm afraid, but I'm hungry, and I want to let the shadows in. I long for it like I've sometimes longed to throw myself off the edge of Mission Crater Ledge. All my life I've done the right thing, I've stayed apart, alone, even when it's meant my own suffering. Is it bad to be selfish just this once?

But if I let the shadows in, if I blacken myself with all the muck and fear in the universe that ever was, I will become who I really am. I don't know that I'm ready for that.

"See you tomorrow!" Cami chirps, like there isn't a storm inside me. Inside the room. Inside us all.

"Sure," I say, surprised my voice sounds normal. "How are you feeling, are you feeling okay about all of this?"

"Sure," Cami shrugs, "it's just one moment of bad in a lot of spliffy stuff, right? Plus, it's important to the story." She's gone.

Caran stands in front of me, shins touching my knees. "Fuck all this fucked-up shit," he says. He smells like sweat and, for some reason, pepper.

I rise and thread my fingers into the perpetual tangles of his hair. "You don't hate me for what I am?"

"I hate everyone," he scoffs at me. "But you don't give a shit about what I am, so why should I give a shit the other way 'round? Fuck the rules. Fuck 'em all."

The darkness curls around us and we fuck in my office again, and then again, emotions and sensations tangled up. I am him, and he is me, and we are we, and I want someone to walk in. I want to be found out. I want the secrets out. I want to die. I want to be born.

(The next day the link forms without transition, the three of us tumbling together. Caran on the sofa. Cami in the chair. Me at my place opposite, only I am not opposite because we are seated in a circle. We are Cami now.)

Abia Bennett enters the cell's doorway, along with two other guard-types I don't recognize. They lead me through a twisty maze of underground passages, and into a part of Ellison's castle I recognize.

Except everything looks smaller now, and all kinds of off. That used to be a white sofa, but it's now a set of red chairs. The curtains are new maybe, or is it the carpet, maybe the lights? The end table's been replaced by an elephant—I actually know what kind of extinct animal that is!

Wait, what?

That makes no kinds of sense. For there to be an elephant, not for me to know what it is. I do know some animals.

I shake my head, sparks of color floating like tears in zero g. I've never been in zero g, but that's what it looks like on the Flowers Powers show.

Corridors blur and colors spark and sparkle. That's not because eight years have passed, and someone's redecorated the place. It because there's EM everywhere and I can't shut off seeing it somehow. Why am I seeing it, I should be able to control which wavelengths I'm seeing, I feel all woozy like I've been drugged—

Foolish Cami, foolish trusting Cami!

What am I, six years old? Doesn't matter that Nannie's never done anything to hurt me. I'd eaten that cookie, eaten it like it was all benign, like I was back in the kitchen with good-cop Nannie watching her take them fresh out of the oven. Like Nannie was ever anything but Ellison's minion. Or like someone couldn't have put something in Nannie's dough without her knowing it.

I'm strong. I'm brave. I'm self-sufficient.

I'm wearing a princess party-dress and white gloves and a bow. I'm being led to the man who gave me everything I asked for except my parents back. Except to go outside. Except friends and homework and being able to relate to anyone else at all. Except an hour without fear.

Something snaps the wrong way 'round and it's like the last eight years on the street don't matter at all.

Back to eight years old and terrified, I am.

Back to—

The rotunda of the ballroom.

Last time I was in the rotunda I played with constructors, building circuits. No clue if it was a Cami-have-some-fun moment or if it was another experiment to get me talking to Dividia. Back then, sensor-eyes glowed above, watching, always watching. Back then I never knew the point of anything until it was too late, and someone told me I couldn't have dinner until I got it right.

The sensor-eyes are gone. Human eyes watch the rotunda today. As far as I can tell, anyway. My vision keeps slipping wavelengths. I press the spots of hurt on my cheeks from Abia's blows. Flashes of clarity pinch through the nip of pain. The room's dressed up special, too, just like me.

Someone's redone the marble-chip floor from an abstract rosette to the seal of Ganymede. The youth tips his cup for the eagle to drink from within a deep blue circle of stars.

And around all that, someone has placed a bunch of random objects. Pieces of machinery, the kinds used in refineries, but mangled and sludging goo. A damaged flank of shuttle. A worker's uniform, bloodstained. Other objects, ones I recognize from the experiments with Dividia. Ritual items for a Dieuvéssau of an evil god. And there, there's the bottle made of microwaves that held Dividia itself—

The spirit's bottle is broken.

Bad, bad.

I flick my eyes away fast as I can, so's not to see the piece of meat and bone sticking from beneath a broken lift-wheel. So's to avoid the feeling that all this badness is somehow my fault.

The circle in the center of the rotunda is juiced with electricity. Like Margaret's shop, it's juiced but not wired; there's no reason why current should flow and yet it does.

But there is a reason. The reason is the presence of an élan vital.

From the margins curl tendrils of black fog. Dividia is everywhere.

It licks away before I can see it straight.

My knees go goopy, and I lean back against Abia and Nannie, resisting forward motion.

They shove me on, the cold mouth of a litegun in Abia's hands now at the nape of my neck.

I'm bigger now, I've got skills. I'm self-sufficient. I can slip this. Slip them. Run. Get outta here. Find the backways. Find the circuit paths. Break the circuit. Make the circuit. Lose the battle. There's no hope, no hope at all.

I've got to get a hold of myself if I'm going to face Ellison. If I'm going to get intel about his plans and get out again.

But that plan's a bust now, isn't it. *Oh Caran, we miscalculated.*

Ellison's here all right. I catch his lines through the corners of my eyes.

Abia and Nannie pull me to the center of the rotunda, smack in the middle of the juiced circle, and leave me there.

My feet can't move. Something's stuck me to the spot. Maybe my own fear. Maybe the drugs in the cookie. Everything's falling in flashes of color, slipping between worlds.

There's no hope of anything at all.

I pound the pain spots on my face.

Caran stands next to Ellison. He's ditched the clothes he'd left Freedom with. Now he's draped in a soft, rich, white wrap that might even be real fur. His flushed face and red-rimmed eyes make me figure he found some rum. I wish I could call Stella to me, set up a link to talk to him in my head. To beg him to get us out of here. To tell him I can't move my feet. We never should've let ourselves get separated. He needs me to keep him straight. Djen's gonna be so mad.

Caran shifts his stance, putting his chin in his palm, making sure I see it.

My eyes go wide as I realize what he's doing and force my lids into a long blink to clear the fear. My feet can't move but my hands are free. I reach up slow-like to put my hair behind my ear, so that the freedomtech com ring goes up where I can hear it.

"In the end, trust the song," Caran's voice whisper-sings a lyric from "The End of the World," barely audible, surprisingly sober. "In the end, trust the song / trust the love / trust the rage." Then he sings from a song I'd never heard before, in a triumphant hiss of notes, "If you can still feel anger, you have not yet been defeated."

Ellison says something to Caran then, laughing, and Caran puts his hands down by his sides, laughing back, a perfect echo.

"Hello Camilla," Ellison comes to me, stopping just outside the circle. Groomed and tailored, just like my bad dreams.

"You'll never win, Ellison," I say, and it almost sounds strong, "because I'll never play!" Anger. Right. I've plenty of that. Especially for Ellison. I bite my nails into my palms since my arms have gotten too heavy to lift, just like my feet. "I'm not a kid anymore."

Ellison laughs. "And when and where, exactly, did you grow up Camilla? Somewhere between L1 and L3 on the less savory streets of Ganymede? With pirates and grifters for role models? No, I think you're too good for that, Camilla Morgan. I think you've been waiting to come back to your castle where you can be princess again for a long time now."

I'm not going to fall for his lies. "Those pirates and grifters treated me hella better than you did. I was just your guinea pig!"

"Yes, I'm sure they gave you plenty of food, love, and toys as well."

"They didn't treat me like a guinea pig! Whatever a guinea pig is."

"Oh Camilla," Ellison lets out a long-suffering sigh, "is that how you've twisted it around in your head over the very small number of years you've been away?"

I blink and Research and Development is there, standing next to Ellison in pale yellow lab coats, the color of fear. Have they always been there? Or just appeared? All hundreds of them?

No, four. There are four of them. There are always four of them. Everything runs dry with fear.

"Are you ready for an experiment?"

Who said that? Who?

Ellison comes closer but is careful to stay outside the circle. "I wish I could turn back time Camilla. If you'd stayed, if you'd done better with your lessons, it might not have ended like this."

The experimenters from R&D make a swirl. A hot buzz, juiced noise, whines. Dials set, energy discharge. The floor feels like the hot end of a battery terminal. I'm standing in the center of a circle for summoning Ganymede. The world's a splatter of light and dot and shadow and edge and none of it no-ways processes.

They're going to kill me.

Foolish child Cami, too trusting, I've let Caran and Ganymede be captured both. Let the plan all fall apart. Stupid, child Cami.

<if you can still feel rage—>

Was that Caran or Ganymede or my own thoughts or some-thing else? "You can't do this! You always said that I was special! I can be—I can be useful to you! I can talk to the spirit now; I can do all those things you wanted me to do! You said if I succeeded, I could see Daddy! Please let me try again, one more time, please, just one more..." No breath left.

I can't do any of those things.

Ellison is hard, mean, a face colder and less movable than the stone of the hills. "Well, Camilla, you *were* special. But you are not anymore. You do have one use left though, and you are right, you will fulfill it."

"No, I can talk to the spirit now—I can—" my words come out in a transparent whisper.

"Whether or not you can is irrelevant. Your father did. He coaxed Dividia into maturity and fed it his fear. His fear for you, Camilla, I thank you for that. In the end it was his fear for you that gave Di-vidia so much strength."

"My dad would never! He'd been swindled by you!"

"Your dad was a pirate and a grifter. And anyway, he's dead now."

"No!" I exhale loud now, but it's too late, he's penetrated the walls of survival, and there's nothing left but fear.

"You're nothing now, Camilla Morgan. Nothing. Not a princess. No castle for you."

Current pours into/around me, every hair on end, as I cry out to the élans in one last burst of hope that maybe they will save me. <HELPME *!* PLEASE!>

—and Ganymede comes. Not from the credit slip around my neck, but from the floor beneath my feet.

The youth on the seal lifts up, folds out, and stands before me. His crinkly coat crumples in folds of metal on the floor.

<*sadness/regret*> the élan projects, opening his hands into a cup.

Inside the cup sloshes black oil, smelling of rust and sweet decay, and it drips down onto the floor and coils back up into the black smoke of Dividia.

<GET LOST!> I yell at Ganymede with all my will.

But I don't have any will anymore.

I'm not strong. I'm not skilled. I'm not self-sufficient.

Dividia draws Ganymede through me and all his metal colors realign to darkness, second by never-ending second.

Beyond, a legion of aliens are pushed one step too far; their voices scream in rage at what Dividia has done.

They turn.

They come for me.

◊

"I didn't see it when Dividia realigned Europa." Caran in the here/now transmits through the link that sits somewhere inside the there/then. "I'd been focused on driving the rover when Dividia realigned Io. But this time, I *helped* Dividia realign Ganymede. Realign Cami. Her pluck. Her stupid, gorgeous, misplaced faith in me. Helped with a grin on my face because it was so horrible what the fuck else could I do?"

<but it had to be done> sensations rustle around me, whispers and scrapes.

"What the fuck is hope, anyway? Cami and I were caught in Ellison's sticky-trap, and it happened to be the same sticky-trap I'd been in all my life. Lie or die."

I say to Caran through the hot wash of dissolved boundaries, "Take the abuse, or give up everything that matters." I don't know if it's my thought or his or theirs, or maybe all of ours.

<yessssssss>

◊

I stand to the side, watching. Dividia coils from Ganymede's cup, visible to everyone, lurching and pooling around Cami. The oily fluid turns to black mist as it falls, formless. The boy—the corner of an image of an alien being that lets itself be known as Ganymede—fights back with a twisting scream of jagged metallic light. But, attached to Cami as he is, the battle does not last long. The sparks drop into darkness. The boy unravels and reforms into a child made of shadow. Cami falls, a tiny tumble of taffeta and ruin.

Ellison crosses the perimeter of the circle, nudges her with the toe of his hard, black shoe. She trembles, but that's all.

Dividia's coils come after me in earnest now, curling demonic dust caressing my thighs, my neck, a lover's touch. The vibration of electrical charge, the tickle of hairs raising in the static air; it's good. It burns the nerves, like an echo of an NQ rush. Like Muse, my companion, a light in the dark.

But it isn't any of those things.

It's the abyss whispering that alone is all I've ever been, and all I'll ever be. Is what I deserve. That everything bad that's ever happened to me is all

my fault.

Ellison watches me, face bland with a slight, inquisitive twist-of-the-lip. Curious, perhaps, what form his machinations will take now, at their fruition. Through Dividia's resonance I catch a slippage of Ellison's thoughts, <ah yes i knew you two would get along>

Within the alone, hate waits. Patient like death. Always there for me. Always there to relieve the pain. Always to make pain no longer matter.

With a shiver of relief, I let Dividia have me.

◊

When we come out of the link, Cami is gone.

Ganymede is too. Another élan replaced Ganymede in the link and I don't know when or how or who.

Caran narrows his shiny black eyes at me. "You know who."

I do. And I know it's still here, still linked in, resonating with us both, how else is Caran reading my thoughts so well?

"What do you want from me, Steven?" he asks. "I mean besides someone to fuck the hole in your soul?"

"I don't know. Maybe I want you to destroy me. Maybe I want to destroy myself."

The arms of darkness eddy around me, probe inside me, into my most hidden places, my most destructive moments, every hair on my body standing on end in the static field. "Plans to jump off Mission Crater Ledge?" Caran laughs as I curl in my shame. "That'll do it. But you didn't jump, of course you didn't, not any more than I swallowed eleven drops of NQ. We don't get to be destroyed, Steven, people like us, we don't get to have our greatest hopes come true."

He stands over me. In the unnatural darkness, and in the smallness of my fetal gesture, he towers. Barely over a meter and a half, he towers over me. Larger that human. Larger than me.

"False modesty," he snarls, "false walls, false distance because you never belong. Wake the fuck up Steven Kwon, wake the fuck up and own who you are. Stop being"—his laugher vibrates off the shadows that crawl inside my mouth and take all the moisture away—"*afraid.*"

PART 4:

CALLISTO

SESSION 22:
CARAN & JORDIS & NOA & CAMI / DIVIDIA

High in orbit 'round Jupiter's pulse
Fair Liberty she spun
And singing with her lovely voice
Cried, "Still your frantic run!

Be still the winds, be still the rads,
A shelter here to stay."
And as she said, did they obey,
So thus Callisto sang:

"Welcome friends from every world
Where freedom's still to reign;
Come to me from every star,
Sweet Liberty to gain!"

"That's Freedom's Call," Caran says, after he's done polishing off the last note.

"Yours?" I ask, though even without the link I know it's not his style. I ask aloud for the record. Because it's the sort of thing I'm supposed to ask.

"No." Jordis tilts a small smile and makes a sound too bemused and sad and proud to qualify as a laugh. "It's a revolutionary ballad."

"We don't know where it came from," Cami sighs on the edge

of boredom. She's ceded the chair to Jordis and sits instead cross-legged on the floor. I asked my research assistant to bring in more furniture, but the levels of bureaucracy on such things are apparently deeper than I was previously aware. *Tomorrow at the earliest.*

"Eighteenth century. Earth. North American continent." Noa telegraphs from her spot beside Caran on the couch.

"I don't think they knew about radiation from Jupiter back then," Cami frowns.

"Noa means the original song," Jordis clarifies.

"Yeah, we know where the original song came from, just not who picked it up and modded it for Callisto." Caran whistles the tune again.

Black smoke curls, making the hairs on my arms stand on end. Dividia's presence should disturb me. It does not.

This is the first time I've been with the four of them together (five of them? do the élans count? how much of Dividia have I seen before now?)

<all of me. all the time. every time.> A sensation of contempt swirls along with the communication, then slurps back in on itself with an exquisite sensation of bells.

The four humans are comfortable with each other, bodies open and eyes soft. I've become sensitive to how Jordis allows emotional warmth to seep beneath the political smoothness of her face. The way Noa rests her hand inside Caran's personal space on the cushion of the sofa. In the way Cami examines her fingernails, chipped and a little dirty with what might be machine oil, in a childlike gesture she'd never allow when wearing the armor of Worldly Adult. And Caran, who is typically too big, too open, takes too few measures to hide either his vulnerability or his barbs, is quiet. No twitches, no hand-flaps, eyes half-closed in a kind of peace I've not even seen after orgasm.

It seems another man who once felt threatened by them, ganged up on by them. Our placement is a circle; our fates linked. My experience is catching up to theirs as I experience what they experience and we experience—

LINK IN

(no—this isn't a link; this is something else—)

<steven isn't going to like this part>

Who said that?

The room blurs, cants sideways.

I hear my pulse; is it panic or am I having a heart attack? Am I dying?

<hush; it's just unity>

<*cruelaughs*>

<steven doesn't have to like it. we didn't like it. why should he?>

<don't be mean mean mean mean mean —>

I can't tell who said what to whom. There is no center to hold.

A feathered white dragon explodes centimeters from my face and twice my size. I scream.

Pull yourself together! You are a scientist!

I fight for breath, unable to tell if the dragon is a projection on the 3V, or a telepathic vision of Caran's Mem presentation, or an élan creating illusions. The borders between the real world, the virtual world, and the élan's world have dissolved.

Caran, it's just Caran, no matter what it is, it's incorporeal, it can't hurt you, there's nothing to fear.

The dragon pumps its wings as it squats on two short hind legs with clawed paws. The body is a snake-like Chinese dragon; its head the delicate wedge of 20th century fantasy art. Crests of plumage stream behind it. It blinks its beautiful black eyes. At me.

Its eyes hold all the light like cores of stars.

This is both deeper and more than a link I'm in. I can sense everyone like it's a link, but I can't locate anyone as a distinct entity. Or, rather, everyone *is all the same entity*.

<welcome, steven> the dragon part of us think/feels <to the unity. share our collective consciousness>

◊

The water in Ellison's pool is warm. I deduce this from the steam fogging from the bubbling surface since my nauta senses can't feel the heat. Courtesans brush by. Don't want them. They're nice, but they can't fill the hole. I want to be alone.

Well, not really alone.

Dividia and I reach out together, murky and loathing, and touch Ellison's toys with <*discomfort*>. The courtesans withdraw, damp and disgruntled, not knowing why. Most had hoped for more; a few for less. All for something different. We drink their anxiety and sneer at their passivity.

We relax back into the water until only my nose is above surface. The sense-deprivation soothes; ears below the surface mutes sound. Breathe myself naked, ego-diffuse.

<*extension*> Think/feel the idea of a formal, disciplined Mesh at Dividia: a weaving of our resonances with each other and with the fabric of human informationspace and natural ambient signal. Teaching it.

<*confusion*> Feelings burning redoubled-dread.

<*EXTENSION*> I absorb the dread and slam memories of Muse and me making a Mesh back at it: openness between intelligences, latching onto/into frequencies, layers of overlapping

worlds through many minds at once. Finding bandwidths, aligning to/with wavelengths, generating shared thought-space with human information systems and minds, with electricity and the radiation of stars. *Meshing in.*

Thrashing <idonotunderstandsharing>

Stupid thing can't even grasp the simplest concepts. Can't even play recorder. Anyone can play recorder. I try again: <see: we-are-1 followmylead *EXTENSION*>

<*extensssssion*> the abyss echoes back, dragging nightmare through the feedback loop between us.

<yesssssss nightmare is us now>

The Mesh clicks as Dividia remembers how to spread itself into ambient signal and share it with me. We are the eye of nightmare, the cold, hating place in the center of terror where even fear freezes away.

We are larger than we've ever been.

<tuneinto signal from camillamorgan>

We pass through walls and seek heat. She's so bright, Magnet Cami. Delicious treat.

She lies on her side, radiating. Wave and spark, glow and scream, jabber and blare and streak and burn. Around her, the old, mobile élans have returned from outside of inhabited space, so angry for Dividia's/our existence. For what humans have done in weaponizing an élan. <*BROKENHUMANPROMISESSUFFERSUFFER*> the raging élans writhe. Seeking an opening to align the magnet to them. A way inside of Cami, to fill her, to use her body for their revenge.

We listen in on Cami's thoughts: <the doors are open. open. loud. LOUD. TOO FUCKING LOUD>

Dividia approaches the other élans; they recoil like the legs of an insect poked with a stick.

Query to the Mesh: find Noa.

Tumble half a moon away. What is this place?

Spaceport.

We find Noa's frequency easily because, like Cami's, it is already resonating with ours. We observe as Noa communicates with Fish in the Mem. "Find me a shuttle. Now. Before the spaceport closes."

We lick our lips; she is tasty-filled-hate.

"I don't think this is a good idea. You don't stop one war by making another one," Fish replies.

"War is part of the equation. I have run the maths. If RealsOlutions is allowed to flourish, many Operators die. There is a 98% chance of our freedom if I destroy their base before they start."

We observe Noa through the sensorcams at the space port, watching arrival and departure feeds.

Now that three moons amplify us, humming at our frequencies, we are so much larger and more powerful than Stella. So much larger and more whole than Muse; Muse was a broken, partial thing. We are large like Zaos and the other old ones. We are one of the old ones too, just lost, displaced, alone. Returned broken. Damage cannot be undone.

Intuit into Ganymedian Meshspace: Details on RealsOlutions, Io, Reals movement.

<get out of the hot tub and share a drink with me and i'll tell you>

That is Ellison's thought! Ellison is in here with us.

I, Caran, slap Ellison's mental voice back down into an unconscious level of the Unity. <hush (*notime4Uyet*)> I can't kick him out, but I know what I'm doing; I can keep him below the threshold of consciousness.

Mesh returns from human informationspace: The humanitarian group RealsOlutions has passed another approval milestone in its application for a non-profit corporate charter. Slogan: "Keep it Real." Mission: To protect the rights and values of humanity against Operator threat through education, research, and action. Proposed headquarters: Io, Sol-Jovian system, industrial. "While unusual to place a corporate headquarters on an Industrial-class orbital, the unique electro-magnetic interference around Io will protect us from Operator influences."

Caran: STOP

We shift to the signal around Europa, seeking Jordis Ansari.

A thin whisper wraiths through the Mesh: "Someone's going to find us, someone's going to find out that we've broken our hobbles." Not Jordis.

But then, "Shhh, it will be OK," Jordis answers. We observe.

"They've executed two of us at this location already, because they think it will draw out the GLF terrorists. Except there is no GLF to draw out!"

<*scoff*> "You have control of Europa's environmental systems, yes?"

"Everyone's afraid. Two of us already—" a babble of networked signal—

<*triumph-amusement*> from Jordis. "There is no place in this game for cold feet. You knew that when you started."

Jordis shifts her awareness from the Mem to the physical world. She is in a back room at Mentist Corporation, planning a meeting with the Captains of the Galilean Black. Planning war on two fronts. One with Ammiel's rebels in the Mem and one with Ray Ansari in the flesh. Neither knows the other's there. But Jordis has command of the entire playing board.

We return to Ellison, pulling him back across the threshold of the collective consciousness. <hello ellison> I let him sample the sensation of sharing Dividia's awareness of ambient signals, the barest touch of the Mesh.

<is this what the alien can truly do? even more useful than i expected, and my expectations were high. it's going to be so easy to stoke fears of feebles with this kind of control. you are doing very well, caran, you will need to teach me what you know>

But his feelings are guarded—or maybe he's just bad at giving control over into the Unity—and we can't read if he's speaking sarcasm. <later> I tell him.

Unity fragments as I, Caran, release its focal point, falling back into the building, the spa, the body floating numb in nothing, beyond love or fear or caring. It doesn't matter anymore that this badness is all

my fault.

There will be no more song.

Open my eyes.

Above, the Milky Way sprawls across the glass ceiling, brilliant in the thin Ganymedian atmosphere. Singing to me of life and hope and joy and dreams, and a Muse of rainbows in a field of wheat and blah blah blah, blah blah.

I do not sing back.

I climb out of the pool, the weight of my body tugging like I've gone from zero g to 8 g. Tired. Empty. Hard and dense and cold. Everything turned to platinum.

Dividia coils in shadow spilling dread, blame, the coming war.

For the first time since I found my mother's well-stocked liquor cupboard thirty-one years ago, I do not want a drink. I do not want drugs, or sex, or song. I am weary of myself. I don't need to fill the hole inside of me because it has filled with hate.

"Ellison." I call. When no one answers, I fill my lungs with Dividia's foul fuel and shout louder, reaching through our resonance with Dividia to echo on two planes at once: "Ellison!" <ELLISON>

Youth dressed like Ganymede come scurrying, courtesans or servants, or maybe slaves. "Take me to Ellison." I'm wet and unpleasant, pulling words from scripts I memorized the day before. "Time to go home."

◊

"So what was that time period like for the rest of you?" I indicate Jordis-Noa-Cami with my thoughts. We're so much one just thinking all-inclusive is enough.

A chorus of shrugs through the link.

"About like what you just experienced." Cami's tone is thin and strained in a way that makes me think of saw blades screaming.

"Caran's perspective is not inaccurate." Jordis flicks something off the cuff of her jacket. "We didn't experience Caran's perspective directly, exactly, or the entire time. But Europa and me, Io and Noa, Ganymede and Cami—we were all so well-aligned with Dividia that we kept seeping in and out of Unity accidentally. Our individual consciousness kept seeping into a collective consciousness, though most of the time it was more of a collective unconsciousness. You've been tasting it yourself, Steven, for weeks now, as seepage. It's 'like a thought of your own from outside'—that's what you put in your notes, right?"

"You read my notes?" I feel defensive. "They're confidential, pre-analysis."

Jordis laughs. "I was sitting there when you made them."

"No you weren't. It was Caran who was sitting there when I made them. It was the first time Muse spoke to me directly."

Jordis shrugs. "Thoughts and feelings leak. It's hard to escape seepage—moments of accidental Unity—once resonance occurs. The three of us share knowing. Sometimes."

"Not all the time. Not even most of the time," Cami says quickly. "Don't get worried about that."

"Caran and I have spent a lot of time tangled up in each other's thoughts." Jordis smiles at me, and it even feels warm. "Rest assured, it takes more than a few months of resonant linking to build up significant seepage."

Seepage. I'd not heard the word before. File it for later. They are trusting me more to share their secret idioms.

"I think we should give Steven a clearer picture. Of our individual activities. At the time." Noa says.

"Yeah, that's probably a good idea." Caran curls his legs up under himself and wraps his arms around his knees.

"I'll start," Jordis says.

◊

Jordis: "Madame X's Empire of the Moon will not let the bombing of Hanger 19 pass." I wag my finger at Primo Capo Som Bliss across his office. "Ray Ansari cannot go rogue with CryCorp and blow up the Empire's cargo as a play in his pointless war against Operators. A play, I might add, that he kept secret from his Captains and Advisors. If he'd told you, 'I'm going to blow up our trading ship to generate media spin about a fake terrorist organization,' I'm guessing you might have answered, 'I advise against decimating our profits and enraging our associates.' Our Syndicate hasn't persisted since the dawn of human history by pissing on its laws and subverting its generals."

Som purses his lips and sighs, fingers pressing heavy on the shiny surface of his desk where he stands. "No, you're right, it's just..."

"Embarrassing?"

His eyes flash anger and then he sees my expression: one raised brow, flirty lashes, apologetic-yet-amused twitch of my lips—all programming to reduce threat-perception and enhance rapport. Because of course I know bringing the facts about the bombing to the Council is embarrassing for Som and the rest of the Captains. I would have known it even without Europa-élan slurping up everyone's ambient feelings and broadcasting them to me. Som says, "Yeah, pretty much. Ansari is King, but he's supposed to wool his competition, not his Captains." He laughs.

I am allowed to laugh then, by normie rules, and I add more honey. "Ray Ansari didn't, in the end, wool you, though, did he? The truth came out and now you know." I leave out the part where I, Madame X's Enforcer, brought that truth to him. *Soon, soon Daddy, you will reap what you have sown.*

In the Mem, the flash of Ammiel's ping troubles my vision. I split my consciousness, one thread on Som, the other reaching through the channel back to Ammiel.

"Okay." Ammiel's patchwork tunic is colored excited-scared-angry. He flicks his thick red braid behind his back and rubs his hands together in a gesture I'm guessing he also makes in the physical world when he's overwhelmed. "Okay, that's the last of the Operators on Europa. We've found them, and they've agreed to join us. I think we can do this; we really can do this."

It's a sentence said out of fear, not hope—a sentence said to self-reassure. For a nanosecond I consider comforting him, but fear is a powerful motivator. Instead, I say, "Normals have exploited us for too long. Regardless of who survives, you are the heroes of today. History will tell of how Ammiel and the Operators of Europa broke their hobbles and took the moon." Too much? The implication that many could die? At least this way we die on our own terms. "How far have you gotten on gaining control of Europa's environmentals?"

"Almost done," Ammiel says. "We just have the scientific sector left; that's the hardest because it's oldest and no one understands how some of it works anymore. But we'll get there."

"Good."

In the physical world, with Som: "So you'll call a special session of the Galilean Council to address King Ansari's role in the bombing?"

Som sighs and turns, his back to me so I cannot see his face. But I feel his feelings. <*resignation/ambition/fear/hunger*> His feelings synchronize with Ammiel's. With mine. With all of Europa's. "Yes," he says. "I'll com the rest of the Captains. If they agree to hold Council, I'll make sure King Ansari is there."

◊

Noa: Fire.

FIRE FIRE FIRE I SEE FIRE.

I shake the flames from my eyes. Not mine. Not my eyes—Io's eyes. Io-élan, but changed, not the same. An angry, panicked version of Io-élan. <you need me, hush, let me guide you, let me show you what we need to do> I assert to her, as she doubles back in walls of flame.

I smash her down again <my *RAGE* is stronger your *RAGE*

is why you rage in the first place so *QUIET AND LET ME DRIVE*>

I am driving a shuttle through space toward Io. I stole it through a series of altered station records. They show me, Noa Oki, as the shuttle's rightful owner. It is fitting; it feels good. Good to own something that was never mine to take. *You own us Operators, but we were never yours to take. Now you pay.*

I growl low in my throat like the jacklets. The jacklets murdered by the greed and hate of normals. *It is time to make you pay for that as well. Nobody lives. Nobody gets a diamond.*

I see Io through the thick, transparent window of the shuttle. She's a bright spot now but will get bigger quickly. She will be as big as my rage soon. She will be wiped of human blight. Free of CryCorp. Free of RealsOlutions. Free of hate. All washed away in sulfur-spew and seismic shift. Just like we did to Markus.

<*iamready*> Not-Io-élan communicates to me, not in words for she is poetry, but in knowing. We know together.

I feel the fire beneath my crust. I have the power to break free.

◊

Cami: Voices scream. They scream to me:
<you betrayed our trust!>
<you broke the last remnants of our pact>
<how dare how dare how dare>
<*vilefilthrage*>
<NOMORE>
The élans continue to return to human space, covering vast distances and multiple dimensionalities.

<you change CHANGE change us like you promised you wouldn't corrupt corruption WE ARE NOT YOUR WEAPONS>

<sever. sever the connection. kill the humans make them pay>

They are angry because of Ellison and the shadows and me letting Dividia realign Ganymede and it's all

my fault.

I think I'm in a room, on a bed, on my side. I think I exist, but I don't know. I think I'm still dressed in the princess clothes but who knows the din is so loud so strong and I don't know where I belong. To them? I am theirs now, aren't I? They want humans all to die.

But I don't want be theirs. I don't want to die.

I wrench my eyes open to the human world.

I see my old room in Ellison's castle, smelling like time and dust and I don't think anyone's touched anything in eight years. Flowers Powers pictures on the walls. Piles of tinkering toys and an old 4V for playing games, and the radio I built from scratch. Closets and dressers of clothes.

I see these things from my body, but I don't feel like I'm in my body. The élans are slipping in and out of me, wearing me like I wear the dress.

<how dare you do this to us>

<how dare how dare how dare>

I pinch myself to make sure that I'm awake. It helps. I have to pee, and I fall off the bed and move, more by body memory than volition. I make it into the bathroom and pee forever. Forever and ever.

Don't fall asleep, Cami.

I pull my panties back up, and somehow end up wearing shoes.

<that's right, we are driving this bus>

The communication wells from the screams. The screams scream. They scream to me:

<you betrayed our trust!>

<*vilefilthrage*>

Resisting the élans is hopeless. I'm just so tired. Tired of having to take care of myself, pretend I'm an adult, pretend I'm not scared and alone and in danger all the time from Ellison and street thugs and cops and nasty people who want to take advantage of a kid. I'm so tired. Whatevs.

They're tired too—the élans. Tired of trying to find a solution to the problem of human thoughts changing them into things they don't want to be and doing things that they don't want to do. They're tired of fighting us, and running from us, and having to decide what to do about us. Their experiences were better when there was no us, only stars. Whatevs.

<go ahead> I tell the screams. <you can drive the bus>

They rush in like wind or tidal force and push me away to some small, bright place beyond myself where I can lie down and sleep—

They fill me, like Ganymede did to bring me out of Ellison's castle all those years ago.

My feet walk me out of my old room, down the hall, to a rover, and the creatures inside me set the coordinates for Iron City Center. I check out.

◊

"Caran! Where have you been! We were so worried! You've caused so much trouble. Are you safe? Where are you?" Mindy's olive-brown face on Europa lurches in the camera as she fights with LaRoque's shrimp-pink one for angle. She wins, of course, being a gigantic bodyguard.

"Hi, Min." I reach for words memorized before leaving the Grizwald squat, repeated over and over with my linguistic programming turned off until I'd gotten them right, just like memorizing a song. But there's no music in my voice. "I'll explain everything, but not on Europa. Lockdown and bombings and people hating on me, you know." *And Callisto has no native élan to complicate things; it has no inhabitants at all.* Dividia channels a dry laugh through me, bones on sand.

"You better explain or I'll—" LaRoque wrestles himself some turf in the corner of the 3V.

Mindy shoves him off with a meaty shoulder. "Where are you? We'll come get you right away. Are you all right?"

"I'm all right. There's a communications station on Callisto. It's got atmosphere, pressure, rad protection. No terrorism. Meet me there. We have a lot to talk about." I go off-script now, echoing words from Ellison. "We're gonna do a benefit show for RealsO-lutions." Then I sing, artlessly, "It's gonna be better / it's gonna be the best."

I angle the camera to get Ellison in the frame. Give a subliminal shove via Dividia to goad the man into speaking for me as I've no words of my own.

"Caran, you're not going to—" Mindy starts.

But LaRoque succeeds in pushing her out of the frame this time. "What's the idea then? Who's there with you? RealsOlutions, eh? That could be usef—interesting. We can't leave Galilean space anyway, might as well make use of our time here. What are we talking credit-wise—eh, wait, who are you?"

"Ulric Ellison, Meta-owner and CEO, CryCorp." Ellison tips a business-like smile. "I fully fund the benefit event and you take sixty percent of the yield."

"Eighty."

"Seventy."

"We coordinate everything," LaRoque clarifies.

"Of course. CryCorp is aware that 100 Worlds Music has full charter on the artist. This would be a ghost-fund, not an amendment to either of our company's doctrines, temporary-amend or otherwise. My legal people are ready to touch yours, at your go."

"Depends on the details—we need to loop in Legal, yes—but that could work for us. What with the difficulty leaving Galilean space right now this could also really work to—well, I see mutual benefits. And since Caran wants to do it…"

"Caran wants to do it." I echo, echo.

"We'll see what Legal says." Mx. Manager LaRoque's pink rat-cheeks have flushed. What better way to prove I'm not an Op, and thus retain me as an asset, than for me to do a benefit that dooms the entire caste? Certainly better than submitting my biological matter to a DNA test. That wouldn't go anywhere good, and La-Roque knows it. Not that he'd admit it. Mx. Manager continues, "There are a lot of details, a lot of fine lines. I can't speak for 100 Worlds Music at the same level you speak for CryCorp, so I need to bring in higher auth."

"Of course. There are fine lines for us too. But as you said, mutual benefits."

These negotiations always go on forever, with their need for normie-style useless extra banter, so I shove Ellison out of the way and finish up with the rest of my planned script—Dividia or not, the show goes on. "Min."

The bodyguard appears in the corner of the crowded lens. "I'm here Caran, what do you need?"

"Collect up everything from the Mnemosyne Hotel. Everything. All my stuff. Kinetikosonus, personal items like my favorite old boots and my personal lockbox. Pack everything into *Sonica*. Everything. I want the feel of my own things again.”

Mindy’s lips make hard lines. I’m not making her life easier. The collecting up my stuff part is easy. But not the getting clearance to bring it all to the old Callisto com station while protecting me from everything at the same time part. She won’t say no though, because this plan’s the best chance any of them have of getting out of the uncomfortable situation I’ve put them in.

“I think we can arrange that.” Mindy adds breath, like she’s going to say something else, but she lets it out with just a curious look on her face. Not a look I’ve seen before. But then nothing looks like I’d seen before, since I’ve never seen it without the filter of NQ. Never seen it with the hum of Dividia-plus-three-moons aligned into the same resonance as me. “You’re looking good, Caran,” Min says. “Rested. Relaxed. What are you on?”

I shrug-grin in a gesture co-opted from Noa. Nothing, I hope the gesture communicates. Nothing.

“You feel good?” Mindy keeps looking at me like I’ve become someone else.

“Yeah!” I flash my best grin, the one that forgives me anything to anyone. I sing, hitting notes only I can hit, “It’s gonna be better / it’s gonna be the best / I’m bright and shiny today, got my egg in the nest!”

Inside, Dividia flutters, whispering hate. Anxious to be set free.

◊

“Set me free,” I lean against Caran after the others have left. This time I have come to him. I am next to him, on the sofa, my old place opposite, abandoned. It’s a whine; it’s a plea. I know he can’t free me from me.

He doesn't try.

He and Dividia suck me into three-way Unity and all boundaries dissolve as i-am-him-fucking-me and i-am-me-fucking-him and we are all three bound together by muck we didn't ask for yet somehow fucking got. Please, someone, something, save us all.

SESSION 23:
CARAN & JORDIS & NOA & CAMI / DIVIDIA

The next day in my office we again become a boundary-less multi-mind: Steven, Caran, Jordis, Noa, Cami, Dividia.

The room fogs over. Shadows curl around our ankles; Dividia bends light to let in the darkness. They don't care so I don't care.

The multi-mind shifts into Caran, waking up.

◊

"Caran. Caran, we're here. Wake up." Ellison's voice in my ear, too loud, too bright. Finger on my shoulder, too light.

I jerk, blinking. Wipe drool off my lip. "Up," I echo, "up, up." I see Ellison's small hairs stand on end; feel mine do the same. Fear-feeding-fear. Hate-feeding-hate. Black shadows curling from everywhere. *Good.*

"Up?" Ellison's tone is a mocking mirror of my own echo. Contempt, maybe, for my drinking or my drug use, but then also maybe for my DNA. I could know if I wanted to. I could use Dividia to pull the thoughts straight from Ellison's head. But I don't care. Stay low. Hush.

"Up." I confirm, and to show it stand into a long, vigorous stretch. Followed by a stomp to the shuttle's lav for a long, vigorous piss. Behind the closed door, splash cold water on my face.

Shake out the fluttering of my heart by fluttering my hands and push wet hair from my eyes. Sweat in anticipation of that vial of NQ waiting for me with my stuff when we get to Callisto. All those drops of dark, blue lies.

Deep breaths. Opera breaths.

Dividia twitches along the edges of my fear, trying to find purchase. Stupid thing can't figure out if I'm scared or not. <*hate* hateU> I think/feel at it, deliberately amplifying its resonance with ugly things.

Bare my teeth into the mirror. That's right. I. Hate. You.

Strike a pose. Imagine the hot shutter-snap of flatshot cameras and the hum of the media. Suck up Dividia's quivering fear to fuel the cold candle of hate, black eyes glittering cruelty in the white everbulb's light. This is the end of Caran Watts. The end of the song started when Djen Pathfinder rescued me from hell and carried me to Freedom. The end of the song that I re-wrote when I ditched Freedom to make my art. The end of all songs.

Don't think about it. Too many minds might overhear.

One more breath.

One more splash.

One more shake-the-tension-out.

Okay.

Go.

I hit the landing platform whistling, shadows pulling in from all sides of Callisto's dead com station. My full entourage stands in the shuttle's lights, lights that don't reach the edges of the hangar so I've no idea how big it is.

They're all lined up to meet me. Mindy Ming in front, trying to tear off her own hands in anxiety to get them on me, wedge herself between me and anything that might cause a bruise. I give her nothing.

Jonathan LaRoque a half-step behind Min, greed like a twin brother gnawing through the low-grade empathy Dividia creates. He stretches out an arm to touch me, prove his valuable corporate asset's really here. I give him nothing.

Hair and makeup and wardrobe, eyes on my skull, my flesh, the hem of my vest, dicing me up with their eyes into component parts to polish and shine.

Roadies and techies looking hopeful, assessing if now might be a moment when celebrity slips and we can discuss the nuanced difference between an Auawia700 resistor and a T-15 resistor. Nothing, nothing for any of them.

The strange gaggle of useless doll-people paid to look like friends on film. LaRoque picks them out of concert crowds, invites them after Min runs background checks, because they'll play nice in visuals with me. Pretty, but not upstaging. Don't know their names.

Behind them, I see the delicate matte-black skin of *Sonica*, absorbing photons like a singularity. A black hole into which I can't wait to fall. *Inside her is my vial of NQ.*

The dim light fragments and brightens; figure-ground flip-flops as my scrambled nauta perception reasserts itself. Minutes, that means I've got minutes before the U4 runs out.

"Hey Min. Hey JL. Hey." Strike a pose. Flash that rakish grin that forgives me anything to anyone. "Let's make some music!"

I form Unity and a Mesh with Dividia and blink into observations of Jordis' rising war.

◇

"You brought that here?" The Junior Capo's color is high, as is the pitch of his voice. He is pointing at me. "At a time like this?"

Primo Capo Som Bliss keeps his fingers firm around my upper arm. As though I couldn't kill them all if I wanted to by a brush of the poison needles in my fingertips.

"'That'," Som snaps, "is Key Enforcer Gala Baudin from Luna who has assisted our investigation of the bombing and represents the Empire of the Moon, so tread lightly."

There are twelve Capos in the room, the captains of the Galilean Black Market. Three Primos. Nine Juniors. And Daddy. King Ray Ansari, sitting all the way across the expanse of the table at the opposite head. I'd been expecting emotions. I'd braced for their impact, packed ice around me to keep cool when I saw him. But I feel nothing. Nothing at all. His proximity is too unreal.

He is tall like me. He's thick around though; I presume my slenderness comes from my murdered mother. *My mother you murdered, Daddy, to hide your shame.* We have the same long, thick, auburn hair. His constrained in a ponytail; mine wrapped in my signature bun. We have the same nose. Different eyes. These observations flicker through me, compare against memory-indexed flashbacks of childhood. He hasn't changed much. But I have. *You don't even recognize me, Daddy.*

He doesn't. I don't just know it through his body language, but through the feelings I receive like a communications hub. All of them in the room, I feel what they feel. Heat, electricity, I am a filigree jelly in an enclosed space with a school of my prey.

Som guides me into the seat beside him, the two of us opposite the King. Som bangs the table with a battered wooden gavel. "I, Primo Capo Som Bliss, call this one-thousand nine-hundred and seventy-fifth meeting of the Conclave of the Captains of the Galilean Kingdom. All are present; all are strong. As siblings we compete; as siblings we complete, as siblings we agree for the good of the Kingdom now and for the generations to come. So be it true."

"So be it true." Everyone echoes the formal opening and sits.

Som glances at me, a barely-there gesture. Asking with his eyes one more time if I want to pass this point of no return. I nod. Of course I do. I have wanted to since I was born. Though Som doesn't know the half of what I will unleash.

"It is for unfortunate business that I call you here," Som begins. "But I'm sure that surprises no one considering the unfortunate condition of our beloved Galilean space." He nods toward me to speak.

"Europa has closed her borders," I keep all tones neutral. "I just came from Io where CryCorp has bought out three major contracts from Io Mining Corporation and cleared four of our Syndicate-controlled holdings for its own use. This is unusual, and not in Our interests. It is also"—I look at Som and bite my lip, as though I need his permission; Som nods—"symptomatic of the larger problem I was sent here by the Empire of the Moon to investigate."

There are predictable dismissive grunts, but lanky Bella clears their throat and affirms, "What she says of Io is true. I just got off coms with a very confused distributor. No one informed me that we were pulling the Marcón Operation."

Good. Bella's one of the more conservative Capos. There are more grunts of concern than sighs of dismissal now.

"Why?" one of the juniors asks. "What's a giant like CryCorp want with a bum-hole like Io?"

Som's eyes fall on me, glittering like light off water. "The real question is what's a giant like CryCorp want with control of Galilean space. Including our portions of it."

I watch my father closely. His face is largely neutral, with a thin film of amusement. It is not because he is amused. It is in preparation to laugh down the truth he must sense coming. *You can try Daddy, you can try.*

I make a gesture of deference to Som, asking permission again. We scripted this in his office an hour ago. But we make it look good.

Som returns a gesture of go-ahead.

I stand and unfold a mid-sized 3V projection plate on the top of the table. I could have used the 3V in the room. I could have pre-programmed what I wanted to show them and brought in a dataslip for an assistant to run. I could have done many things to make the Capos and my father more comfortable, to help then forget that I'm an Operator. But I want no question in any of their minds of what I am.

"As you know, I rank as one of Madame X's Enforcers." I straighten the legs of my gray suit. "I was sent to investigate the bombing in South Bay, a tragic incident affecting both our assets. What I found, in joint investigation with Som, is cause for alarm."

I click on the 3V with my thoughts and split my consciousness. Thread one: Speaking to the Council. Thread two: controlling the 3V. Thread three: capturing and analyzing the expression on every face in the room, the shift of every shoulder, the shuffle of every knee. Who is on my side?

Europa's frightened, angry hunger flutters in my chest, jaws wide to swallow unsuspecting prey.

Over the projection plate, I display the evidence. My father's deals with Ellison and CryCorp, how they created the GLF and were responsible for the bombing, how he manipulated the media and the public consciousness not to benefit the Galilean Black Market as is his sworn role, but to fuel his personal hatred of Operators. *Of me.*

The room floats in a long silence. However, the airwaves scream as the Capos communicate with their crews through their coms. Confirming what I have uncovered.

Ray Ansari releases his prepared belly laugh. "What entertainment Madame X has sent us! Apparently, we were meant to enjoy its cute attempts to act like one of us."

But no one laughs back. Because none of them have found a reason to refute the evidence Som and I have laid out.

Someone clears their throat. "King Ansari, it is my honor to serve in Devotion to you. Surely there is information you've yet to reveal, something that explains your plan."

"I believe," I raise my brows as though my words have little consequence behind them, "the missing piece of information is the Operator taint in his genes."

There isn't as much of a gasp as there might have been, and a-ha expressions flash around the table like a ripple over water. It never was a secret why he killed my mother. Nor a secret that he'd produced no heirs besides Jordan and me. No one will say it, but they all know he's to blame for his daughter's full-blown and his son's borderline Operator status.

"How the simple simplify." Ray Ansari's voice is a low rumble of condescension and fear paved over by hate. The shadows boil in ways that do not make sense with the direction of the light. "You would take the word of this retarded creature, this abomination of nature, over the wisdom of your own King? Even if she were not a feeble, she is Madam X's Enforcer, a ranking officer from our rival syndicate. Obviously, X sent her to weaken us. To stir things up. How did my Capos get so easy to fool, so weak on Operators?"

Indecision shivers over the room. But it doesn't stick to everyone.

"I've confirmed through my crew that the media spots were

fixed," one of the Capos starts.

"The findings check out," another interrupts, the bur of betrayal in his voice. "And it's not just Enforcer Baudin's investigation. It's ours too."

"Is this true, Som?" Fear feeds the shadows. No one wants to believe the King is acting against Family interests. The small hairs on my arms rise, a feedback taking place. I do not fully understand it, but I will use it.

"It is true." Som says simply. He and I make a field of calm. An eye in the storm. But the eye is a lie.

"You are King," Bella speaks up. "And we have sworn Devotion to you. But your personal vendetta has gone on long enough, at Kingdom's cost. It is time we let it rest."

I smile inside, but it does not move the glacier of my angles. Bella is one of the oldest, with both the most and least to lose. They were old when Daddy took over for Great-gran, and that was years before I was born.

"You think climbing in bed with a bunch of feebles will get us ahead of the Empire of the Moon?" Ray Ansari rises, face red now with rage. Whatever else I inherited from him emotional incontinence is not on the list. Or is that Madame X's training? I can't process now; the room is moving quickly.

Bella speaks up again. "I say Oust."

"And what, put Jordan on the throne?" Someone scoffs, their identity swallowed in the clatter that follows, everyone talking at once, tossing names onto the table like antes in a poker game. Arguments over precedent and how no King or Queen has been Ousted since whatever date in the past two-thousand years like any of them even knows until Som smashes his gavel and yells, "STOP."

Silence.

Som wasn't exaggerating when he said this conflict of opinion between the Capos and my father has been brewing for a decade. I give him a side-ways glance; my respect for him grows. But not enough to save him.

"One issue at a time," Som speaks into the silence, concerned but unaffected. "We are a civilized Council. Primo Capo Bella Tu, do you make firm your proposal to Oust Ray Ansari?"

"Aye, I do." The lanky shrew smacks their lips.

"This is preposterous!" My father shouts, pounding the table hard enough to shake its massive weight.

"What's preposterous," Bella says, "is that we have let this continue until it has reached this point. That is on every one of us in this room. Secret meetings with corporate CEOs for the sole purpose of destabilizing the system and destroying Operators? Even if it did us any good in terms of credit or power, you did not consult with us. That is against the Proclamation of Ethos ratified by Council in 2508, and, speaking for myself, I am done looking the other way."

"Does anyone else feel this proposal to Oust rests on solid ground?" Som cracks his gavel.

A rumble of "ayes."

"Then who among us seconds the Oust to place another on the throne?"

The pause comes then. The glances at my father. He is a wall of a man at the head of the table. His power is a silent, living rage, pooling from the shadows. His presence stops them. The fear he summons. Oh so, so much of the room is fear.

But none of it directed toward the true threat.

"Capo Deng Thao?" Som acknowledges a gesture to speak.

The man stands, his angry eyes on me. "We're taking word of

a retard for all of this. I know the crews confirm what she claims, but she's a fucking k-dromer. She can make information say anything she wants. There's a reason our King doesn't let her kind into our ranks, and a reason we don't consider the voice of her kind in our deliberations. This crisis has you thinking with your panic, not your brains. Kill the fucking retard and start over. I'm sure there is a reasonable explanation if you take the time to find it." Deng sits.

I favor him with a smile at the edge between subservience and pity, and signal Som for permission to speak. I rise shakily, eyes downcast. "I recognize that regardless of my rank within the Empire of the Moon, things are done differently in the Galilean Kingdom. My respect for local custom is true. I am lesser than you, and, in your custom, my rank as an Operator takes precedence over my rank as Enforcer. But I ask you to consider this."

I level my attention at the group, straighten my spine, and push power through my words. "Madame X has led the Empire of the Moon in domination of the Shadow World for two hundred years. She has trusted me as Key Enforcer, and as liaison to your domain.

"You are right to ask yourself what an Operator might bring to the table, particularly in discussing events related to Operators. But perhaps you should also be asking yourself what X's Enforcer brings to the table. In fact, you should be asking yourself why Madame X sent this particular Enforcer.

"Actually—" I let a hungry smile spread over my mouth, pleasure-violence rising from the depths of Europa's ever-hungry ocean and mixing with all the fear "—you should be asking yourself right now how I might take the Galilean Kingdom as my own."

Even Som's jaw drops.

I snap my fingers for the drama as simultaneously in the Mem I engage the shadow-network of Ammiel and his rebels. "NOW."

Throughout Europa, the rebels exert their control of the electronics. Environmentals in halls, smart arts in bars, tubes along their beds of sound, the lights along the city streets, the seep of air and the suck of scrubbers—the body of the Europa torus switches from automatic to manual control.

The Capos know it. Every one of them around the table knows it from the coms implanted in their cochlea, the reports from their crews flooding in.

The lights throughout the torus flash "Europa is ours" in binary code; some tinker somewhere will recognize it and then—

"All right, Ammiel," I say in the Mem. "That's good for now." Everything goes back to automatic. Just enough to get a taste, to let Europa know who is in control.

Oh how the authorities are scrambling now, terrified, just as much as the Capos. The whole of Europa is realizing that an invisible army has taken over, and no one saw it coming.

The Europan Operators have broken their hobbles and the Dreaming City is ours.

"What have you done?" Som's face is livid, body rigid with betrayal.

I laugh, full, warm, open. "Done? I've done nothing dear Som, nothing but come home. For I am not Gala Baudin of Luna. Have you never asked yourselves why Madame X would place me in such confidence? Oh, she has Operators a-plenty on her payroll, but none ranked so high as Enforcer, and certainly not among her personal favorites. I am Jordis Ansari of Europa, and I am heir to Ray Ansari's kingdom, your Princess, by name, by blood, by talent, by training, and by temperament. Should we Oust here today, it is I who will be your Queen."

I pull myself to full power, all facades washed away. "Do you really think my brother fit to lead us? Moreover, do you really want my brother to lead us? Him with his set of paints and his fragile artist's soul? He is heir by virtue of my father's hate alone.

"No, I think it's better we leave Jordan to the pursuits he has talent for, let him have the life he wants. You will find I already have my brother's blessing."

Som relaxes; he is a smart man. I feel with the room filtered through the soiled soul of the moon; I know Som is processing quickly, rearranging his childhood memories of me, of my willful, bossy disregard for the subservient role assigned to me even at so young an age. He is furious with me, but he respects me.

My father is pale as a quarana as he floats back down into his seat. All of the fear he commanded is mine now. It always was mine. The ice around me melts. I smile. My father is afraid of me.

"No," Bella gasps. "No, we cannot have an Operator for a Queen."

I shrug. Bella's reaction is disappointing, and makes things more violent, but ultimately it will not matter. I am at peace with beginning my reign by quelling a schism. I am at peace with blood. Blood in this room. Blood in the streets of the torus.

Voice steady but hands shaking, Som stands and addresses the Council, delaying the killing for a short time more. "Your points are considered, Bella Tu. Recess two hours. Then we vote on whether or not Ray Ansari is fit for the throne."

◊

On Callisto, there are so many things that have to happen *right now*. Ellison must keep up with his Dividia timeline. LaRoque must prevent All Worlds Music from dropping us at any second. Mindy pushes me from station to station on *Sonica*, wardrobe in the spare room, security and sound together in Mindy's suite, the CryCorp lawyers and a special com channel to 100 Worlds Music's uppers on Cass-Prime in the cabin where LaRoque sleeps—

In the hangar outside, a posse of strangers coordinates how to get the donors and the sponsors and the meta-owners to Callisto for the show. Oh and maybe a few regular people too, for the cameras, for the press, to go home and talk about how wonderful it was later. A lottery of disappointed concert ticket holders?

Good thing I slept on the way over. Is this frenzy typical? How had I managed this on never enough sleep?

With NQ.

Awareness of the lockbox in the next room loops, an endless visual verse, a constant beat, a sheen of sweat across my palms. I near the door to my cabin only for someone to push me away before I can enter. No relief. Not yet. Not ever fucking yet.

No way to quiet the splintered sound, the roaring colors, the confusion of the senses making me unable to track what the fuck is going on. Always a beat or two or three behind. Slow and dull. Stupid. Forgetting where I am in space and bumping into everything.

Luckily everyone is used to me being a space wreck. Technicians push me down pathways of preparation like a train over prelaid tracks. Signatures, hair, fitting, roadies, tuning, signatures again: a machine made to produce a show out the other end. I'd never really processed it. There's even someone following along behind with a cloth wiping up anywhere I might have shed a skin cell. Can't have the wrong kind of fan get a hold of that, no. How much do they know, Mindy, LaRoque, and the crew? How much do they *want* to know? Doesn't matter. Any which way I'm fucked. Thinking of my gig back at Jeanie's Hope, rough and tumble and all my own, I laugh empty notes. Fame is ridiculous.

Dividia provides a nervous, hysterical edge to everything. No one is having fun. Worry for job security, political tensions, that there might be a bomb on the station, worry from the Op-loving members of the crew who'd always wished I would turn out to really be an Operator—

I press my eyes until I see sparks. Noise crashes from the angle of the walls; walls of sound collapsing onto my shoulders. Pressure.

The hair guy weeps because there aren't enough styling nanites to re-do my hair, and the choking sobs needle into my skin in sense-scrambled confusion. I lean back in twitching discomfort as the man struggles to make sense of the tangled black waves, as confused by my hair as I am by my perceptions. I slip into Unity and Mesh and close my eyes to find: Noa.

◊

I scream in multi-frequency, the pain of my people, the pain of my moon. We cannot find a way through the storms.

The owners are down there, the defilers, the haters. The hitters and punchers and destroyers. They do not care if their actions set humanity back to a darker age. They will trample Operators as they trampled su-bees and fomori mice, prometheus laurels and jacklets.

They deserve to die.

But we can't get through the storms.

It seems like we should be able to, for I am Io, and Io is me, and Io is below the storms. But I am above the storms, so our connection flickers in-and-out and which Io am I? Io has changed.

We are fire and volcano and death.

Nobody lives.

Nobody gets a diamond.

We will raise a storm to snuff the haters in Milktown. The people of Milktown are not my miners anymore. They are CryCorp. They are the enemy. They gather in buildings bought by RealsOlutions to slam the force of oppression down ten times harder on the backs of we who have already paid. And paid. And paid again.

WE HAVE WEAPONS

A hole appears in the storm, and we try to slip through.

It closes; we fail.

What will we do once we get there, once we find our way inside Milktown? So easy to open airlock doors. To sever emergency life support.

But that is not what we are. We are lava and tide. We are plasma storm and spitting stone. We have killed this way before. This is our nature.

I, Noa Oki, clutch the diamond in my hands. It is so cold it burns. Burns me with barrenness. All the life I built is gone and CryCorp took it from me.

So easy to kill everyone on Io, huddling under just the one dome. But the howling EM storms will not let us though. Try again.

You love me Io. You love me so make me a little pathway back to you.

But there is no safe passage yet.

◊

"No safe passage yet," I murmur in empathy, soliciting a "hm?" from the makeup man. I turn the echo into a quavering hum, so it sounds like I'm working out a song. But the notes fall flat, and the man gives me a funny look.

I haven't been able to seal the small surgical opening where my navis slips through. Would need time alone in my room for that. Time alone with my lockbox. With my vial of NQ. Did the hair guy notice the slice? Or was he too distracted by the knots that never comb out? Doesn't matter. Nothing matters. It's the fucking end of the world.

Ellison stirs. <everything matters more than anything in your life ever has, or ever will again>

Ellison's thoughts react to my vibrations in the Dividia Unity like a spider reacts to a shiver in its web. He's sucked in with me every time. I'm not sure how much he's conscious of.

I reach out to observe Cami.

◊

The spirits are here, the screamers and the sparkers. <*angry-ANGRYbetrayal* betrayal by humankind. our kind taken, manipulated, turned into something that should never have been. DIVIDIA-DEFILED>

They ebb and flow, sometimes filling me so much there is no me, but other times they let in fragments of reality. I have no control of my limbs or awareness, and then I see a flash of Iron City. Financial district, big biz. Leveled.

Leveled? I shake my head, blinking away the slide-blur.

Level—

Screaming pours through me again. The wrath of uncountable alien consciousnesses. The hunger of the Galilean Black Market. The rage of an Operator rebellion. Other people's screams seeping through and confusing me into thinking I am other people too.

But I am other people too.

I am all the people there are. I am stars.

I am screaming here, in Iron City's financial district. There's screaming all around me. People, flesh and blood people, screaming. At me.

No, screaming *because* of me.

What am I doing?

What have I done?

I can see light and heat shooting out of my hands and feet.

I can see buildings on fire-glow. I'm doing that. I'm setting the buildings on fire. No, not me, the élans, but no one can see them, so it looks like it's me.

People scream. People are on fire. They're on fire because of the energy the élans are shooting from my hands. A person hangs suspended by a geyser of electricity, buffered off so he's aloft but not frying, he's screaming along with the others as the black tendrils of Dividia curl from the ground and into them, burning everything in blue-hot light and the horde of angry élans kill even more—

◊

"Caran, are you there?" Snap-snap in my face. I cower from the sound, too loud, too bright. Don't know who or where it's coming from.

"Yeah. There." I echo. What Cami's doing sure isn't going to play well for humanity's first impression of the élan vitals. Oh well.

"You don't seem OK. Should I get Mindy?"

"No." I shake my head, the world in a tumble. "Not okay. Time out?"

But no, not yet. No time for a time out. Soon, they promise, soon. Have some wine, take some breaths. Can you last a few more minutes? Off to another round of rooms and sounds and lights and would-this-do-as-a-performance-stage and check the acoustics, check-check-check.

And then, without fanfare or clean transition, I am alone in my room. I am alone with my vial of NQ.

"Ten minutes," someone says. Ten minutes to do what I have to do.

I lock the door. Run my fingers along the surface of my platinum-coated lockbox. Heart speeds in anticipation of slowing down. Years of dosing here, in this room, every eight hours, every part of me twitches like I'm gonna do it again. Readies itself for the rush. Floods my bloodstream with adrenaline to counter the endorphins that are about to be unleashed by the miracle of nyquolium-quadrolate. I can't wait I can't wait I can't wait.

I set the box gently on the soft carpet, back two paces away.

Dividia curls around the pale metal, curious; it does not understand. It never has. I want to laugh at how wrong I'd been in Noa's rover thinking that Dividia had any care at all if I was high, if I was exposed as nauta, any of it. Dividia just wants me. All it's ever wanted is me, no matter what state I'm in.

Well, it has me.

It always has had me.

"Mindy." My voice is too small and thin to carry through the closed door.

I take a breath and try again. "Mindy." My breath whispers out, impotent.

Excited by my fear, Dividia sets my small hairs on end.

I lurch back and hit the panic button beside my bed, screaming for me since my voice holds no power.

Mindy comes running then, breaking through the clasp on the

door like I always knew she could even though I'd so meticulously locked it all these years. Locked it against what? Does she really not know what I am? She really does not want to know.

Well, tough fuck, Mindy Ming. Now you're gonna know.

The wisps of oily fog vanish at Mindy's entrance, but Dividia remains.

"What's wrong?" Mindy scans the room, my shivering, sweating body. "Are you sick?"

I shake my head. I point toward the box. Through the disintegration of my senses, the platinum surface roils with light, like a living skin.

Mindy squints, confused. She's huge, and muscled to the teeth, a tranqgun forever strapped to her hip. She's older than I remember, or maybe just more worried, crow's feet and pensive chasms between her brows. What does she think of me? Does she care about me at all?

Dividia probes outward, following the trail of my attention. Seeking resonance with Mindy's fear. Hooking into the adrenaline that spiked through her at the chime of the panic button.

Fear for what? For my wellbeing or for her job?

Doesn't matter. I hate her for all the times she's known my weakness in so many intimate ways. Dividia can have her. I point toward the box again and jerk my head.

Mindy bends, the figure-ground of her shifting, and I blink against the disarray. Now she's standing very close, the box in her hands. <*concern*> vibrates toward panic as Dividia forms resonance with her frequencies.

I reach with hands I can't feel on arms that don't belong to me to guide her elbows, bringing the box to my eye-level. I can't touch the box. It is an acid that will vaporize me on contact. I put my eye near the retinal scan. Click goes the lock.

I jerk back, wiping sweat from my nose. The vial of NQ is inside. Right there. The dark blue lies that make all of this go all away.

I command Mindy through our shared dread. <remove the vial and stick it in the waste reclaimer>

Mindy's eyes are saucer-plates. Her knees tremble. Here is a threat she cannot shoot. Here is a life she cannot save. I am a behavior she can neither understand nor control. Fear that I'll die on her watch, and she'll find the body, and it will be her fault.

<doitNOW> I think/scream before she can think her thoughts all the way through. <NOW>

Dividia adds a push, learning—or, rather, remembering—how to puppet a person for its own purposes.

Mindy shudders as air vibrates from her lungs. She turns the box so the opening faces her instead of me. She doesn't know what's within, but she knows it's so terrible there will be no return from the knowing.

Mindy cracks open the lid.

She picks up the crystal vial in her thumb and forefinger.

The platinum-coated lockbox falls to the ground. It lands heavy on her foot, but she's such a thrall of Dividia's she doesn't notice.

She tilts the vial upwards. The indigo liquid twinkles like all the stars in space.

I want it. I want it.

<*NOW!*> I send the inferno-blast of terror building in my belly straight into Mindy, fueled by fear fear FEAR itself.

Mindy screams the broken-chaos sound of the damned and flings the vial into the waste reclaimer in the corner of the room.

<turn-it-oN NOW *NOW!*>

Her fist hits the reclaimer button with the snap-crack of fracturing bone, blood smearing the white surface, Dividia/Caran rejoicing. Laughing with her panic. Laughing with the death-mask Fear.

<leave now> We push into her. <NOW! *hate* you *HATE!* now!>

Mindy turns her bloodless face toward me, grasping her shattered hand, confusion and fear and the sharpness of pain leaking off of her to pool on the floor into Dividia's black fog forever building and collapsing, never holding form, visible now, a monstrous mist.

Me.

I am the monster.

She is afraid of me. Not for me, *of* me.

She's called me a monster before, in her private thoughts and in conversations with LaRoque. But until now, she never admitted that "monster" is no metaphor. I am not human. I am a terrible, painful, nightmare, genetic-defective thing.

Mindy runs from the room, slamming the door behind her.

I push a chair under the knob.

I kneel by the platinum-coated lockbox gazing into an interior emptier than my hate.

I lift the false bottom. The pale blue rectangle of my navis lies beneath.

<*?disappointment*> Dividia becomes small; curls of black fog withdraw. It does not understand the significance of what has just happened.

I put my face in my hands and weep.

◊

We come out of Unity.

I, Steven, put my face in my hands and weep.

(We return to Unity, only with an added layer of signal and sharpness now that Caran has access to the human Mem and all of his programming and we are in the fullness of what he and the élan can truly do——)
Falling.
Through blades of tears.
Suffocating.
Stinker. Stinker Watts.
Stinks don't talk and neither does Stinker Watts!
Ha ha ha
<SHUTUP DIVIDIA>
<*!*>
<iamincontrol>
<(((*smallsorry*)))>
Breathe.
Breathe.
A panic bigger than space.
Airless.
Breathe.
(colored tinkling, ringing bells, resounding slipstream in wake of the fluid weave humming waveform tangling, don't forget to)
Breathe!

Breathe. Breathe!

<better with navis computational amplifications?>

<...?>

<better somehow?>

<..."better?">

{concept   allatonce   betterness   comparison:morebetter-from-lessbetter}

<better—*yes*>

OK.

BREATHE.

Together now—

My (Caran's) consciousness breaks into the Mem, my dragon-tail anchored in the élan's abyss and white wings beating sound. My nose touches the membrane of local signal, breaking it open until my head is through and I can survey the local informationspace. I'm no Pathfinder like Djen, but I learned a thing or two in the decade I ran with her. All of local knowledge spreads before me, not muddied as it had been through that nasty old navis from decades ago that I'd used on Ganymede, not thin and slippery like the Mesh where only Dividia could perceive signal. This is the Mesh through my custom-made, recently calibrated, properly-programmed navis flush with Dividia nestled into the crystal matrix and both of us equally sharp in our perceptions.

Shift perspective. Real-world view of my cabin on *Sonica*. Sensory-motor-linguistic routines running, full functionality. Everything should make sense but none of it does. What are these things? This dresser, this bed, this carpet the color of my fucking puke when I drink too much red-berry schnapps, these pieces of abstract light-art on the walls—these are not my things. Picked out by others, arranged, a perfect performance of a self that never existed.

I've never had any things. I'd left Agrippa with nothing, left the *Stella-Maru* without much more.

My fingers curl around the platinum-coated dataslip at my neck, the one that once-upon-a-time Cami stole. It contains Ellison's encryption patterns, useless now. Nothing here but the navis is mine.

I sing a scale, a vocal warm-up, make sure I still can.

Notes come out sweet and true.

Heart pounding. Raking sweaty hands against the slimy silver fabric they've dressed me in.

I reach out and pull Jordis, Noa, and Cami into the Unity with me and Dividia, but leave them on an unconscious level, below the threshold of full sensation. I presume Ellison's also sucked in, but he doesn't get an invitation. I'm going to have to be very careful about what I think and feel with him in here, got to keep him out of my plans. Good thing I've so much practice at lying.

<we are *hateful*> Comes from all of them; unconscious whispers of the shape of things to come.

<you have no idea the shape of things to come> I intuit back into our collective unconscious.

To Dividia I think: <if the people outside this door see blue on my forehead, we die. they kill us. the end. need to work a glamour—hide it.>

Creature laps up my fear, feedback strengthens, buttressing our Unity. Well, great. But does it understand what I'm asking it to do? To bend the light, like a tiny version of Jordis' fan, keep people from seeing the blue across my forehead?

<you know this, right? you remember doing this? we've done it before. when people walked in while i was recording. you were small and couldn't do it much then. but you're huge now. you're vibrating

with all the moons. you are whole. you can deceive them all.>

Scraping sounds and infected wounds.

Yeah, great. I push a bunch of my awful hair into my face for good measure. Guess there's only one way to find out.

I clear my throat. One last test. "Hello everyone. How's it going with the setup?" I affirm spontaneous spoken word, now that I have my navis, will come.

An unconscious echo from Cami in the Unity: <good, good>

I pull the chair from under the knob. Step into the light. Dragging myself through everyone's darkness.

◊

Jordis: Som Bliss colors with rage once we're outside of view of the Council. "YOU SHOULD HAVE CONFIDED IN ME."

"And I was to know sooner that my father was behind a conspiracy to destroy his own Kingdom exactly how?" I can't sit. I stand in the center of Som's office, hands clasped behind my back so tightly they are numb, as I fight the need to pace. To check the tightness of my bun. No matter how many resources I put into motor control programming, the alien energies I'm connected to have me too spun to stay still. Suppressing tics is like holding back Jupiter's tides.

"No, you should have told me you were Jordis Ansari," Som snaps. "There are ways we could have fixed this thing years ago. The right way!" He picks up the vase from his desk and smashes it against the wall where it rains orchids.

I arch a brow. "Feel better?"

The man billows a sigh and sinks into the padded leather of his chair. "Sit down, Jordis. This isn't just about your birthright and you know it. And yes, I'm on your side no matter how much Bella and the others want to see me crowned. They're going to have to figurehead Jordan if they want someone other than you, because as much as I don't like your play, I respect your blood."

I scoff, replaying Jordan's tears of relief when he realized I could offer him a real way out. "If Jordan lets them crown him."

"Jordan is weak. He won't stand any more chance against their pressures than he has against your father's. Sit Jordis, fucking sit, you're making me even more nervous than I already am."

My head shakes a tight tic-y jerk of a negation, and I let the pacing escape. What does it matter anymore? I've won, haven't I? I don't have to make myself act like a normal in front of Som, not anymore. "Jordan is stronger than you think, and he's stood up to Father more than you know. Plus he sees this situation as a chance to have his own life; he's never been interested in the business."

"Maybe. But you're changing the subject." Som swivels his chair to track me as I stride one end of the room to the other. "Let's set aside the fact that crowning you is going to cause a war within the Galilean Black. And probably a war with Madame X too, because I'm sure she didn't send you here on the assumption that she'd lose you. No, you're too valuable an asset to her, and you're breaking your vow of Devotion if you stay. Let's set all of that aside—what are you going to do with a nation of rioting Operators, Jordis?"

I show him a rare smile with teeth. "I can think of a few things."

"Okay, let's say you get everything you want. You get the throne and the world knows the truth about the Genetic Liberation Front. The authorities clear the Operators of terrorism. There are eighty thousand on Europa, Jordis. Eighty thousand. That's eight times the number of people currently initiated into the whole of the Galilean Black. Those Operators have no place in the business. At least not all of them, and not right now. It's not like you can engage in negotiations with the Europan government. All you'll be as far as it's concerned is the owner of the Argus Hotel and Casino, and they're not going to listen to you any more than they listen to your father. The government here's just as frustratingly straight as when you left, our people in law enforcement and customs notwithstanding. For Chyte's sake Jordis, will you fucking sit still!"

<and that's the best-case scenario> The words are not mine, but they come from within. Like the tumble of whispers before but stronger, buzzing through my connection to the Mem.

<that's right. this is me, dragon, from freedom. remember me? older and wiser, and no longer taken by your games, you machinating fucking bint.>

The gasp escapes before I can ice over my expression, and I stop, still.

"Jordis?"

"I'm sorry Som," I point to my ear in the universal sign for incoming com call even though I don't, obviously, have a com, "I've got to take this." I snake around the display shelves in the corner, the ones sporting Som's collection of Mentist's smart art awards. I wedge myself out of his eye-line in case I show feelings I'd rather keep private.

<what is this? you're not on a normal channel. why are you a voice in my head?>

<this is freedom's secrets, just like you wanted>

<well, about that, i could use instruction on exactly what and how—>

<shut up and listen. by taking on your father, you're going to make things worse for the operators. *good*>

What? <you want things to get worse?>

<i want you to file for colonial status for callisto.>

What?

<and yes, worse is good. worse is great. better than the best. rip 'em all down. destroy the fucking jovian system, jordis, huzzah!>

<but—>

<since when did you respect anything i had to say? *amusement*>

<*anger* what are you gaming at dragon?>

<callisto. colonial status. just do it. why be queen of servitude when you can be president of freedom?>

What?

<and take a look around io while you're at it. there's someone there with equations that can predict the future who can help strategize your war>

I clutch the dataslip around my neck. Warm. President of—

Everything is going according to plan. Daddy's throne is one vote away from being mine. Ammiel and the Europan Operators have control of the torus. The Operators will be free. I will be free. But—

I straighten the seams of my suit; I check the tightness of my bun. I step back into Som's view. I split my consciousness and send a query into the Mem's public 'pedia. "What's it take to file for colonial status on an uninhabited, class F, bio-hostile moon?"

On the thread I hold in the physical, to Som I say, "I value your perspective. What would you do, were you in my place?"

◊

Caran: The roadies and technicians have set up a makeshift performance area. It looks tiny in a space made for assembling massive communications arrays. Someone's pulled the grav generator from *Sonica* and stuck it below the room so the weight of everything feels near Earth-normal. And no horrified looks my direction either, so Dividia must be doing its bend-the-light job on my forehead. I stay in the shadows for good measure.

On the stage rest eight meters of glossy 4V plates for me to dance upon, the kinetikosonus with its glass and brass and wires, towers of pipes, frills of bellows, and glitchy synth circuits. I hear sleeping Callisto, beautiful darkness, rotating with bass drums building so gradually no one realizes the sleeping power of the timpani until—Bam goes the tick-tock-clack and the beat of feet on golden-tiled streets echoing off facades and the fake blue ceiling-sky. The bells of aurora tinkling over the broody bass of hard lava and rumble-wub of the rover's wheels scraping stone on beat. Clang-rang, clang-rang; wind whistling through railing rungs and patter-pat hands on cables—

The Jovian Symphony.

I run my fingers along the surface of the instrument. Want nothing more but to sink my mind into it. Produce the sounds I've been hearing since waiting for clearance to land on Europa, when I first saw Callisto's disc. To let the music free—

But there is no freedom. There is no music. There is no Symphony.

Mindy is nowhere to be seen. The remainder of the security team shadows me like assassins, but until the credit holders and hand-picked public arrive, there's nothing to protect me from. What did Mindy tell LaRoque about her busted hand? Did she tell LaRoque what I am?

If Min said anything, LaRoque gives no sign.

"You come up with this idea for a benefit concert?" Mx. Manager asks me, shoulders like sword blades in his sharp, stylized jacket.

"Nah. Ellison did." I bend so the hair stays across my face, my frame out of the light. Making it easy for Dividia to maintain its glamour. "Trying to make up for how shitty CryCorp treated me on Io, I think."

"You think?" LaRoque laughs in contempt for my egotism.

No, actually, I think Ellison orchestrated this scenario because I'm the perfect storm.

Ellison stirs in the subliminal levels of the Unity <yes, that's right>

There's so much anxiety in the assembly bay that we might as well be breathing Dividia instead of air. Everyone's holding it together though, in a grim, determined way as though the normalcy of the show set-up can counterbalance the uncertainty of the universe. They have no idea Jordis is about to unleash an army. Noa is about to obliterate a city. Cami is already a conduit for extinction-level alien rage.

◊

Noa: I float above Io in zero-g, hair spread in webs, eyes open and seeing through the hole in the storm I have found. I HAVE BE-COME A MOON.

We tremble ground.

We arc lightning across the Milktown dome, watching people scream. Feeling them gasp in strangled, icy terror. Feeling how good it feels to cut off their breathing just as they cut off my screams with their slaps.

With each tremor-zap the dome weakens. Soon it will fracture and fragment. It was built to withstand quake and storm but not like this.

"Everybody pays." Our voice sears through Milktown's speakers.

The RealsOlutions crowd cowers and covers their ears.

"Not so powerful now!" We hiss at them, "You can hate us and hit us and take away our dignity and call us less-than-human but you will not control us. We know now. We hold the power. No more are we held by your lies of our less-thans. We are *more-thans*, more than you, more than the worst you ever feared." We tremble ground and watch them fall down.

<noa>

We shake off the voice. It is not of the fire.

<noa it's me>

We shake it off again like a quake shakes soil, but it doesn't slide away.

It is a part of us.

It is Dividia-Io-resonance.

<if you can still feel—>

We bare our teeth, chittering the challenge-call of the sulfur-crickets.

<*the sulfur-crickets echo back*>

No, that isn't right. The sulfur-crickets are dead, destroyed by Dividia. Trampled by CryCorp. WHICH IS WHY WE MUST KILL.

<hush; listen: *su-bees hum and jacklets trill, rippling through the breezeless jungle, songs of things with fur and wombs, with cilia and exoskeletons, chirping insect-song*>

We pause, confused.

<what does io make? in the furnace of her heart, what does io give to us?>

<*deathrage!*>

<listen: *the leaves of the laurels shiver silver and violet, the su-bees whisper a dissonance. And io, io, flame and fire—io dances within, around, inside.*—what does io make with her sul-

fur-spew?>

   Precious crystals forged in rage: <diamonds>

<diamonds>

"Everybody gets a diamond," we exhale through the Milktown speakers.

<everybody gets a diamond>

We shake away the spell. It's a flashback; it must be a new short in my navis. Experience cannot be un-felt. History cannot be mended, only avenged. Nobody lives! Nobody gets a diamond!

And yet—the music, all rumple-trill and the soaring sonics of aurora-flux, breath threading into the symphony Io and I share for the first time with— <caran?>

<shhhh... *nullidentity* if you can still feel anger you have not yet been defeated.>

My hand is in my pocket. Io's diamond, cold as the surface of the moon for so long, is heating up. Radiating. Pulsing flicker-flash. Diamonds. Heat. Rage. Revenge— <?we can make diamonds *?*>

<*!YES* we can make diamonds! talk to jordis she has an army for your anger.>

We flood with signal, floating in freefall, clawing for the handles and straps of the shuttle, stuttering toward control.

Io lies below, red and yellow, black and white. Distant.

I take the diamond from my pocket and place it so that it floats between me and the window. Right. There.

Io-above and Io-below.

<jordis> I think/feel, not by opening a channel in the Mem and connecting with her but because—I suddenly realize—we are literally part of the same mind. We are a multi-mind.

<hello noa. caran tells me your mirai equations can predict paths into the future. interested in analyzing a battle scenario?>

With the question comes the fullness of what Jordis holds: eighty thousand Operators able to control every electrical system on Europa at a moment's thought. Including the defense systems. Between us—me and Io and Jordis and Europa and the un-hobbled Operators—we can destroy two moons. Two-thirds of the inhabited Galilean system.

I lose breath to terror of my own self, gasping like the masses in Milktown, fighting for air.

I was a scientist once. *What have you let the world turn you into?*

But I don't care.

Nobody lives. Not even me.

None of us get a diamond.

◊

Caran: The big shuttle from CryCorp arrives on Callisto with all the booze and streamers. Catering rides in on its tail, and the shuttle of PR people from CryCorp's stable follow. The PR people start prepping the after-party. The corporate dealing. The benefits rolling in. The representatives from RealsOlutions click and hum appreciation at the banners and tablecloths, not speaking a word about what Noa's doing to their brethren in Milktown. Rumbles from Ellison: <makes our case, makes it clear why hundreds of thousands of operators have to go, cull them right back down>

"We are so grateful to you," the RealsOlutions PR woman gushes, taking my hand. "It means so much to know you're behind our mission."

"Alternatives must be explored!" I let her pump my arm.

"Exactly!" the man from RealsOlutions's marketing department joins, not wanting to miss a chance to touch genius. This is so much more tedious sober, and it was tedious enough drunk and high. The man finally stops pumping my hand. "There are ways to end our reliance on the k-dromers, and we will find them. It's time for our indenture to them to end."

"And their indenture to you." I tip a sly smile and flirt with my lashes, letting Dividia's apprehension ooze from me and all around. Reverse-Muse. "It will be nice to see them put in their proper place." My genetic material is all over their hands now, their palms, their knuckles, dead skin cells mixed with sweat from the glands of everything they fear. I squeeze their shoulders, mashing it in. Satisfaction churns in the hate I hold for them, for how they forced me to destroy myself to do the work that I was born to do. The fact that it is all

their fault.

<you would have found some other way to destroy yourself; all you've ever been is hate and fear>

<fuck you dividia>

Dividia's veil over everyone's perception holds though. The cursed creature needs me, still. It understands, still, that we must maintain the self-destructive secret. Loves the self-destruction, feeds off it, wants the endless looping of self-inflicted wounds to never end. Good thing I've an endless supply.

"Catch you in the after-party," I tell them, "and the rest of your band too. Gotta sound check."

Unity: What's happening on Camymede?

◊

Cami: Dead people litter Iron City's Rieza square like spare parts. In my shadow, my curls spread in savage static. I'm still wearing the evening dress Ellison put me in, the bow around my head undone and ribbons dripping down my jaw. My lips mouth words that come through in multi-frequency from every crystal and ceramic surface: "WE ARE NOT YOUR WEAPONS." My eyes have rolled back, yet still I see.

No, *they* see. The hordes of élan vitals filling me.

<talk to them, cami> Murmurs from my subconscious.

Mainfeed broadcast seeps into my awareness: "We've confirmed the chaos in Rieza Square is not a new threat by the GLF but something else entirely. There is nothing unusual about the girl to explain the high levels of electromagnetic signal coming from her, nor why she remains alive. Dieuvéssaus on Ganymede claim the gods have descended to ride in the end of the world, while the team provided by All Worlds Scientific has interpreted the force filling her as alien in origin. At this crux of crises, humanity is being attacked both by its own Operators from within and by a hostile alien force from without. We still don't know—"

<cami, listen to me>

There is something different about that thought, something clearer, stronger, more annoying than all the other not-my-thoughts. It is the dissonance between the chaos-élans and a stable, singular voice. Caran/Dividia.

<just kill me i can't make them stop> The dust of Ganymede runs muddy rivers down my bruised cheeks. I have dirty, dusty hands. Bare hands, bare arms, bare shoulders. Infra boils around me; I see heat waves. The élan vitals—they are keeping me warm in Ganymede's sub-zero air. I wish they'd stop and let me die so I would stop killing people.

<cami. you need to stop giving them all the control. talk to them.>

<i can't i'm tainted by dividia, i'm blowing it all, it's all your fault, i'm blowing it all because you didn't let me save you, and i couldn't save me, and it's all gone wrong!>

<get a fucking grip, cami. you're still you. *look*>

A push and a click and a pain of the heart so intense I'm not likely to survive, and I'm somewhere I've never been.

A dark plane shot through with pulses that reveal the surface of an invisible fabric, like a woven rug. Like a circuit map. And I'm face-to-face with a shiny black eye.

I gasp and pull back.

The eye pulls back as well; a delicate, feathered white dragon stares at me with cruel intelligence.

Fear boils visible, an inky oil; this is some kind of black Dividia matrix. I'm done for, for real—

<get a hold of yourself cami> the Dragon arches its neck and says in Caran's voice. <don't be such a kid>

<i'm not a kid! i've been major for more than a year *irritation*>

The Dragon smiles, a toothy grin. Caran's toothy, roguish grin. <see? told you that you were still you.>

<hey!>

A graceful tail, tipped with blade-shaped plumage, curls around my feet, flicking a beat. <we're in unity. a proper unity created by a major élan. not that thin thing stella makes.>

<in a unity with dividia?>

<yeah. with dividia. suck it. things don't always work out the way you want them to. the other élans won't come here because they don't want to pick up any more resonance from dividia than they already have so it's quiet, but i can't hold your full consciousness for long 'cause i'm busy.>

<but—>

<shutup and focus on your core>

The dragon cocks his head, closes his shiny black eyes. Sways to the beat of his tail. Starts to disappear.

The quiet place falls away and I fall back into the hot-screaming battering of the Horde.

If I'm still me, is there something I can do?

◊

Caran: The guests arrive. Corporate bigs in private shuttles, dropped off by chauffeurs to cluster in glistening swarms of privilege. Hand-picked fans in transport vans, chittering and tossing, hair done up like mine before I'd killed all those expensive styling nanites and made the hair guy cry. Media with their glowing cheek-tattoos, attended by clouds of feed-dust and camera crews.

The tables for the after-gig glitter with food and crystal, more food right there than I'd gotten the whole first decade of my life.

The handlers whisk me away before I can get to work on the bottles behind the bar; "Mindy's orders" they say, though still no sign of the bodyguard.

There's a make-shift backstage area in the hallway behind the assembly bay. A bit too cozy for the crowd of handlers who occupy it, but I don't mind. This is the last time I'll have to do this after all.

One by one, the handlers leave. The weird fake friends, fawning strangely even as stage management shooshes them away. Makeup next for touch-ups—never anything but efficiency from him. Wardrobe, with a last frown and torrent of hand-wringing angst over the fact that I'd exchanged the slimy suit for a simple, sleeveless white dress and bare feet—not that wardrobe stands a chance against the presence of Dividia. They're all scared of me. So, so scared of me. Good.

The hair guy is the last of the trivial ones to go, eyes still watering over his inability recreate the proper shade of purple, to sculpt the hair into its trademark spikes. There are a thousand kindnesses I could give the man, but I snarl instead. There are a thousand kindnesses anyone could have given me to keep me whole, and no one did. And anyway, what kind of privileged prick cries over insufficient styling nanites? Let him suffer. The man doesn't know real suffering anyway.

Only the stage manager, LaRoque, and Ellison remain: the conductor and the directors. And of course me, their living sack of credit, plus my crawling shadow, the élan vital of fear, dampening the mood.

"You're really good for this?" LaRoque looks scared for the first time I can remember. Not that I remember much but being high.

"What, you filling in for Min in the paranoia department?" I laugh.

The small, pointy man shakes his head, breaking a nervous, unhappy smile. "You're gonna be great, my man. Gonna be the best."

"I'm gonna be like nothing you've ever seen." The words came out viciously, slipping vitriol to feed Dividia. Fucking LaRoque, company man and his selfishness and his greed. Time for the user to become the used. A fitting end it will be. A fitting death for you Jonathan LaRoque—

Ellison's eyebrows shoot up; my thoughts must have seeped into his through the place he occupies in the collective unconscious of the Unity.

<well, you didn't think you'd get a war without casualties?> I kick his way.

<of course not>

"We have a go from sound and lights." The stage manager calls status, tone distracted as she listens to her com, holding up a finger.

Ellison stares at me, tendrils of his psyche brushing mine. It had seemed outrageous when he'd first said it, but Ellison and I really do have quite a lot in common. Well, really only one thing in common, but it's a very big thing.

<don't worry> I let him feel my confidence <benefit's for us both, right? just wait and see what i can do with dividia. that's one of the things you wanted, right? let me show you how to control the monster fully and then you can try it yourself>

Ellison twitches a smile.

Okay. Time to feed the beast again. I conjure memories of Agrippa. Alone in the dark, unable to scream, no one coming even if I could. Stupid. Stupid good-for-nothing Stinker Watts. Good for nothing but music, and even then too stupid to play a single instrument, can't even play recorder, everyone can play recorder, and taunts and smacks and laughter and stupid good-for-nothing will be all I'll have to look forward to if I don't sing this benefit for Ellison and RealsOlutions. Get the world back in balance on the right side of the transgression line. Prove my genetic innocence. Kill all the birds with one stone. Can't lose the fans, the handlers, the private dimship, the love. By all the gods that ever were, I can't lose the love. Can't be alone.

Dividia thickens in response to my fear; I watch the stage manager pat down the small hairs on her arms. Shadows deepen. Monster fills me, a black smog through my breath.

Ellison grins. And relaxes. <my monster likes you>

<well, that's what you hoped for, wasn't it?>

"We have a go from front-of-house," stage management calls.

I start my warm-up vocals and LaRoque gives me a mock punch

in the shoulder, like we're friends.

Ellison merges into the shadows.

Unity grows stronger as I feed it. The stronger the fear, the stronger Dividia, the stronger the Unity, the stronger everyone's connection, integration. Dividia amping itself for the show. Amping itself so it can sink its tendrils into millions of terrified fans, all chanting genocide.

<yesssssssssss>

Stage management intones, "We've a go from media, secure net's ready to transmit to Galilean Local Broadcast and Interstellar New Media Productions."

"All right, then." I pace one small, tight circle, shaking out my hands. I tear the fake dataslip from around my neck, dropping it to the ground. "Time to go." Push toward the stage.

"Wait!" Stage management wedges in front of me, hands out in a stiff panic. "What are you doing! Your dataslip! All your music!"

"It's okay," I hiss through a jaw locked with terror as I shove her aside hard enough that she yelps as she hits the wall. "I'm not going to fucking need a dataslip this time."

◇

I'm shaking. Oh shit, I'm shaking, and my bowels are weak, and I'm worried for a moment that I'm shitting myself in my office because even though I knew these things from the news feeds when they happened I didn't *really know*.

They stare at me, all of them, Caran and Jordis and Noa and Cami.

All I taste is acid fear. It's coming up, I'm regurgitating terror, fear I'd stuffed deep, deep down into the shadows, fear I'm not entitled to hold.

"I think," Caran says, his vocal cords tight and high, "I need a moment alone with Steven."

The others stand in an eerie unison, as though they are a hive-mind. They are a hive-mind; they are still in Unity. They leave as one body; only Caran remains.

The Unity dissolves; we are alone facing each other.

"Spit it out, Steven," he says. "If there's ever a time to unburden yourself it's now, because this is the unraveling time. You can't resist the resonance."

But I can resist. I can. "No."

"Why not, Steven, why not? You asked me to destroy you as I stuck my prick in you and fucked you in feedback loops that were almost, but never, enough. Why not?"

"Because I don't deserve it!" I yell. "Because I've no right to what I feel!"

Caran laughs, and I can't stop the story that tumbles from me—

"Yes, I grew up in the woods, and yes, I got teased because I'd rather understand a tree than cut it down. But I had a family that loved me and teachers that tried to stop the bullying. I could at least communicate what was happening even if no one could stop it! My parents spent their life savings to send me to Toronto University to live with my cousin. And yes, he was violent towards me when he was drunk, and yes, he took credit for my research, and told me I was a piece of shit before apologizing and swearing things would get better. But compared to what Noa took? Compared to the sacrifices Jordis made? Compared to what Ellison did to Cami? Compared to you? It's nothing.

"I've made a way to live with my 'muck,' and that is to stay alone, outside, and then you walked in here and destroyed all that. This is the most important project the anthropology department will ever do, and I have compromised its integrity beyond correction because all I want is you. Because I am a selfish piece of shit I've sat here for weeks falling in love with you, and I haven't told anyone. I haven't told anyone because I don't want to confront the truth of the matter, which is that I, Steven Kwon, PhD, Senior Professor of Anthropology at All Worlds Scientific, *want* to fuck my life up. The same way and for the same reason you want to fuck yours up. Your self-destruction resonates with me, but my story is an insult to yours. I'm just feeling sorry for myself."

My mouth opens. Closes. There is nothing more to say.

"The thing about damage," Caran says, as though I haven't just spilled my shame all over him. "Is it doesn't matter how it happened or what kind of beating we took. It's still damage. Pain is relative to personal experience alone. We all carry our own constants for it. Makes no sense to measure your pain against mine." He shrugs. "I don't measure mine by yours."

I'm frozen, jaw-locked. He's sprawled on the couch in a pool of relaxed calm, eyes lidded, one hand resting on his chest as it softly rises and falls with his breath.

I close my mouth.

"Do you mind," I say in a small voice, "if I take a break?"

I go to the bathroom and put my head under the tap of the sink.

No one gets an All Worlds science job without being at the top of the smarts, including the person who cleans the floors in Lab D. But these are all intellectual smarts. In anthropology especially, we're trained to be observers and report dispassionately on what unfolds before us like unedited mainfeed. Yet Caran's pulled a profound understanding of me from the shreds I've let slip, put them together seamlessly, and handed me back—what? A mirror image of myself, made meaningful.

That is what artists do.

The stage is dark.

The audience shuffles in the floating beyond, also in the dark.

Heart beats with a terror-pulse fast as NQ withdrawal; throat's dry as it had been on the diamond plains of Io.

<we like fear> Dividia transmits <*grins*> and <*daggers*>

We spread through the room, weaving collective apprehension through the five hundred hearts assembled before this stage. Forming a Mesh with local informationspace and seeping into the secure broadcast network to touch the five hundred million hearts tuned in to watch.

Mic-dust shimmers the air currents; I feel it pass me in the dark.

I exhale. Turn on the mic-dust with a thought. Feel the distress of the sound techs as they realize they've lost control.

The audience shifts; aware of a presence on stage.

At a normal show, they'd've gone wild sensing a body arrive, even if it just turned out to be a roadie. But everything's damped in the slip of uncertainty, the unsavory rumors of my genetics and terrorist alliances, the ambiguity of my recent whereabouts. For all they know, the lights will rise on a sentry turret blasting them all the fuck to smithereens. Which, come to think of it, is about what the élans are doing through Cami on Ganymede.

I split my consciousness.

Thread One: Flowing into the stage systems, light and sound and signal control.

Thread Two: Entering the kinetikosonus. Slipping inside electronic controllers built for real-time operation from my navis—not for any of that dataslip pre-programmed shit. Sound made direct from the music of thought. My hands shake in the key of terror, thumping a silent melody against my chest. Dividia thickens around the instrument, curious. Curling into amps, confused as to why they feel familiar. Growing stronger in the feedback of the fear it feels over its own inexplicable reaction.

<that's right, be afraid you creature of fear, eat what you have cooked and call for seconds, shall we both?>

Thread Three: Reaching out into the Unity.

<*RUready?*> I intuit in the direction of Ellison. <am i where you want me?>

<exaaaaaactly>

Thread Four: Aloud, too-loud through the mic-dust, voice too thin and nasal, "Can I have some lights here? Who wants a show?"

The scream goes up then, the revelation that it's me, really me, on the stage so close to them. But the scream's edged with anxiety, and the room remains in darkness because I'm in control of the light.

Thread Three: Intuit into the subconscious layer of the Unity where I've cordoned everyone else off from Ellison, bringing them up into full conscious awareness of each other and the whole— < jordis-noa-cami it's time, combine, follow the fear into the pain we become>

◇

ONE.

Where are we?

How did we get here?

Who's here?

...shhhh (the sound of wings, feathers sliding over air)

We've slipped into resonance with each other. Through the moons.

Well now, aren't you the smart one.

Someone tell me what is going on!

Dividia realigned us. All of us have changed.

(claws clicking, landing. cold. dark and cold.)

An anxious yellow glow emerges like neon through murky ocean. A body follows, black-and-white, Jordis Ansari with her crisp black bun and her smart Vemi business suit, yellow anxiety glowing at her heart.

The knife-edges of Noa's butterflies follow, fluttering nervous orange-red, the rest of her a-blur.

A whimper: Why can't I see me? Why can't I ever see me?

A shiver-shake and Caran's dragon is the last to form, tail curled around his haunches and silver-white feathers limp in the no-where. <sorry that took so long. been busy.>

SCREW YOU, WHY CAN'T I EVER SEE ME!

The dragon beats dust from his wings; it twinkles in the ane-mic not-light before skittering like iron filings to reveal oval bands of force.

<that's you cami, you're a force here, not a form> Caran arcs his graceful neck. <only felt, never seen, not unless you have a navis which you never will.>

<*pout*>

Jordis laughs like a mean girl.

Caran lashes out, a zap-slap. <*hate* don't do that. never do that. never feel good about anything. can't afford to feel even the smallest bit of good about anything even if it's coming from a place of bad. *especially* if it's coming from a place of bad.> He snaps his jaw and clatters his claws. <*he's* in here with us and i can't guarantee he won't overhear.>

Others: <he?>

Caran: <him, ellison. are you listening?>

<collectiveYES>

Caran: <in the end, trust the heart, trust the song>

◇

On Callisto, I bring up the stage lights, blasting myself sightless as the roaring of the crowd blasts me with sound. I stand motionless in terrible, empty light.

Wait for the audience to quiet. They wouldn't have ordinarily; the stomping-screaming-flailing would have escalated into a wall-rattling pitch until I rewarded them with sound. But not today. Today they peter out. I wait for the silence to become uncomfortable, and then wait an awkward seventeen beats beyond. *Fuck you all.*

I crack a clap with my hands, echoing in the poor acoustics. "Welcome to the CryCorp RealsOlutions benefit gig. I know there have been allegations about my genetics. That I've been working with the Genetic Liberation Front. Well aren't you all a gullible lot, huh?"

An uncomfortable shuffle, scattered, nervous laughter because what did I really just say? *Awkward ambiguities you fucking pricks, because I wouldn't be much of a perfect storm if I told you it was all going to be okay.*

I punctuate that last thought—which maybe they heard on some level via Dividia's telempathic seepage—by kicking over one of the smaller, less useful amps. The audience gasps. The anxiety of the roadies—and the techs, who still can't figure out how they lost control—reaches pants-pissing heights.

From Ellison, with <*frowns*>: <what are you doing, caran?>

<making you your benefit money, ellison. clearing my name for laroque. demonstrating how to use dividia>

<then i suggest you generate a bit more warmth, or you'll lose the crowd.>

<do i tell you how to do your job? you asked me to do this and i'm doing it, watch and learn> The long stink of Ellison's appraisal drags itself through my hate-dulled feelings. *Whatever, Ellison. Do your worst. I'm exactly where you want me to be.*

"Well you all are a bunch of wet fucking blankets today," I laugh at the audience's discomfort. "Let's see what we can do about that."

I shake out my hands. "Over a thousand years ago, Galileo Galilee pointed his telescope at the sky and saw this moon we're standing on right now. His discovery of Callisto—and of Ganymede, Europa, and Io, the Galilean system—changed everything everyone thought they knew about anything.

"Landed Galileo in jail too, and the powers-that-be tried to bury the truth.

"But they couldn't cage Galileo, fuck no, because he was right. And truth has a way of always getting free.

"Because it's fucking real.

"And because Galileo's truth set us free, we live on Galileo's moons today."

I draw Dividia's shadows around me, like the élan is a new anti-lighting effect. All attention's fixed on us, so I tap out a beat. "I'm telling you this because even though I'm called Nuevo-Beethoven, I have more in common with Galileo Galilee. Because today I'm going to show you something that will change everything you ever thought you knew about fucking anything."

◊

Into the Unity: <jordis, you ready? your song's up first.>

Inside our collective consciousness, the black mists of Dividia shiver, for a milisec, with multi-colored light.

Jordis blinks. There is something else in here, something more than just the embodiment of fear and the realigned vibrations of Europa. Something more than the realigned echoes of Io and Ganymede. <something more than us>

<whatisit?> Cami's thin thought whispers.

Jordis' chest burns magenta suspicion. She snaps her black-and-white eyes at Caran. <what's your game?>

He laughs, dragon-feathers rustling. Dividia responds to his hatred of Jordis, his delight at her discomfort, by thickening its darkness. <jordis ansari can't figure out the game, how rich is that!> He stops the taunt, the fluttering, and stares at her dead-still with shiny black eyes. <you tried to kill me for freedom's protocols, you bint. three times.>

<only the once back at the hotel>

<and how do you think things would have ended if your stunt with my dataslip had been discovered? if i'd been forced to play my show live? muse would've hidden the blue across my forehead, sure, but do you really think i'd have survived a three-hour set in nq withdrawal?> All the hate, all the rage he's ever felt for her, for how she took advantage of and twisted his weakness and pain to

her own ends, all the loathing of why she is in his life at all, stupid fucking Freedom making unwise deals with the fucking Luna Black Market, Freedom too frightened to come into the light.

Jordis folds her arms. Knows the authorities have executed another five hundred and sixteen Operators. Instructs Ammiel's rebels to take five hundred and nineteen normal lives in return by manipulating the airlocks in Building West Red Two and letting the ocean in. <at least i have always been true to myself>

Caran, into the Mesh: What is our death-count now?

All-of-local-knowledge: Operators in the past three hours: eight-hundred and four. Normals in the past three hours: five-hundred and eighty-nine.

Caran has become a stranger to Jordis since she dropped him on Io, hard and cold as anything she's ever been. She asks, <do you even still want to stop dividia?>

◊

Back on Callisto, it's time to drop the punchline. "I'm going to share something with you now," I tell the five hundred in the room and five hundred million watching on the mains, "something that, like Galileo's revelation about Jupiter's moons, will destroy everything we ever knew. But I'm counting on us to have learned a thing or two since Galileo's time about how the truth can make us stronger. Because of Galileo's truth we are no longer live in some shithole ass-pit back-water crap-stop dark-age village can't tolerate the thought Earth moves around the Sun." I pause in challenge.

On Callisto, silence, confusion.

"Well, haven't we learned a thing or two since Galileo's time?" I demand, pumping my voice to command the crowd.

A collective shout of defiance.

"That's fucking right!" I shout back. "We've built cities on Galileo's moons, people, fucking cities on *Jupiter's moons!*" Pump my fists in the air.

A thousand fists push upwards before me, a billion beyond pushing for the sky out there, screams echoing in answer to the challenge.

◊

<of course i still want to stop dividia> Caran plunges his wing-claws into darkness and pulls out waves of rainbow light. <the real question, jordis ansari, is are you willing to give up the syndicate to save the world? you'd fucking better be.>

Jordis' chest flashes lightening-white surprise as the opening chords of a symphony break and she recognizes what else is in the Unity with them. Recognizes it because once it grabbed ahold of her in a hotel room to save Caran's life. <oh my stars. *wecandoit*> the thought/feeling escapes her, all ice melted in a single flare.

◊

"New music today everybody, you're the first to hear it. *Let's take back our moons!*"

No time to wonder if it's going to work. No time to fear for my life. No time to think if now is the time to reveal the élan vitals or if I should have asked them their permission first. No time to be afraid of anything at all, I take hold of the anxiety thick through the crowd, thick through all four moons and every person on them, thick through the élans raging through Cami. Fear is all I've ever been anyway, all I've ever learned or known. I hold it. I own it. I cherish it. I enter the cup of wounds in the center of the monster that is me.

Igniting into sacred anger.

Igniting into art.

The first note is a scream through the lungs of flutes, the light of the kinetikosonus' controls flaring from the 4V plates to die into darkness while sound still shrills. Into the shocked silence of the crowd, I send an arpeggio spanning five octaves with my voice and they explode into screams of their own. I stream through teasers from my best-selling songs, until the warmth's returned. Until I have their hearts. Hungry for their love like the filigree jellies and the quarana and the endless night of Europa's ocean. Hungry like the tourists at the slots, play it again, play it again, run it again, give me that ante one more time. I start the Jovian Symphony. I start Europa's song.

◊

I am Jordis but I am also Caran. We are we in unity. We are the crouch-and-lurk of illegality, the uncompromised integrity of self. We are the heat from Caran's dataslip that contains the uncorrupted fractal copy of Europa-élan.

The music on the Callisto sound stage flows from instruments, but it imitates Europa's Casino Row so well one might, at first, confuse the two—

Tick-tock-clack go drums to the beat of feet on the golden-tiled streets, echoing violins off facades and the fake blue ceiling-sky. A brassy rush of laughter and whoots from trumpets, trombones, breaking up the percussive chatter of the crowds. Live adverts whistling from corners. Sad voices whispering from the margins, please, just one more token for the probs, I'll win this time I know it, please, please give me one more chance… Into the shimmer-tinkle of an ambient electronic abyss where sea-creatures swirl theremin hiss in their hunting forever-hunger, never sated, the pleasure of eating, eating, eating…

I, Jordis, am every longing chord. I am Europa. I am on the stage. I am here, in the office of Mentist Corp, waiting for the verdict on my father's Ousting. Waiting for Noa's equations to tell me who and how many to kill next in order to free Europa's Operators and reach my father's throne. The symphony comes through the speakers in Som's office; streams live in my mind.

The change occurs so slowly that I can't pinpoint when it starts. It's a dip in the temperature of the room. It's a whispering voice across space. It's coming from me, around me, in me; something from the dataslip is *drawing forth*. Summoned, as Stella was in a closet while I watched.

I open my mouth into a keen, echoing Europa-élan, echoing Caran hundreds of thousands of kilometers away, as the version of her clear of Dividia's influence emerges from my throat. She floats above the ground haloed in backlight from a seven-pointed star. Hair the color of ice half-hides her delicate white face, and her black garment refracts light like deep sea water. She runs a hand along her necklace of pale, alien bones. She is beautiful—until her torso ends just above the waist where brackish water trails and drips from where the rest of her should be. And that is beautiful too.

The office crackles with static electricity and fills with the black fog of Dividia.

Europa and I scream defiance, and Caran loops our cries through the kinetikosonus. Amplified by her own sound, Europa overpowers Dividia's darkness with the endless hunger of my ambition.

And she is free, realigned to what she should be. Europa-élan flows into the Europa City Torus visible to all. The people scream.

Europa screams! <I AM THE SOUL OF EUROPA>

Everyone stops, and asks in wonderment, *what is happening?*

◊

It is not a weakening of Dividia but a shift in its resonance that i, caran, experience as the Europa movement progresses. Colored sparks flit like dizziness, feedbacking with the monster inside me. Dividia/Muse, Muse/Dividia.

I weave Io's theme into Europa's, fade Europa's out. Bring up the Io movement.

Into the Unity: <are you ready noa?>

◊

I am Noa but I am also Caran. We are we in Unity. We are want and will, the demon-angel of the diamond planes. We are free. We are the heat of Cái Morgan's diamond as we glow.

On stage on Callisto, a bash of drums collapses into the bells of the aurora tinkling over the broody bass of hard lava. Fragile flutes and analogue synths float wisps of ash, repeat, sustain, until it becomes predictable and then! The brass shimmer of a diamond's spark. The sound paints in orchestral strings a sky-full of fairy-light in red and green and violet against a backdrop of Jupiter. Icy electronics and brassy fire and the sub-bass rumble-wub of rover wheels across landscapes lit by the longing of flutes and unstable beats. The rustle-hush-THRUM whisper-rustle of life under the dome and the beat of a human heart. THRUM-THRUM two human hearts together, hand-claps, foot-stomps.

I, Noa, growl low like my extinct jacklets, and the sound snarls back. Back from where?

Back from Caran, my connection to him in the Unity.

Back from my physical ears too: from sound spitting through the shuttle's radio, shot through with static from Io's electro-magnetic storms. The static is part of the song—it retransmits, looping, on the stage. We are hundreds of thousands of kilometers of vacuum apart but singing the same song.

It's the song Caran composed in my lost dome.

My dome is not lost. It is in his song.

Caran sings:

◊

the volcano she will keep you warm
when shadow's turned you cold
when nothing else can thaw the burn
she'll storm away your void

◊

I sing back. Tap the beat I'd slapped against Caran's palms, trilling to bring the jacklets out, celebrating our ecosystem of broken hearts.

Static crackles inside the shuttle, more texture in our duet.

No. We are a trio.

Io-élan heats the diamond that floats before me. It burns and melts the dash, lifting my hair in electro-static charge, breaking sweat across my chest.

In a violence of drums. Io-élan bursts from her diamond flicker-flash, on, off, cycling, sparking. Restless! Oh-boy-restless.

Plunging toward the storms, she manifests above the moon. Bigger than herself. Big enough for all to see. An unstable woman-shape rippling and flaring with the aurora, glowing with the fire-color of the corrugated lava plains, crackling blue-white live-wire. I glimpse a face, long and lean, not beautiful in any traditional way but seductive all the same. I want her. Want her with decades of desire from a million miners who turned her from whatever she'd once been into a spirit of savage human need.

Io-élan flashes above the deadly plains, reclaiming herself from Dividia. She howls piezo-electric wails through the silicates in her soil.

We, Noa/Caran howl back, a triumph of sound. Three voices push through the Milktown speakers, and the trapped miners (*my* miners) pause in their choking, panicked run. Stop to listen to the song that speaks their loss. That gives it space to ache.

◊

As Io realigns back into herself, weakening Dividia, I stumble onstage. Get back up. Hold it together just a little longer. Time for movement number three.

Grab those loops I've been saving in my memory, sound of the clang-rang of boots on metal catwalks and the whistle of wind through rungs. Filters change the sound waves to emulate the quality of noise in the big, cold outside. Of noise off the sides of buildings and echo-plummeting into the canyons of Ganymede.

Sequence of synthesizers, bells, and the glass harmonica like the children laughing and the tong-ping tong-ping tong-ping howl! of playfulness in a dark, cold cave.

Tiny triangles make the tinkle-ring of water over ice, flutes whistling pressure-pipes, clamoring xylophone keys and the corrugated putt-putt of industrial rhyme. Screeching musicality, heavy-industry and the cymbal-shiver of snowflakes over the shining brass brilliance of innovation.

Innovation like you, Camilla Morgan. Remember what I told you!

◊

I am Cami but I am also Caran. We are we in Unity. *In the end trust the song, trust the love, trust the pain—*

Ganymede's theme in the Jovian Symphony summons me, Cami, from the Horde like a hook in the chest. I remember those sounds. I was there. They are mine.

I fall to the ground, the ice-packed dusty-red ground of Ganymede.

I've got my body back.

Everything around me's in a shattered shambles; smells like burning and ionized air.

Bad, bad.

And really mad! <i didn't give y'all permission to use me like that!> I scream to the Horde of élan vitals.

Something else is happening past the din of the screams in the real world and the screams from the élans that really want to fill me again.

Something's happening from the battered green credit slip around my neck, the one given to me by BlackJack.

First a shimmer.

Then a finger.

Then Ganymede is pulling himself out of the slip. He can't help himself with Caran playing his very own sounds.

We're not hearing them just through the Unity either; we're hearing them with our ears, out here on the street. The music's piping in from a still-functioning mainfeed somewhere. Good, good!

I tear the credit slip offa me, finally, and fling it as far away as I can.

Ganymede slouches the rest of his way out in his endless metal coat, neo-Roman curls touching his long, soft lashes and perfect nose. He grows tall. Tall as the buildings, tall enough to see all the way over in Minot Plaza. He duplicates himself, visible Ganymedes spreading across the moon. Making even more screams but hey! He's not killing anyone. Real good!

All the Ganymedes everywhere pull their hands from their pockets. They cup them into goblets filled with gold and the smell of dust and ice.

<*stop*> / "Stop." Ganymede sends into the Horde and vibrates through every piezoelectric surface everywhere so the people of Ganymede all hear <*hope* we will find another way>

Tipping the cup, sanctuary spreads over scorched ground, stilling the blue bolts of the Horde, silencing the human and élan screams.

My breath comes back to me in a flutter of wonder.

Caran's song goes gentle. Low, feathery woodwinds, and the hum of his voice lilting like a lullaby. Well, Ganymede was founded as a waystation for weary travelers. That's something no one, not even Dividia, can take away.

No one can take away all of me, either. There'll always be a piece of me that can't be ruined. If I hold onto that, I bet I can communicate with the Horde. I bet I can draw the summoning circle not around them, but around *me*. Summon Cami inside and none can cross.

I breathe Ganymede's crisp air and draw a circle in the dust around my feet. "Y'all can't cross!" I yell aloud and also <y'all can't cross!> into my mind. I plant my feet. And open myself to broadcast. Let the élan vitals talk to me on my terms this time.

<y'all just exposed yourselves to humanity big-time, and you can't take that back, you know?> I tell them, hoping they'll understand some fraction of my human words. <like ganymede said, no more hiding and no more killing—we've got hope now, *HOPE*—so you gotta announce yourselves more gentle and proper-like. let ganymede show you the way>

Ganymede, resonating with his song, makes a Mesh with local informationspace and me and the Horde.

We pick up Caran's transmission from Callisto and connect it to the communications arrays just beyond Saturn.

The arrays shoot the signal through dimensional loops to Phoenix Station around Cassiopeia Prime, which relay it out to Nerion Station where the next mass of dimensional arrays push the song deeper into inhabited space and—

<all of the inhabited worlds hear us>

<let our existence/presence be revealed>

◊

Fourth movement. Through Ganymede's melody, i weave Callisto's theme. So subtle at first with the bass drums that no one notices the sleeping power of the timpani until they resound, bigger than Jupiter, bigger than fear.

I am alone in the Dividia Unity with Ellison.

<caran, what have you done> he hisses into the curling blackness.

I send him dragon-y smiles. <same thing you did, ellison. you transformed hope into fear. you had so many hopes for your empire, and so many fears of losing it, for losing all your fucked-up power, that something was attracted to you out of nowhere—a wisp of darkness resonating with your hateful, coward's heart. a bit over thirty years ago, am i right?>

<*suspicion/surprise* howdidyouknow?>

Holding the final Callisto movement on stage strong, I say into the Unity, <because the same thing happened to me around the same time, alone in the dark, hungry, afraid. hoping for a better life. wanting my voice to be used for something good, for kindness and freedom, to make people happy.

<you took your hope and built an empire of fear and hate, gold turned into shit.

<i took my fear and hate and turned it into hope. turned it into art.

<too bad for you, because that's what artists do: transmute shit back into gold. my hope has always been bound up in what i fear. dividia and muse, muse and dividia, they're the same fucking entity, you hateful fuck. the creature that visited me and the creature that visited you were two pieces of a divided whole> The darkness of Dividia becomes waves of rainbow light.

The Unity collapses as Dividia's resonance collapses; I silence the kinetikosonus and bring the stage to blackout.

The audience is silent.

One breath.

Two.

A hesitant clap.

A whoop, a cheer—the darkness explodes in screams and applause.

<they really liked the jovian symphony *!!*> Muse-Dividia

think/feels.

I'm grinning in the darkness, grinning all to myself, and to the creature, and to all five hundred in the room and five hundred million on the feeds and—<well that's good because they're not going to like my next number> But it's hard to feel pessimistic because the audience is shrieking and clapping and pounding like I've just saved their godsdamned mother from explosive decompression and I'd know even without a telempathic alien monster taking a read on the crowd that they liked it. Hot shit I missed this! Best enjoy it because it's probably the last time.

Time to end the dark blue lies.

I command a spot to follow and walk in its light to the edge of the stage where I sit before the audience, cross my legs. The intimate gesture silences them. They lean forward. The nearest ones could reach out and touch me if they wanted to.

I pick up the dataslip reader, which no one seems to have noticed I haven't used. I hold it up in the light. So much of my life for so long has depended on this thing and I don't even need it.

I chuck it off the stage.

The crowd gasps.

Bits of dust and lint float in the beam of the single spot. Barefoot in my sleeveless white dress, I hum the opening bars of "The End of the World." The crowd roars. Not my top-seller, but it's a song with legs. With personal meanings for people. Least that's what the fanfeeds say. It's got a few meanings to me too. Seems appropriate. A cappella, I sing:

◊

beneath the sky

i'm holding tight
holding in
smaller than
smaller than a star

◊

I start a loop, a synth, tracing patterns in pale light, build something for them to sing against. Here comes the chorus so I send the mic-dust outward, into the crowd. *Take a risk, take a risk you cowardly shit because this time it really is the end of the world.*

Sounds of pleasure and surprise come through the mic-dust in a whisper-rush "—he wants us to sing—" some of them murmur.

Yes. Please. Please-oh-please do.

I mouth the lyrics and five hundred voices chorus back.

◊

please tell me it's
the end of the world
and nothing matters anymore
so i could tell you
tell you then
tell you i—

◊

Yeah, they know the words.

I turn up the charisma I can never fully turn down and lay in more synth. Screw my eyes shut and pull the mic-dust back to myself because I don't want to know how the audience responds to what happens next. I *can't* know. Not right now. Not this moment. They could rush me and pluck me from the stage and rip me apart. If I know, I can't continue. Okay.

<dividia-muse—drop the glamour. let them see what i am.>

<ruSure?*concern*>

<gotta hope, right?>

I know it's done it because I know it's done it. Because Muse's presence relaxes. Because I can't help but catch the edge five hundred people taking a collective, startled breath.

I angle the spotlight so tzaddium blue flashes strongly across my forehead. Steady voice. Verse two. Can't look yet.

◊

under the rain
i'm holding in
staying tight
much too small
to block the night

◊

My voice chokes then, chokes on the last note because I'm pointing the mic-dust back to the audience and and and—*Will they still sing?*

Five hundred voices chorus back.

◊

please tell me it's
the end of the world

and nothing matters anymore
so i could tell you
tell you then
tell you i—

◊

I open my eyes to Muse manifesting rainbow waves from the amps and the cables and the lighting fixtures, the whole of the space filled with colored light and static charge.

I split the mic-dust with the audience so together we can sing:

◊

inside the dawn
you're holding me
breakable
i can't breathe
to tell you that I—

◊

Oh yes, building into full orchestration and all together still—

◊

please tell me it's
the end of the world
and nothing matters anymore
so i could tell you
tell you then
tell you i love you

i love you
i
love
you

◊

Cut the instrumentation, pull the mic-dust back to myself, and in multi-frequency through every ceramic surface, Muse and I whisper the rasping coda.

◊

in the end, trust the song
trust the love
trust the rage
that holds us at the end of the world

◊

Before anyone has a chance to process what the fuck just happened — including me — I return control of the lights and the sound and the mic-dust to the crew, throw up the full-stage of 4V motion-controlled instrumentation switches, and slam into "Blood Deeps" as the crowd claps along and I reach my voice out with all the power of music that is mine, and theirs, and ours, always and forever.

"Everyone's gone." It's a dumb thing to say to Caran. A dumb normie thing. Of course Jordis, Noa, and Cami are gone; we said goodbye at the spaceport last night.

He doesn't make me feel bad for my statement, just shrugs with rue and presses his hands to his eyes in a tell that means he's weary. We did stay up too late, the five of us, laughing and talking. And the three of them—Jordis, and Noa, and Cami—at various points telling me to break things off with Caran, that we're bad for each other. That we're too alike, and too different, and we'll just end up in wounds.

Caran and I haven't said much to each other since my outburst, but it's not because things are awkward. It's because things are comfortable. Fifteen minutes of catharsis never solved anything complicated, but it does grant a temporary reprieve from the muck.

"I'm surprised they stayed as long as they did." Caran says distractedly and veers toward the sofa. He catches my hand on the way.

"I'm surprised you're staying even longer." I follow to sit beside him, in Noa's spot. "You have just as important a job as they do."

He chuckles, and the sound is music. "My 'job' keeps on ice better. But I'm leaving tomorrow anyway because Djen's stopping by Callisto for a few days before she heads to you, and I want to be there to meet her." He shoves a strand of tangled black hair out of his eye and the light shines iridescent off his forehead. It reminds me of the wings of long-extinct blue morpho butterflies. He pushes me around on the sofa until he's got me pressed against the arm and turned a bit, and then he lies on his back with his head in my lap and closes his eyes.

<dividia—you were muse and vice-versa all along> I direct the thought to the invisible presence, confident that it will catch the thought for reasons I cannot explain.

An image of shadow-arms that terminate in rainbow waveforms rises in my consciousness and falls away, not visible this time, just a telempathic transmit. <we were apart and alone. then we were not> Muse/Dividia tries to put its experience—badly—into human terms.

"It's an oversimplification," Caran says, "but you can think about the élans like sentient ideas. They don't die, but they're sensitive to mutation. They can lose what we think of as 'ego' to each other or to our thoughts and feelings. That's what makes them so defensive around us and makes us so dangerous to them, even though they find us fascinating. The old, vast, mobile ones, they all left after the Runner Wars because we deliberately tweaked them in ways they didn't like. Ways exactly like Ellison did with Dividia. But some—like the ones that live around the Galilean moons—have fixed domains. Got to develop different kinds of defenses."

"So Europa, Io, and Ganymede saved copies of themselves prior to Dividia's influence in various crystal matrix devices, waiting for an opening to differentiate themselves again from Dividia." I stroke his kind of awful hair, run my fingers over his fantastic skin, golden and butterfly-wing.

"Pretty much. Was the only defense they really had."

"But they didn't know about your Jovian Symphony?" I'm suddenly skeptical.

He laughs, eyes still closed, and curls over on his side as though he plans to go to sleep on me. "Of course not. For all they knew it could be a billion years before they could climb out of those storage devices. *I* didn't even know about the Jovian Symphony until Ellison's shuttle landed on Callisto. Although I knew Dividia and Muse were reunited pieces of the same entity from the moment I was forced to confront it in Ellison's summoning room. I mean, I knew it sooner, much sooner, my resonance with Dividia was too strong and too familiar, but I denied it right up until the point that I let the creature in. Then I couldn't deny its familiarity anymore. Plus it made all of Freedom's complaining about Muse being 'incomplete' make sense."

"So you'd gone into that benefit show with no plan?"

"Oh, I had a plan. Take back the fucking moons from what Ellison had done. Just hadn't worked out the details. Then I caught a glimpse of Callisto through a window and the song that I'd started when I was hanging in orbit 'round her back at the start of the whole mess came to me. I had a song from each moon. Just had to patch them together."

"He says, like composing a symphony in two weeks during intense personal crisis was no big thing," I laugh.

"It's not if you've been doing it for near-forty years and you're fucking brilliant at it to begin with." He nuzzles his face into me. He has two modes of personal space: back-the-fuck-away and let-me-climb-inside-your-mouth. I don't consider that bad.

"I'm hopeful," I say, gathering him up so he lies on even more of me. Curling myself around him.

"You should be, considering what you're in resonance with right now." Light amusement, teasing.

<i am hopeful too> Muse says.

<you *are* hope, silly thing. that's what i meant> Caran extends his light teasing to it, reaching up in the air perhaps at a manifestation of it only he can see.

<i'm also scared about what happens next> I think/feel into the link.

<i am too> Muse makes the shadows move.

<and again, of course you are> Caran sighs.

I take a deep breath. Not quite an "opera breath." <all right> I communicate to Caran in the closeness between us <tell me how this part of the story ends. i don't know what's going to happen with the part after that, if i'll still be around for the second set of interviews, but this part, tell me how this part ends>

◊

LaRoque and Ellison fight over who gets to sue me for Breach of Contract.

Ellison's sure he has rights as more than half the donors for RealsOlutions backed out when I pulled my "little stunt" as he's calling it.

LaRoque and the lawyers from 100 Worlds Music insist I played the benefit as contracted, regardless of if it had the desired effect, and anyway, the remaining donors more than doubled their offerings so RealsOlutions lost nothing. Ergo, 100 Worlds Music has rights to sue me as illegal to be on a 100 Worlds Music contract in the first place.

Ellison counters that bad choices on the part of 100 Worlds Music aren't CryCorp's problem, and therefore he's got dibs.

They work themselves into a circular froth. When the amusement factor gets old, I cut in. "Hey, if you want someone to blame, might try government medical on Agrippa. They're the ones fucked my DNA test; my records've always been on the up. I'm certified normal. Not your fault. Not sue-able over this. Technicality. Sorry."

LaRoque stares at me like I'd just sprouted a second head. "Yeah, that's right, I'm alive in here, Mx. Manager."

Outside this actual closet we're stuffed in, I hear the concert after-party running on laughter and the tinking of crystal.

◊

"Wait, you were having a party? Right after?"

"Yeah, of course, where were you, hiding behind an asteroid with no dimensional array?"

"No! I was—" I'm blushing. "Well, I missed the actual start of the event because I was teaching and it was nearly over by the time someone came and called us out of the classroom, but then I had to go watch it and do some—some research on it."

Caran cracks one eye open to peer at me. "I give the most important concert in the history of music and reveal the existence of a meta-intelligent alien life form against a backdrop of a three-moon war climbing upwards on claiming two thousand casualties—which my concert and the élans put an end to—and you not only miss it, you go off and do research?"

"Well, I am an anthropologist." I say sourly and then realize he's teasing me.

"You are too much, Steven," he says, the edges of his lips twitching to stop a smile. "What were you researching?"

"Um. Stuff."

"Stuff?"

"You."

He laughs that musical laugh. "You're such a stiff."

I sniff, but he's right.

"Yeah, we were having a party. It had always been planned—Ellison's Benefit Party—just wasn't for Ellison's benefit anymore. If you'd been paying attention, you would have first been caught up in the weird euphoria that happened as the fighting stopped, and then experienced the awkward afterbirth of 'what the fuck just happened—woah aliens we can talk to? After centuries of exploring the galaxy?' It was a bigger fucking deal than even me for most people.

"Luckily, Jordis, Noa, and Cami came to their senses fast enough to contact their local governments and, along with the élans channeling through Cami, explain resonance well enough to avert total disaster. The authorities were eager as fuck for any explanation they could back up with facts and that gave them a quick return on stopping the chaos, and there was a special magic in that moment of first contact."

"'We are an ecosystem.'" I quote Noa's simple statement that was first to appear blazing across the mainfeeds.

"Yeah. Noa's reputation with All Worlds Scientific and her mirai equations didn't hurt any. Her pitch and Cami and the élans and Jordis with her silver tongue convinced the populace pretty fast that feeling happy and relaxed would enable first contact to be, well, happy and relaxed. So we were having a party. Largely ignoring all the nauta frictions for the moment, but they'd stopped killing us, so we could catch our breath before the real work started."

"And everyone turned themselves in. You, Jordis, the rebel leader Ammiel, Noa, and Cami?"

"Yeah." He snorts. "Not that they could touch us. We had become ideas. Even without the élans on our side, we had already become big as ideas."

◊

"Look," I say to LaRoque and Ellison, pressing my fingers into my eye sockets because I'm suddenly so fucking tired post-show, post-whatever-the-fuck-I'd-just-done, "you can argue all you want about who gets the blame for contracting with me, but truth is, whatever you negotiate won't get you out of the legal cesspit you're in because of me."

Both of them, plus the two lawyers each of them dragged along, all look at me. Like they can't believe I'm there, or real, or something. Except this is the first time I've ever been real.

"Law says I've got to be persecuted and executed, but that would piss our alien friends off into consequences not even Ellison's hate-squad wants. So what the fuck do we do? I don't know, but no one's going to kill me or throw me in jail. You've made your billions, LaRoque and 100 Worlds Music. And Ellison—I gave you something for your haters to rally around. RealsOlutions is getting its charter, regardless of what I've done. Not even Noa and Io could kill all the haters everywhere. I'm still and forever resonating with the Dividia part of Muse, and now you've got hope from the creature like you never did before. We're locked together now, Ellison, you and me, for better or ill, no knowing which of us'll win the fans in the end. But bickering about Breach of Contract isn't going to do a thing for either of us because no reasonable person can claim I didn't do my part to give your movement legs."

LaRoque and Ellison are piles of glares, but the lawyers on both sides nod.

Some person I don't recognize walks in without knocking. "*Sonica's* cleared to return to Europa."

Independent, neutral Europa. Perfect place for the actually important negotiations. Callisto to Europa: right back where I started.

At least I'll have an hour in transit for some wine and a nap. Finally.

An hour later I wake up from a post-show stupor in the executive room of Europa's Diplomatic Center Building. Room's full of flags—mostly Europa's teardrop and the Federal Banking Worlds' eagle, plus a smattering of others that, if I cared enough to look up, would probably be Trewal and Arcadia and the rest with independent or near-independent status. Red City's woman-with-the-trident is there even though Cass-Prime's a Federal Banking World.

Europa's President Nye sits at the head of the round table. Not sure the purpose of having a round table if everything in the room points itself clear to the space having a "front" and a "back." He's frailer than the mainfeeds show him, tall and dark in Europan indigo robes. Wonder if Nye feels the same about me, diminished by reality. But Nye's barely looked at me twice; he's focused on Executive Roger Killian from the New Organization of Federal Banking Worlds to his left, and Jordis Ansari to the left of Killian.

Jordis is smiling and it's terrifying.

She's not smiling at me, luckily. Nor is she smiling at pale, red-headed Executive Killian or President Nye, but at Djen. Djen who, of course, glares crankily at everyone. Djen, next to me in her red spacer's suit as always, with a death-grip on the small, dense cube of *Stella-Maru's* dimension drive in her lap. It must be making her looped to not be able to communicate with Stella, but the terms of the negotiation are clear: everyone on the same level, ergo no telempathic links between the negotiators and the élan vitals. Except for Cami.

Cami sits at Nye's right. Except she's not Cami. Eyes closed, lids twitching. Yellow curls spread in the static field that surrounds her. Mouthpiece of an alien race.

I reach for Noa's hand to my right. Not sure she'll take it. Taking a risk. I'm shaking. I'm so full of fear and hope I can't breathe.

Noa cups her warm fingers around my cold ones. Her squeeze trembles, too.

"Welcome everyone," Nye begins, shifting his focus to Cami. No, not to Cami, to the élan vitals that fill her. "We sit at the brink of a fundamental shift in our understanding of the universe. We can take this moment and make war or take this moment and make wonderment. In this room we define our relationships to come. Thank you all for being here."

"Embassssssy." Cami hisses in multi-frequency. "No more Free-dom-seeeeeee-krets."

"Oh come on," Djen rolls her eyes at the élans, forgetting to appear unable to cope with gravity in her annoyance. "You're the ones who made us keep you secret in the first place and you know it."

"Hush," Jordis directs at both the élans and Djen. She shifts her weight toward Nye and Killian to her right, face a politician's mask of invitation covering a roil of machination. "Thank you, President Nye, for your kind opening and for providing a neutral territory for this negotiation. And thank you for your blessing on Freedom's proposal for colonization.

"Thank you, Executive Killian, for your willingness to consider Freedom's charter to the New Organization of Federal Banking Worlds.

"And thank you, Djen Pathfinder and the Conglomerate of Élan

Vitals, for assisting me in representing the interests of Freedom—and for generously allowing me to represent those interests in the first place."

Killian makes eye contact with Jordis, steady despite being on foreign soil addressing an Operator ex-mob Enforcer who has the power to destroy the Galilean system with a thought. Bravo to him. I tap out a four-four beneath the table to let some tension out.

The government man skims a pile of digipages. "Colonial status is not a charter we give lightly, and especially not with concurrent Independence and Neutrality clauses. There are responsibilities. For example, to achieve Emergent status within one hundred and fifty years of charter date, Earth standard. Ceding the deed to a body as large and valuable as Callisto is a serious matter."

Jordis makes her smile into something both humble and confident. Shit, she's good. "I think we can manage that; we have Noa. She assures me Callisto is much easier to terraform than Io, and considering her success there?"

"Emergent status requires more than sufficient square meters to support a population of over ten million. It requires the capacity to govern that population as well." Killian pokes around his digipages. "Governance gets more difficult with an Independence Clause. You won't have the support of the New Organization of Federal Banking Worlds to assist you. In fact, you will have additional barriers given the complexity of visa and import-export laws."

"Independence from the New Organization of Federal Banking Worlds, as well as political Neutrality, is necessary to maintain the élan's embassy." Jordis' quiet words answer Killian, but she directs them toward Nye. Yeah, Europa would benefit from another independent, neutral nation next door. Help get Callisto functional and it'll be harder for the Federal Banking Worlds to pressure Europa.

I stifle a surprised laugh. Killian and Nye were so afraid of the élans exerting a coercive force in this meeting, when it's Jordis-fucking-Ansari they should've put up defenses against. Cami-as-conduit emits <*satisfaction*> with the direction Jordis is taking. Shit, I can't believe I survived Jordis.

"Yes, the embassy." Nye's face pinches with repressed envy. Salt in the wound of Europa's latest disappointment with alien contact. The first being when Europa's native life turned out to only be interested in eating. Nye straightens his shoulders and makes another play. "Europa is already both nationally Independent and politically Neutral. Our strong, existing ambassadorial infrastructure can support more nations, and we have centuries of experience organizing inter-political coalitions and negotiations. We would be honored to host the élan embassy here." He turns his focus to Cami.

"We don't want that," the élans speak, vibrating the ceramics in the room to make a chorus with Cami's throat. "Freedom we trust <*sortof*> only."

"We've an established relationship." Djen grumbles. But her eyes crinkle with satisfaction. "Embassy needs people to translate, integrate, navigate the path between the worlds. Embassy'll need Freedom's Pathfinders. It's what we do."

All two of you? I wonder, but keep a lid on it. Glad right now there's no link.

<*agreement*> the élans think/feel while echoing through Cami's larynx. "Alignment with Djen Pathfinder, her location please."

Nye does not smile. But he doesn't make another play.

Killian cuts the silence. "Assuming you can produce a viable Hundred-Year Plan that includes consideration of Independence and Neutrality, I'm afraid you're still short of the necessary credit to purchase Callisto by eight-hundred million c's."

Jordis stares at Executive Killian like she can reduce that figure to a handful of u's by sheer force of eye-gaze.

Noa crunches my hand. My eyes go wide; she's gripping me hard enough to hurt.

Killian continues, "The problem isn't just on the books, it's practical as well. Independence requires a substantial amount of additional paperwork and negotiation—treaties drawn with the other sovereign nations and then there's the high cost of the Neutrality clause which to date has only been given to a handful of corporate entities such as All Worlds Scientific—Europa's special circumstances notwithstanding. So even beyond the cost of the moon itself, there are line items—"

"My songs."

"What?" Killian's eyes bulge at me. Well, it is the first time I'd anything to say.

"My songs. I'll give you the rights to all of my currently existing songs. Only thing of mine I never signed away to 100 Worlds Music, but they're worth the world. Seven set releases, Galaxy winners every one. Colonial status for Callisto, including citizenship for all current members of Freedom, for the purpose of sorting human-élan relations, in exchange for all of my songs."

Killian nods. "That might work. We'll have to run a detailed accounting of the numbers."

President Nye nods to Cami-the-Conglomerate of Élan Vitals. "We appreciate the need for neutrality due to the embassy—" his focus turns back to Jordis "—but if Callisto is both Independent and Neutral, and it's primarily run by Operators, then every Operator in inhabited space will want to immigrate."

"That should tell you something about your current policies," Noa gnashes, and I stomp her foot. She communicates resistance with the set of her shoulders but doesn't continue the thread.

"We'll just need to be very clear then about the Colonial status then, won't we?" Jordis says over the élans' growling response to Nye, a sound that should not be coming from Cami's tiny mouth. "Everyone knows Colonial status means restricted access, limited resources, special visas. Even this close to Core worlds."

Killian looks at Nye, communicating in primitive eye-stares as normals do because they lack any sort of real communications technology. Dividia-Muse raises the hairs on my arms as it detaches itself from the Conglomerate filling Cami to tangle with my heart.

The fear is thick as the hope when Killian rises and shakes Jordis' hand, handing her the initial papers to sign. "I'll expect your Hundred-Year Plan by the end of the week. In the meantime—" he turns to Noa "—I'll need your list of startup resources."

◊

"That was less complicated than I'd imagined." I twist his hair around my finger.

"That's because I didn't understand any of the legal shit. If you were sitting here with Jordis' head in your lap, you'd get a different story."

We both laugh at that image. But my laughter cuts short—"The others. Jordis and Noa and Cami. It sounds like everyone was okay afterwards, but you weren't, were you? None of you really were."

"What's 'okay' even mean?" Caran sighs and buries his face in my lap. "Are *you* okay, Steven?"

I shiver from the question. No, no I'm not at all okay. And I'm very okay. And I'm unmade but not yet reborn. And I'm—"I'm confused. Mainly."

"Yeah. That's what happens when the masks come off."

"But I spent a lot of time in your head. In all of your heads. You all are basically okay now. Kind of?"

"And a few heavy years fall between then and now too. And a lot of other stories. And how do you even know if what you got from us is all we could tell you. Just because we can share each other's thoughts and feelings doesn't mean we share each other's souls. But we were okay enough for a moment. Just like here, now, you and I are okay enough for a moment."

"All right." I shift on the couch, curling up around him in a little circle of warm body heat. I don't want the interview to end. I don't want him to go home. "Tell me how it ends."

◊

(It's two weeks after they signed the charter. I know because I know, in the funny remembering of something that never happened to me that comes through the link.)

Above, past the shimmer of the atmo-dome, Jupiter's sphere swirls in blue, red, and gold, casting spooky shadows from the temporary buildings in the not-light. None of the shadows move. Darkness makes everything look less hastily constructed. More magical. Can't see the scars. Noa and Cami stand next to me, and we stand next to a coil of thick, green ribbon on the cold, black ground of Callisto.

"When are they gonna get started already?" Cami huffs at the packed dust with her furr boots. Her voice is hoarse, and her eyes red-rimmed. Don't know if it's from crying or from being the voice box to alien consciousnesses for days on end. At least there still seems to be a Cami.

"Politicians." I shrug. "So whenever they fucking feel like it."

"Mind the media," Noa says, twitching a shoulder in the direction we decided to call south.

Cameras and feed-dust over where the event's going to happen have focused on me. I give them a wave and a smile. Eat it up. Yeah.

"Not helping." Noa says.

"What?"

"I think Noa's saying that they're waiting for the media to stop focusing on you," Cami says.

Oh! "Oh." <hey, do something> I think/feel to Dividia-Muse and take a step back.

<like what? *frowns*>

<like hide me or something>

<i don't think that will make them less fixated on you>

Shit. Oh—I lift my arm and point first at the coil of ribbon at my feet, then to its twin coil, ten meters away at the other side of the new Embassy Square. I nod and nudge to Noa and Cami. "Hey, point at the other side like you're actually interested."

Media follows our fingers like a charm—OMG WHAT'S CARAN WATTS LOOKING AT—and falls on Jordis Ansari talking it up with President Nye, High Councilor Ang from the New Order of Federal Banking Worlds, and reps from the other independent nations of Trewal, Arcadia, and Faraday. Everyone who'd just signed the treaty with Callisto and toasted with disappointingly small amounts of champagne.

But it doesn't last. The cameras follow right back to me.

A pulse of light in the long space between the two spools unfolds into rainbow waves. Media swivels to focus on it. Swivels and stays. <i thought of something> Muse says.

Jordis notices and detaches herself from the knot of leaders and move toward Freedom's side of the gap.

"Finally," Cami mutters.

"Soon I can have a lot more champagne and finally sleep," I add wistfully, even though I've had more sleep the past two weeks than I ever would've on tour.

"Soon I can get to work," Noa grinds. "Everybody lives."

Jordis reaches us. She's come out best from this, even if she didn't get her wish to be Queen of the Galilean Black. She seems not pleased, but at least satisfied that Som Bliss is now King.

She smiles at me. I remember her taunting me with NQ and look away.

It really is quite dark on Callisto; it only seems light-ish because my eyes have adapted to Jupiter's dim proxy-light. Thin, cool air smells like new things and boxes, and the siliplas walls of the structures set to support the members of Freedom's cells who will relocate here. To support the two-hundred additional residents yet to arrive in the next few months. To support the handful of staff that's already arrived, including, to my surprise and kinda discomfort, Mindy Ming wanting to work on our security. To the "north," on the other side of the square, the dome of the embassy building arches, adorned with a spindle of old radio antennae. We apparently got the old Callistoan com arrays along with the deed to the orbital, though they're not going to work without a lot of repairs.

Jordis flicks non-existent lint off the sharp shoulders of her suitcoat and checks her bun. She smiles at the small crowd. Clears her throat. Speaks with graceful, icy pride. "Today Callisto becomes an independent, neutral colony. Today we have completed the groundwork for future relations with the first meta-intelligent beings like ourselves that we've found in the vastness of this ever-surprising, ever-giving universe."

Head Councilor Ang—at the opposite coil of ribbon—returns: "Today we have completed the groundwork for peace between our nations and cultures, and for an open dialogue between our paradigms. Today we will not cut the ribbon on this new city we name Hope—"

"—but," Jordis completes the script, "we will unite the ribbon whole."

Electricity crackles from Dividia-Muse, followed by sparks like fireworks from other élan vitals.

Jordis and the Head High Councilor bend and pick up their ends of the ribbon, green coils unwinding like waveforms as they walk toward the center point.

"Everybody gets a diamond," Noa whispers.

I find her hand. She lets me hold it. She presses hard enough for me to feel it.

Cami's face is pensive, her fists tight. She must be concentrating to keep the élans out, to keep them from resonating with her. But she manages to smile a little at me anyway.

President Jordis Ansari and Head Councilor Ang hold the ends of the ribbon together as Muse fuses them with heat.

Callisto's lights come on, the noontime blaze of our new home.

◊

"You could," Caran whispers to me like he's on the brink of sleep, "you could follow me home. To Callisto. You could come home with me."

"I don't know," I say. We are a tumble of brown and golden limbs.

"Don't know what?" He shifts.

"I don't know...don't know if that's what I want."

He frowns. "If what's what you want? You mean me, Callisto, what?"

"All of it. Any of it. My job. My life."

"What life?"

"I'm senior faculty in the Anthropology Department at All Worlds Scientific."

He sniffs, untangles himself from me. "Yeah. Of course you are." His tone mocks.

"Yes—no—I mean—I don't know what I am." *Except broken.*

"Except broken." Caran presses his fingers to his eyes and stands.

"I—I don't know what I want." *I want you to choose for me. To tell me what to do. To tell me who I am.* But he can't. I'm as empty of self as Cami when the élans filled her.

He moves slow to the door, giving me one last chance. His eyes catch and hold the light like tiny stars. His mouth twitches with darkness and pain and dreams of destruction he longs to realize but never can. His movements as he pokes tangled, wavy black hair out of his face fascinate me. Every flutter-of-an-eyelash, every angle of muscle and bone beneath his golden skin.

"Well, when you figure out what you do want, Steven, if you think it includes me, you come tell me. You come sing it loud."

CODA:
DJEN / STELLA

Djen Pathfinder clomps into my office, near two meters tall and dressed in a bright red spacer's suit and light-up mag boots. Her hair falls in coils to the small of her back. She glares around my office like she's shooting lasers from her eyes.

She bursts out laughing.

"What?"

"Your office. I can see what he meant about you."

There is no need to name "him." My knees forget themselves and I find myself on the ground.

Djen towers over me, hands on her hips and head cocked to the side. I can't read her expression, but a sensation of <*concern*> washes through me. Stella.

"I can't eat; can't sleep; can't think." I blurt. "He's gone. He's gone back to Callisto."

Djen arcs a thick brow at me, sensations of <*amusement*> falling around her. "He does live there, you know."

"I know but—" I burst into tears.

"You love him," she says.

It's a statement of fact. Her tone says it, my heart says it, it's just a fact. *Does he love me back?*

"Only way to know's to ask him. And only way to ask him's to follow him home. And the only way to do that's to tell your team what all's been goin' on. You'll feel better for it, get it out of your system. Then go tell *him* how you feel, get that out of your system too." Djen's eyes crinkle in amusement.

"You're not going to try to stop me? The rest of them, they all tried to stop me. Told me we were bad for each other. Too alike. Too different."

"Hey, look, you and Caran are grown men. You can do whatever you want. But if what you want's my permission, I think you're good for each other. If you let each other be good, anyway, and that's not a given considering your mutual tendencies toward self-destruction." She sniffs.

I wipe my eyes on the back of my hand like a six-year-old. Djen doesn't help me to my feet.

She sits on the couch in Caran's usual spot, moving heavy like she weighs 800 kilos. She looks like she might be scrawny beneath the thickness of the vacuum-ready coverall, but it's hard to get a gauge. It's hard to get a gauge on her demeanor, too. Unlike Noa and Jordis, Djen never went through Operator Socialization; no one taught her how to act like a normal.

"Sorry." I'm not sure I can act like a normal either because all I am is the wreckage of hope and fear. But I need to try, for the next hour and this last interview at least.

"No cares." Djen sprawls out.

The hairs on my arms go on end as Stella becomes more present. It's a different feeling, Stella's presence. At once more crisp and less accessible.

"Stella's not like the élans you've been linking with," Djen says like she's in my thoughts already. Probably she is. "Stella was made to hold a link, made to make a Mesh. She's a fragment of the big old one Strange Navigator, so she's not her own thing entirely."

<i am a starship; i am all points bound>

"That doesn't mean she's shy," Djen smiles large and radiates <*pride*>.

I smile too. I like Djen. I miss Caran. "Before we get into what happened after the founding of Callisto, I'd like your take on the ribbon-cutting event. But first, I'm curious—what's so funny about my office?"

Djen smiles large again, this time radiating <*bemusement*>. "*Stella-Maru's* an explorer class dimensionship. Exploring's what we do. Been to more untouched words than likely anyone else, 'least in the forty-five years we've had to roam. And you know what I've got up on her walls? Flatshots of all of them. All the places we've been. You're a scientist, Steven, an explorer like me. You've been inside human minds and cultures like I have worlds, and what've you got on your walls? A decades-old certification of education that's the least of what you care about. It's the blandest office I've ever been in. Caran told me you were scared to let your real self hang out. Guess he meant that literally." She laughs at the pun.

Over Djen's left shoulder, a globe of light forms, flaring like a miniature sun. Blue eyes open, silver plasma trails tracing into Djen. Stella's mental tone feels like bells: <you are an explorer steven will you come with us?>

<i would love to, stella> I think/feel back like I'd been born communicating with élans.

The plasma flares across the room to me. It's harmless, a bending and molding of ambient light, not real plasma; it hits me, goes through me, feeling like a puff of heat from a vent. I'm not sure what to say to Djen about my bland walls so I say instead, "Were you on Callisto for the ribbon joining?"

"I was not." Djen sprawls even flatter, thumbs looped in her empty utility belt.

<we were 469,098 light years from callisto in uninhabited space> Stella says.

◊

(Djen's mind is hurricanes of light and sound and information datum structure tumble BIGNESS OF IT ALL—)

Darkness: shut the information off.

A glitter-scape of stars, twinkling in the black of space through the windows of the *Stella-Maru's* egg-shaped common room.

Pick the information from inhabited space back up again and punt the flow to the 3V display on the front wall. Don't want it playing direct in my head. Don't wanna make it real.

From Callisto:

"Today we will not cut the ribbon on this new city we name Hope—"

"—but we will unite the ribbon whole."

I push off, float to the center of the room. Push my hair out into a cloud.

Look at the stars.

<*hope?*> Stella noses.

<nah, *grumpy* gimmie silence; silence with the stars>

But there's no silence for me, even this far afield. Flickers of information flow seep back in around the darkness. Feed. Mesh. All of human knowledge flashes, crash-changes. New narratives blossom like peri-lotus on Mau. Like those weird pod-things we saw on that planet with the indigo seas.

Feed over the 3V jabbers with after-comments, Caran and the

rest long gone to whatever food, or intoxication, or nap, or screaming session, whatever people did after unleashing something like that on the universe. Slit their own throats. What do I know.

Well, I do know one thing.

I frown and cut the feed to the 3V. Send a puff of air out to roll and float toward the door to the pilot's nook.

<stella, there's gonna be a revolution>

◊

I walk out of my office and shut the lights behind me. There is no trace of myself inside. I com my research assistant, subvocalizing, "Zizi?"

"Steven! How'd it go with Djen?"

"Good. Go ahead and process the recording." I turn left toward the Ethics Office. "I have an appointment with the Review Board; it should last a few hours."

"Okay. Everything all right?"

"Yes. Everything's fine. Book me on the next shuttle to Callisto."